BLUE FLAME

Z.N. ARNSTAM

Printed in the United States of America

First Printing, 2017

ISBN 978-1947426900

Winters Publishing Group
2448 E. 81st Suite 5900
Tulsa, Ok 74137
www.winterspublishinggroup.com

Graphic Design Image by Jeff Langevin Art & Design,
www.jefflangevin.com

Author Photo by Ward Hooper, www.wardhooper.com

Cover Design by Z.N. Arnstam

CONTENTS

ACKNOWLEDGMENTS

Nobody's gifting, dreams or calling ever comes about apart from contributors. Even though I spent an endless amount of hours alone writing, I cannot say that I wrote this book alone. Whether it was at the old wooden desk tucked away in the nose of my construction trailer while on a job site — the dim light of a 40 watt bulb glowing overhead, sawdust floating across my keyboard, and the sound of 120 psi nail guns firing in the background — or in a local Idaho coffee shop typing away; I was never alone. I have a small crowd of individuals to thank for making this possible. Beyond what my own abilities can produce, I owe much credit.

First of all, my good God and Father is at the center of it all. To Him alone belongs all the glory and honor for any and all achievement I get to participate in. His love is magical and unending. He's the source of endless creativity. When I was just seventeen and seemingly insignificant, He saw me, recognized me and branded me with purpose. His greatness permeates my life for no other reason than that He loves me. To belong to Him is enough. Thank you, Lord, for the ability even to write, to be alive, and to be a part of the economy and culture of heaven.

Secondly, there's just no other way to say it — I am married to the most selfless, auspicious woman on the planet! Laura, my beautiful wife, for every hour you allowed me to spend writing, you sacrificed an equal amount of time raising our children, cleaning the house, paying bills, doing our taxes, and most of all encouraging me to keep going and to not give up pursuing what I love. In moments when I felt this whole thing was useless and a waste of time, you were there smiling, reminding me of who I am to you regardless of success or failure. Thank you for loving me with crazy love and for everything you put into the vision of making this story a reality. I appreciate you and simply couldn't have done this without you by my side. I'll spend the rest of my life trying to pour into you what you've poured into me. I love you.

Thirdly, I dedicate this book to my mother. You always put my brothers and I first. You lived to provide for our needs. You toiled and you worked and you lived to make everything possible for me. If nothing else — during my childhood and adolescent years — if I lacked all things but still had you, I would've been just as prepared for a great life as anyone else. There's no one else like you. You never bridled my imagination, you never discouraged me, you never lacked faith in me, you never withheld the fulness of your heart from me, and you were the most constant person I had growing up. Thank you for all you gave. And thank you for always believing in me.

Furthermore, I cannot refrain from mentioning my mother-in-law. Lilly, you're amazing! Your smile and your prophetic words have been invaluable fuel for me. Thank you for always speaking truth into my life and for showing me what authenticity looks like. I admire you.

Lastly, I want to thank Scott Winters and Bryan Norris and the entire Winter's Publishing Group staff and editors. Thanks for not growing weary of the back and forth, the phone calls, the emails, the process of producing this story. Thanks for believing in me and for believing in this project. You all have contributed so much and I couldn't have done this apart from your team. Thank you.

I dedicate this book to all of the desperate truth seekers hungering for the supernatural, thirsting for more and searching for their purpose.

#

Water

Everything could have been different if it were not for *them*. Two-thirds of humanity, lost. Maybe some predicted it would all go down like this, life being reduced to the simplicity of water. Maybe not. Good? Evil? The dividing line has been dull for too long.

2077 means the earth has been dying for more than two decades now. Slowly and abnormally, its aged heartbeat barely surging. Like a deadly virus infecting the pure crimson blood in a man's veins, earth's water supply came under assault and has yet to recover. What remains of the ocean, lakes and rivers, from the crest of the northern hemisphere to the bottom of the southern, has been dwarfed by the same rotting death. All is sick and dry. The spread of poison so broad, so dense, the atmosphere has never been the same. Rain and snowfall becoming scarcer as each year tucks itself away into the sleep of the ages.

The only thing certain anymore is the phenomenon — the isolated Redfish Lake, cloistered in the mountains of central Idaho, is miraculously uncontaminated. Its ability to continue producing fresh water somehow immune to the poisoning, becoming known as nothing less than the prized headwaters to the last fresh water supply in existence.

The coveted watershed — every stream and river connected to Redfish — might have been salvation to those thirsting to death. But under *their* power it has become a curse of destruction. The northwestern part of the United States is nothing more than bloodstained, war-torn real estate. Parched, dying souls have flown, fought, ran, sailed and crawled from all over the globe to get to the water. Yet most were not even able to reach the watershed's immediate vicinity, dying like scorched dogs with festering tongues hanging out of their mouths. Many thought they were coming to a divine well, but instead were confronted by a sinister gatekeeper.

Fortifying the water supply, *they* have cut off all access and are policing it selfishly behind bloody knuckles and smoking pistols for leverage to create a one world system of tyranny and corruption. At first, some were ignorant to think this was all about water. Though it is clear now the callous overtakers were not only voracious for the water but for the creation of a new generation, a new people, devoid of all spiritual underpinnings, all forms of faith, all systems of hope in any and every so-called supernatural reality.

Slavery or death, an exception here or there, the options for those at enmity with *them* are limited. Under *their* crushing thumb, the purpose of life has been reduced to technology and what can be proved by means of science, nothing more — absolute zero toleration for spirituality, religious names and language banned. So much so that some have had no choice but to form new vocabulary for the metaphysical. For the oppressors, *flesh* is all that is real anymore, s*pirit* no longer exists.

Nevertheless, a few have taken refuge inside the best kept secret in all of history — Adullum. Some of them barely clinging to life, some of them refusing to ignore the signs of a new awakening, all of them fighting for their lives.

TWO
Rock Man

I t was exactly the way he remembered it — majestic, clear, and cold as ice; no surprise. Every time his foot touched the water, he was ignorant to think it would somehow be warmer than it was the last time. The lake was cold; it was always cold. Middle-of-winter cold, dead-of-summer cold. What could he expect when its belly was filled with the melting snow of the Sawtooth Mountains? No sooner would the tip of his foot poke through the surface, a riveting chill would course through his limbs. It was not long before he realized *one body part at a time* was a bad idea, it left too much time for negotiation; a mindless plunge was always the way to go. Graced with fleeting youthfulness, his ability to assess risk was dulled by adrenaline. No matter how many times he stumbled home shivering, his tiny teeth chattering, he would just go back out the next day and jump in again. The glacier-like water was cold, but it was life – a wake-up call to let him know he was still alive. It was home.

Punks! Thieves! There's a lot of lakes out there, but none like this one. None! Dad? Is that you? Dad? We gonna catch a fish today?

The boy hears a static, broken voice issuing from an approaching figure with an unrecognizable face, "We will, son. I promise."

Crazy! The place is still the same! Hard to believe how clear the water is, at thirty feet deep I can see straight to the bottom. And they're always there — those salmon! Swimming around like monsters! So many times I cast my line right into the middle of 'em and didn't get a bite. Not one bite!

Dad, you always told me it was cause they were old, they weren't looking for food anymore, they'd come to the lake to do one thing — die.

The same static voice, "Son! I got one! Come on, reel him in!" The figure hands the rod to his son.

The boy fights the fish with all the strength his puny young arms can offer. *I can't! I can't! Dad! Help!*

Silence. The father figure disappears. So do the fish and the rod. So does the lake.

Dad? Where'd you go...dad?

Life's not fair. Life sucks! My whole childhood's been drowned here. I wish I could go back to the beginning, back to when I was young, back to when life was as simple as the lake. The smell of pine trees! The sand! The water! Water! Water! Clean, clear water! I'd give anything to be back here again.

The boy sighs, looks up and stretches his gaze to the mountain side. *I can't believe it — there he is. Could almost reach my hand out and touch him, Rock Man! He's huge!*

Why couldn't anyone else could see him? People thought I was crazy, but I wasn't. His face was right there, carved into the rock skin of the Sawtooth's.

A faint voice coming out of nowhere, "It's just a mountain...dumb kid."

No, it's not. Rock Man's real! He came out of the ground so he could get some fresh air. Can't you see him? But they couldn't. No one could, just me. People were scared of Rock Man, that's the only reason I can think of not wanting to see him. But he never scared me. I always believed he was the guardian of the lake — looking down from above, protecting a sacred place.

Those criminals. They ruined everything. They don't deserve this place! All this was mine, and they took it! Whatever I have to do, I'll find a way to get back here. I will!

□

Nathan woke up. He whispered profanities to himself while being confronted by the harsh winter draft that blew through the cave, slapping him across the face while making an eerie growl that was anything but comforting. His frozen body lay motionless on top of a dingy coil-spring mattress that had stains all over the fabric, most of it held together by duct tape so the cotton would not fall out.

Before he could think, a rush of anger flooded his mind. The faint scenery of the lake and mountains began to disappear just as quickly as they came. No matter how hard he tried to forget about the place, even though it had been more than twenty years, powerful images and memories of the lake were becoming a regular occurrence at night. Many of the feelings and voices, once dormant and hidden away behind a veil of pain and passivity, were coming out of the dark just as unwelcome as they were unannounced. Regardless of how bitter he was, or how much he refused to acknowledge the existence of the place, that small piece of water was still haunting him.

Shaking the frost from his trashy blanket, Nathan crawled over to Iris's stock-still body lying on another mattress next to his, and spoke into her ear, "Grandma."

There was no response.

"We gotta get up," he said.

Not getting an exciting response, he was greeted by a heavy snore and the subtle flinch of the old woman's eyelids.

"Every morning…" he complained to himself as he waited a few seconds, then nudged her on the shoulder.

"Grandma, get up," he said in a louder voice.

Finally, after a few minutes, there was an answer. Iris's frigid lips moved slowly even though her mind was less than half awake.

"What?" she snapped, and then after a short pause, "be quiet, I'm sleeping."

"I know. The sun's gonna be out soon…time to hunt."

"Hush," said Iris with her eyes still closed and her back turned toward Nathan.

"You wanna eat or not?"

"Life's not all about food," she answered, "ten more minutes."

"It is when your belly's as empty as mine. You're something else, you know that?" Nathan grumbled. *Ten more minutes is all I'm giving you, then you're getting up,* he thought to himself.

Nathan lifted his strong adult body off the mattress, his joints were still frozen from the evening. He moved through the early morning darkness, feeling his way past familiar objects, until finally latching on to a gasoline can. He could tell there was hardly anything left, but there was enough. He opened the cap, poured a few drops onto a pile of scrap wood, and then pulled a flint knife from his pant leg pocket. He rubbed a piece of steel against the knife until the sparks ignited a modest fire.

Wrapping his fingers around the handle of an old cast iron kettle, Nathan filled it with a small amount of water from a plastic jug, before placing it on a large rock next to the flames. Looking back at Iris, who was still immersed in her slumber, Nathan crouched down beside the fire and waited for the cold to leave his bones while he rubbed his hands together in its warmth.

Nathan watched and waited with heavy eyelids. As the fire grew, it brightened the place, casting a soft glow across the walls of the cave. The blaze flickered. Shadows danced, weaving in and out of each other, appearing and disappearing, enabling the archaic words to manifest again. Through the light of the flames the words were static, but looked as though they were moving, playing hide and seek. *Here I am, find me.* Nathan could hear them whispering, taunting him with a spectral moan. Every morning, for years, he was confronted by the same sentence: *NOTHING IS IMPOSSIBLE WITH THE NAVIGATOR.*

He was not trying to notice them, he just did not have a choice. That solitary phrase was written everywhere: spray painted, etched, scribbled, carved, engraved, painted, penned, and plastered across the walls of the cave — messy, without order, side to side, top to bottom; it was everywhere. Iris's handiwork had invaded the walls so much that it became the room's wallpaper, even masquerading the granite surface behind it.

As Nathan vacillated between gazing at the wallpaper and trying to ignore it, the thought occurred to him, that he could not recall a time when the words were not there. Yet by now, they were no longer special. Nathan was used to the phrase, to the point where he was unmoved by its significance, if it had any at all. More than once he desired to pour white paint all over those walls so he did not have to see it anymore, but he knew Iris's identity was too bound up in all the graffiti.

Nothing more than a common phrase to Nathan, the words were meaningless. He paid more attention to the dirt under his feet than he did to the *Nothing is impossible with the Navigator* thing. Unlike Iris, who felt the words comprised not just a sentence, but an anchor, for Nathan it just reminded him of the drudgery that greyed his existence in the cave. He noticed the words, but he was as cold as steel to them, morning after morning overlooking them. *Gonna take a lot more than that sentence to get us out of this mess,* he thought.

The kettle started to steam, causing the lid to shudder. Nathan slid it across the rock away from the flames, opened the top, then dropped his last two bags of cheap black tea into the water. Letting the tea steep, he walked back over toward Iris and nudged her shoulder.

"Wake up, Grandma," he said.

Again, there was no response.

This time Nathan spoke louder, "Wake up." His voice was firm, but far from a yell.

And then, as if being annoyed by a fly buzzing around her face, Iris slapped Nathan's hand and pushed him away, mumbling, "Ok, ok. I'm getting up."

Nathan was relieved. On any given morning there was no telling how much effort was involved in rousing Iris. She was a heavy sleeper to say the least. Her excuse to Nathan was that she always saw the world better with her eyes closed than open.

"Made some tea," said Nathan, raising one eyebrow, curious to see Iris's response.

"Don't mess with me," she responded, her voice still coarse. She was in disbelief, "Thought we didn't have any."

"It's the last of it…saved it for hunting."

Nathan anticipated an excitable *thank you,* but she just stared at him in a fancy way, "Put cream and sugar in it?" she asked.

Nathan shook his head back and forth, uncertain whether he should smile or just ignore her foolish question. "You know we don't have cream, haven't had it for a long time. And sugar? Absolutely not."

She shrugged, "Well, you never know."

"Whatever you say, Grandma." Nathan kept the rest of his comments to himself. *Actually, we do know…Reapers can't get their hands on things like cream these days,* he thought. He helped her get up off the mattress.

"Cold morning!" Iris blurted out, not wasting any time making it over to the fire.

"Been a cold winter…just not enough snow," Nathan complained in a low voice.

Iris sat down on a crummy military box while Nathan wrapped a dull elk hide around her shoulders, then picked up two dimpled metal cups. For a second, he admired their blackened burn marks before filling them with tea. No sooner did he pass one to Iris she started sipping away, her slurp being louder than the crackling fire. Nathan watched as the movement of smoke greeted Iris, brushing across her leather-worn face, her cheeks and eyebrows graced with admirable wrinkles.

Iris moaned, letting the steam from the warm drink engulf her nostrils. She closed her eyes and recited to herself, predictably, as she did every morning, "Nothing is impossible with the Navigator. Nothing is impossible with the Navigator," and on and on multiple times.

From Nathan's point of view, her recital of the phrase was either psychopathic, or just simply *Iris.* He sat across from her in silence, gazing into the fire, inwardly shunning her meditation. No matter how many times those words poured out of her sincere lips, the caverns of his heart remained numb. After all the disappointment, after all the injustice, the war, the chaos, the unanswered questions – after all the defeat, the death, the thirst, he still did not understand how she could hold onto that purposeless phrase. It was lifeless, yet she clung to it like it was the edge of a cliff; the familiar words coming out of her mouth almost as much as oxygen itself.

Nathan knew Iris was certainly mortal, she was human — prone to error, weak in some ways, frail. But she was odd, kooky to some, intimidating to most. To Nathan, she was a complete mystery, a riddle he still has not quite figured out. He loved her, regardless of how different and confusing she was. She had a way of clutching to things Nathan deemed worthless, and letting go of things he thought valuable. She rode through life in a sense with no saddle, and was a rare woman possessed by conviction that was unnatural, often times seeing circumstances in ways that no one else could. It was never certain whether she would make a confusing thing simple, or a simple thing confusing.

Although there was much about her Nathan could not unravel, he was sure of one thing — he did not want to live without her. Since boyhood, Iris was all he ever had. At times, if the despair of life was unbearable, she would somehow find a way to release the fragrance of hope. She was Nathan's gatekeeper in more ways than one – a powerful shaft of light, without whom he would be left groping about blindly. Unusual? Yes, she was. Misunderstood? Definitely. Crazy? Without a doubt. Nevertheless, she had become a critical piece to Nathan's survival in a world that had grown unrecognizable to itself. She could take someone's answer and turn it into a parable, and in turn hand them a piece of understanding that they were confounded by.

As soon as Iris finished reciting the wallpaper, somewhat immersed in another world, she opened her eyes and looked directly at Nathan. He was peering down at the warm metal cup situated between the palms of his hands. She was quiet and waited for him to lock eyes with hers. When he did, she spoke up in a soft voice, "Don't be surprised, Nathan, my son." She paused, "Don't be surprised…"

"Don't really care" said Nathan, clenching his jaw, not in the mood to hear what she had to say because he knew it would be something in reference to the current state of his inner man. It also was not easy thinking about anything other than food.

Iris did not seem put off by his carelessness. "Don't be surprised when *good* overcomes *evil,*" she said.

"Yeah, right," Nathan shrugged. "Sure looks to me like that outcome's already been decided."

"Depends on what you're looking at."

"You act like you don't live in the same cave I live in," argued Nathan.

"I don't," said Iris in a sharp, but loving tone.

"Figured you'd say something like that."

"We both live in the same world, son. The difference is…the cave you live in, I know is temporary, and the cave I live in, I know is eternal. Just need to be living in the right one, that's all."

"Please…just leave the spiritual stuff out of it today. There's only one thing on my mind and that's hunting. Food."

"Nathan, how long will it take for you to realize *this* is who I am. Son, you know for me there is no divide between spiritual and physical, other than that of disbelief. The *unseen's* always been superior to that which is *seen.*" Iris could have left Nathan alone at this point, she knew the heart behind his comments. But love does not always leave people alone just because they are irritable. So she furthered the conversation in a kind way. "Nathan, you stink this morning," she said, with no guile.

Nathan was too numb to be offended, he laughed instead, "We both stink, Grandma. Don't know about you, but I haven't seen any showers around here lately? And you don't quite smell like a field of flowers."

"Scrubbing that dirty skin of yours won't do a thing for the *stink* I'm talking about. You're hopelessness is smellier than usual today," Iris was quiet for a moment. "The anger in your eyes is getting worse."

"Doesn't matter. What makes you think I'm gonna be any different this morning when everything around me is the same as it's always been — depressing."

"We don't get to choose the time or season we're born into, son." Iris could tell that Nathan was more isolated in his thoughts than normal. It was easy for her to discern the disconnect behind his comments. She took a wild guess and spoke up again, "You were dreaming about the lake again, weren't you?" she asked.

Nathan did not immediately respond. He stayed quiet for two reasons; one, he hated the fact that she always knew, and secondly, memories of the lake either made him sad or angry – probably both.

Iris gave the silence some space and then continued, "I miss it too, you know. That lake wasn't just your home, it was mine also."

Nathan's anger welled up inside and he found it difficult to keep from talking, "We'll never get it back," he groaned. "We're outnumbered by those bastards! I'm gonna lose my mind if something doesn't change around here soon."

Iris held back what she really wanted to say, *losing your mind might just set you free once and for all*, and instead tried to connect with him on his level. "You miss *Rock Man* don't you?" she asked, in a mischievous voice, not trying to trigger Nathan's childhood because of the pain, but because of the beauty.

"Grandma," answered Nathan, looking at her with serious eyes, embarrassed to an extent, "I'm a man now, it was just a mountain. Rock Man's fake…always was."

"Maybe, maybe not? You were such an amazing boy, always loved how you were the only one who could see *him*. No one could convince you otherwise. You're greatest gift as a boy was your imagination, it always was."

"There's no imagination left anymore — it was stolen, just like my childhood."

"Maybe," answered Iris, "but...nothing can be taken from us that we don't willingly give away. Nothing can have power over us unless we allow it to." Iris took a sip and then repeated something similar to what she had said earlier, "Don't be surprised when you find *that* hope, *that* imagination flooding into your veins again. A person's influence, their ability to bring about change, is always determined by the amount of *hope* they carry." Iris looked into Nathan's eyes with a sturdy compassion. She was familiar with what he had been through. Her love for him was so strong that every loss of his was a loss of hers.

By now Nathan was starting to warm up as he huddled next to the fire. For a moment he thought about Iris's uncanny encouragement and then refocused again, concerned more about the warm drink pouring down his throat than how much life was in the words she was trying to impart. Yet after a few minutes he found it hard not to respond.

"I don't need surprises, I need food!" declared Nathan. "Aren't you hungry? Aren't you tired of eating cans of refried beans or nothing at all?" Nathan picked up an empty can that was covered with a fancy Mexican label and then threw it across the room. "I'm so sick of this crap!"

Nathan stayed quiet for a few seconds while he waited for Iris to say something about his aggression, but for some reason she refrained, respecting the silence. Nathan spoke up again, "I don't want to think about the lake anymore. If I had the choice I wouldn't be dreaming about it either!" he exclaimed. "Can't seem to get that place out of my mind!"

"Maybe that's because you're not supposed to," she answered. Nathan looked at her in an odd way, not understanding what she meant. "Let the memory of the lake smolder in your mind. See it! See it! And see it again! Until, at last you find yourself back there. No matter what lies ahead of us there's one thing you must promise me — promise me you'll never lose your vision. Sometimes it's all you have, but it's enough. Choose to live with *hope*. Don't imprison your spirit, son."

"We need to get ready and get out there while it's still early," said Nathan, changing the subject.

"Son," Iris paused, "first…promise me." Iris looked at him with intensity.

Nathan already knew she would not be satisfied without a response, he would be pestered the rest of the day if he chose to remain silent. "Fine," he answered casually, "I promise." His words were empty.

Normally, Nathan was not caught off guard by Iris's philosophical prodding, especially in the mornings, but today she was being more aggressive than usual. He knew she wanted to help him, but sometimes it did not feel that way. Most of the time, he preferred being left alone in the dismal pit of his own memories — fragile as they were. It was hard to hide stuff from her. When she sensed something, she did not hesitate to call it like it was. Nathan's thoughts, no matter how deep, or dark at times, were only a look away when it came to her. He learned to accept Iris for this. She was marked by a strange wisdom, and an ability to discern people's hearts. Even if in the moment she was not making sense, Nathan would eventually get the revelation of what she was saying, though it may have been days, months, or years later. In spite of that, he did not agree with everything she said. They argued often.

THREE
One More Time

omewhere in northern California, the lead from his pencil crushed into pieces as the little boy scribbled mercilessly against the greasy piece of paper. The stains underneath his fingernails caked and thick, his hands small and boney. He wore an oversized pair of faded blue Nikes, two sizes too big, with the outer edges of both feet falling out through tears in the fabric. The boy's eyes were intense for his age and zealous as he watched his own drawing coming to life. He was on his knees, hunched over the paper, paying no attention to his mother standing behind him with her arms crossed and salt streaks dried on her skin. Her face was tired, her eyebrows heavy, her pupils glazed over in such a way that anyone could tell she had been sobbing, but now emptied of her tears.

She stood there, watching her boy stop to sharpen his instrument against the rooftop concrete, and then start drawing again. It was all she could do to keep herself from ripping that pencil from his hands and breaking it.

"This is the last one," she declared, trying to ignore the cold winter that was seeping into her bones. The boy knew what she meant, he knew she was serious. He had seen enough at this point.

"One more time," he answered, not looking up at her, hurrying to finish the drawing before she changed her mind.

She stayed quiet until he was done.

"Finished!" the boy exclaimed. He stood to his feet and waved the drawing proudly in his mother's face.

She did her best to act as though it were her first time seeing it. "Just get rid of it," she ordered.

Without hesitation, the boy walked to the ledge of

the building, took in a panoramic view of the valley, closed his eyes, stretched out his arm and let go. Immediately the drawing was carried away by the wind.

FOUR
Bear Trap

athan heard footsteps coming down the corridor of the cave. The sound was broken up by a soft, but sharp whistle, followed by a familiar voice calling out, "You two ready?"

The footsteps grew louder as Annak walked out of the shadows, Max and Silas were behind him. The glowing fire lit up their faces when they entered the room. They were unapologetic about forgetting to knock, as if there was a door in the first place, or some kind of unspoken cave etiquette. All three of them were decked out with appropriate attire: layers of warm tactical gear, guns hanging off their shoulders.

Max carried himself as he always did — big and bulky with an uncommon athletic build, though it was easy to tell he had been malnourished. Part of his toughness was given away by his shaved head. His cheekbones were edgy and always looked as though they were swollen from a fight. He was just shy of six and a half feet, and with pure brawn weighed close to two-hundred and sixty pounds.

Silas was not too different; he had been battered by the same world Max lived in. Silas's skin was fair and he had dirty blonde hair that he kept pulled back in a ponytail. Both of them were in their late twenties, close in age to Nathan.

Annak was divergent, he was older, but there was a confidence about him that was alluring. His personality was unshakable and his ability to survive was ruthless and calculated. He rarely made mistakes, let alone lifted a finger if he knew his energy would be wasted. Because of his dark black beard laced with streaks of silver and his slicked back hair Nathan always assumed he was Spanish. Though, Annak never liked to talk about his nationality or made it a priority to do so. He was somewhat quiet, but revered. Nathan always knew it was him. The sound of his voice was unmistakable. Because of Annak's partial hearing loss he spoke in a deep voice that was rough and slightly nasally, though Nathan could never make sense of the fact that Annak heard just fine during conversation. If anything it was less of a defect and more of a trait that contributed to Annak's potency and seriousness. Aside from that, Annak walked with a shoulder that looked permanently dislocated, yet it never seemed to be a glitch that ever slowed him down.

"Morning," said Annak. His voice was intense, and deep.

"We'll be ready in five minutes," replied Nathan, he knew they were running late. Iris nodded to acknowledge all three of them, but was still consuming her warm cup of tea as Nathan left the room and made his way into another one filled with junk. Against the back wall there was a rustic steel safe, more than six feet tall. Nathan pressed his finger against the key pad and entered the numbers: 156780, *Click.* The safe unlocked and the weighted door crept open. Reaching inside, he pulled out an MP7 assault rifle, two Walther handguns and one Blaser R8 hunting rifle — all loaded.

He closed the safe and walked back into the other room, "Here," he said to Iris. She reached one hand out and reluctantly took hold of a pistol. Nathan set some extra blocks of ammunition on her lap. "Don't leave these behind."

Iris looked at him in a suspecting way.

"You act like we have a choice," said Nathan. "You, like me, should refuse to go outside Adullum without one."

"I'm not going to change, Nathan."

"And I'm not going to argue with you. How about you stay behind today and let us do the hunting?" Nathan was well aware of the fact that Iris was in charge of everything that went on at Adullum. Still, it did not keep him from trying to tell her what to do.

Iris looked around the room. Annak stared back at her in a way so as to communicate he did not want to be involved in the matter. Even though she was the leader, no one was fond of her refusal to carry a firearm. As they continued to hunt, Nathan was growing more uneasy about her coming along, it was too dangerous, and she was getting older. But he knew her protocol by now; she rarely, if ever, let him out of her sight.

"If it's my time, I'd rather die out there with you guys," said Iris, with a subtle wink as she stood up with gun and ammunition in hand. Her long grey hair was draped down across the sides of her face, which she brushed away, revealing her intense burning blue eyes, that for most were more frightening rather than comforting. Because of the energy that was there and the way in which she carried herself, she could be quite commanding to say the least.

In the moment, Nathan was reminded how unpredictable she was, almost as if she was all four seasons at the same time, consistent in some things, but sporadic in others. Like the queen in a game of chess, it was uncertain whether she was going to stay put on the back row of the board, hiding comfortably next to the king, or come out early in the game and tear things up. She was pure electricity — always stirring. Regardless of gun in hand or not, he knew Adullum would not have been kept alive this long without her.

As she finished getting ready, Iris caught Annak helping himself to her tea. She glared at him and gave him a good jab in the gut, "I'll get you for that. You know how evil it is to steal an old woman's tea don't you?"

"Oh, come on," said Annak, as he wrapped one arm around her, "you know I'll make it up to you. Besides, you're not a normal old woman."

Iris pretended to be humored. "We'll see about that," she said, as she took the cup, tipped her head back and drank the last few drops.

No one needed to communicate about the urgency of the day, they all knew it was best to go out as early as possible. The five of them did not waste any time exiting through the front of the cave and into the sobering morning air — it was brisk, and windy. A thin sheet of frost was covering the ground.

As Nathan set his eyes on the Crawlers he asked Max, "When's the last time you put water in these?" Both the engines were hissing quietly.

"Each of them got a gallon last month," Max answered.

Nathan glanced at the gauge on the inner console and was reassured. He knew Crawler's were uncommon machines; transformative ATV's fueled by water, clean or contaminated. They would run another 300 miles before the tanks needed to be filled again.

Iris got into one of the passenger seats. Annak buckled himself into the driver's chamber while Nathan jumped in the back. Max and Silas got into the second Crawler. When Annak took hold of the suicide nob he unlocked the emergency brake, shifted into gear and called out, "Everybody ready?" Max gave him a nod from the other driver's chamber and they took off down the dirty white road.

"Annak, you getting worried?" asked Nathan. Annak was quiet and focused. Nathan kept his eyes alert, scanning the forest, his machine gun aimed halfway out the roll-bars. Sporadic tree branches were breaking under the weight of the snow and falling to the ground. *Crack... humph. Crack...humph.* Everything was eerie and more quiet than normal because this was the first time the snow had insulated the forest in a long time.

"Worried?" answered Annak.

"Yeah, *worried?*" repeated Nathan. "This is the only snow we've had all winter...if you could even call it a winter."

"I'm well past worried," said Annak, in a calm voice. Nathan knew what Annak meant and for some reason had the inclination that Annak's *worry* was far different than his own.

"When this snow melts, there's no way we're gonna make it through the summer with the amount of water we have — it's impossible," declared Nathan.

"One day at a time, Nathan," said Iris, "we've made it this far haven't we?"

"Barely," answered Nathan. "Our food's almost gone. I'm sick of –"

"I know," Annak interrupted, "beans." Iris was in the passenger seat shaking her head, probably at the amount of energy Nathan was still producing just to complain. "You say that all the time," continued Annak. "You should be thankful we even found all those beans in that abandoned car."

"Well, it's been a long time since I've had fresh meat. You think anything's waiting for us at the Pass?" asked Nathan.

Eight miles from Adullum was a thick patch of sequoias, a place still known as Badger Pass, one of the many trapping spots they had set up around the radius of the valley. Normally, it did not take more than thirty minutes to get there depending on visibility and weather. Today was clear, and frigid, the slightest wind felt like needles scraping across their faces, making them eager for the rising of the eastern morning sun.

"Hope so," answered Annak.

"Hardly any animals out there anymore," said Nathan. "Last week our traps were empty, and the week before."

"Nathan, you act like I don't already know that," said Annak. "Today's a new day."

"We better find something," Nathan grumbled, "I'm restless."

Iris spoke up again, "You know what I always say about that."

"Yeah, I know, *I can either rest, or wrestle something,*" answered Nathan. "Neither one sounds good. Tired of both."

"You better not," Annak reminded. He could see Nathan in the mirror, pointing his gun in the air with a hint of carelessness, sensing that he was clenching his trigger a little too tight.

Nathan curled his eyebrows, "I know the rule – don't fire unless you have to, no unnecessary noise."

"Can't afford to waste bullets," said Annak.

It stayed quiet for most of the drive. When they reached midpoint, the sun's rays starting to pierce through the tree-line, grappling its warm fingers across the land. Within minutes, the sky was filled with gold, pink, amber, blue, and shades of green. Numerous clouds stood out, looking as though they had been spattered across the firmament, like paint flecked from a brush. According to Nathan, the sunrise was one of the only things that was still beautiful in the world. No matter how gloomy the landscape was, the sun never ceased to pour out color on all that was sick.

Annak slowed down when they neared the entrance of Wawona Tunnel, easing his foot off the gas. They listened for any off sounds, the darkness of the tunnel putting everyone slightly more on edge. Max and Silas were close behind, Silas aimed his weapon, watching the rear, his feet dangling off the back of the Crawler. Nothing could be heard except the sound of cold air moving through the hollowed-out concrete cylinder.

That was until Nathan realized he never cocked his rifle. No sooner did he do so that the subtle noise echoed, causing an intense flutter of wings to burst forth over head. *WHOOSH!* The light from Nathan's gun shot upward.

"Calm down, don't fire!" shouted Annak, before anyone could act out. A swarm of bats flew from the tunnel and then, like a dense cloud, they dispersed into the forest. Nathan was surprised that many bats were even still alive.

When they came out the other side, Annak turned left and pulled off the road. Three miles of wild terrain lay in front of them. There were no more defined roads, just snow, ditches, falling timber, and dead wood. With the click of a button on the driver's console, the entire lower section of Annak's Crawler transformed. In an instant, the wheels sunk into the cavity, and stout tank treads appeared in their place. Max did the same. Two snow machines now made their advance, gripping and churning across the white landscape, puffs of steam shooting out of the exhaust pipes while the engines revved.

After long, at just two hundred yards out from the trap site they turned their ignitions off. With no verbal communication, everyone knowing what to do, they grabbed their weapons and hiked through the last remaining stretch of snow, cautious with every step.

Annak lifted his arm and wiped some of the glistening rime off his beard. He was eager, but not as anxious to examine the site as Nathan and the others were. It had been a while since they checked this location, and if any of the traps caught game, it could have easily attracted a predator. Annak took a few more calculated steps, his boots halfway engulfed by the powder, and heard a snag break off one of the trees. Looking up, not feeling the need to move, he watched the descending branch miss his left shoulder, and sink into the snow. For a brief moment he admired the sequoia, thankful for the fact that they were thick enough in this area that they did not need to worry about being spotted by *Gnats*. The concern was more about other hungry animals looking for meat — people were not the only species trying to hang on to life.

Coming closer, Nathan noticed a rack of ivory-colored antlers protruding from behind a bush. He began to salivate and could not believe his eyes. In his excitement, he took off running, passing Annak, and then dropped down next to the dead animal. Clenching his fists, he looked up into the sky and yelled, "Yes!" Without delay, he started brushing the snow off its fur.

Max came up alongside the kill and shook his head with delight. "It's a bull elk," he shouted "Can you believe it? Sucker's big!"

Silas hit Max on the shoulder like they were kids, excited to get a morsel of bread that had fallen from the table.

Annak approached, knelt down and rubbed the animal's neck, then ran his fingers across its gums, "Dead no more than a couple days," he said quietly.

The others were ecstatic. Nathan looked up at Iris, he could feel her staring at him, not saying a word. He did not have to guess what she wanted to say, her voice was already running through his mind, *We always seem to have just enough, don't we?*

Nathan glanced back down at the elk, its hind leg was crushed between the metal jaws of the trap where a thick flow of blood had clotted and froze. The expression on his face turned from excitement to fleeting remorse. Even though he was starving, his stomach turning in knots, he could not ignore that quiet grief he felt every time he looked into the soul-less eyes of a dead animal. It was not the hunt that bothered him, just the killing. For some reason he could not stand seeing breath stolen from a living creature. As a young boy, watching a caught fish gasping for air always sickened him just a little. Something inside told him that, *things were never meant to die*. Yet, he really did not have time to regard his feelings about life and death. Surviving at Adullum involved trapping and killing, there was no way around it — no kill, no food. Nathan knew the brutality of other things could not compare to trapping. An animal could be caught and suffer for weeks before actually dying. Trapping was ugly, and cruel, but necessary. Every time Nathan baited and set a new trap, he just reminded himself it was the lesser of all the other atrocities that had ruined the world. Nathan could worry about animal cruelty all he wanted, but then he would simply starve to death.

Annak took his knife and hacked the leg free of the trap, unbothered by gore. He was seared by the trenches of war more than anyone else. He had to discern when, and to whom he would show his mercy. For Annak, animals did not need mercy; they needed to be eaten.

"Thank you, Navigator," Annak said quietly, pausing for a moment, before cleaning the fragments from the trap, then re-engaging it.

As Nathan overheard him, an awkward tension arose. "I can't believe you're still thanking Him," said Nathan, "This elk didn't come from the Navigator, I'm the one who set this trap, and I'm the one who's gonna carry this thing back to the cave!"

"Nathan," said Annak, acknowledging only a part of his frustration, "no need to get into that right now."

"You're as crazy as my grandma!" he exclaimed. In a moment, as if bipolar, Nathan erupted concerning an allusion to something he was not fond of.

"I can thank whoever I want," replied Annak.

"Just don't give Him all the credit," warned Nathan, "He's the reason we're in this mess."

Annak glared at him, yet not in the sense that he was offended, or that his feelings were hurt. He grieved for Nathan's negativity, and for his propensity to speak foolishness concerning things he did not understand.

Nathan looked away from Annak and had nothing left to say. He was uncomfortable, not because of Annak, but because of Annak's faith. Even though Annak was the closest thing Nathan knew to a father, he still hated hearing about the Navigator. Whatever spiritual current ran through Iris and Annak's veins, Nathan wanted no part of it. All it did was make him aware of the residue of doubt and bitterness that still lingered inside his own heart.

"Go check the other trap," commanded Annak, in a firm voice. "I'll start getting this one ready."

Iris looked at Nathan, "Staying behind with Annak," she said.

Max and Silas followed Nathan down a sixty yard ravine to where they hoped to find another banquet table. At first it appeared promising when they saw a small white tail deer lying in the snow, it was still alive, its head barely moving from side to side. But, then Nathan's eyes were quickly drawn to the rotting flesh on its body.

Nathan tried to hold back his disgust, "It's no good," he jeered.

"Looks like the water already poisoned it," added Max.

"That's 150 pounds of meat!" Nathan vented. He pressed into the animals tough flesh with the butt end of his gun, then turned and looked at Max, "shoot it."

Max had a pistol with a silencer on the barrel. He leaned over the deer and shot it.

Nathan knelt down, unhooked the trap from around the deer's neck and reset it. "You guys see the fish hook anywhere?" he asked, looking through the snow for the shiny piece of metal they used as bait.

"Right here," answered Silas, holding up the fish hook with a tarnished pink flair on it, and then handing it to Nathan, who set it back down in between the trap on a small plank of wood.

At the top of the ravine, Annak and Iris continued preparing the elk, when out of the corner of her eye, Iris caught a glimpse of something beyond Annak's shoulder. "Annak!" she shouted. Annak turned around and was stunned by the sight of a grizzly bear ripping down the side of a steep hill, coming directly at them. The panting bear was huge, its shoulders jolting back and forth as it ran.

Grabbing his shotgun off the ground, Annak aimed it dead-on at the beast's head. *Crack!* Without hesitation, he fired a blast but failed to deliver a fatal shot. The spray from the shotgun spread out just as the bear passed a large tree. The shot sent exploding fragments of bark and snow flying through the air, only part of it catching the bear's rear leg, causing the beast to stumble slightly, but barely slowing its pace. The bear's rage only intensified.

As Nathan and the other's lamented the loss of meat, they heard Iris's voice and the deafening noise of the gunshot ring out. Nathan scurried up the ravine as fast as possible, Max and Silas trying to catch up.

Annak re-cocked and aimed again at the bear, not more than twenty yards away by now. He pulled the trigger, but to his disbelief, the gun failed to fire. He pulled the trigger again, still nothing happened. Again and again, trying rapidly, he could not get the gun to fire. With no time to figure out the malfunctioning gun, Annak threw it down, got up off his knees, pulled a sharp diver's knife from his belt and braced himself for the charging beast. Just as he was able to rear the blade up in front of himself, he was face to face with a roaring mouth twice the size of his head. The bear hurled itself onto Annak, clobbering him and driving him into the ground. At the same time Annak's back sunk into the snow, he plunged his blade deep into the bear's chest.

"Nathan!" Iris called out. "Nathan!"

When Nathan reached the top of the ravine he saw what was happening — Annak grappling with the bear, being tossed around like a pet's gnawing-bone. Yet rather than going to help, Nathan held still and refused to move any closer.

"What are you doing?" yelled Max, as he caught up, "he needs our help!"

Silas started yelling at Iris, unaware that she had neglected to carry her weapon from the Crawler, "Shoot it! Shoot it! Take it down!"

Nathan was furious, knowing that Iris made the mistake of not carrying her firearm. From a distance, he watched Annak thrust his left forearm into the bear's neck so the beast could not wrap its jaws around him. With his other arm Annak sunk his knife deep into its belly. The bear snarled viciously and growled at the top of its lungs, writhing in pain, and then clutched its massive paws around Annak's shoulders, digging them into his flesh. Annak was pinned under the weight of the bear and looked as though dead. The bear snapped its jaws at Annak's face. Annak flung his head back and barely escaped its teeth. Drool and the warm breath of the bear's mouth filled Annak's nostrils.

Again, Annak pulled the knife out of the bear and tried to slash it across its throat, but his arm was stuck. Feeling as though he was being crushed to death, he cried out from the pain, but was then able to get his arm free. He stabbed the bear again. The beast reared back and roared like a monster, falling even more so onto Annak's chest and knocking the wind out of him. The bear, still alive, was growing weaker, but so was Annak.

By now Annak was not only trapped, but suffocating. The pressure from the bear was so intense on Annak's sternum that it was close to breaking. The beast continued to growl, swiping at Annak and gnashing its teeth in countless attempts to deface him. One of Annak's arms was still pressed into the bear's throat, holding it back as best he could.

Then in a state of pure adrenaline and shock, Annak went crazy — stabbing the bear repeatedly, like a sewing machine threading fabric. With every strike, the bear was slowing down and losing strength, yet still somehow able to summon reserves of aggression. Even though the bear was getting stabbed, Annak was still getting mauled at the same time, neither beast nor man was giving up. Annak struck the bear as many times as he could, but then lost his grip on the knife and was not able to recover it.

Max grabbed Nathan by the collar and urged him, "Come on man! We need to get over there!"

"Stop!" snapped Nathan, "We don't have time, I'm taking the bear down from here!"

Max and Silas were unsettled. A rush of thoughts flooded Max's mind, *We're far enough away that there's no guarantee Nathan will hit the bear – or miss Annak, for that matter.* He knew Nathan was not joking.

"Nathan, you can't!" exclaimed Max, "I'm going after him!"

"If you run, you'll only be in my way," warned Nathan, "You know Annak would want me to take the shot!"

Nathan was difficult to argue with, and he did not want to waste any more time letting Annak get killed. A sliver of faith ran through Max because he knew that Nathan was a gifted marksman. He got out of the way.

Nathan quickly flung his black rifle from around his

back, and pressed his eyebrow against the cold metal sight of the gun. Without flinching, let alone taking time to breathe, he fired twice. *Snap! Snap!* The shots resounded throughout the forest corridor like two large marbles dropping onto a hardwood floor. Max and Silas stood behind him and watched in slow motion as the rounds sunk into the bear, blowing its head apart and splattering blood across Annak's face. The beast fully collapsed and smothered Annak in the snow.

Without wasting any more time, Nathan ran toward Annak, not sure what to expect. Iris pressed herself against the burly creature and tried to roll it off Annak's body, but with no success. "Hurry up!" she yelled at Nathan. "Annak!" she cried, pressing down on his forehead, trying to open his eyes.

When the other three arrived, Annak could barely get the words out of his mouth as he struggled for breath, "Get…this thing off…me!"

All four of them got on one side of the bear and pushed it off. No sooner did they clear the wreckage that it became uncomfortable to look at Annak; his face was bloodied with gashes, his jacket torn up, claw marks and lacerations covered his body.

"Don't move," urged Nathan, trying to take off Annak's outer layer so he could examine his chest and ribs.

Annak grabbed Nathan's hand and flung it to the side, "I'm fine, just help me get up." Nathan was caught off guard for a moment, but then let off. He knew Annak was angry and shaken up. He grabbed him by his hands and helped pull him to his feet. Annak bent over, picked his knife up off the ground, and then thrust it into the bear's side one more time for personal edification, before cleaning the blade off in the snow.

Nathan picked up Annak's shotgun and handed it to

him, "What the hell happened?" he asked, "Why didn't you shoot it?"

Annak was silent. Still perplexed, he pointed the shotgun straight up and pulled the trigger, *Crack!* The round fired out of the barrel and into the open sky. "Interesting," Annak said, as he wiped the blood from his face, and stuffed a handful of snow into an open wound across his arm. "This gun's never done that before."

"You mean, it just didn't fire?" asked Nathan.

"Maybe the Navigator thought I could use a good wrestling match," said Annak.

Nathan shook his head. He could not believe Annak's attempt at humor amidst what had just happened. He ignored the comment, knowing Annak had been threatened by much more dangerous odds than an underfed grizzly bear and a jammed shotgun; this was not the first time he had survived death. Still, he was baffled by the fact that his shotgun, which he cleaned every day, had jammed — it did not make sense.

Annak grabbed Nathan by his cheek and looked at him, "You took those shots? Didn't you, Nathan?"

Nathan did not say anything, but just looked back into his eyes.

"Fair shots," said Annak, with just enough gratitude so as to let Nathan know he was not deserving of all the credit.

Nathan simply nodded as if to say, *you're welcome.* But then so many thoughts flooded his mind. Caught up in the moment, he could not keep from opening his mouth about the comment earlier. "So, the Navigator likes seeing people get killed by bears?"

"Am I dead?" asked Annak.

"Where's He at when you need him?" questioned Nathan. "Seems pretty foolish to put your faith in someone who doesn't even protect you when you need Him. No bullet in the Navigator's gun?" he said, squinting his eyes confidently.

Annak looked back at him, "I like your questions, Nathan, I do. They let me know you're somewhat open. Are you actually looking for an answer..." Annak paused, "or just a fight?"

Nathan thought for a minute, "You actually got an answer?"

"You serious?" asked Annak.

"Sure," said Nathan.

"This far and no further," said Annak.

Nathan waited to see if that was all Annak had to say, looking at him awkwardly, "What's that mean?"

Annak spit some blood out of his mouth, and adjusted his jaw, "It doesn't matter if it's a bear, a Screener, or a gun pointed at my head — when it's my time, it's my time. But until then, it's *this far and no further*," he said slowly. "My days are numbered." Nathan was quiet in a way that let Annak know he was not tracking. Annak continued, "The Navigator knows when to intervene and when not to."

"Well *He's* either in control or *He* isn't," Nathan shot back. "It's that simple."

"Not always," said Annak. "He steadies Himself to see what's in our hearts — courage or fear? And sometimes," he said again with more emphasis, "*sometimes*, He will use a person, even if they don't acknowledge Him."

"For what?" asked Nathan.

"So that we can share in His glory — so that we can know what it's like to have some of the victory. He's not the only one with all the bullets in this life."

"That doesn't matter. Despite all your nonsense, one fact remains — they were my rounds that put that bear down, not His. Mine! If it weren't for me, you'd be dead."

"And if it weren't for me, you'd never be that good

with a rifle," said Annak.

Nathan was silent, reflecting on the first time Annak taught him how to shoot. Regardless of natural gifting, Nathan could not deny his blue-ribbon marksmanship was attributed mostly to his mentor.

"And more than that, Nathan, my life's always been in His hands, not yours. Just remember that," warned Annak. "Nonetheless, I would have told you to take the shots."

Nathan made a simple stride over to the Elk and started to wrap a chain around its legs so they could haul it, "I'm ready to go."

"What about the other trap?" asked Iris.

"Water already got to it," answered Max, "Kill's no good."

"We're taking the bear, right?" asked Silas.

"We'll scrap the bear best we can," answered Annak.

"Let me drive," Nathan said to Annak.

Annak stayed with the elk while Nathan and Max went to get the Crawlers. Max backed up to the bear and Nathan to the elk, where they chained an animal to each vehicle. When both animals were secure, everyone got into the Crawlers and headed back toward Adullum, with the meat slowly dragging behind them. Nathan knew that despite the poisoned deer, and the bear fight, it was still a good morning. There was never any guarantee during hunting excursions that they would find fresh meat at all. And even though Nathan's heart was unsettled about many things, he was thankful that Annak was still alive.

FIVE
Stinkin Six

 hen they returned to the cave, Iris and Nathan spilt up from the others. Annak was confident he could nurse his wounds by himself.

Butcher responsibilities fell to Max and Silas and a few others for the week. They got started cutting up the meat and preserving it by means of smoke and salt. The rest of the animal, bones and all, were divided and used as necessary; there was no question that Annak would be getting the grizzly coat.

"Fire's still going," said Iris, as she walked into the cave and sat down. "What's it gonna be Nathan? You gonna gauge the pools or check on the watchtower?"

"Get somebody else to check the pools," answered Nathan, referring to their limited reserves of water, "I wanna make sure Alex hasn't gone insane up there."

"Well, if you're going, you need to go now. Only a half day of sunlight left, and you can't be out there when it — "

"Grandma, I know," Nathan interrupted, "I'll be back before it's dark." Nathan opened up his rifle and reloaded it. He placed an extra round into the pocket of his coat. "There it is again," Nathan complained. "The Worms! Don't know how much longer I can take of that noise."

"I'm surprised you're not use to it by now," said Iris.

"How can I be? Twice a day, like clockwork, for how many years? And the vibrations are only getting stronger." Other's had gotten used to the tremors, but for Nathan they were impossible to ignore. They felt like the waters shuddering when a large ship would pull into port, or a massive underground jackhammer chewing away at the earth's core.

"When are we actually gonna find out what the hell that is? Isn't there something we can do? I'm getting sick of all the mystery around here. I've heard that sound so many times it makes me nauseous! How is it that out of all the people in Adullum, no one has an answer for the Worms? Especially you, grandma?"

"I don't know, Nathan. I'm sure the answers will come to pass eventually."

"It's just one more thing that I don't get," said Nathan. The monotony of Adullum was beginning to eat away at him more than normal. He was like Annak, pinned under the weight of the bear, feeling suffocated and mauled by the routine of survival, and the lack of answers that pressed him on all sides.

"I mean, come on, Grandma. Day after day, we just measure our water supply, hunt — many times not finding anything, and try to go undetected by the Screeners? All we do is play defense. And we wait? What are we actually waiting for?"

"Nathan, you know how many people have been lost going up against them," Iris replied. "The only guidance I have from the Navigator right now is to wait."

"That's what you've said for a while now, but what if He's trying to get your attention through the restlessness of your grandson?"

Iris grinned, "Not so sure about that. I don't move unless He tells me."

"Ok, let's just keep doing nothing until we starve to death." Nathan raised his voice. "Have you noticed the winter's getting shorter? There's not enough water out there. And what about the Gnats we've captured? It doesn't matter if we've broke into them and shut down their tracking devices, it's only a matter of time before the Screener's find us. This place can only stay a secret for so long."

"Nathan, there's nothing I can say that will put you at ease. I'm not sure what's to come. All I know is that no one's more aware than I am, of the plundering our world has experienced at the hands of evil. Adullum's been revealed to us as a place of survival, a means of escape. And for now we're safe, that's what matters."

"Well, maybe our safety's paralyzed us. Maybe we should take some risks and do something to get the lake back?"

"Nathan, you were just a little boy. You haven't seen what I've seen. You're naive, son. It's not just about the lake, it's about getting back what's beyond the lake."

"I'm not a little boy anymore, I've seen enough. And for me, it's all about the lake."

"We have to take risks, but they need to be the right ones," said Iris.

"Yeah, but look at this cave — a huge granite dome of safety and we can't even figure out what this place is capable of. All this potential and we're stuck here with no electricity to run it! The government obviously meant for this cave to be a fortress, and we still don't even know how vast it is in here. We can't even get into the Tree House without power, and that's the nerve center of the cave!" Nathan was referring to the huge concrete structure inside the cave, exalted on four enormous columns, with an elevator shaft running through the center of it, down through the ground. At the top was what appeared to be a control room, locked by a stout electronic door.

"Nathan, we don't know how deep or far Adullum goes. And there's no telling what could be in those tunnels. The Tree House is obviously impregnable for a reason. Even if electricity does unlock the door, who knows what's in there?"

Nathan took a deep breath, "I don't care about being safe anymore. I need to get out of here. I need to see what's beyond Adullum...need to know what's going on out there. What if there's more we can be doing? What if there are others just like us, hiding, scared, not willing to go out and find an answer to this depression we're all in?"

"*All* is vague, Nathan. No one knows how many people are still alive out there. After this many years, it's unlikely that anyone's alive outside Geospark's reign, other than us. But, I do believe that one day we can get the lake back. Nothing is impossible — "

Nathan interrupted, finishing her sentence with skepticism and mockery, "With the Navigator..."

"You declare that sentence with carelessness, but one day you'll know what it means, and you'll be owned by it," warned Iris.

"I know what it means, grandma."

"Sure. Just because you've *heard* something a thousand times, doesn't mean you *know* what it means. Just because you can say *it*, doesn't mean you've been gripped by the revelation of it. Without *faith* you can do nothing. In the best expression of your own human strength you can try to go up against those monsters, but it will be in vain if it's done apart from Him." Iris paused, looking intently into Nathan's eyes. "Nonetheless, I can only tell you so much, Nathan. You have always been a risk-taker and a young man of courage. Yet, you go by what you feel. You know as well as I do, how many Reapers we've lost in the attempts to go outside Adullum. Right now we sit tight and we wait. We don't change a thing until I receive further guidance."

Nathan stiffened his shoulders and looked away, "Waiting around here for some kind of *revelation* or *strategy*, is stupid." He was silent for a moment, "Is that all I exist for?" Nathan's tone went from frustration to sobering introspection, "I'm not going much longer without answers. I need to know what's causing the Worms, I need to know what happened to the water. I need…" he paused, "I need… to know what happened to my parents."

Iris gripped Nathan's shoulder with her aged, strong fingers, "You will, Nathan. You will. But you need to surrender your life to the Navigator. If you can't do that, you'll be groping around in the darkness the rest of your life."

"He's the reason they're gone. I'll never give my life to the One who's responsible for all this. Never!"

Iris responded, "I do believe one day we'll see the goodness of man prevail once again in the land of the living. But how or when, I don't know. I have nothing more to say to you at this point, Nathan. Just know that I love you very much and I'm here for you. There's not much time left so if you're going, you need to go now. Do not get caught outside the walls of this cave when darkness falls."

"I know."

"I mean it, Nathan, no messing around."

Nathan turned around, made his way from the wall of El Capitan and started trekking through the valley of sequoia trees. He was on his way to MX-Peak, Adullum's primary watchtower, located at the top of Half Dome.

The sun was hidden behind a collage of scattered clouds. Still cold outside, Nathan tightened up his collar and moved quickly. The trails were too small for a Crawler so he hiked through the ravine, and in little over two hours, was up the side of the mountain and at the entrance of the bunker. With the butt end of his rifle he slammed it into the metal door three times. *Clank! Clank! Clank!*

A rusty hole, the size of a penny, opened up where an odd looking eyeball pressed against it from the other side, and then shut again. Nathan waited as multiple latches and gears shifted inside the door; the hinges creaked with age, allowing the metal slab to slowly swing open.

"What's up, Nathan?" said Alex, in a squirrelly, but confident voice. His Latino face was perky and optimistic when compared to Nathan's, which was rigid. Alex was dressed in worn out military garb with a peculiar red Christmas scarf wrapped around his neck. He wore a thick pair of broken black eye glasses. Two other watchman sat behind him peering out one of the windows.

"How's everybody doing in here?" asked Nathan, walking into the bunker, Alex making sure to slam the door shut behind him and lock it quickly.

"Cold! How do you think?" complained Alex. "Still alive though."

"Everybody's cold," said Nathan. "Brought you guys a half gallon of water. Make it last." Nathan handed the container to Alex. He embraced it in his hands like it was pure gold. "What's that smell?" Nathan declared with disgust.

"What do you think it is?" Alex asked back, "you see any showers around here?"

"Well there's fresh snow, at least put some of it in your crotches and armpits!" said Nathan. "Smell's terrible in here."

"Yeah, like you don't stink man!" Alex snapped back, with a slight chuckle.

"Activity in the last week?" asked Nathan, changing the subject.

"Of course - Gnats," answered Alex.

"Out of the ordinary, or just the same?"

"There were three fly-overs this week," said Alex, "and that's just what we saw on our end. They're sending more and more this way. Not only that, but they're getting sporadic and hard to predict." Alex started getting hyped up a bit more, probably because he hadn't seen anyone outside the bunker in the last week. "If this bunker wasn't made out of reinforced concrete, we'd be dead by now."

"What happened?" asked Nathan.

"Two days ago one of them dropped a nuke and it detonated just to the side of us, the whole place shook. When it circled we had just enough time to take it down. What about the other six bunkers? They're made of scrap metal, man!"

"Still standing," answered Nathan, "Don't know if it weren't for their extra artillery. Those bunkers also aren't as exposed as you guys are."

"They know we're here, Nathan, they have to," warned Alex, "this place is no secret anymore."

"I know."

"Every Gnat we've shot down we've disabled as quick as we could, but that's not working anymore. They're eventually gonna find out where all their drones have gone missing. Geospark, and its forces aren't that far off, there's just no way. Stuff's gonna get hot over here real quick. I'm getting anxious."

"I know. Me too. Just chill out, ok. You guys good for now? You only have two more days in your shift."

"Yeah, we're hangin," Alex looked at the other two watchmen, both of them pale and worried looking, "Wouldn't be able to do this by myself man. You wouldn't believe the noises we hear up here at night, they're not human. Don't know what I'd do if there wasn't twenty four inches of metal and concrete between us and whatever's out there. Gnats aren't the only thing I'm worried about."

Nathan did not respond. He heard Iris's voice echo in the back of his head, *Do not get caught out there when darkness falls*, and then dismissed the thought just as quickly as it came. "Annak got attacked by a grizzly this morning," said Nathan.

"You serious?" asked Alex, "Didn't think there were any more out there. He alright?"

"He's cut up pretty bad, but he's alive. Thinks his forearm is broken. You wouldn't believe Annak's strength to hold off this bear - it was massive. He must have stabbed it fifty times."

"Knife?" asked one of the other watchman. "Why didn't he shoot it?"

"Shotgun wouldn't fire."

"I don't believe that! No one's more OCD about cleaning their weapons than Annak!" exclaimed Alex.

"He fired the gun right afterwards and it worked fine; still doesn't make sense to me."

"So where's he now?" asked Alex.

"At the cave, probably in his room. Didn't want anyone around him."

"Annak's a crazy dude. Not as crazy as your grandma, but still crazy," said Alex.

"Well, I still don't understand either one of 'em," replied Nathan.

"Hey, before you go, check this out," said Alex. He picked up a complex gadget from the ground, "It's a revolver I took out of the last Gnat we brought down near glacier point. Keeping it as a souvenir."

"Souvenir? You think you're gonna live long or something?"

"Geospark's technology's getting more complex, man. I'm trying to figure out how it works. Look!"

Nathan took the heavy mechanical ball into his hands and examined it's intricacy, admiring it with confusion. Alex called it a revolver, but it was much more complex than that. Parts of it were still sparking as if it ran off limitless energy. "How is this thing supposed to shoot a bullet? And what are these?" Nathan reached his finger inside one of the cavities and was about to pull out a small capsule before Alex snatched it back.

"Nathan! Don't touch that!" he yelled.

"What is it?"

"I know it's just the size of a speck, but that's no ordinary bullet — cause an explosion big enough to level this hillside!"

"Why you messing around with it then?"

"Why else — curiosity?"

"Curiosity's gonna get you killed."

"Before we took this one down it shot something across the bunker. See that over there?" Alex pointed out the bulletproof glass window to a large crater in the ground. "That little thing rocked the whole side of the cliff. I'm still trying to figure out how they're making this stuff. They're gun powder isn't even a *powder* anymore - it's a fluid!" Alex paused, then joked, "If I get blown up in the next couple days, you'll know why."

"Sure you wanna keep messing around with that?"

"What else am I gonna do around here? I gotta figure out some of their technology."

Nathan noticed how fast dusk was approaching, "My time's up, I need to go."

Alex gave him a brief hug, "Better hurry, man. I'll see you in two days."

Nathan did not waste any more time in conversation, he flew out the door of the bunker and began his descent. It was roughly three o'clock in the afternoon, which gave him maybe two hours to make it to the opposite side of the canyon before nightfall. On a normal day this should not have been difficult. Typically, from MX-Peak to the cave, two hours was plenty of time; even if weather was bad. But in Nathan's world there were more factors at play than just the weather.

With the day closing, and the entrance of Adullum at the front of his mind, he hustled southward, descending the rocky crags through a long rift in the mountainside. As he continued to get lower into the valley, the timber thickened around him; and even though the sun was still out, the atmosphere was darkened.

Everything was fine as he paced himself until his feet reached the dried up banks of the Merced River — he felt a sharp pain rush through his forehead. In a split second, surges of heat flashed through his body. He quickly became aware of the rising temperature in his flesh. *There's no way! There's just now way this is happening*, he thought. *No! Not today!* he muttered, as the chemical balance of his nervous system went out of whack. He picked up the pace, turning the cadence of a hike into a run. He knew exactly what was happening, and he did not like it. Yet, helpless, as if his whole body had suddenly been whacked with a sandbag — he had hit an invisible wall. He was quickly paralyzed by blurred vision and overwhelming disorientation.

With no choice, he stopped and forced his back against the nearest tree. He knew he was on the cusp of having to defend himself. Closing his eyes, he clenched his rifle tightly to his chest and tried to manage the dizziness — hot enough now that he could feel the sweat leaking through his skin. "This can't be happening!" he said to himself, tearing off his gloves, jacket and shirt. Naked from the waste up, the cold air brushed against him, but he kept sweating. Reluctantly opening his eyes, he swung his head frantically back and forth, trying to reassure himself of the natural world, trying to cling to something familiar - the snow, a rock, the dirt, anything! It was all there — the elements of the valley, but then, before he could reach out and hold onto it, the entire scenery folded up as if it were a rag scorched by fire.

And suddenly he did not know where he was. The

only reality surrounding him was a perplexing labyrinth of hallways and corridors, stretching back into nothingness. All of the walls looked as though they had been smeared with black coal and layered with soot. No matter how far he looked he could not tell where the hallways started and where they ended. He closed his eyes, but nothing changed. He opened them — still the same.

He knew they were coming next, just like they always did. Six towering figures appeared out of the darkness and began making their way down the hallways, from all directions. They moved and twitched methodically like beetles. Nathan slapped himself in fear and tried to come out of it, but nothing changed — eyes open or not, did not matter. They crept towards him like phantoms; each one abnormally tall, wearing long black trench coats. At first, they always appeared to be human, but something about them was *off*. Their skin was deathly pale and they had no eyes, just empty sockets. Nathan could see their hands rotting, their fingernails were thickened and long as if diseased.

Moving slowly and coming to within twenty feet of Nathan, a terrible smell filled his nostrils. The pristine mountain air turned to the odor of decomposing bodies, with a hint of sulfur, burnt hair, rubber, and the stench of polyurethane. "Get away from me! Get away from me!" Nathan yelled, as he lifted his weapon and opened fire. Like every time before, he was foolish to think that bullets would do something — they never did. He was up against something much greater than flesh and blood, and he knew it, yet he shot at them every time, then watched in dismay as the bullets passed right through their decrepit bodies. They only came closer, quicker, sneering and whispering rapidly; all of them at once, simultaneously. Their collective voices were sharp and powerful — sounding like clanking metal and razor blades scoring pieces of glass. Nathan could not cover his ears fast enough. Unable to do a thing, he curled up into the fetal position and started rocking back and forth — just like he always did.

It did not take long for him to sense their smelly bodies lingering over him. Their voices were only louder now, clear enough for Nathan to make out their words, "Alone! You're alone...punk! Piece of crap little boy — scared, scared, scared little boy!"

Not only hearing the words audibly, he felt every fetid, rotting emotion that was encased inside each syllable. As they spoke, Nathan was encased in this feeling of forsakenness. Forsakenness from people, forsakenness from things, from himself. The collective power of their whispers overwhelmed him to the point where he became directionless. Nathan lost his focus, unable to think, his mind raptured in a whirlwind. His only real feeling became a cold awareness of the complete absence of anything *good*. In a panic, forced to go to a deep place in search of refuge, he did the only thing he could think of, crying out in a loud voice, "MOOOOOOOM!"

He cried again, "MOM!" and again, "MOM!"

But it did nothing. Their whispers were still cutting like knives, "You belong to us...just a mistake...all you are." They kept tormenting him with cruelties, even bending over and pressing their festering lips to his ears, "Only a matter of time, Nathan..."

He could feel their sickening vomit and saliva pouring down his head. And then, just as he was sure he would be drowned in it, they were gone. The horrid smell of their presence retreated. The black hallways were gone. The endless labyrinth of corridors vanished, and suddenly, the only thing in front of Nathan was the natural order of his familiar world — the overcast sky above, the frail valley around him.

The heat in Nathan's body dropped, and the pounding in his head went away as if it had never been there. He came to himself and started shivering, the sweat turning to frost on the surface of his skin. He could not get his clothes on fast enough. The only thing he could think to do was check his rifle's magazine cartridge, and to his shock, all the bullets were there, not one round had been fired.

"What am I doing?" he asked himself, unable to figure out why he was curled up on the ground. Everything around him was the same, but one thing was different — a type of paranoia attached itself to him as a leech would. Though he could not remember any of the words, the residue of the whispers clung to his bones.

Dazed and violated, but somewhat slowly gaining back his ability to think clearly, Nathan realized what was happening. It was obvious he had forgotten it was day 60, and now he was pissed off at himself as a result of forgetting something so important. Overcome with anxiety, he knew that the next 48 hours were going to be terrible. The thought of being mentally paralyzed out in the woods by these *things* increased his discomfort.

He stood up and started running again, hugging the banks of the river, as it provided a tangible measuring line to the entrance of the cave. At this point there was no certainty what would happen, or when. The *episodes*, as Nathan referred to them, were predictable every 60 days, but once they started, there was no telling what they would bring. Being out in the open, Nathan's worst thought was that he would become disoriented to the point of not being able to find his way back.

Nathan despised the episodes. *Despised* probably is not even sufficient enough to describe the hate he harbored for *them*. At times he wished he could be someone else, anyone, if it meant he would not have to suffer whatever these things were. Nathan never knew how to make sense of *it* — the occurrences, and the regularity of them, that is. They started out as nightmares when he was five. Nothing too peculiar there, what five year old does not have nightmares when the lights go out? The visions, the voices, their faces only showed up while he slept, and mostly when he was sick with a cold or the flu. But then, the nightmares started happening more frequently. A couple years later, Nathan sensed, as best a seven year old could, that something was different. He woke up during one of them, thinking everything would go away, but it did not. All the aspects of the slumbering vision stayed the same, even solidifying more intensely as he woke up and opened his eyes. Alone in his bedroom, lying on his back, he would pull the blanket over his head and try to escape the terror — it never worked. Every vile thing that was outside the blanket, was inside the blanket. Plagued by the reality of the vision, he would grope for something safe and call out for his mother, until at last, she would come rushing into the room, flick on the light, and hold little Nathan tightly in her arms.

Mommy — the single noun, that for Nathan, represented the entire world's security system. *Mommy* is the end to the means, the answer to the question, and the refuge from the storm. She is the healer, the pacifier. But then, even then, when she would hold him, nothing changed — none of the fear left, none of the panic, none of the demons. Nathan could never make sense of the fact that even *mommy* was unable to comfort him. What kind of mother cannot stop a ghostly nightmare and crush it under her heels? It did not make sense. At least not for Nathan.

Life is not supposed to work that way. Mothers are supposed to be divine; unmatched in their selfless ability to protect the fruit of their womb. Maybe so, but in Nathan's world that was not how it worked. The episodes, whatever they were — were different. Nightmares? Night terrors? Seizures? Open visions? Euphoric migraines? Temporal-lobe epilepsy? Nathan did not care about the etymology or the definition, or even the diagnosis — the episodes were powerful, and debilitating, they always were. It did not make a difference if she was crying out, *I'm here, Nathan. I'm here! Mommy's here! It's ok, son! Mommy's here!* For what seemed to her like an eternity, she did her best to stay calm even though her son's eyes were rolled back in his head and his arms were wagging helplessly all over the place. Thinking he was suffocating to death, she would squeeze his cheeks and say, *Breathe! Breathe! Little Nathan, breathe!* Then, to her astonishment, as if nothing ever happened, he would calm down, not even remembering a thing.

How Nathan always wished to have had the episodes just be something as simple as nightmares. At least then they could have had the chance to grow weaker and less intimidating as he aged. But, with the passing of each year he was greeted by those he named *the Stinkin Six* — with uncomfortable regularity and precision. It was as if they held the page to a calendar, about which Nathan knew nothing about. Without fail, every sixty days, it would happen — the temperature change, the influx of head pressure, the smells, the whispers, the vomit, the aloneness. All of it was there, each time lasting for a few minutes and then subsiding for another half hour, in bipolar intervals for the next 48 hours, and then receding for another 60 days before starting again. For years now, Nathan has kept them a secret, hidden away from others as best as possible. When *they* do come, it is easy and familiar to play them off as migraines and say, *I'm tired, gonna sleep for the next two days.*

It was not hard to predict the episodes, but for some reason, today he had forgotten about them. Annak's encounter with the bear, and Nathan's inner restlessness had cluttered his thinking to the point where he was caught off guard. The only two things he knew to help, he did not have — sleep, and a confined space. In the open wilderness, on the cusp of black-out was no good. The Stinkin Six, were always more mischievous in open spaces. Regretful for having made the attempt to check on MX-Peak, Nathan continued running back toward the cave with increasing anxiety.

SIX
Dark Visitor

I t had been exactly 30 minutes since he got his clothes back on after the first episode. Closer to the cave now, he felt his body being taken captive again. The sun had almost completely disappeared over the crest of the valley by now. "No! No! No! No! No!" he said to himself rapidly, unable to summon enough strength to run any faster. Once again, the heat in his body became unbearable and then, there they were — the black hallways, the Stinkin Six and their rotting flesh. Barely conscious of whether he was still moving or curled up into a ball on the ground, he did not even need to look over his shoulder, their presence was noticeable enough.

Despite his delirium it still felt like his legs were moving mechanically underneath him. Knowing they were behind him, he could hear their whispers and chants, "You scum! Hated! Alone! We're gonna get you!"

They howled with conviction, sending chills down Nathan's spine. It was almost impossible not to be crippled by the emotions of despair that were flung at him. Not knowing how, he kept moving, even though for what seemed like an eternity, they continued taunting him, and twitching. One of them came so close, Nathan could feel it rip the edge of his jacket off. "Get away from me! Get away!" he yelled. And then, just as they had hundreds and hundreds of times before, they vanished.

Coming out from under the oppression of the vision, Nathan's clothes were cold and damp with sweat. He stopped to catch his breath, and looked around, raving to an extent that he was able to keep running despite their crippling taunts.

Then he realized it was completely dark. A pile of question marks littered his mind. The day held enough complexity already, he was not looking forward to being confronted by any more enigmas of the darkness. Not knowing what else to do, he reached into his pocket and groped for a flare or even a flashlight, but there was nothing there. "There's no way!" He said to himself, remembering that he had cleared his pockets of extra weight before making the hike. Looking up though the crowded tree branches, there was a sliver of moonlight coming through, reflecting off the snow. Nathan thought it would be enough light to trek the rest of the way. Even though he had memorized the path by now, the uncertainties of the night made him uneasy.

Nathan and the other Reapers knew the world was broken. It was hard enough surviving during the day. But the oddities that took place at night were another story. There were beast-like sounds, the appearance of things moving, strange echoes, and voices that were hard to explain. At night things dead would come alive — a *lurking*. It was not uncommon for a Reaper to return to the cave, after being out in the darkness, only to have lost his mind, or not to have returned at all. After multiple disappearances and losing innocent victims to insanity, it became a solid rule to get one's business done before dark — no matter what.

Nathan knew this, and the knowledge of it troubled him. He was confronted with two choices: allow fear to paralyze him, or maintain some level of confidence that he could make it to the cave unscathed. He chose the latter.

Continuing to move, he knew he was less than a mile away. His breath was heavy with every stride. The hike, the lack of food, the cold, and both episodes sapped most of his energy. *I know I'm close. I can make it. I know I can,* Nathan thought to himself.

Then, in the seriousness of the moment, something

peculiar happened — an old joke came to mind. It was the last thing he would have expected. *Can't be serious,* he thought. Of all things, Alex's wisecracking lips were chatting in his ears, telling that same worn-out story. Nathan felt his consciousness being pulled into the humor, but then roused himself to stay focused on the sobriety of his predicament. *Just run,* he thought. But there was nothing he could do when the first line of the joke kept battering the door. The more he tried to ignore the humor, the louder it got. The sound of Alex's voice was intrusive, as it was so many times before. A replay of the dialogue took over.

"Hey Nathan! I got a story for ya," said Alex.

"Same one I think it is?" asked Nathan.

"Maybe not. Only one way to find out."

"Fine."

"An old man was sitting on the porch rocking in his chair…"

"Oh come on, Alex. You know how many times I've heard the stupid *old man* story?"

"Doesn't matter. Whether you've heard it or not doesn't make a difference, you're still grumpy. Maybe this time you'll laugh."

"Whatever, I'll just pretend I haven't heard it."

Alex's voice took over in Nathan's mind, "So, an old man's rocking in his chair when someone walks by and notices how content he looks. *Wow! Sir, you look so happy! Do you mind me asking, what's your secret to life?* The old man says, *I smoke five packs of cigarettes a day, drink a case of whisky a week, eat whatever I want, and don't exercise.* Stunned, the passerby asks another question, *That's unbelievable. How old are you?* The old man replies with a smile, *26.*"

A smirk spread across Nathan's face, the thought of the joke caused his nerves to settle a bit. His energy was still low, but he was only moments away from reaching the cave. A few more minutes, nothing more than that, and he would be there. His nervousness started to give way to a sense of calm at the thought of surviving the day.

Yet suddenly, just as he was able to see the outline of the entrance to the cave, something strange happened. Nathan was startled by the noise of branches cracking under feet that were not his own, accompanied by the gust of an eerie wind blowing. The wind was mixed with some sort of thick black smoke. He knew he was not having another episode, the feeling was different. Before he could discern what was going on, a dark figure appeared out of nowhere and stood in front of him on the trail. Nathan was running too fast, and unable stop, slammed right into it. When his head smacked into the its chest, he bounced off and fell backwards to the ground. With his eyes wide open — no trance, no temperature change, no headache; he beheld what looked like an awful monster; it had the form of a tall man, though strangely contorted with long arms. The *thing* towered above Nathan easily by more than 3 feet. In a moment, the same unbearable smell of the Stinkin Six filled Nathan's nostrils, but somehow he knew this thing was not one of them. Something about it was different, this thing possessed a greater authority than the Six, and commanded greater reverence. It was not a phantom or a figment of his imagination — it was real.

Nathan roused himself, sprung up from the ground, and tackled the creature, crashing violently into its stomach. When he collided with it, the creature did not budge. It was stout, and braced. No sooner did the sharp pain run through Nathan's body, that he knew his shoulder was dislocated. He stumbled backwards, clenched his jaw, then violently shrugged his shoulder socket back into place, letting out a yell. Resolving not to charge at it again, Nathan aimed his rifle and pulled the trigger multiple times. *Crack!* But, then stood back in shock when he watched all four bullets go right through the creature, opening wounds in its flesh that immediately closed back up.

Nathan stepped backwards as the creature came toward him. Through the dim moonlight Nathan tried to make out the details of what he was looking at. For a moment, he was convinced the thing was human, but as it got closer he noticed it was more edgy than a normal man. The thing was attractive in the sense that there was something supernatural about it, yet mangled at the same time. Its shoulder blades protruded and were obscure. Its head was elongated, hunched down toward its chest, and its face was recessed. Nathan was unable to discern its gender, somehow appearing to be neither male nor female. The creature was frightening. Whatever it was, Nathan knew it was not a Reaper or a Screener, and he had the hunch that it was not confronting him in order to bring good news. Not sure what to do, Nathan relied on his rifle one more time, but again the bullets did nothing.

As the creature came towards him, easily more than seven feet tall, its glowing red eyes — flickering with some sort of static electricity — pierced Nathan's. As soon as their eyes met Nathan felt his body tense up as if he was being restricted by something. Nathan struggled to move, but found himself slowly unable to escape, somehow being bound up by the creature. Powerless, Nathan fell prostrate on the ground. He felt like his body was being covered by an invisible sackcloth blanket and was mysteriously being put into a coma. Yet, just when Nathan did not think it could get any worse, he felt his stiffened body begin to levitate off the ground. Within seconds he was floating in thin air.

The creature marched toward Nathan and stood over him, not lifting a finger, continuing to raise him off the ground with some sort of invisible pull. Soon enough

Nathan's face was right under its skeletal looking chin. Out of pure fear, Nathan tried to yell, but could not, his voice just as stiffed as his paralyzed body. The thing kinked its neck and slowly scanned Nathan's body from head to toe like he was a victim on a coroner's table. Nathan could not help noticing how gross the thing's mouth was — there were no lips, the opening was huge and intimidating, vibrating and quivering like it was about to release a deafening roar. There was a pulse beating in its throat. And after a period of silent inspection, the creature spoke.

"Hi," it said, conjuring up words from its mouth even though it appeared to have no tongue, or teeth.

Hi? Nathan thought to himself, scared no less. This was not the sort of word he expected to come out of whatever this was. He was reminded that there are some things he never wanted to hear *hi* from — death, for example. This *hi* had that tone to it. As the simple syllable rolled out of the creature's face, Nathan sensed the totality of all dread being poured over him, having no choice but to listen as it spoke, its voice sounding like two rusty machine cogs grinding together, mixed with the tenor of hundreds of rats screaming. Its breath reeked of sulfur and pneumonia. The stench was so bad that Nathan hoped it would not speak again. Yet, his false hope was soon exposed.

"Nathan," it said slowly, silent for some time then speaking again, "you have no power over me."

How the creature knew his name was uncertain. The question ran through his mind, *What are you?* Then a strange sensation came over Nathan's body, as if a thousand worms were crawling through his torso.

"I am many names. Unbound by identity," the creature answered, discerning Nathan's question telepathically as it cranked its neck from side to side before pressing its face closer into Nathan's.

Nathan was confused and intimidated. The creature paid no respect to Nathan's questions.

"One year," it said, "one year from today you will surely die. I'll be there to carry you away."

As the word *die* fell out of its mouth, Nathan felt his heart stop. A shock ran through it, as if a small needle had pierced the main artery. The creature began taking deep breaths, its eyes twitching rapidly with electricity, as Nathan started to feel the air being sucked from his lungs. He knew he was starting to suffocate. The pressure in Nathan's chest and head increased to the point where he felt like he was going to implode.

Then unexpectedly, as Nathan was almost completely unconscious, he heard the racket of a two-stroke motor howling in the distance. The sound was familiar and reassuring — the angry rev of a throttle, the burning of gasoline. It got louder. Trying to shift his gaze from the creature, he looked down the trail and saw two headlights racing through the dark. Nathan squinted his eyes until he was able to make out the silhouette of someone on a four-wheeler. The machine skidded to a halt, kicking snow up into the air right where the electric-eyed thing was still levitating Nathan off the ground.

Nathan soon realized it was Annak. The creature somehow redirected its power, causing Nathan to hit the ground, and then turned its attention to the new intruder. Annak leapt off the four-wheeler and rather than bracing himself for the hideous thing, started rushing towards it. The creature, not backing down, responded, moving swiftly toward Annak. But Annak, instead of leveling out a gun, or a knife, simply stretched out his arm. Nathan was trying to catch his breath while he watched in amazement as the creature stopped just feet from Annak's hand, and was hindered from moving any closer.

Annak was half the size of this thing, but all it could do was hiss, snarl, spit, and flail its arms violently. Like a rabid animal it tried to do everything possible to crush Annak, trying to make contact, trying to crush him. As the creature lashed out violently, Annak held his position confidently, his eyes radiant and smoldering blue, impassioned by a deep vehemence toward the creature. Annak gazed at it, reveling in some sort of impassioned delight, as he watched the creature struggle like a spider trapped inside a glass jar.

"I come against you by His authority!" yelled Annak.

The creature immediately began to pant, swinging its head rapidly from side to side, and then buckled in on itself and collapsed.

Annak continued to speak with force, "I bind you and command you to leave!"

One more time, the creature tried to surge toward Annak in an attempt to devour him.

Annak yelled, "NOW!"

It was as if a cannonball had just been shot into its stomach, the creature's shoulders bent forward, its arms folded inward, and immediately disappeared into the forest. Annak was not impressed or surprised, nor did he linger. He went right over to Nathan and pressed his hand firmly against his chest. For Nathan, the smell of stale coffee and motor oil could not have shown up at a better time. Soon, as Nathan sensed a peculiar heat issuing from Annak's hand, the sensation of worms crawling through his body was gone. Nathan took in a huge breath of air as Annak pulled him up off the ground.

"Get me outta here!" said Nathan. "What was that thing?"

"No time," answered Annak.

They mounted the four-wheeler and sped off toward the granite wall of El Capitan that was towering above them in the distance.

SEVEN
Words Become Worlds

Nathan held on tight, pressed his head in between Annak's shoulder blades and closed his eyes. He had no idea what had just happened back there. "Was all that real?" he asked.

Annak chose not to respond. In a few minutes they passed by two Reapers holding machine guns, guarding the opening to the cave. The sound of the motor rang off the rock tunnels as they slowed down and pulled into a large cathedral-sized room. There were a few sporadic camp-fires, and some shabby candles burning throughout the place with various people gathered around them.

"NATHAN!" yelled Iris, rushing up to both of them, Annak barely getting a chance to slow down. "What happened? Where were you?" She clutched Nathan's chin and looked over his body. "What were you thinking? Let me see your eyes! Let me see your eyes!"

"Grooma, ooouh...ah...I. I joost," Nathan had a hard time saying anything with his cheeks pressed together by Iris's fingers. She loosened her grip. "I just lost track of time...that's all."

"Nathan, how dare you! Don't you mess with me!"

"I was just going over stuff with Alex, lost track of time."

"You're lying to me! Son, I know when you're lying!"

Annak looked at Iris and said one word, "Sarx."

"Annak?" she questioned.

"I'm positive," he reassured.

"Sarx?" asked Nathan.

Iris snapped back, "Annak, don't mess with me."

Annak said nothing back, he just stared at her. Iris knew he was being honest.

"You saw the current in *its* eyes?" Iris asked.

Annak nodded to affirm.

"Its mouth?"

He nodded again.

"Sarx haven't shown up in years!" Exclaimed Iris.

"Iris, I'm certain. There must be a shift taking place," said Annak.

Nathan's nerves were becoming more unsettled.

Iris got quiet and started pacing back and forth, before speaking up again, "Tell me it didn't open its mouth," she said to Nathan.

Nathan was alone in his thoughts to an extent, *Shift? Open its mouth?* He was certainly feeling like the victim of something he was not ready to know about.

"Nathan, tell me," she commanded.

He thought about it, and for some reason stuttered with shame, "I…I…I can't remember." And then with a little more courage declared, "You guys are freakin' me out!"

"Nathan!" Iris said as she shook him, "this is not a time for lies! If that Sarx spoke to you, you're only chance at staying alive is telling me what it said. Right now!"

Nathan's heart was beating, he started to realize the severity of the situation. With hesitancy, compelled by Iris's tone, he answered, "Yes."

Iris looked even more stunned now, "It can't be," she mumbled to herself. "Not Nathan." There was an awkward silence, "What did it say to you?"

Nathan looked as if he had seen something far more frightening than a ghost. Iris's intensity was starting to frighten him more than the creature did. He hesitated, looked at Annak, then back at Iris, "I…don't know."

"What did it say, Nathan?" she asked again. "If that

thing spoke to you, its *word* can become a *world*.

"One year from today I will..." he paused, looking down, feeling a slew of shame and angst.

"What?" demanded Iris.

"Die," Nathan blurted out.

Iris took a step back, letting go of Nathan's shoulders, her eyes widened as she became deeply enraged. Not responding, she turned around and left the room.

Nathan's angst hit a tipping point. He was confused by Iris. She could have at least offered some sort of comfort, given an explanation about what just happened. But instead, she walked away and turned a cold shoulder to Nathan.

Annak was no different, he looked at Nathan, "I wouldn't bother her for the rest of the night if I were you."

"What's going on, Annak?" responded Nathan. "Why am I left in the dark about so much of this crap?"

Annak held the side of his own arm, the bear wound was leaking blood through a bandage, "You just encountered a legion of the abyss, Nathan."

"Abyss?"

"Hell, in other words. Those things haven't been around in a long time, and they rarely allow themselves to be seen. It's strange, but you have to be famous in a sense, to get one of those things to notice you."

"What's that supposed to mean?"

"Famous in their world, not ours. It knew your name didn't it?"

Nathan nodded.

"They don't show up in our dimension for anyone. The only way to summon *one* is through the dark arts, magic — and even then, the encounter is rare; for those foolish enough to beckon the dark."

"Well I wasn't doing any of that, don't even know any magic. I was just trying to get back here."

"That Sarx knows something about you, or else it wouldn't of shown up."

"What?"

"It's afraid of something that's inside you."

"That thing wasn't acting scared, pretty sure I was the victim. It said I had no power over it."

"Cause you didn't. And you don't."

"Obviously."

"Not yet, at least. You could if you wanted to," said Annak, less like a warning and more like an appeal. "There's something about your life that it knows, and wants to keep it from happening."

"Just like everybody else around here, that Sarx knows more about me than I do. Annak, all this *darkness* stuff creeps me out. I only care about one thing and one thing only — getting the lake back and going home."

"Unfortunately, you don't have a choice now. Some people seek darkness out — those who are weak minded and ignorant. Then there are those who seek after good and, as a result, darkness seeks after them. Darkness goes after what it's intimidated by."

"That seems unfair, why?"

"It's an attempt to get as close to the light as possible, so it can hide within the shadow of its wings. People only get adversity when they're moving. But not just moving — moving in the right direction. With all the dams stationed along the Columbia River, the Snake, the Salmon — those few remarkable fish still find a way to make it upriver from the Pacific ocean all the way to the famed Redfish Lake. That's over seven hundred miles."

"I'm still not getting you, Annak. You go after goodness, and darkness follows? Doesn't seem right."

"Nathan, listen to me very carefully. That Sarx marched out of the dens of hell for one purpose — to shut you down, to keep you from your destiny. It knows that you're carrying something."

"Carrying something?"

"I don't know, but it's something great. And you're the only one holding it back."

"Maybe I was just caught outside in the dark at the wrong time."

"Nathan, you need to understand something. That Sarx opened its mouth to profane the sanctity of your life. The words it spoke to you carried poison, and it's already taken root inside your heart."

A nauseating look came over Nathan's face, "What do you mean?" Nothing's in my heart that I haven't allowed to be there."

"Did you feel a needle poke it, like you were on the verge of having a heart-attack?"

"Never had one, but probably," he paused. "Hey! How'd you know that?"

"When that Sarx spoke, it released the very nature of its own darkness over your life. Like Iris said, their *words* become *worlds*. What it speaks can become reality, it's a prophetic curse. Words carry things, whether we realize it or not. Sarx have been sickened, trained to speak only what can ruin and destroy. At some point in time you must have given permission for this to happen."

"There's no way. I might hate Him, but I'm not friends with demons."

"You must have, Nathan. As long as you're keeping Him out, you're leaving yourself open to darkness. If you're not seated at his banquet table, you're seated at theirs."

"He's the only one who's kept me out because he let my parents die!" Nathan answered in anger.

"You have free-will, but there's a consequence to staying bitter. It opens your heart to all kinds of vile things…

spirits.

"There more of those things out there? Sarx?"

"Unfortunately, there are many. But, it only takes one of them, with one word, to destroy a single life that's not under complete reign of the Navigator."

Nathan shook his head, "One more thing in life that doesn't seem fair."

"If that Sarx had power over you, it was simply equal to the amount of rejection you've shown the Navigator. Those demons can only take what we give them."

"I didn't give that thing anything!"

"Yes you did, Nathan. You've given it your anger, your doubt, your fear, your lack of reverence."

"Why didn't bullets work?" asked Nathan.

"Sarx can't be shot, they can't be stabbed, they can't be blown up, tackled, chained or anything. Bullets don't work. The weapons of flesh and blood don't sting a Sarx. There's much more involved than that. You didn't have power over it because of your maturity."

"What, my age?" Nathan shirked, "Cause I'm only 27? I'm tougher than anyone else in this camp."

"I'm not talking about age, I'm talking about your inner man."

Nathan rolled his eyes and balked, "Oh my goodness! I am so sick of hearing about all this *spiritual* stuff. What is it with you and my grandma? Why do you guys always have to crack open the doors of the so called *unseen world*? I believe in what's real, Annak! The trees, the snow, the dirt, gasoline, and nothing more than that! And whatever that was out in the forest, I'm sure there's a natural explanation for it."

"Nathan, you're a strong young man, you're tough. But you need to know there's a world among us that you can't see with your natural eyes. If you don't learn about the unseen world from Iris and me then you're gonna learn about it eventually, and it won't be from the right side. That Sarx carried a power that you should be scared of. But there's One among us much more powerful — it's Him you should really fear."

"And what about you? Why weren't you scared of that thing?" asked Nathan, almost disregarding his comment about *One much more powerful*.

"Because I'm not afraid of *creatures*," said Annak with emphasis in his voice. "I'm not afraid of anything *created*, I only revere and worship the One who's uncreated and the One who made all things. Whatever thing you fear, that's what you exalt, and that thing will always possess you and have the most power over you. If I didn't have the Blue Flame, you would've seen something different out there."

"The Flame? That's why it couldn't touch you?"

"Yes. But, that's the short answer, there's a lot more to it than that. You want me to tickle your ears or you want the truth?"

Nathan thought about it for a moment.

"It's up to you, I can make you as comfortable as you want. If your inner man is still an infant I can give him a pacifier, swaddle him and rock him to sleep. Would you like that?"

"You're an edgy guy, Annak, still can't figure you out. One moment you're saving my life, and the next? You're making fun of me."

"I'm not making fun of you, Nathan. You just can't tell the difference between someone trying to save your life and someone trying to kill it. Even right now you feel *put down*, but I am trying to help you. You need to know that. You're irritated by something you don't have. Whenever the Blue Flame or the Navigator's mentioned, you squirm, because it hurts. The surgeon's blade is trying to heal you, not harm you."

Nathan was silent.

Annak waited for a moment, knowing that Nathan wanted answers, but often was not willing to wade through the spiritual matters in order to find them. "So, you want the truth or not?"

"Fine."

Annak began, "Sarx have dominion over the natural world, they exercise as much authority as they want within the boundaries of what's seen. From the core of our planet, to the outskirts of the sky, they can mess with whatever, and whoever they want, possessing and destroying souls one at a time. They have unlimited power over anyone unaware of *their* existence. Sarx can hijack a mind and plumb it to insanity, causing the victim to commit their own suicide. Yet the very person being demonized doesn't even have a clue that those suicidal thoughts aren't coming from themselves, but from the Sarx. Their power relies on other's naivety and ignorance. The only reason that *thing* couldn't touch me, on the other hand, is because I didn't do anything."

"What? What do you mean — didn't do anything?"

"*I* didn't. It wasn't me, Nathan. It was the Blue Flame. The only thing more powerful than a Sarx is the One who created it. The creature comes from the Creator, not the other way around."

"The Blue Flame created those things?"

"Sort of, the Navigator did. The Blue Flame is the — "

"Alright," Nathan interrupted, "that's enough for me right now." Nathan rubbed his eyes as a reaction to fatigue.

"Listen to me very carefully, you can only make it out there for so long without the Blue Flame."

Suddenly, Iris came out from her room. She was decked out in heavy winter gear, marching right past Annak and Nathan. She refused make eye contact, and acted as if they were not there. Nathan was more bothered by it than Annak was. They both watched as she left the cave.

"Whoa! Whoa! Whoa! Where are you going?" asked Nathan, "you can't go out there?" He immediately went after her, but before he could cut her off, Annak grabbed him by the jacket.

"Calm down," said Annak.

"But that thing! That Sarx! She can't go out there by herself!" exclaimed Nathan.

"Iris knows how to take care of herself. She's your only hope at staying alive now. Just let her go."

"She's crazy!" yelled Nathan, "doesn't she know what just happened?"

"Of course she does. That's why she's going out there, to wage war for your soul," Annak peered into Nathan's eyes. "You have no choice but to let her go."

Nathan was not about to fight with Annak about whether or not he should go back out there. What he experienced in the darkness was a reminder that there were things in the universe much stronger than him. Sensing the onset of another *episode*, Nathan started to walk away from Annak so he could lay down.

"Nathan, DO NOT leave this cave," he commanded, "I'll be watching you the rest of the night."

Nathan went into his room. He had no energy left to deal with the Stinkin Six. He flung his guns and pack onto the ground and plopped his body onto the mattress, clothes and boots still on, and then he fell asleep.

#

The Lodge

here was a long, rectangular mirror suspended on the dull concrete wall. He bent over, pressed his hands against the polished metal countertop and gazed into it, admiring his reflection like a rare piece of art or lunar eclipse. The room was empty, pristine, quiet, and dark. Except for the light that was coming from behind the glass. The florescent light beamed softly, creating a brilliant frame around the mirror, adding a tungsten-silver glow to his image. There was a lingering scent, like the smell one would find in an informational server-cellar or a hospital room — clean, and uncomfortably sterile. Nothing in the room was as important as the mirror. That single plate of glass, no more than half an inch thick, was the focal point of his stronghold. It was the tangible, daily reminder of his existence. By looking into it he was greeted with pride, and became aware of the totality of all he needed to know, the sum of all he cared about.

There I am. I am everything, he thought to himself, enthralled with contours of his face. Grinning from ear to ear, he marveled at his flawless teeth — white, perfect. His fingers ran haltingly through his crisp-black hair that was as sleek as a sheet of ice. His skin was without blemish. He had to be certain that everything was just as good as it was the day before. He was the epitome of perfection — alluring and attractive in every sense of the word, and unparalleled in his beauty; primed and ageless.

After a generous amount of time gazing into the image of his own glory, Onyx slowly backed away from the mirror — its glow disappearing from his face like a curtain as he left the inner atrium. Two massive, mechanical crystal doors, as clear as day, opened up in front of him where he made his way onto the floating steel deck.

Waiting for him, resolved and at somber attention, was Gabriel. The frigid morning wind swirled around his body as he stood there quietly. As Onyx approached, a subtle flurry of snow blew between them.

"The dams." said Onyx, stiffening his neck. He looked into Gabriel's eyes in such a way as to communicate that he cared more about those stoic river blockades than any human life that still existed. His stare was more bone-chilling than the weather.

"Winter hasn't been good, but they're still supplying power," answered Gabriel.

"How much?" asked Onyx.

"30,000 megawatts."

"Less than we've ever had." Onyx clenched the cable railing that ran the perimeter of the deck, and looked out across the the jagged Sawtooth mountains, still covered with a small sheet of snow. "The Dalles?"

"It's been twelve hours now."

"Twelve hours ago you told me the powerhouse was down, three turbines stalled, and the generator dead. Why aren't they fixed?"

"They don't know if it's an attack or a malfunction. The outflow pipes are clogged. The engineer's still working on it."

"Reapers?" Onyx's eyes were beaming.

"There's no way," Gabriel reassured. "Nothing left of them anymore. They've all been wiped out."

Onyx stared down at the frozen lake below, "Gabriel, I've made you Chief Steward over all this. I've given you command over the entire watershed. The whole purpose of your existence is to prevent these glitches. And, yet, they're still happening. The Dalles supplies one-sixth of our power. The system needs to be perfect, nothing less. You're responsible!"

"I have the Adler and thirteen Screeners ready. I'll take care of it," Gabriel responded.

"Don't return to Icon until it is." Onyx squared his shoulders and looked away so as to say, *Get out of here!* Gabriel knew him well enough by now, to know what he wanted.

Gabriel took a few steps back and slowly made his way to the edge of the deck. Two Screeners were standing at the top of a long steel staircase that was staggered across the face of the mountainside. They were waiting to hear about the conversation that transpired with Onyx; curious, grim and unsettled all at the same time.

"What did he say about the drones that went missing over northern California?" one of them asked.

"Nothing," answered Gabriel, sternly.

"Nothing?"

"Didn't tell him."

"Why not?"

"Why do you think?" Gabriel looked down at his chest, and dialed a digital knob on his armored body suit that was used to control vital signs and monitor GPS information.

"But what about —"

"Shut up!" Gabriel interrupted, grabbing the curious Screener by the throat, holding him off the ground and glaring into his eyes. "Get the Adler ready," he said, then lowered him back down.

"Yes, Gabriel," both men nodded in unison, turned around and rushed down the stairway.

Gabriel glanced over his shoulder and looked clear across the deck. Onyx was standing on the other side of the crystal doors, hands folded behind his back, and an eerie stare transfixed on his face. A heavy loathing came into

Gabriel's heart. He allowed it to penetrate for a moment, and then turned and ran briskly down the middle of the deck. Hitting the digital dial on his chest, he leapt off the edge, spread his arms out, and fell like a base jumper into the metropolis below. As his body cut through the air, he observed the details around him. Onyx's floating glass precipice, built stoutly into the side of the mountain peak, towered above the valley. Ahead of him was the frozen lake, a thin layer of fog still hovering over it. Surrounding the lake was a cluster of towering buildings and factories, woven throughout the forest. The place resembled that of a tyrannic military establishment from another world; all of it made of various kinds of metal, concrete, and glass. It was a mountain city that fostered a sickened culture of technology. Sinister science was its foundation.

In less than seven seconds, Gabriel neared the ice. Two small canopies released on each side of his ribs. His body slowed down in mid air and hovered over the ground. Touching down, he made his way through a shaft-like gateway that led him onto the snowy shore. All over the place, Icon was bustling and chaotic. In a strange methodical way, Screeners moved about, marching around on assignment like empty souls; bound as if under a spell, lifeless and death-strung. The place was depressing. As Gabriel moved vigilantly, everywhere he went they saluted him, fearful as he walked by. He was the closest thing any of them ever saw to Onyx, who never left his glass tower. Some even denied Onyx's existence, thinking Gabriel just went up there to talk to himself, or to hoard his secrets. Yet they were just ignorant not to believe the rumors that a seemingly flawless human being lived up there.

As he walked between the buildings, a fleeting picture ran through Gabriel's head. For a second he remembered what the place looked like before Geospark took over and renamed it Icon. The memory was gone. He passed a multitude of soldiers, and came to the front door of the last original building left standing — the Redfish Lake Lodge.

Gabriel walked through the door. Inside, it was the way it always had been, nothing was different. The old hardwood floors creaked when he stepped on them, the dense smell of pine, fish, and smoke still seeped through the timber-log walls. Even the same old, decrepit dirt-stained Victorian rugs were there, not much left of them. The few single-paned windows were murky and brittle; most of them broken and lined with mildew. The walls still hosted a gallery of crooked pictures that were dated and covered in dust, all of them portraying moments of families camping, catching fish, eating, smiling.

It was odd, really. The fact that Gabriel was willing to do whatever it took to keep that lodge standing. For some reason, he did not want any trace of the new world touching it. The lodge just sat there, suspended awkwardly in time, out of place, dwarfed by all the dark ultramodern structures surrounding it. It was nothing more than a building reminiscent of an era that no longer existed. Whatever was there, in that shabby place, Gabriel wanted it to remain exactly the same, no matter what.

NINE
The Dalles

fter spending no more than a couple minutes staring at one of the pictures on the wall, Gabriel went to the helipad where the Adler was just about ready. As he walked onto the landing, about a dozen soldiers lined up, all of them were strapped with body armor, an array of blow torches, guns and explosives. Gabriel nodded to show approval and okayed their boarding.

Two specialized pilots were manning the whirlybird. It was roughly the size of an old Boeing Chinook, yet able to fly without the use of propellers, relying instead on technology that harnessed the earths natural magnetic field.

Once everybody was inside, one of the pilots spoke the coordinates into the system and in an instant the Adler lifted off the ground.

In less than two hours they arrived at the dam. It was late in the afternoon, the peak of Mount Hood was in the distant background, shaped like a dark dagger pointing up through the sky. No sooner had they landed, the lead engineer — a scrawny, ugly looking man, accompanied by two Nephilim, came out to meet them. Gabriel stepped out of the Adler first, followed by the other Screeners. The engineer, along with the two Nephilim, did not hesitate to bow in reverence and intimidation. Gabriel having to show up was never a good thing. The Nephilim were snarling and breathing heavy like beasts. Even though they were bent over, their shoulders towered above Gabriel by a few feet.

"Commander," stuttered Sloan, "please, this was just an accident. It won't happen again. I…I can explain."

"Shut up!" exclaimed Gabriel, as he motioned with his index finger for Sloan to stand up. "Look at me!" Gabriel's eyes burned with irritation. "Don't waste any of my time."

"Yes, commander." Sloan turned around and started waddling away, dragging the weight of his short, heavy body. Gabriel and the others followed him across the main bridge of the dam, where they entered the control room just next to the powerhouse. Once inside, Sloan opened a laptop that projected a virtual display of the dam. A translucent blueprint was quickly broadcast across the wall.

"It's right there," said Sloan.

Gabriel examined the display and saw a snowflake-size cluster of red debris flashing on the screen. Sloan zoomed in on the cluster, which by now, looked like a geothermal X-ray of the massive outflow pipes. "It just appeared overnight. The debris has been hindering water flow, compromising the turbine canal," said Sloan.

Gabriel was well aware that the outflow pipes allowed the river's current to push water through the turbine canals, enabling the generators to store power. "Why is it still there?" he asked.

"Dangerous," answered Sloan.

"Dangerous?" repeated Gabriel.

"Only the Electrets go down that far," said Sloan, referring to the programmable droids that were specifically used to maintain the dams. "None of them are charged because the power's been down. Can't we fly in two others from another dam?"

"I told you not to waste my time. We're not waiting for reinforcements to the care of this."

Sloan got a nervous look on his face.

"Get two men," Gabriel commanded casually. "Suit them up."

"You're serious?" responded Sloan.

Gabriel did not answer back. He just stood there.

"But commander," Sloan hesitated. "The Electrets

are programmed for this. I can't send two men to the base of the dam, not in these conditions. A clog in the outflow pipes isn't that simple. It's freezing! Do you know what could happen to them if that clog comes loose from the pipes all at once? That's easily twelve tons of pressure. They could be trapped! Killed!"

Gabriel moved closer to Sloan in a way that put everyone in the room on edge. Except for one Nephilim that stepped in between the two of them. The thing was enormous, its veins protruding and pulsating as it snarled. It held a long graphene machete, notched with titanium teeth, and rocked anxiously back and forth, communicating to Gabriel that it was not fond of the fact that Sloan's life was being threatened.

Gabriel noticed the Nephilim's Adam's apple, the size of a man's fist, and its body armor easily weighing a couple hundred pounds. The Nephilim was drooling, a mutant foaming at the mouth, peering down at Gabriel as if he was a rabbit about to be eaten by a wolf. At first, Gabriel was somewhat surprised he was being challenged, but then remembered how many brain cells the Nephilim could have lost during experimentations. He knew the steroid induced half-man half-beast was mindless, and that most of the chemicals killed its ability to think rationally. Nonetheless, Gabriel's command was being challenged.

For a moment Gabriel looked as though he were going to back away, yet the deception was short lived. Standing plumb straight, Gabriel looked into the Nephilim's bleached-white eyes and then pulled a seventeen inch blade from around his back, and before the giant could engage its own weapon, Gabriel slashed the blade across its stomach. The piercing sound of the knife cutting through flesh was heard throughout the room. At once, like a water balloon had been punctured, the Nephilim's bowels spilled out.

THUD! The control room shook when its body tumbled over and hit the floor.

Gabriel wiped off the blade, put it back into its sheath, stepped over the dead body, and came face to face with Sloan. "Do it now," he commanded, not raising his voice.

Sloan took a deep breath, trying hard to control his inner panic. He had never seen a Nephilim killed before, let alone by the hands of one man. Gabriel and the fifteen Screeners waited while he logged on to the maintenance system and verbalized some instructions into the intercom.

Before long two men walked into the control room, completely suited in elite scuba gear. Sloan spoke quickly, briefing them on what was taking place. Their task was simple: dive to the bottom of the dam, unclog the outflow pipes, and swim back to the top safely. The men nodded, not too concerned about the danger of the task, probably because they were grunts, and contrary to Sloan, were unaware of the treacherous jeopardy they were entering into.

When Sloan was done, all the Screeners walked outside, Gabriel was the last to exit. They made their way to the fringe of the spillway wall, where they stood atop a massive concrete bulkhead that overshadowed the river. Bolted into the side of the four-story wall was a rusted out rebar ladder that disappeared into the water. The weather was bone-chilling. By now the day had progressed into the evening and the sun had slipped down behind the rim of the gorge. The flood lights kicked on. In an instant, the eight thousand foot length of the dam was lit up, the men's faces glistened with silver as a light fog moved through the light.

The two divers descended the eighty foot ladder until they reached the bottom. Their bodies disappeared through surface of the water between floating slabs of ice. The river was black, except for the white wisps caused by its swirling eddies and tides. Sloan watched in silence, uncomfortable.

It was quiet for a while until one of the diver's spoke into Sloan's earpiece, "Thirty feet." He peered over the railing, listening. "Twenty feet," he could see their slack lines jerking back and forth, rubbing against the concrete. "Ten feet," silence for a few more minutes. "Here."

Even though they had reached the bottom of the river bed, clinging to the side of the dam, they still had a fifty yard lateral swim to make it to the obstruction. The problem was that along the way, some of the outflow pipes were still flowing. To prevent from being swept down river, they clutched onto the grab bars — slimy, and covered with greenish black moss, and advanced one hand at a time.

Twenty minutes later the same diver spoke up, "Made it," he said. It was evident in his voice that he was out of breath. He and the other diver were now directly in front of the 9 foot diameter outflow pipe. Both divers were struggling to see through the dark mirky water, even with their headlamps on. Sloan could barely hear the sound of their drills, muffled by the water, *zip-zip*, as they took the pipe's grate cover off and moved it to the side.

One of the divers unhooked a spotlight from his hip and aimed it through the tunnel, "Can't make it out yet, but whatever it is, this thing's packed full of it!" he exclaimed. Swimming further down the canal, they came close enough to discern what the debris was. The same diver responded with astonishment, "Unbelievable!" he exclaimed

The other diver's voice echoed in the background, "Crazy!"

"What?" asked Sloan, anxiously.

"You're not going to believe this," they said, starting to hit the large condensed cluster in order to break it free.

"What is it?" asked Sloan, not getting a response. He listened carefully as an exploding static erupted in his earpiece. Down below, as the divers were hitting the clog, the bulk of the debris came loose and a violent swell of water broke through the tunnel. All at once, the brute force of the river's back-flow unleashed on the men.

"Hey!" yelled Sloan, in terror. "Answer me! You guy's there?" He turned to a man standing next to him, "Do something!

Gabriel was not too concerned for the men as much as he was about the pipe being cleared. Inside the pipe the divers were racked against the hard interior walls. Like ants being flushed down a toilet, they were shot out into the open water. Their slack line snapped and flew past the faces of the Screener's standing above, opening a gash on one of the men's foreheads, nearly taking his eye out.

Surrounded by freezing water, the divers were smothered in the congealed chunks from the clog, the force of the current so powerful that it wrapped one of the diver's legs around his head, spinning him into a ball. He was killed instantly as his head smacked against a boulder in the riverbed. The other diver was swept down river with the tide, doing cartwheels fifty feet under water. From the top of the wall the others looked out on a myriad of currents bubbling up to the surface. Fragments of ice were broken and scattered everywhere.

It did not take long for a motor-powered raft to come jetting from around the navigation lock and into the rapids. The raft smashed through the crashing waves and swirling water, carrying a search and rescue team of five men. Their stout spotlight scanned back and forth across the water.

Gabriel looked out and could barely see the debris floating up to the surface, unable to discern what it was.

"Whatever it is, there's tons of it," said Sloan, slapping a pair of binoculars to his face for a closer look.

"Get me some of it," ordered Gabriel.

Down below, it did not take long for the men in the raft to find one of the mangled bodies floating on the water's surface. They hauled it in and confirmed the diver's death, before skipping over more rapids in search of the other one. Even from a distance, Sloan could tell what was going on. He paced frantically back and forth across the spillway wall.

After a half an hour, Gabriel had waited long enough and commanded Sloan to direct the raft back in. Unable to find the other diver, the raft turned around, the men snatching up a sizable portion of the drifting waste before making their way in.

Gabriel, Sloan, and the others walked back into the control room, the water from their clothing pitter pattering onto floor. They waited until the door flung open. Two of the men from the raft were holding five gallon buckets filled with the debris, which they set at Sloan's feet.

Sloan reached his hand into one of the buckets, pulled something out and quickly looked puzzled. "Fish?" he said.

"Sir, there were tons of them," said one of the men who brought in the buckets.

Sloan replied, "Fish? There's no way. Thought we took care of this problem at the Graveyard." In the back of Sloan's mind was a fleeting image of the mouth of the Columbia River spilling into the Pacific Ocean just above Astoria. "We eliminated all fish migration with the blockades. It doesn't make sense. This amount of fish is impossible!"

Gabriel moved closer and reached into the bucket, pulling out a cold, wet fish. He studied it carefully, "These didn't come from the graveyard."

Sloan was confused.

Gabriel ripped one of the fish in half.

"They're putrefied," said Sloan.

"These fish have been dead a long time," added Gabriel.

"How on earth did that amount of putrified fish get into the outflow pipes?" Sloan wondered.

"*They* didn't," answered Gabriel. "Someone," he paused, "or something, put them there." He grabbed another fish out of the bucket, strange markings behind one of its gills caught his attention.

Sloan moved closer to look at the same thing Gabriel was staring at, "It's just a scratch," he said.

"It's more than that." Gabriel got another fish and handed it to Sloan, "Look. Two fish with the same mark, in the same spot." Gabriel kicked over the buckets, the fish spilled all over the floor. One by one, they each had the same identical dirty white scratch in the same spot.

"Looks like a *V*," said Sloan.

"That's no *V*," said Gabriel, knowing exactly what it was. The sight of it made him seethe with fury — perplexed not so much by the insignia on the fish, but rather, disgusted to see it after all these years. He took one more fish, tore it to pieces and threw it across the room. Then, without hesitating, jerked Sloan's head backwards and put a knife to his throat. "Don't let this happen again," he warned, before marching out of the room.

TEN
Broken Mirrors

Nathan's head was pounding as he woke up and planted both feet on the ground. His boots were still on. They were the same boots he had been wearing for years. The leather was cracked and stitched up in various spots. For how old they were it was remarkable the soles were still attached. Nathan refused to wear anything else. The boots were the last thing he had left of his father's. Even though they were uncomfortable, he was used to them. Crossing his arms and clutching onto his jacket, he moved about, trying to get warm, trying to make sense of what day it was.

"Grandma?" he yelled.

He waited and heard nothing, breathing into the palms of his hands then yelling again, "Grandma!"

A modest shaft of light was coming into Nathan's room, he shielded his eyes like he had been in a hole for the last two days. He assumed it was sometime late in the morning. It would have been normal to hear Iris mumbling to herself, reading one of her books, or perhaps singing some made-up melody, or sleeping.

"Grandma!" he called out. Yet, there was nothing. No sound, no movement. Nathan got up, zipped the collar of his jacket tight to his chin and walked out into another open room looking for signs of Iris. "Annak?" He heard only the sound of his own voice echoing off the walls. *Where the hell is everyone?* he thought. Things were uncomfortably quiet. Something did not feel right. This was the first time since boyhood he had ever woke up to find Iris missing.

Leaving the large room, he took off down a hallway and busted through a metal door. To his comfort, a couple lanterns were burning around Annak, who was standing in front of a fractured mirror shaving his neck.

"You're finally awake." said Annak, leaning over an old wooden hutch and dipping his razor into a copper basin filled with mirky water.

Nathan hesitantly unloaded a series of questions, "What's going on around here? It's quiet. Where's grandma? What day is it?"

Annak looked through the mirror's reflection and gave Nathan a less than satisfying blank stare.

"Seriously, where's grandma?" Nathan didn't like how calm Annak was acting. Nor did he like the fact that Annak was casually shaving while Iris was missing.

Annak lifted his head, stretched out his chin, pulled the bottom of his dark beard out of the way, and stroked the side of his neck with the wet razor. "Two days," he said.

"Huh?"

"You've been sleeping for two days. I've been checking on you. You were having some fierce dreams...or nightmares. Talking to yourself a lot."

"Sure don't feel like I slept for two days. I'm exhausted."

"Just because your asleep doesn't mean that your mind isn't still at war," said Annak.

"You gonna tell me what's going on here or not?"

"She's still out there."

"What do you mean she's still out there?"

"Out there, Nathan. She's in the wilderness. Probably on the mountain-top."

"And you haven't gone to get her? Why hasn't she come back yet? She's all alone out there."

Annak kept shaving, not feeling the need to respond immediately.

"She could be frozen to death by now! Attacked!

Or something else!" Nathan vented, but all he could hear in response was Annak swirling the razor around in the water.

"Nathan, Iris is your grandmother, but there's a lot you still don't know about her."

"What's that supposed to mean?"

"She's doing business, she's not stupid. As far as I'm concerned, there's nothing out there more intimidating than her. Believe me, she can handle herself...been doing it for years now."

"But, why isn't she back?"

"She's warring," answered Annak.

"Warring?"

"She's contending for your soul, Nathan. If I know Iris, she's probably not coming back until she's got what she's fighting for."

"She's trying to break that curse off me?" asked Nathan.

"You're the last relative she has, you're all that's left of her legacy."

"I know that, but — "

"She's not gonna just stand by and watch you get torn to pieces by darkness," Annak interrupted. "She'll come back when she's ready."

"But she doesn't even like carrying a gun, let alone a pocket knife! She left here with nothing!"

"That's because Iris doesn't fight with guns, Nathan. She's not of this world. Your grandmother has a measure of the Blue Flame I haven't seen in anyone else. She's done things that I never thought possible. That Sarx is certainly a threat. But all your life you've been raised by a woman who's much more threatening. If anyone can protect themselves out there, it's her. She's the only one who knows how to break that curse."

"How?"

"You sure have been asking a lot of questions lately," said Annak.

"I just feel something different around here."

"Something spiritual?"

"I guess, if you want to call it that," said Nathan, reluctantly.

"The greater intimacy one has with the Navigator, the greater power they have over darkness. It's best you just let her do what she needs to do and stop worrying."

"I'm not worried, I'm just...well, it doesn't matter." Nathan changed the subject, "I never thought the smell of your nasty beard would've been so comforting."

Annak laughed.

"Thank you for helping me the other night."

Annak's face perked up, "One of the things I hated most about being a *SEAL* - I couldn't have facial hair. I used to love going out on long assignments because I had an excuse not to shave." Annak stroked his neck a few more times with the razor then continued, "We were overseas one time, off the coast of Russia. Just successfully completed our mission, but we still had another three months of duty before we could go home. The commanding officers got this crazy idea," Annak smiled. "They wanted to surprise us by flying our wives and children over for an unexpected visit." Annak sighed, "I hadn't seen Victoria for six months! It was terrible. They didn't tell us our wive's were showing up. I looked like a different person when I was out there at sea."

"You mean, like you do now?" Nathan laughed.

"Exactly, only I was younger then. Before we knew it, our families came bursting through the door. Victoria ran into my arms! We held each other for the longest time. Not sure how or why, maybe I was in the submarine's engine room before seeing her, but all she could say in between her tears, was that I smelled like coffee and motor oil. When we got back to the states and tried to piece together some sort of civilian life, there were times she'd ask me to put coffee grounds and motor oil in my beard. I laughed at first. Thought she was a little crazy, but she was serious. She loved it. For some reason it spiced up our romance," Annak winked. "She said it reminded her of one of the best days of her life, seeing me after we hadn't been together for so long."

"It all makes sense now. I always thought you were weird because of that smell...well, I still do."

A sobering look came over Annak's face, "I *loved* that woman," he declared. "She was everything to me."

The mood in the room changed. Nathan was not sure how to respond, so he stayed quiet.

"I guess...I still put the stuff in my beard, because the smell reminds me of her. Sometimes I think she might come back, and I can hold her in my arms. But I know I'll see her again. Someday. Maybe not in this life, but in the next."

"You think there's life after this?"

"I didn't always used to, I spent a lot of years not believing in anything. Then one day my eyes were opened and I realized that life after death was real, whether I chose to believe it or not."

"Just like that, huh?"

"There's a lot more to the story. But think about it, if there's nothing after *this*, then what's our purpose? Born from nothing only to return to *nothing*?"

"Yeah, but how do you know?"

"Nathan, it's hard to explain. But when you know, you *know*."

"That's all? You just know?"

"How would you describe life outside the womb to a baby who's still in the womb? How do you try and tell that little baby what it's like to eat ice-cream, or what the sand on the beach feels like? Or explain the color green?"

"You got a point."

"You can't. All that baby knows is life inside the womb, too premature to comprehend anything outside of it. I can only convince you of what I believe to a point, but there comes a time when you just need to exit the womb for yourself. There's a whole lot more that exists outside the walls of time, space, and matter than you might realize. You see this mirror?" Annak pointed to the fragmented thing hanging above his makeshift sink.

Nathan nodded.

"It's old. It's fractured. It's dim. The reflection in this thing's less than perfect. When I look into it, I can barely shave without cutting myself, almost have to shave my neck by touch. This mirror's ability to give a reflection of what I really look like is limited." Nathan was intrigued, listening. "Some people spend their entire lives trying to figure out *who* they are, but the whole time they're looking into a mirror like this. They're trying to figure out what the purpose of life is, but all they do is cut themselves because they can't see clearly."

"Sorry, Annak. I'm not following."

"As long as we look inward, or try to define ourselves by this world, the reflection will always be dim. The image is only as good as the mirror. People who don't believe in an afterlife, are simply looking into a broken mirror. Listen to me very carefully, every single thing in the visible world is defined by the world that's unseen. But when you come awake, when you finally stop looking inward, and look beyond yourself, you behold that perfect reflection where you're able to see clearly."

"What perfect reflection?"

"Him, the One who created you," answered Annak. Humans were never meant to define themselves. That's like a gun trying to call itself a quilt. The only one who has a right to tell you who you are is the One who made you. All I can say is that for a long time I didn't know anything beyond myself. Then one day I saw my reflection in the right mirror. Nathan, you're still looking into a broken, dim mirror. You're confused, incomplete, catching only glimpses of the unseen world through fragmented pieces of glass."

"One day you just woke up and things were different?"

"Waking up? Coming alive? You could call it a lot of different things. I was a rebel, Nathan, filled with hatred and pride, trained to be a professional killer, and taught to put down anyone who threatened this country. Many times I was surrounded by death, yet never thought much about what would happen after I died. Didn't care. Anything outside the present moment, the current mission, didn't concern me. For years I defined myself only by what I could see through the scope of my rifle, nothing more. I was numb, not realizing I was just a dead man walking." Annak continued shaving.

"And what?"

Annak closed his eyes, "Then…I lost her."

"Victoria?" Nathan asked, cautiously.

"She was everything I'd ever loved on this earth — *everything*. And in an instant she was gone."

Nathan was quiet.

"When the closest thing to you…the only thing you see any value in, is taken from you, there's a choice you have to make, and it's a hard one — quit or go on. I'm not even sure how to explain it. Never knew I had bones until she died. Rather than growing more numb, I started to feel every fiber of my being. My body groaned with pain. I cried out for understanding, for an answer to *why?* How could something like this have happened? Losing her wasn't fair. I thought about committing suicide. I had no reason to go on living without her. But the closer I got to ending my own life…I started to sense something surrounding me. I felt something hindering me from killing myself."

"What?"

"A small voice. A prodding, something that told me there's got to be more to life than *loss*. There's got to be some sort of *gain* involved in all of this, some sort of afterlife, some sort of reckoning and reconciliation; where all that gets lost in this life, gets redeemed, restored...made new in the *next*. I'm sorry to say it, but her death is what triggered my awakening. It's at that point, when I despaired of myself, that I started to grope for something more. And to my surprise, I found it. However, the means by which someone is awakened to that other world is different for everyone. Pain is often the common thread."

Out of curiosity Nathan could not hold back the question, still stuck on the *loss* of life, rather than the *gain*, "How'd she die?"

"Maybe another time."

There was an uncomfortable silence between both of them, probably more so for Nathan. Rather than ask another serious question, Nathan veered from the spiritual and inquired about something more light-hearted. "You got any good stories?" he asked.

"Plenty. What kind?"

"Navy stories?"

Annak shirked, "Got tons of those. What do you want — funny? Gross? Violent?"

"I could use a funny one. Gross too."

"My *funny-gross* might be more than you can handle."

"Guess we'll find out. Tell me."

"Awhile back, probably before you were even born, hadn't been in the Navy for more than five years..." Annak paused, "I used to drink a lot. We all did. I mean, I could drink."

"Hold on a second, you?" Nathan asked in unbelief. "You, drank?"

"Heavily. Definitely an alcoholic."

"That's hard to believe knowing you." Nathan wasn't alluding to alcohol being inherently evil, as much as he was pointing to the fact that Annak never seemed like the type to drink.

"Well, I have a past. Besides, alcohol's not the problem, I just abused it. Or maybe it abused me. Our ship was docked at the Bay of Naples, in Italy. If you don't know what that place is, it's an industrial shipping yard, one of the biggest in the world. Used for a lot of drug trafficking and trading. We had a couple days down time, so my buddy Lance and I got curious. "

"Curious?"

"About what was at the bottom."

"Of the shipping yard? Why?"

"Because that place is old, I mean *really old,* one of the most historical and congested shipping yard's you'll ever find, probably the size of Marseille, France. There were rumors of all kinds of crazy stuff being down there. We had nothing better to do, so we geared up and went diving. The only problem was that the night before, we both had way too much to drink."

Nathan was shaking his head, curious to know more.

"Little by little we followed the chain of the ship all the way down to the anchor. Easily more than 100 feet under water by the time we reached the bottom. You wouldn't believe all the stuff we saw, it was ridiculous! Still the filthiest place I've ever been in!"

"You sure about that? I don't really think this place is all that clean. What was down there?"

"Old broken statues, cables, scraps of metal, piles

of broken concrete, rusted barrels, trash, vehicles, war junk. Remains of things I won't even mention."

"Cars?"

"Tons," answered Annak. "It was an underwater salvage yard." Annak laughed, "There we were, shining our bright lights all over, throwing hand signals at each other trying to see what we could find. Can't remember quite what happened, but I did something funny, made a joke I think. Well, Lance lost it, he started laughing. He was hung over enough that he laughed so hard he puked." And not just a little, a lot!

"That's disgusting!" exclaimed Nathan. "Seriously?"

"Gets better. There was so much vomit inside his mask that it clogged his oxygen tube. He started throwing hand gestures, panicking because he couldn't breathe. In seconds the moment turned from excitement to terror. There was no way we were making it back to the surface in time."

"Dang! And you were that deep under water?"

"I've helped some people stay alive in my day, but this was the nastiest thing I'd ever done to keep someone from dying."

"What did you do?"

"I pulled his mask off, took mine off, puke floating everywhere, and we buddy-breathed all the way back to the surface. It was scary at the moment, but we laughed about it later."

"Nasty! I'm guessing you stopped drinking after that?"

Annak raised one eyebrow, looked away from the mirror and stared at Nathan, "Course not."

"You're something else, Annak," said Nathan, trying to let the story lighten up his mood, but still feeling heavy inside.

"Next time I'll tell you about the time we stole a

golden toilet seat from a Persian prince's night club in the Middle East."

"You really are crazy," said Nathan.

ELEVEN
Lewiston

Nathan walked around the room while Annak splashed some of the dirty water on his face. "That bear…" said Annak.

"The one we killed just a couple days ago?" responded Nathan. "What about it?"

"Max and Silas opened it up and found a tracker."

"Did the bear eat it or something?"

"It was surgically planted."

Nathan looked somewhat surprised. "They're getting creative aren't they? "How much longer you think until they find us out?"

"Don't know, but it can't be long."

"So we just wait for an ambush and let them put an end to us? How many of us are here at Adullum now, almost 300?"

"*How many* isn't that important."

"Annak, I'm not the only one getting anxious around here. There's gotta be something we can do before they get to us. Aren't you tired of all this?"

"The war's different now, Nathan. It's a matter of *when* and *how.*"

"Same thing Grandma keeps saying, I still think it's a bunch of crap."

"It's about being consumed by the Flame and being led by Him, Nathan — when to move, when to stay put. There's a spiritual heartbeat to our world, a pulse. It's something we have to tap into in order to go about things the right way, not just the immediate way. Your grandmother, myself, and some others — we have our fingers on that pulse, and you need to trust us. Iris isn't ashamed about her refusal to be led by anything other than the Blue Flame. You and anyone else operating apart from that anointing is dangerous. There's a lot more strategy involved than what you're aware of."

"Oh, come on. For so long we've just been surviving! But for what? What are we doing? Don't lie to me Annak, you know there's not gonna be enough water to get through the year. You know it and I know it!"

Annak looked concerned, but still composed, "Possibly."

"None of this makes sense, it just doesn't. Spiritual or not spiritual, I think we're being stupid and scared and none of us are willing to do anything about it."

"Well, you and I must have two different definitions of *stupid*."

"Annak, what about this cave? Why aren't we *going* to explore these tunnels? Look at all this crap in here — the electrical, the networking, the plumbing, the HVAC! All this equipment and resources and all we need is," Nathan paused, "POWER! Annak, I know you know how to get the power on in this place."

"It's just a rumor, Nathan. No one knows if it's true or not."

"Well, what if it is? We should at least find out, or die trying! I mean, who put all this in here? For all I know, everything we need could be right here at Adullum. Right here!" Nathan was silent for a moment, "And the lake? Don't even get me started. I know you've never been there, but that place was my home…and they stole it from me!"

"Nathan, that lake was your grandmother's home too. Trust me, she'll do whatever it takes to get it back."

"We'll see," Nathan scoffed. "You gonna tell me how to get the power on to the place or what?"

"I said it's just a rumor."

"But what if it's not?"

"Then…it would still be difficult."

"I heard that the whole power supply for this place runs underground, that it comes from one of the dams."

"Yeah, and it's a dam that's far away. And none of us have seen what's outside Adullum for a long time now."

"So is it true? Was this place really supposed to be some kind of top secret military bunker?"

"The government started building this place for a reason. But there's also a reason why it was abandoned."

"And after all this time how could the Screeners not know about Adullum?" Nathan continued prodding, as if Annak had all the answers.

"Because whoever started excavating this place, did their best to hide it, even from Geospark and the Screeners."

"We gotta to do something, Annak. Either we start taking back the waterways, or we find a way to get the power on to Adullum. If we don't do anything, we're just going to die."

"Nathan, if there really is a fuse box to this place, and if it's at the dam I think its at, then it's no easy task getting there."

"We need to at least try. What dam is it?"

"I won't tell you."

"Oh, come on," complained Nathan.

"No way. That dam's over seven hundred miles from here, deep in the Columbia River gorge. How do I know you won't just take off alone and do something foolish? I'm not doing anything apart from Iris's leadership," declared Annak.

"So what's her answer to why we've been doing nothing for so long?

"She's convinced that we haven't just been *doing nothing*."

"How's that?"

"Waiting for others to find this place, so they can take refuge here, and we can build our strength. That's one reason."

"Yeah, but the Screeners are building their strength too, and controlling all the water as they do it!"

"But they're building differently than we are. Their foundation is sand, ours is rock."

"Just tell me which dam it is, enough with the metaphors."

"Nathan, I've known you long enough now to be cautious. When you get information there's no telling what you'll do with it. Why do you think Iris and I have kept so much hidden, not *from* you, but *for* you. There's too much out there you're not ready for."

"Yeah right! I know how to survive! I know how to fight! As a matter of fact, I'm starting to think you and Grandma might just be teaching me how to die here."

Annak laughed heartily, and slapped Nathan across the shoulder as he walked away from the hutch, "If you only knew."

Nathan didn't think anything was funny.

"Nathan, that dam, and all the others, have been dominated by the Screeners for years now. Their garrisons are everywhere along the Columbia. Every river connected to Redfish Lake, from the Pacific Ocean and in between, it's all theirs. It's not as simple as just *taking a dam*."

"Well, when times get scarce, maybe it is."

"There's no more electricity left on the earth. All that's available is what the dams can produce, and only, may I remind you, *only*, the dams connected to that lake. They're all fortified."

"Annak, I know all this. What's your point?"

"They're savages, Nathan. They'll do whatever it

takes to protect those water-ways. They're dangerous, most of their force isn't even human."

"I don't care," Nathan complained, "We need water, and we need power. Let's do something!"

Annak's voice lowered, "Nathan, you seen a Nephy yet?" He asked, referring to the Nephilim.

"No. I've only heard rumors."

"You ever fought against one?"

"Doesn't matter. I've taken down Gnats, I've taken down bears, moose, other men! I can deal with a Nephy."

"They're giants, Nathan! Ten? Twenty? Hard to say how many bullets it takes to bring one of them down. And they're heartless.

"Well...thats good, means we don't have to feel bad about blowing 'em up."

"Screener forces outnumber us, Nathan - by a lot. They're inventions, machines, experimental giants — it all stands between us, and getting that water back."

Most of this was not new to Nathan. He paced back and forth, "In that room over there," Nathan pointed outside Annak's doorway, "where I sleep, where Iris sleeps, all over those walls — you know what it says. My Grandma lives by that one single sentence: *Nothing is impossible with the Navigator.* You too, Annak! You guys give me all this spiritual crap — all this faith, all this hope — and tell me that nothing is impossible. But when it really comes down to it we do nothing. Nothing! You say, *His ways our beyond ours!* But in these last ten minutes all you've done is tell me how intimidating the Screeners are. And how *impossible* it is to take back the water ways! Look at our reservoir! We're down to gallons, Annak. Gallons! And the damn alkali flies are swarming over all the water thats left out there, none of it's clean anymore. Death and sickness is all over the place! And you tell me there's a *supreme being* over all this? The

Navigator?"

"I never said *it* was impossible, Nathan. I'm merely stating the reality of what's in front of us. It is possible to defeat them, but there's a way to do it. And regarding that *way*, Iris hasn't received further revelation. She's the last living seer, she moves when the Navigator moves, and I move when she moves. Not a matter of *can*, but *when*."

"You think she's a prophet, but I thinks she's gone mad," scoffed Nathan.

"Be careful. She's done more for you than you'll ever know. And she loves you deeply. She knows what she's doing."

"It shouldn't be this complicated. You don't need a supernatural revelation about what to do when you know you're gonna die if you don't do something."

"Just trust. Wisdom has a lot more strength than adrenaline." Annak put his arm around Nathan, "I know a lot doesn't make sense to you right now, but it will."

There was a tattered Polaroid photograph next to Annak's bed. Nathan picked it up. Annak was in the picture, standing next to a young woman. They were on a Naval dock with the vast ocean behind them. "Is this Victoria?" Nathan asked.

"Yeah."

"Wow, she was beautiful."

"I know."

"Dark skin."

"Most gorgeous woman I ever knew."

As Nathan gazed into the photograph, something peculiar gripped him. Maybe it was the peaceful countenance between Annak and Victoria. He was not sure, but whatever it was triggered a flashback and in an instant he was just a little boy, wrestling with his mom and dad on their living room floor. All the original childhood feelings of the moment came back to him, and then in an instant were gone. Refusing to let go of the picture, Nathan gazed into it and beheld its tranquility. Annak left him alone and started cleaning one of his guns.

Just as Annak walked away and sat down, Nathan heard the subtle whisper of the Sarx in his ear, the residue of its scratchy voice was no less familiar, "*One year from now... one year from now.*" The peace triggered by the photograph quickly disappeared, and Nathan sensed a cold aloneness come over him. The hairs on his arm stood up and his heart palpitated, and he found himself suddenly trying to catch his breath. "Annak!" he blurted out.

"You alright?" Annak answered, seeing that Nathan was acting strange.

Nathan caught his breath, "Uh, yeah. I'm fine. I just..." Nathan tried to calm down and decided not to make much of it. "What's my grandma really doing out there?"

"I told you."

"No, I mean what's really going on? How is a curse broken?" Nathan asked hesitantly, still not wanting to believe in curses, or blessings, or anything spiritual, but having a hard time dealing with the onset of unwelcome symptoms brought on by the Sarx.

Annak was staring down the barrel of one of his shotguns, wiping it with a rag. He set it down, then looked at Nathan, "You're asking because there's one of two reasons behind your question, both maybe — you're either curious, or just plain scared. Doesn't matter, really. I'll put it simply - Iris is invoking the Navigator over your life."

"And?"

"Sarx can only speak what is dark. They don't have the capacity to speak life or light. But whatever it pronounced over you, can only be altered by the Navigator. Not everyone who knows the Navigator, actually walks with Him."

"What do you mean?"

"Your grandmother doesn't just have the Blue Flame - she's possessed by it. The Flame is the Navigators personality, His nature, His DNA. Because she's walked with Him for so long, she carries not only the audacity, but the authority required…"

"Required?"

"The authority to invoke the Navigator to do something on your behalf. Listen to me, the greater the cost, the greater the wrestle. The Navigator will, and can intervene, but…" Annak paused, and looked as if the next thing he was going to say weighed a few more pounds than the words before.

"What? What is it?"

"There has to be a trade. In order for Iris to get what she wants — in this case the preservation of your life — the Navigator has to get what He wants."

"What would He want?"

"Something of equal value to what she's requesting."

"Hold on, you mean…" Nathan hesitated, "life for life?"

"Your grandmother's the only one involved in the exchange, I don't know."

"That *thing* really has the ability to say when I die, and now my grandma has to give her life in order for me to keep mine?"

"Not what I said. It's complicated."

For years Nathan had been bitter. He was skeptical about hearing anything spiritual concerning the Navigator or the Blue Flame. Yet, the events of the last few days had shaken him to the core, and he was beginning to feel the weight of his life hanging in the balance. In a way, more so than in the past, he was becoming desperate for the right answers. Whether he hated it or not, he could not deny the supernatural flare he saw in Annak and Iris.

In the moment, Nathan thought about how Annak rebuked the Sarx, "Did you always have it?" he asked.

"Good looks? Of course I have."

"I mean, the Blue Flame, Annak"

Annak leaned the gun up against the wall. Nathan was hardly in the mood to find out about Annak's inner life, let alone be doubtful and scared by it. Yet Annak perceived that in the moment Nathan was vulnerable, "The Blue Flame's not an *it*," said Annak. "He's a person."

Nathan listened.

"He's the personality of the Navigator, as expressed through a yielded vessel."

"The Blue Flame's the Navigator?"

"Yes and no. They're one, yet distinct."

"That doesn't make any sense."

"Sure it does. Whether you believe it or not, you're made of three parts — body, soul, spirit. All three parts make up one person, but all three parts operate in very distinctive ways. It's called the human trichotomy."

"No wonder it's so easy to become schizophrenic."

"Only when you're not in unity with yourself and Him. But when your spirit's alive, your soul is in submission, and your body is the vessel that carries out your destiny. Similarly, the Navigator is the divine heartbeat of all that exists, the Blue Flame is the revelation of who He is, and His *body* is made up of those who are willing to be totally consumed and used by Him."

"How do you get the Blue Flame?"

Annak laughed, "You don't."

"What do you mean, *you don't?*"

"He..." said Annak, "gets you. And then, you get all that He is. The Blue Flame is a gift, but you have to lay down your life first. You have to be willing to empty yourself. The

Navigator's Spirit is divine power, but He can't enable those who don't allow Him to. He desires for all to share in His nature, and make's Himself available to everyone. But here's the key — He only allows Himself to be discovered by those searching for him. When you come to the end of yourself, you come to Him; hide and seek. He's generous, but He's jealous, and only discloses His ways to those who are open."

"What's it mean to be *open*?"

"You have a soul — it's where your emotions and your will reside, it's a delicate place, and it can easily be kept closed to His ways. Many things — unbelief, anger, bitterness, pride, selfishness — all these things are like poison to the soul. Whatever a person carries in their soul can help them or hinder them. If you're carrying all that stuff, you're gonna have a hard time being open to Him, because all you're thinking about is your own hurt. But it's not easy stuff to get rid of. A person turned in on themselves doesn't always know it. Unfortunately, sometimes the only way to get free of all that stuff is to get radically shaken, broken so badly that you come to the place where you have no choice but to say, *Here I am, help me!* And if you're groping is sincere, then He will come. Listen to me carefully, Nathan, the eyes of the Navigator are fixed on the earth, looking for those whose hearts are ready for Him."

"And what about you?" asked Nathan.

"Well, I didn't start searching for answers until after Victoria died. But, receiving the Blue Flame happened years later."

"How?"

"*How* someone receives the Blue Flame is unique, and different for everybody. But I do know this, that ever since that day my life's never been the same." Annak stalled. He wasn't sure about whether or not to share the story, it was special, and it wasn't something he told just anybody. Nonetheless, Annak perceived a sliver of sincerity in Nathan's question. By now, he knew Nathan had stuck around either because he was lonely, or because he was finally interested in spiritual matters.

"Lewiston," said Annak, "it happened in Lewiston."

"Idaho?" asked Nathan, "You mean Lewiston, Idaho?"

"Yeah, you were just a little boy when the breakout of the war was still fresh. Geospark had just been alerted to the phenomenon of the lake, and was making its attempt to take it over. I was constantly leading Reapers on raids directed at key locations along the waterways. There were maybe 50 of us. We knew they were about to take Lewiston — a small town, but when the water contamination happened, that little town was put on the map pretty quickly. It's the junction where the Snake River and Clearwater River join together. A substantial amount of water was tied to that town, allowing the Screeners to take control of Lewiston meant the death of thousands of people who would be hindered from accessing it."

Annak continued, "When we got to the outskirts of town, the place was already shot up and decimated. There was a second story bank building on the corner of 5th and main, we charged into it and posted up." Annak sighed, "It was a worthy day, not because we were successful... but because all the men fought with their lives. We held ground for a while, but just didn't have the technology or the power they had. When they started deploying Gnats, it was all over. I still remember exactly what it was like when it happened. I had my rifle set on the edge of a window that gave me a 180 view of the river below. One after another, I was taking them down, for a while, until a fly-drone, the size of your hand, flew through the window. By then it was too late, none of us could do a thing. In the blink of an eye the Gnat dropped a mini nuke and…"

"What happened?"

"We blew up," said Annak.

"You blew up?" Nathan asked, in disbelief, making sure he had heard Annak correctly.

"All of us did, everyone in that room — gone. Everything went black, I couldn't see, couldn't hear, couldn't feel, didn't even know where I was. I knew I was dead. It wasn't until I started to feel pain shooting through my body, that I realized I was still alive. To the best of my memory, the building's roof collapsed on us. I called out every name I could think of, screaming, yelling for anyone who might have survived, but there was no response. When the smoke cleared, I realized I was pinned under the rubble — brick, stone, mortar, beams. It didn't take long to notice my left arm and leg were both completely blown off and my skin was boiling from the chemicals released by the nuke. The worst sensation of all was the feeling of all the blood leaking out of my body. I can honestly say it was the first time in my life I'd been *that* scared."

"How were you even alive?"

"Don't know. All I wanted to do was die. We'd been fighting the Screeners for nearly a year at that point, and I was exhausted. But something strange happened, call it shock, nerves. From deep down within, I summoned up enough strength the get out one word — *Help.*"

"To who?"

"To Him, I guess. I had what I believed would be my last thought, *if You're real, if there's any good left on this earth, than help me.* And that was all. I waited, all the pain was still there, the silence. But, then I heard a voice."

"A man's voice? How'd you know it wasn't a Screener."

"I just knew, it was unlike any voice I'd ever heard.

Like thunder, or roaring water, but peaceful. As soon as it spoke, I forgot about the pain."

As Annak spoke, Nathan could not help but contrast that voice with the voices he had been hearing all his life and the one from the Sarx just a couple days earlier.

"The voice," continued Annak, "asked me a question: *Will you give Me your life?* It was odd, though. The first thought I had was, *what life?* I was blown to pieces, seconds away from the blackness of death, what kind of life did I have left to give? No matter how hard I tried to rationalize how ridiculous the question was, I was captivated by the sheer weight of the voice. There was a credibility, a genuineness, a…hallowed reverence. It was a voice that expressed perfect calm and command over everything I was. And for some reason I knew I could trust it."

"What did you do?"

"I knew this was one of those moments in life where everything seems to come to a point, and I could feel the gravity of the question. I didn't know how static my life had been until that question."

"Static?"

"It's like someone listening to a radio that doesn't work their whole life, all they know is the sound of static. And then one day, without warning, a clear voice comes through. I was overcome with desperation. I said, *YES.*"

"That simple, huh?"

"No sooner did the word come out of my mouth, that the voice spoke back again, *Then I will give you mine.* But what happened next will always be something that's hard to explain. Not everything's easy to put into words."

"What was it, what happened?" asked Nathan.

"You could call it a light — that's what it was, but much brighter than anything man could produce. There was a radiance that came into the building. As I was lying there, the light was so blinding that I was forced to close my eyes. Then, at once, all the light that was in the room materialized into the figure of a man standing over me."

"A man? Like a ghost, or something?"

"Not a ghost, no way — He was real, very real. It was like someone standing before me who had harnessed the complete energy of the sun, but greater. His face was like that of a million different faces, all their expressions shifting and changing simultaneously, yet forming one universal face. Every human emotion and countenance you could ever imagine, it was all there, in one single moment." Annak's face lit up as he spoke, "I can't even explain it, to be honest with you. His clothing was split in half down the middle of his body, yet seamless. Half arrayed in an unearthly-looking white tuxedo, more pronounced and stunning than anything I'd ever seen; definitely not made by human hands. And the other half....well, the best way I can describe it, was like a white shimmering body armor. It wasn't metal or anything we would think of, it was something more, much more. Its strength and material couldn't be measured or comprehended and there were radiant jewels embedded into the armor like it was part of His flesh."

"A tuxedo and body armor? That's weird."

"I know. In the same moment, He emanated with royalty and nobility, and reigned as an unearthly warrior. In awe of Him, the only thing I could feel was complete terror. Regardless of what I was seeing I was scared to death! Yet, I had this strange feeling that I was safe, for the first time. And something else, His whole body was on fire."

"On fire?"

"On fire, but not burned. He was aflame with brilliant blue and sapphire flames."

"How is that even possible?"

"Don't know, but it's what I saw, and I'll never forget

it. He spoke again," Annak was quiet for a minute.

"And?"

"I can remember every…single…word," Annak got quiet, looking as though he was in another place and almost forgetting Nathan was there. "He said, *I'm the Navigator, the One who formed you. The One who holds your past, your present, your future. From now on, you will carry my healing balm. You will look after, and protect the next generation of those whom I've chosen to redeem the time and live for my cause. This is your call and destiny. As long as you walk in it, you will be successful in everything you do. For you, I'm opening a door that can never be shut.* And that was it."

Nathan was unsure what to say. Part of him wanted to deny everything Annak was saying and write it off as a complete fairytale. Yet part of him burned inside as Annak spoke.

"He's spoken to me many times since then," said Annak. "But listen, here's the moment I want to tell you about, the moment when I received the Blue Flame. After He finished speaking, He took in a huge breath, and blew on me. I remember feeling like I'd just been hit with a 1000 volts of electricity. And then all of the sudden I fell asleep. As soon as the power hit me I didn't even have a chance to respond or do a thing. The next thing I knew, I woke up in the grass alongside the Merced River, right out there beyond the walls of Adullum."

"What about your leg? Your arm?"

"When I got up, I was twitching and pulsating. There was a new current running through my body. Something I'd never felt before was running through my veins, and I knew I was now being dominated by something bigger than myself. Everything was healed. My leg, my arm — it was all there. Like nothing ever happened. Even the boils on my skin from the nuke were gone. As I looked down my left arm and wriggled my fingers in disbelief, I couldn't help but feel that something was healed inside as well, not just physically. There was a new resolve in my heart. Up until that point I felt like my whole life had been in black and white, and now in an instant, the lights were flicked on and everything turned to color. There was a new tension, a new reason to go on living."

"Just like that? You were healed?"

"Not just healed, but empowered. Filled! When I searched my body for wounds, all I could find was one small mysterious mark."

"Like a scar?"

"You could call it that, more like a divine stitch mark, though, two of them, one where my leg was healed and one where my arm was healed. It's the only visible thing I have left as a reminder of what happened."

"Ok, you gotta show me or else I'm not believing any of this."

Annak laughed, "You always want evidence, Nathan." With nothing to hide, Annak pulled back his shirt and revealed the skin on the front of his left shoulder.

Nathan leaned in to see it, "Looks like a tattoo!" he exclaimed. "But, it's like nothing I've seen before." Nathan kept staring, "Kinda looks like a dove doesn't it?"

"It is," answered Annak as he covered it back up, then showed Nathan the one on his hip.

"The exact same thing! Nathan was bewildered, "So, you got blown up? Healed? Then transported back here to Adullum from Lewiston? Just like that? But when did you receive the Blue Flame?"

"Honestly, I believe I received the Blue Flame when I said, *YES* - no sooner, no later."

Nathan was stirred up, and was not about to let the story fade into the back of his mind. His curiosity was triggered even more so by Annak's miracle and the marks on his body, "So, whats all that supposed to mean?"

"For me, it means a lot," answered Annak. "I've seen remarkable things since then; signs and wonders, things I never thought possible. For the last twenty years I've lived by the words He spoke to me on that day — waging war against all injustice." Annak stopped and thought to himself for a moment, "Don't know if I'll be there to see the day when we take the watershed back, but I do know that Geospark and the Screeners will fall. Not sure how long my journey will last, but I do know this: watching you grow up has made things very clear for me."

"What do you mean?"

"You're different, Nathan. I've been sent here for many reasons, but above all others, the main reason I'm here is to see you through to your calling, and to help you realize your identity. You're part of the next generation I've been giving my life to protect. Though you're not ready yet, I do believe you'll be a part of those who bring the *giant* down."

"Hope so," replied Nathan.

"You were made for greatness, Nathan. But you have to come to a place where you can let go of your hurt. You have to surrender your life to the Navigator, or else all you'll be doing is fighting in your own strength. It's easier to fight with an abandoned heart than it is with a stiff neck. Stop resisting, and you'll find that all the power you need comes from Him," Annak spoke with a firm voice, then repeated himself, "It comes from Him, Nathan."

Nathan sat on the edge of Annak's bed and was quiet. Compared to Annak, there was so much about life he did not understand yet, let alone what it meant to live with *purpose*. *He* could not shake the feeling that there was something significant about Annak, his words and his stories. He knew the road ahead was strewn with the gravel of uncertainty, complexity, and trouble. So much had been stolen they had yet to take back. So many pieces to try and somehow put back together in the midst of reigning chaos. The world was unfair and treacherous. Nathan's thoughts were a mixture of the echoing curse of the Sarx, Annak's miraculous story and ethereal convictions, worry concerning Iris's return, and much more. The mysteries inside the cave paled in comparison to the mysteries inside Nathan's head. No matter how drab and monotonous Nathan felt their life at the cave was, there was always a lot to think about.

TWELVE
Time to Move

I t reeked of dirty rags, sweat, and the musty bone marrow of a wild animal. The smell was strong. No one was talking — too hungry, too thirsty. They both knew there was only an hour left until the meeting. Annak was shifting a pot back and forth over some flames, melting a modest amount of snow while Nathan chewed on some of the elk meat.

Nathan was wiping the grease from his lips when he heard frantic mumbling coming from outside Annak's door. The voice was repeating something familiar, "Nothing… nothing is impossible. Nothing is impossible with the Navigator." He immediately knew who it was.

"Annak!" said Nathan, "she's back!" Nathan ran out the door and saw Iris coming down the hallway. "Grandma!" he yelled. "Are you ok?"

Annak quickly followed behind. As Iris approached, still mumbling, she stretched out her arm, "Nathan, don't touch me!" she warned.

Nathan came to a halt, not sure why, wanting to embrace her. He looked at Annak.

"Just stay back," said Annak, echoing Iris. He came up behind Nathan and braced his arm across his chest. "She's been smeared."

"What?" asked Nathan.

"I need water! Hurry, get me some water!" begged Iris.

Annak rushed back into his room, brought out a tin cup and gave it to her. Iris's hands quivered as she held the cup to her mouth, trying to drink, some of the water spilling over, running down her chapped lips and weather-beaten neck.

"OH! Goodness!" she cried. Iris gasped after finishing off the cup of water, she was still shaking. "It's time! It's time!" she declared.

Nathan stared at her, thinking, *Time for what?*

Iris directed her gaze at Annak, in a way acting as though Nathan was not there, "It's time!

Annak knew what Iris was alluding to. An excitable grin spread across his face as he looked over at Nathan, "There you go."

"Bonneville!" Iris exclaimed. "The Bonneville!"

"That's the one, Nathan," said Annak, "that's the dam." Annak knew it was a moment of divine fortuity, the fact that he and Nathan had just been talking about that location moments earlier.

"What? The one that's got the power switch to this place?" asked Nathan.

"It's time to move," said Iris.

"What do you mean, *move?*" asked Nathan "Are we finally going on the offensive for once?"

Iris held the cup upside down over her mouth and smacked it, groping for one last drop of water. "However you want to look at it," she answered.

"We're finally gonna do something?"

"Nathan, slow down," urged Annak, "you don't even know what we're doing."

"Sure I do, we're gonna kill some Screeners, and go after the water!" he answered.

"Am I too late for the meeting?" asked Iris.

"Just in time," said Annak. "First, let's get you some food."

Nathan was anxious to see what the meeting would be about. Following Iris into Annak's room he noticed how well she looked. He knew she had not eaten or drank any water in two days. She was out in the raw elements, yet appeared vibrant. There was a remarkable radiance about her. Her eyes were wide-open, her body trembled — seemingly not from weakness, but from a power that was on her and through her. Nathan was intrigued by how intense it was, still curious about why she did not want anyone touching her.

Iris was unwilling to sit down, too on edge. Annak handed her a small plate of meat. Outside the door they could hear people making their way out from different parts of the cave. "Take your time and eat," said Annak, "they can wait." Annak stood up and threw a strapped rifle over his shoulder.

Iris took a few bites of food, but was having a hard time sitting still. "Let's go," she said, motioning for Annak to start walking in front of her as they left the room.

At the center of the cave was a massive room the size of a towering cathedral. The Tree House was in the background. From it, a myriad of tunnels and rooms broke off in all directions like spokes shooting out from the hub of a wheel. The entire body of Reapers were gathered in the middle, waiting for Iris to show up. The majority of them were huddled around the smoldering bonfire. The place was reminiscent of an abandoned industrial-construction site that had been overtaken by a ton of homeless people — everything one would expect to see from a site roughed-in, but never finished. Long corded lightbulbs spanned across the ceiling overhead, all of them blacked out. Huge mechanical runs and fabricated metal trunks pierced through the rock walls and dangled loosely like a ton of slinky's. High voltage electrical and low voltage network wiring —red, green, yellow, white, concrete forms, steel framing studs, and a slew of junky scraps were all over the place. Whatever leftover lumber there was had all been reserved for fires.

Iris, Annak and Nathan, took their place in front, standing on the stout steps that lead up to the Tree House.

Staring out across the multitude of people they saw a crowd of restless, worn-out faces — almost three hundred — most of them foreboding with angst and uncertainty. They appeared tired, dirty and beaten up. The only Reapers missing were those manning the watch towers and those guarding Adullum's entrance. There was a dense racket that lingered in the atmosphere — coughing, faint whispers, babies sounding like babies, hands fidgeting. The mood was intense aside from some chuckling teenagers wrestling around in the rusted body of a 1969 Ford pickup truck. Some toddlers were playing on the hood, banging on it with pebbles and stones.

No sooner did Iris start to speak that things grew quiet.

"Reapers," she announced in a voice that could be heard by every listening ear "We're still here. Some of you have been with us since the beginning. You've come from all over, to seek refuge from a land torn by poison, greed, and wickedness. For all I know, you're the last remaining fragment of what's *good*. You've lost houses, wives, husbands, children. And much more. Geospark's taken something from all of us. I've lost my whole family, except for my Grandson, Nathan. Our land was on that lake, it was our home. Our lives depended on those rivers. Those of us here at Adullum are fighting for the same thing — restoration. Many of you have given your last ounces of hope to protecting this body. This place is what we have left — it's our cleft in the rock, our safe haven, our high place in the trees. Apart from this granite fortress, many of us would've never survived this long. But...we have — still hunting, still scavenging, still finding ways to get water."

There was silence for a moment, then an abrupt voice cried out from the back, "What is this place?"

Annak stepped forward, with gun in hand. No one interrupted Iris while she was speaking. Whoever it was must have been unfamiliar with the meetings. "Who's asking?"

A tall black man stood up, looking not more than 30 years old, "My name's Easton," he said confidently. "I've been here a week. They took everything from me." When he spoke, some of the others were stirred up, their anger fueled.

Annak allowed them to vent for a bit and then commanded them to refocus, "Listen up!" he yelled. "Check his wrist."

Some of those standing next to the man pulled up his sleeves and checked. "He's good!" one of them yelled back.

Annak looked at Iris for a moment to get a sense of how she wanted him to deal with the interruption. She put her hand up and motioned for Annak to step back. "Easton," she said. "This is a secret nerve center that was set up by the government before the contamination occurred. When I fled for my life, this place was revealed to me in a vision. It's the only place *they* haven't found yet. Any more questions, keep them to yourself for now."

Easton was quiet and sat back down.

Nathan got sick to his stomach and had a weird feeling about the guy. People showed up from time to time looking for safety and some sort of community, but this stranger seemed different.

Iris, on the other hand did not seem too concerned. She continued, "We're living in much uncertainty. The days are dark. Water's not getting any better. Some of you came here out of sheer necessity to survive and some because you refused to compromise your beliefs in what's unseen. There's nothing new under the sun regarding Geospark's zeal to rid the earth of all spirituality. Over the last twenty years they've been creating monsters, using captives, POW's, and slaves like experimental rats; manufacturing deadly machines, and reinforcing their fortresses along the waterways. They control the water, therefore, they control the electricity. The watershed of Redfish Lake is the Screener's only leverage to imprison all of us under their rule. They're trying to redefine the future — without any moral code, without any accountability. At the beginning we went back outside the boundaries of Adullum many times, searching the northwest for food, supplies, weapons, vehicles, other survivors. And in doing so, too many of us have been lost and killed. Every time we've gone out and tried to take one of the dams, we've lost. Every time we've tried to get close to the rivers, we've lost," Iris paused, "yet, the miracle remains — we're still here."

There was an ever-glow about Iris as she spoke. "But there's a momentum in my spirit! Something is shifting." Iris looked over at Nathan briefly, reminded of his encounter with the Sarx, knowing that darkness was on the move, but also aware of the greater light that could once again be opened up before them. "I was in the forest, seeking, and the Navigator spoke to me very clearly, *It's time to move.* I asked what He meant, and if we were supposed to leave Adullum. He simply spoke of one assignment, one mission. That was it. I asked Him, how many are supposed to go on this assignment? He said, *Those willing to go will volunteer.*"

There was a raggedy looking woman sitting in the front, holding her small child, "What are we being asked to do?"

Iris explained, "Before Adullum's construction was abandoned, there was a complete circuit of power set up in here. All the electricity was trenched underground, supplied by a dam on the Columbia River. There's a chance the control panel is still at that dam. I don't know the reason, or what it will do, but the Navigator spoke very clearly. He said, *It's time to get the power on.*"

Someone else asked, "Which dam?"

"The Bonneville," answered Iris.

Another voice yelled out in astonishment, "That's insane! How are we supposed to survive out there?"

Another frantic voice shouted, "How much water do we have left?"

Iris raised her voice, "Listen! We've been given a task, our next step, that's what I know right now. We need as many of you as possible, but the journey's not for the faint of heart. This won't be a sightseeing trip to assess the wreckage that's out there. The fact is, we've captured more Gnats in the last three months than we ever have. They're sending more and more surveillance scouts our way. There's a chance that getting the power on will help us to explore this cave and deepen our resources to fight against them."

Someone else shouted, "We're too outnumbered by them!"

Like clockwork, the hulking vibration of the worm started to shake the walls. The HVAC trunks swayed back and forth, and fragments of dust fell down from the rock ceiling. Iris waited, let it run its course, and then responded, "The reasons for getting the power on are not entirely clear to me, but it's what I heard."

"If we don't?" someone in the crowd asked.

"If we don't, we don't," answered Iris. "We take out chances staying here and we do our best to hold them off when they come. But if we get stuck inside this cave, we're trapped. They either wait for us to surrender, then they torture us, kill us, or we starve to death. The doors to this cave can't be shut without electricity. Not only that, but if we take the Bonneville, there's a chance we can open the navigation lock and allow water to flow this way again."

"I'll go!" a voice shouted. It was Easton again from the back. "I've got nothing to lose. I'll give my life for that dam if I have to!"

Everyone in the chamber was quiet until another

voice spoke up, "Me too!"

"I'm going!" someone else declared.

Iris should have been excited that people were volunteering for the journey, but she did well to hide her zeal, if indeed there was any. Instead, she looked out across the people and asked the question, "How many of you have the Blue Flame?"

A little less than eighty-one people stood up, Easton was one of them. "Come up here," she said, sporadically pointing out a few of them. They made their way to the front and stood in a row in front of Iris. She wasted no time looking each one of them in their eyes, her body still trembling the same as it was when she came into the cave. "What's He like?" she asked the first person.

The middle aged man being questioned looked confused, "What do you mean?"

"The Flame," said Iris.

He scrambled for the right words, "It's...it's — "

"Go back and sit down," Iris commanded very calmly. She moved to the next person, "What's He like?"

The young man was intimidated by Iris's eyes, "Well...I...think — "

"Go sit down." Iris came to the third person. It was the same woman who was in the front holding her child. As Iris looked at her, the woman's eyes widened with sincerity, the child was quiet, waiting to see what would happen. "Well?" Iris asked, implying that she was setting the same question now before the mother.

The woman answered instantly, "I don't know! I...I don't know, but please. Please! I don't have the Blue Flame."

Iris discerned what she was feeling, "You want what I have, don't you?"

"Yes!" she said, with all honesty.

"Hold this child," she said to Nathan, motioning for

him to take the little girl out of her mother's arms.

"Wait a second!" the woman piped up. "What are you doing?"

"Do you trust me or not?" asked Iris. The woman was still a bit uneasy, but, looking into Iris's eyes, decided to hand her girl to Nathan. "Nathan, you'll be watching her the rest of the night."

"The rest of the night?" the woman asked, somewhat concerned.

"Shhhhhh," Iris whispered. "You need to let her go to receive what I'm about to release to you. You came up here for a reason, and because of your genuine desire, you're gonna have what you've asked for."

Nathan took the little girl in his arms, uncertain about what would happen next. Annak shifted and stood behind the woman while the others watched. As Iris lifted her trembling hand toward the woman she simply touched her palm to her forehead and in an instant the woman shot backwards. Annak quickly caught her and laid her on the ground where she was left flopping around and kicking, the woman's chest rising up and down with bursts of power.

Nathan did not know what to think. He held the toddler in his arms and noticed the child was not scared or frightened at what just happened to her mother.

Immediately, Iris stopped shaking. She moved to the next man standing in line, "You said your name was Easton, Huh?" she asked casually, ignoring the woman on the ground.

"Yes," the man answered.

Iris sized him up, "You're young. And strong."

Eaton did not say anything, nor did he appear to be in the mood to accept compliments or reject them. He seemed assertive and meek.

"Let me see your eyes," said Iris. She peered into

them, grabbing his wrist at the same time as if taking his pulse. She held on and did not let go until she caught a flicker of indigo flash through his pupils. She let go and stepped back promptly saying, "There's a peculiar gift inside of you isn't there?"

Easton stuck his chin out and leaned his head away from Iris as if she had revealed something about him he was not proud of or at least something he had yet to understand about himself. He did not answer.

"You do don't you?" Iris asked again.

"Maybe," he said in a strong quiet way.

"It's almost too hard to believe, but I know you have it. He's given you the one gift I always had a hard time understanding. I can't believe it." Iris shook her head. "It's been a long time since I've seen someone with it, thought that gift had vanished." Iris was talking to Easton like they were the only two people in the room. Easton was reserved, not wanting what he carried to be exposed. Regardless of whether or not Iris was impressed, he seemed abashed by it.

After a while, the mother on the ground stopped shaking, she lay there perfectly still, seemingly entranced in another world, with only her eyelids twitching periodically. Iris and Annak were not caught off guard by the woman's motionless body, nor her inability to be cognizant of what was going on. Yet Nathan found it almost impossible to take his eyes off her, thinking something was wrong, wondering when she would get up. Others in the room were undoubtedly just as confused.

"You're a fascinating man," Iris said to Easton. "Don't go anywhere. I want you to wait here until I'm done." She looked at Annak, "Keep your eyes on him," she said before turning back towards the crowd. "There's a lot more than a *carnal* war being fought out there. In those streets, and in that wilderness, there's a war in the spirit realm. Having a skill is good, having military experience is good. Knowing how to hunt…or use a bow…or pull the trigger…is good. But in order to survive, in order to push through their lines, it's going to take more than skill and bullets — much more! Without the Flame, you're just an empty shell and you will crack as soon as there's pressure. Those dams are guarded more heavily than anything else in this world. Nothing's as coveted as that water — not oil fields, not treasury reserves, nothing. Yet this war is far more complex than water rights — it's a struggle for the legacy of the human race, for the eternal destiny of every person. The Screeners are not our only enemy. Behind their faces of flesh is a host of principalities, gatekeepers of darkness, and unseen dens of wickedness. We have to get back the waterways, but we need more than gun powder. We need more than fuel, fire, and explosives. We need power! Power from another world! His world! And not just a few of us — all of us!"

"Listen to me very carefully," Iris focused intensely on individual faces throughout the room, "Your access to that power is wide open. All you have to do is let go…and enter in. Abandon yourself! And trust Him!" It was evident by her sincerity that Iris was not speaking from a prescribed set of notes. She spoke as one who cared more about the heart than the head. "Every one of you, there's a reason why you've been drawn here. Adullum's the place where the broken rise up, where the despairing find hope. It doesn't matter what brought you here, He's the One who's guided you this far. This mother up here is an example of how easy it is. All you have to do is ask. All you have to do is become hungry enough, not for food, but for Him. Then, no matter what happens here in this life, you'll be secure in the next."

Iris let go of that thought for a moment and changed the subject, "It's obvious the winter season has been getting shorter. The contamination is still everywhere we go. We've done our best to save as much water as possible."

"How much?" someone asked.

Iris was less than eager to answer. Nathan felt the urge to speak up in her place so he could increase the tension and stir people up.

"It's minimal," said Iris, knowing they could not have had more than two month's supply of clean water. As soon as she answered there was an increase of patchy whispers, murmurs, and a subtle wave of panic.

Another cry rang out, "Where are we supposed to get water?"

Annak whistled loudly and then yelled, "Calm down! Everyone knows they're supposed to be gathering up as much snow as possible. We'll see how far it gets us."

"Everything's been raided," said Iris. "All that's left is what flows from Icon. It's all under Geospark's control. Any clean water outside of that will be nothing short of a miracle. This next expedition will hopefully open a door for us. For now, the watchtowers will stay manned and Adullum will remain guarded. We'll continue our hunting schedule as normal. Everybody who chooses to stay behind, must continue to occupy their normal tasks."

Some disturbed fanatic broke out, "But you're our leader! Why haven't you done something? We're gonna die because of you! It's your fault!"

"Listen!" said Iris. "My shoulders aren't the only one's our future rests upon. I've never failed to do all I can, but my time and role is limited. Overcoming what's in front of us is going to require something from every single person. Everyone who's willing to complain and do nothing, can leave right now and go join *them*. That's all I have to say for now. We prepare tomorrow and leave the following day. Anyone else willing to go with us, come to the front. Meeting's over."

When Iris finished, there was a hustle in the room, bodies shifted and kids started running around again. One by one, a small group of people came forward. The majority, however, made their way back to their designated plots and routines in the cave. Iris stepped back and sat down on one of the steps. Annak counted those who came forward — there were twenty-five.

"By standing up here, you're committing your life to whatever happens over the next week," said Annak. "At first light tomorrow, we'll meet back here to discuss what we need for the journey. You're dismissed." Everyone left, most of them knowing full well the dangers that would be involved.

THIRTEEN
Scarecrow

The rest of the day Annak stayed near the mother, lying motionless on the ground. There was no use covering her with a blanket or setting her next to a fire, her body was already too hot. Annak knew she was being burned with something not made by human hands. Nathan went with Iris into their room and played with the little girl. It was not long before she grew tired and fell asleep in his arms.

Nathan sat next to the fire and watched Iris reach down and pick something up off the ground. "I'm surprised that thing's held together this long," he said.

Iris held up a dark crimson, tattered book, the binding was barely attached, its pages were frayed and frail. She looked at it as if it were a coveted relic. "It's the last piece of literature I have," she said. "Boreham — always was my favorite. Never found anyone else who could write quite like him."

From the other side of the fire Nathan could barely make out the title on the cover, even though he knew it by heart, *Ships of Pearl*. The imprinted words were dirty, yet still glistened with a small amount of metallic ink.

"You know," said Iris. "I hated reading. I struggled to read. My brain was too slow for it. When I was a little girl, barely able to make a sentence, my dad gave me this book. He said it was children's literature." Iris laughed. "He said if I could read this, I could read anything. It was only later I found out he'd opened me up to the world of one of the deepest thinkers that ever lived. In my humble opinion, of course." Iris thumbed her way through the pages carefully in search of one of her favorite pericopes, trying to keep some of the pages from pulling away from the binding. "I'd be put to death if they ever found out I had a copy of this. Probably the last one out there."

"Probably," Nathan agreed. "Read me some." He looked down at the girl, her mouth was half open and she was snoring lightly with her arms curled up under her neck.

"Just a little." Iris lifted the book to her nose and started to read "*Faith is a bird that loves to perch on scarecrows. She knows that there is a certain amount of risk in doing so. But she knows, too, that only by taking such risks can she enjoy the fruits of the garden. She knows that there are scarecrows wherever there are strawberries; but she also knows that wherever there are strawberries there are scarecrows. If, frightened by the scarecrows, she remains on the tree-tops, the telephone wires, or the fences, she will never find strawberries.*"

Iris stopped reading and began to expound, "There's two birds, Nathan. The wise bird and the foolish bird. The foolish bird looks out for scarecrows so she can avoid them and lives in fear. The wise bird, however, looks out for scarecrows so she can ravage the fruit."

"Birds..." said Nathan, "I get that. But why does there have to be scarecrows?"

"Simple," answered Iris. "Every good thing in life is guarded by something. The best things always cost something."

"Why?"

"Just the way it is. In life, there has to be a way to distinguish between those who are scared and those who are courageous. Good things belong to those who are willing to take them. Living by courage is a sacrifice...but there's a special reward for it. Scarecrows test the heart and reveal what's inside us. There's no glory in getting things that didn't cost anything. Whenever you have to slay a giant in order to get the promise, there's always more glory in the victory. The problem's not that all of us have an appetite for the fruit, rather, it's the fear that strikes us when we see the giant standing between us and the strawberries. Those with the strongest appetite get the fruit. But think about it, the giant's just a scarecrow — an object of baseless fear. The fight's not against *it*, but against our own fears and insecurities. Nathan, scarecrows don't keep people from the fruit, people keep themselves from the fruit. The fight's always against your own inner darkness. If you can overcome yourself, you can overcome anything else out there."

"You make it sound so easy. You don't know what it's like inside here," said Nathan, referring to his inner world.

"It might get harder for you."

Nathan stayed quiet. He pulled out a pocket knife and started scraping some calluses off his fingers. "I have so many questions Grandma...so many. It feels like I was thrown into a world I was never supposed to be a part of."

"Questions reveal hunger," said Iris. "But you're still outside the garden, pacing back and forth, intimidated by the scarecrow. Your inner man is groping for meaning."

Nathan didn't have a response. "This girl's cute."

Iris smiled, "She's at peace."

"What was it that happened out there?"

"It wasn't me, I can tell you that," answered Iris, "I didn't do anything."

"Sure didn't look that way."

"I was just a carrier, Nathan."

"You knocked her to the ground, Grandma."

"No," Iris said. "I didn't. I was just the conduit — the copper that carried the current."

"But why? Why her?"

"If I'd have touched anyone not desiring that current, it would have hurt them, or even worse —"

Nathan interrupted, "You mean, *like her*? Looked like you gave her a heart attack."

"Trust me, she's not hurt at all. She's being touched by paradise for the first time. When I was in the forest, the Navigator asked me to carry something. He said there would be one person, just one, waiting for it. For a second, I thought it might have been you, Nathan."

"Why just her?"

"Only He knows that, son. He searches the earth looking for those whose hearts are ready. She'll never be the same again after what happened today."

For Nathan, the thing that bothered him most about spiritual matters was that there was no way to measure them. With medicine, you can see the reaction of an antidote killing sickness. With science you can witness the exchange of chemicals. But with the metaphysical, the movements of the transcendent are hard to capture. There was no way to photograph the transfer that took place between the palm of Iris's hand and that mother's forehead. All he could do was question, which led to more of Iris's answers, which often times did nothing to clarify matters at all.

"What about that guy? Easton?" Nathan asked. "He's a big dude. You looked at him different…"

"He caught me off guard. I'm still having a hard time believing it."

"You worried about something?"

"No. Just shaken up a bit," Iris responded.

"Shaken? Doesn't seem like you."

"Because of his gift," she answered and then muttered to herself, "his gift."

"What about it?"

"I can't say."

"Why not?" Nathan was a little surprised, seemingly asking a question he was not permitted to know the answer to.

"Because, you wouldn't believe me if I told you, Nathan."

"Oh, come on. Stop messing around and just tell me," begged Nathan.

"Nathan, I'm serious. No."

"You're such a hoarder of secrets, you know that." Nathan shook his head with a hint of sarcasm.

"You can't show everything to everybody," said Iris. "There's things you're gonna have to see with your own eyes and hear with your own ears. What Easton carries can either liberate or cripple someone."

"How can you call it a gift, then?"

"Because it's a gift of edification for those *with* the Flame. If you don't have the Spirit, his gift will tear you up."

Nathan was quiet.

Iris continued, "There's an ancient story of a king who was tormented by evil spirits. He had a young servant he'd summon into his chambers. He would command the boy to sing and as the boy did, the evil spirits would be forced to flee the king's presence."

"And that's supposed to mean?"

"You'll know when you see it."

Nathan had nothing more to say. All at once he realized how tired he was and became quiet. Joining the little girl in her slumber, he fell asleep.

FOURTEEN
Rally Point

Adullum, which was comprised of the valley of Yosemite National Forest, was mostly the only world Nathan knew. Beyond those borders were things Nathan had yet to encounter. There was much he had still to experience beyond the safety and refuge of the cave he had grown up in. He was not unaware of his own frailty. Nathan was a Reaper, and Reapers were at best, peasants outside the city walls when compared to the lot that Screeners occupied. Nathan wondered, *did he and the others have what it takes to make it all the way to the Bonneville alive? And if so, would they be able to get the power on?* What parts of him were untouched by restlessness and naivety were prone to doubt. The Screeners were not only substantially greater in number, but their positions were fortified by means of weaponry that was far advanced beyond what Nathan and the others could get their hands on. Most Reapers had weapons, but they were outdated and archaic. More so, the Screeners had food, storehouses, technology, strength, and most of all, they had access to the water.

Nathan knew the day ahead of him was limited, they only had so many hours to get ready before leaving the next morning. Nathan helped prepare, Annak met with those who volunteered to go, assessing each one's capabilities and strengths, and making sure everyone knew full well what was required. Max and Silas, two of Annak's best men, were at the forefront of the preparations.

When Alex was relieved from the tower and made it back down to the entrance of the cave, it did not take long for him to notice the commotion that was taking place. "I'm not too sure what's going on here," he said to Nathan, who was watching Annak brief everyone, "but I heard rumors that you guys were going to try and take control of one of the dams. Ain't nobody leaving without me!" Alex exclaimed.

Nathan looked at him, "Of course not. I knew you'd find out what was going on. We need you with us."

"I'll get my stuff ready," said Alex, his voice was amped up.

"It's more than seven hundred miles to the dam from here," said Annak, "Fifteen hours by road. That's two to three days, assuming we'll be able to stay on main roads. We'll do our best to stay away from what we think are highly patrolled areas. Interstate 5 is a dangerous section, it's our longest stretch — five hundred miles. Tomorrow, day one, we're trying to get to Redding. Day two, downtown Portland, we'll set up a rally point there. The Willamette River runs through downtown Portland from the Columbia. If the navigation lock's engaged at the Portland dam then the river should still be dried up and the city deserted, as it's been for years now. From downtown we have forty miles to the Bonneville dam and lock."

"Doesn't sound too bad," someone said.

"Here's the problem," Annak shot back, "That forty mile stretch is the I-84, and it parallels closely with the Columbia. It's trafficked by the Screeners daily, more than any other road. We won't be able to drive on that part."

"So…what's your plan?" asked Silas.

"We're packing," answered Annak, in a serious tone.

"You're joking, right?" laughed one of the other men. "You expect us to go forty miles on foot? And then back the same way?"

"Depends on Screener activity when we get there." said Annak.

"I'm not doing that," a man protested. "I'll stay here and look after Adullum." He picked up his stuff and left. As he walked away, his angst infected part of the group, and five others did the same, balking at the dangerous journey.

"Anyone else?" Annak asked, not too overly concerned or surprised by those who left. He offered up a general petition, "If there's any doubt in your mind than you need to leave now, you won't be any help to us out there."

"I'm all in," said Nathan.

"Me too," Max and Silas said in unison.

"I'm going," said Easton.

"We'll engage the Crawlers as much as possible," said Annak, "but there's gonna be footwork. There's a chance we can use the back-roads into Ainsworth Forest — it can shorten our distance by twenty miles. I don't have every angle on this thing...none of us do, all we have is what we've got. There's always unknowns. But we're going, at all costs. Everybody coming is choosing to submit to Iris's leadership, and mine. The chain of command will be no different then it's always been here at Adullum."

Every mouth was quiet, there were no objections. Annak turned and gave some silent instructions to Nathan, "Food," he said, "make sure everyone's rationed for at least ten days — one meal per day, half a quart of water per person...per day. Whatever else we find out there will be extra provision. We leave in the morning at first light."

"Weapons and ammunition?" asked Alex.

"We'll need all we can take," said Annak. "You're in charge of that."

They all dispersed and stayed focused the rest of the day. Nathan scrounged for food and water. Max and Silas scooped limited amounts of puddled water from the Merced River and filled the Crawlers as best they could. The others did what was necessary to ensure they had all their equipment and supplies. There was a lot of quiet activity going on.

As Nathan walked in and out of the cave, he brushed

shoulders with Annak, who was loading up two sniper rifles. "What you think about those guys who bailed out?" Nathan asked, in a low voice.

"Nothing," answered Annak.

"What do you mean, nothing? Every person counts, right?"

"We don't need them out there. Strength of the few we have will be enough as long as He's on our side."

"Yeah, but extra bodies never hurts?"

"Dead weight, Nathan," retorted Annak, "now stop talking and stay busy."

"Hope you're right," said Nathan.

That night, after a long day of preparation, Nathan was fascinated with the woman Iris had touched during the meeting an evening earlier. She was dancing with her daughter in the firelight. He heard them laughing and singing from down the corridor. Physically speaking, she was the same woman, but she was oddly different. She was exuberant with joy and beside herself in a way. Nathan thought it strange to be in the throes of an apocalyptic world, surviving one day at a time, yet finding time to dance. No one danced anymore. In the world Nathan lived in, people no longer played catch, there was no time for games, let alone mindless frolicking. The tone of the atmosphere was always a march not a skip. Yet this woman was taking a moment to celebrate, who knows what, in a time of war. It seemed like being on the beaches of Normandy during the onset of WWII, yet taking a quick moment to sit in the sand and admire the pearl inside a broken oyster shell. It was odd.

Nathan hid in the shadows, leaned up against a vertical iron pipe and watched them. He was dazed by their happiness, because for Nathan there was no room for happiness, too much revenge was inside his heart, too many devils still to conquer. Yet standing there, he could not deny that he was attracted to something. It was as if in this mother's dance with her daughter, they were stirring something up, a whirlwind reminiscent of another world Nathan had yet to discover for himself; one he had yet to see with his own eyes. The short moment was like a firefly flashing on and off as it gently glides through the night, giving off a fleeting spark of light, then disappearing.

Nathan was catching glimpses of something, but then suddenly startled by a hand that hit him on the back of the shoulder. "What's up?" a voice asked from behind.

Nathan turned around abruptly and noticed it was Alex, "Punk!" exclaimed Nathan, "Don't scare me like that."

"How do I smell?" Alex asked, as he nestled up to Nathan and forced his armpit into his face.

"Whoa man!" exclaimed Nathan as he tried to push Alex away.

Alex laughed, "Well?"

"Sure don't stink as bad as you did a couple days ago," said Nathan.

"Not much time to get clean running those towers. Man...I was getting rashes."

"Still not sure how you got rid of all that stink?"

"A shower...a bath, not sure what you call it, just found some melting snow and rolled around naked in it," Alex shook his head. "It was cold!"

A gross smirk came across Nathan's face, "Whatever it takes, I guess." Nathan turned his attention back to the dancing, "You scared?" he asked Alex.

"Depends. Of what?"

"Of what's out there. What we'll encounter," said Nathan, not so much referring to the physical obstacles, but rather to the spiritual. Ever since that Sarx spoke into his life, he had been gripped with an uncomfortable insecurity about the things that were unseen.

"Sometimes I am," answered Alex, "Can't be worse than what we've seen so far, though."

Nathan sighed, "Maybe not."

"Hey, you ok man?" Alex asked. "You're not yourself...you seem more on edge than normal."

Nathan hesitated for a moment, "Just seen some stuff lately."

"Like what?"

"Don't want to talk about it. Just a little nervous about being out there at night."

"Yeah, but you're forgetting something — Iris and Annak are with us. I'll follow them anywhere man!"

"I know, it's just —"

"Hey," Alex interrupted. "We'll do what we gotta do to stick together."

Just then Annak walked by, "Get to sleep," he commanded. "We're heading out early...need all the strength you can get."

"Alright, alright," said Alex. "I'm outta here."

"See you bright and early," said Nathan. The three of them split up.

The next morning, as the sun was creeping over the hills, slowly reaching its burning fingertips through the canyon, Nathan and the Reaper caravan were already en route to Redding. Annak was leading in front with Max. The rest were in the middle while Nathan and Iris took the tail end. It was chilly and slightly windy, yet calm, as they made their way out of Yosemite Valley and onto the tattered asphalt of Interstate 5. Alex was curled up in the tailgate of Iris's vehicle, clutching his machine gun watching the rear, ready to lock his eyes and unload on anything that moved. Silas controlled a heavy artillery gun mounted on the cab of the middle Crawler, his fingers rubbing against the triggers. Nobody was talking, including Nathan. They were too alert and entranced by the miserable landscape — bleak and windswept.

Every single bridge they crossed, spanned what years ago would have been a flowing river. But, instead the riverbeds were dried up basins and canals that reeked with the stench of sickness and death, cracked and bone-dry. Occasionally, as they drove, they were forced to maneuver around ditched vehicles that lined the highway; all of them having shattered windows, blown tires, and missing parts. Any dead bodies still in the vehicles would have been eaten by wild animals by now. The 5 was long, but surprisingly, for most of the day they moved swiftly with little complications. There was a dense layer of fog that did not seem to lift for most of the day. This was a good thing, it provided a canopy under which they could hide from any drone surveillance.

The bulk of the day passed by surprisingly uncomplicated. They veered off the highway and made their exit into downtown Redding. Annak led them to the Sundial Bridge where they set up a discreet camp underneath a patch of dead willow trees hunched over like decapitated giants. They set up temporary camp.

The next morning everyone was stone-cold because Iris did not allow any fires. Without wasting time, they got back on the 5 and continued north. It seemed like just another uncomplicated, overcast day. Yet hours later as they neared the outskirts of downtown Portland, a strange feeling came over Nathan. There was something more depressing about the city than other areas he had seen. Most of the buildings were either crushed, blown apart, or barely standing — they were dark and empty. Nonetheless, it was the only city he had seen in his life. All he knew up until this point was the lake, the wilderness — Adullum.

At some point, Iris and Annak must have agreed on terms as if there was some sort of behind the scenes communication, because as they slowly pulled onto Broadway Street in downtown, Annak knew exactly where to go. He led them into a specific parking garage, a shabby concrete structure barely standing where they slowly spiraled up to the middle floor. Once all the Crawlers were parked in a dark corner, all the ignitions keyed off.

"Where we supposed to be going?" Nathan asked Iris.

"Right there," she said, pointing across the street.

Nathan looked over the balcony of the garage, barely able to read the distorted words hanging off the side of the building, *nitzer c...cert h...ll*. From what he could tell it appeared to be what was once an iconic theatre.

"Get all your stuff," instructed Annak. "Don't leave any weapons, ammo, or food."

The rusty hinges whimpered as they breeched through a rickety doorway in the back of the building. The place was quiet, and smelled stale. The daylight glow that came through the doorway triggered the flutter of pigeon wings in the rafters. Shafts of light spanned across the place from wall to wall, poking through holes in the ceiling. As they got further into the building, more details came into view, elaborate wood-carved millwork, and the modest wink of victorian wallpaper.

Smash! Nathan's foot struck a broken popcorn machine that sent a some starving rats scurrying across the floor. Max and Silas pressed their guns to their cheeks and moved cautiously over various rubble, old theatre seats, fragmented pieces of furniture, and trash. Others plugged their noses as the fetor of urine, and other horrible smells seeped up from the tattered carpets and flooring.

"Oh!" moaned Alex, "this place is disgusting!"

"You act like you've been living in a palace," snapped Nathan.

"Shhhh!" warned Annak, "We need to clear this place."

Nathan was suddenly caught off guard by something. He perked up and aimed his rifle, but soon realized it was just the skeletal remains of a body slouched over a chair. He passed by it, then noticed another lying in the aisle, then another. Carcasses and cadavers, both human and animal alike, were all over the place.

"Split up in groups of five and scout the rest of the building," ordered Annak. "Don't take any longer than twenty minutes. Meet back here."

Nathan and Alex broke off with three others. As they cautiously made their way out into a large foyer, Nathan aimed his weapon up at the ceiling and was bewitched by a huge glass chandelier. Parts of it were broken and shattered, barely dangling, but still attractive. As the dim light hit it, splintered glares shot out in every direction. The floors made a hollowing sound as the soles of their feet cracked against the rubble scattered across the marble tiles.

"This place is nasty," commented Alex.

"Yet, kinda beautiful at the same time," said Nathan. "Let's go up the stairway." He shifted his eyes off the chandelier and moved his body up alongside the railing, its varnish boiled and cracked.

Step after step they inched toward the top of the landing, just as a cold gust of wind blew through the open foyer. The breeze came out of nowhere and seemed to be isolated as if someone suddenly turned on a huge fan. It was strong enough for Nathan to feel like he was being seized in a small tornado, the others equally startled. Nathan hoisted his gun to his shoulder and aimed rashly across the peripheral back and forth quickly looking for an oncoming assault. The angry swirl of wind kicked up a blanket of dust and scraps that went flying everywhere. Everyone covered their mouths and shielded their eyes. Yet between hacking and trying to keep his eyes open, something went sailing through the air that took hold of Nathan's attention.

Without hesitating, Nathan took off running after it.

"Hey!" yelled Alex, "Slow down."

"Do you see it?" shouted Nathan, frantically pointing to a piece of paper twisting in invisible circles up the stairway as it was carried along by the wind. Nathan sprinted after it, unaware that he was quickly separating himself from the rest of the group.

"Nathan! Wait!" yelled Alex, trying to catch up. "You crazy?"

Not letting it out of his sight, Nathan fought his way through the second level of the building as the piece of paper moved about all over the place. Running as fast as he could he tried not to trip over scattered junk.

"Nathan!" Alex yelled. "Chill out! It's just a piece of paper!

But like a horse with a bridle in its mouth, Nathan was not focused on anything but that piece of paper. Finally, after a frenzy of excitement, Nathan snatched the paper out of mid-air, and held it between his thumb and index finger, the paper still shaking in the swell of wind as if it was a fragile leaf. And no sooner was the paper in Nathan's hand, the wind disappeared.

Alex struggled to slow down, and crashed into Nathan. "Nathan!" he said. "We're supposed to be quiet. What's all the panic for?" Nathan did not respond, he was entranced by the piece of paper. Alex ripped it from his hands. "What? You kidding me? Some stupid drawing?"

"Hey! Give it to me!" Nathan yelled, as he pushed Alex and took it back. Immediately, Nathan folded it up and stuffed it into his front pocket.

"Not sure what the big deal is, man," said Alex.

"My Grandma needs to see this," said Nathan. "Let's finish up here and head back down."

"You've already blown our cover," complained Alex. "If there was any danger up here we would've known by now."

Nathan did not care about Alex's remarks, the paper had stolen his attention.

After scouting the second level, Alex and the other three followed Nathan back down to the large amphitheater room. They were the first ones back. Nathan looked for the best seat, climbed up on stage, and plopped himself down on a grizzled corduroy sofa. Just as he did so, the thought of perhaps sitting down a little slower crossed his mind as a cloud of dust lifted up through the burgundy cushions. Nathan coughed as if he had just inhaled a cigar and waved his hands to clear the air in front of his face. He looked around, noticing the shot out stage lights, broken theatre props, and cracked floor boards. Resting his gun on his lap, he pulled the piece of paper from his pocket and stared at it again, admiring it as if it were a complex set of blueprints.

It was not long before the others started trickling back into the theatre. They gathered around the stage and waited for further direction.

"Building's clear?" asked Annak.

One by one, multiple people responded, "Didn't find a thing."

"This will be our rally point," said Annak.

"If anything goes wrong," said Iris, "if we get split up, do whatever it takes to get back to this spot. None of us head back to Adullum until we're all accounted for."

"Everybody find a spot to lay low," said Annak, "We'll rest here tonight and leave in the morning.

That evening, Nathan was responsible for making sure all the doors to the building were shut. It was uncommonly cold so Iris conceded to allowing a single fire. They found anything that was combustible and made a pile below the stage; everyone huddling around it like they were ants on a donut crumb. Nathan, Iris and Annak sat in a row of chairs covered with shabby aquamarine velvet.

"Grandma, you seen Annak's scars?" Nathan asked.

Iris looked at Nathan as if to imply that it was a vacuous question, "Course I have."

"Look at this," said Nathan, unraveling the crumpled piece of paper in his hand.

Annak leaned over, grabbed it, and held it to his face, "Where'd you get this?"

"When we were searching the building," answered Nathan.

"But how?" asked Annak, handing it to Iris.

"What do you mean? I just found it," said Nathan.

"Nathan," Iris spoke slowly, "how…did…you… find…it?"

"This wind came out of nowhere, blew right through us," Nathan paused, "The paper flew across my face. If I'd never seen Annak's scars, I wouldn't have thought anything of it. Never in my life have I seen this image. And then within only a few days I see it twice. Seem weird to you?"

"A little child drew this," said Iris. She held the dirty paper in her hands, looking at the pencil sketch depicting a covey of doves escaping from a treasure chest; it was drawn on what looked like a faded newspaper article. "Not sure if you found the picture…or the picture found you, Nathan. Wind carried it into your hand, huh?"

"You think it means something?" asked Nathan.

"Yes," she answered.

"What?"

"It's a signal," said Iris. Nathan listened. "A sign… whatever you want to call it —"

"More like a torch lit in the dark," added Annak.

"What's it mean?" inquired Nathan.

"Could represent the past...the present...or the future, many things. Hard to say exactly," said Iris.

"Could you be any less vague?" asked Nathan.

"It means there's danger ahead of us," Iris paused soberly, "but...He's with us. He's always with us. There's something ahead for you Nathan"

"That's it?" Nathan shirked.

Iris grinned with compassion in her eyes as she looked at Nathan, "Sometimes that's all that needs to be, son. He's enough. He's pursuing you though, Nathan...sniffing you out like a hound. You can keep trying to run, but He's gonna find you; He's always gonna find you. It's no coincidence you're holding that picture."

Nathan contemplated the drawing, "I don't care what danger lies ahead of us. I want the dams, I want the lake back."

Annak squinted his eyes and glanced over at Nathan, "What do you make of this boy's tenacity, Iris?"

"Keep your eye on him, that's all I have to say," she murmured.

Nathan put the picture back in his pocket and changed the subject, "Why this place?" he asked. "Why not the subway or a warehouse or something?"

"I thought about this location long and hard, Nathan, long and hard," Iris said seriously "And you know what? It's a very insightful matter - I missed these dark green theatre chairs."

"Oh whatever," Nathan shrugged. "You're joking. The Navigator didn't give you some mystical reason or vision for this place?"

Iris laughed, "Nope. Just wanted see these seats again."

Annak smiled, indicating he thought she was a little loony, yet unsurprised.

"Fine memories here," Iris continued, "This is the Arlene Schnitzer Concert Hall." Iris's eyes glossed over as she started to reminisce about the place. "This center isle — right here. It's where I first experienced the sting of embarrassment."

"Stop messing around with me, you serious, Grandma?" Nathan could not help but think there had to be a more rational explanation for choosing this building as their rally point.

"I was never a city girl, still not. But your grandfather took me here for our first anniversary. My favorite singer of all time, Laurie Burn, was performing her last concert on the same night of our anniversary. My goodness, we barely had enough money to leave the ranch in Idaho. But you're Grandpa had a way of figuring things out and making them happen. It was beautiful. Never did hear anyone else who could sing like that woman."

Nathan started to realize Iris was being serious, "Ok, so where's the embarrassment come into the story?"

Iris continued, "That night was the first time I'd ever worn a pair of high heels. All I'd known were old tennis shoes and some cowgirl boots. Even though it was obvious we were *country* people, that night I wanted to impress Grandpa with something different; I thought high heels would do the trick, maybe throw him off a bit. And you know what? They certainly did. But your Grandpa played some tricks of his own — it was the first time I'd seen him wear a tie, it was the last too. Never did like men in ties, I always preferred him in a logger shirt, half unbuttoned with some chest hair showing." Iris smiled.

Nathan laughed.

"Well, during the concert I had to use the bathroom.

We were sitting right over there, just a couple aisles back. Got outta my seat and started down the aisle, when all the sudden I tripped and fell flat on my face. My purse went flying and all my stuff with it, broke the bottom of one of the heels right off. I looked up and all these city greasers were laughing at me, snickering and whispering, pointing their fingers."

"That sucks," said Nathan, "No wonder you're the only Grandma I know who wears boots."

"That's not the best part of the story," she continued. "Suddenly I felt your brave Grandpa's hands reach underneath my arms and pull me to my feet. I can still remember so clearly what he did next," Iris paused as she reflected. "That man was so crazy about me. He looked every single one of those well-suited, well-dressed egos in the face and gave them the best speech I ever heard. *"Ya know who yure laffin at?"* he said," Iris impersonated his voice perfectly. *"This is Iris Loyal! The most beautiful, intelligent woman I ever met. How many you city gals can break a wild mustang, split a cord a wood in twenty minutes, skin a deer, survive in the wilderness with a flint knife? And how many of you can kiss like this?* And then he took me, leaned me over his arm and kissed me with all the passion anyone could ever hope for in a lover." Iris laughed, "Oh, my goodness, he was a real man. The thing about your Grandpa is that he had a way of making me feel like I was the most important person in his world." Iris rubbed her hand across the theatre chairs as she finished her sentence.

"Neat story," said Nathan.

"And just like that, my humiliating moment turned into a redemptive act of grace. The unashamed love of one crazy man drowned the insults of an entire crowd."

Annak was listening quietly, enjoying the story.

"A lot I don't know about you, Grandma," said

Nathan.

"And you may never know all there is to know. Now you know why I picked this place, just a memory, that's all. But sometimes memories are all we have."

"Would've never guessed," replied Nathan.

eryr.

sm.

FIFTEEN
Dirt Girl

The metal door at the back of the stage swung back and forth, its rusty hinges groaned quietly; the sound was subtle, but annoying enough to wake Nathan from his sleep. Strangely, there was no cold draft blowing through the door, just the stillness of a quiet night. As he inhaled, Nathan felt his nose hairs sticking together. Far from being thawed from his icy slumber, he could barely open his eyes. He lay still trying to tune it out, but the obnoxious sound of the creaking door kept rattling on and off. Even though they were soldered together with frost, Nathan summoned up enough muster to open his eyes. He poked his head free and squirmed out of the sleeping bag. He knew it could not have been later than three in the morning. Nathan looked around, in one sense concerned how the door had come ajar, and in another sense irritated that no one else was bothered enough to get up and shut it. Nonetheless, he shivered his way over to shut the door, stepping over sleeping bodies, and at the same time was alerted to an anomaly. It was an uncomfortable sound, like an unruly beast was guzzling away with loose manners. In an instant he realized he was not the only one awake during the twilight hour. Feeling the hair rise on the back of his neck he forgot about the door and slowly turned around.

His uneasy hunch was solidified when the beast came into view — a wild wolf ravaging part of their food supply, it was sickly looking, with a rawboned frame and bloodshot eyes, its body marked with cuts and gashes. The wolf's glaring eyes locked with Nathan's. The beast snarled viciously as a warning, then sunk its canines back into the food, letting Nathan know he was not going to let him get in

the way of his appetite. In an instant, the shivering brought on
by the chill soon gave way to the numbing heat of adrenaline.
Nathan mumbled some ugly curse words to himself when
he realized he had neglected to grab the pistol underneath
his sleeping bag. His eyes rushed back and forth, searching
for the nearest weapon he could find. Midway between him
and the wolf he noticed a steel bar. In a moment, Nathan
leapt towards it, startling the wolf into action at the same
time. The wolf's grin was ferocious as it hurled its open jaws
at Nathan. Nathan dove onto the ground, his back sliding
across the floor boards, and clutched onto the bar before
taking a swing. With great force, the bar smacked against
the wolf's face and cracked its head open. The wolf's frame
went limp and plummeted to the ground. Nathan tried to
gain his composure the best he could, but was still in shock.

"Nathan, what's going on?" Iris said as she poked her
head up.

"Door's open, somehow a wolf got into our food," he
answered, still trying to get up off the floor.

"You take care of it?" she asked.

"Yes, just go back to sleep."

Nathan went over to the door, still swinging open and
closed from the draft. But when he went to shut it, he was
again made uneasy. In the distance, across the street he could
see the deathly Sarx. The demon was glaring at him, humped
over, twitching from side to side, pacing back and forth
inside a blown apart elevator shaft. Immediately, Nathan was
struck with fear; swinging a steel bar at this beast would not
do. Just by looking at it, he felt it almost impossible to move
or speak, let alone breathe. He was confused as to why the
demon was not approaching him. The only reason he could
think of is that Annak and Iris were close by and the thing
was forced to keep its distance. Nonetheless, Nathan could
not shake the onset of his body clenching up. With what little

strength and resolve he did have, he slammed the door shut and braced it with the bloody steel bar.

"Nathan, what's wrong?" asked Iris.

"Nothing," he muttered, "it's nothing." He was scared to tell Iris what he had seen. It was as if seeing the Sarx again gripped him with deep shame to the point where he did not know how to ask for help.

"You sure?"

"Yeah, don't worry."

Nathan moved away from the door, crawled back into his sleeping bag, looked up at the rafters and became increasingly more paranoid. He hated living in a world where the next moment was so unpredictable. Dicey seemed to be the norm. He clutched his pistol tightly to his side and drifted in and out of sleep the rest of the morning. He could not seem to get the events of the early dawn out of his head. The sound of the wolf's skull getting crushed bothered him, and there was nothing uglier than the figure of that Sarx.

Just when he was able to feel his body going to sleep again, he was rudely awakened by Annak's husky face looking down at him.

"Rough night?" asked Annak, as he half heartedly nodded at the dead wolf.

Nathan rubbed his eyes, "You could say that."

Annak snickered, "Whatever happened, looks like you got us breakfast."

"Yeah, nice to know you slept through all that noise," chided Nathan.

"Slept like a baby. I only wake up for the battles I know are mine."

"I'm aware of that."

"That dog get you before you got it?"

"No."

"Good. Now get up, we got a long day ahead of us.

Today's the day things get interesting."

"Just give me a second, alright."

Some of the guys were already cooking up the wolf meat and dividing it amongst themselves. Nathan got up and tried to shake off the fatigue. He was delirious from lack of sleep and felt particularly alone in his thoughts. Yet he knew there was no time to be coddled, the morning was not going to wait for him. Before long, everybody packed up, exited the concert hall and hustled into the parking garage. They keyed the ignitions and moved down to the bottom of the concrete structure. The soft hum of the Crawlers hissed through Portland's downtown streets.

Iris looked over at Nathan, "I know there's more than that wolf bothering you."

Nathan said nothing, clenched his hand around the suicide knob and concentrated on the caravan in front of him.

"You're never alone, Nathan. Not as long as I'm around." Iris could sense Nathan was more reserved than normal.

"A lot of unknown crap out there, you know?" he muttered.

"Of course there is, son. There always will be," answered Iris. Nathan narrowed his gaze and grinned against the crisp air passing through the cab. "Who wants to live in a world where they have all the answers?"

Nathan's eyes widened, he glanced at Iris, "I do."

"When do you think a boy becomes a man, Nathan?"

"Don't know. How bout when he kills another man?"

"There's always going to be things we are uncertain of, son. You're having a hard time with everything you don't understand. I think a boy becomes a man when he learns to steward the tension of mystery and revelation at the same time."

Nathan thought to himself for a second before

responding, "What's that supposed to mean?"

"You have to control your hunger," admonished Iris. "Desperation belongs under the feet, not over the head. You can't let what you *haven't found* kill the joy of what you *have found*. When we hunger for understanding we have to guard our hearts while we wait for the revelation of the very thing we hunger for. If it's a *pure* hunger, a good desire, then the answer will come, it always does."

"No, the answers don't always come," argued Nathan.

"They do, just not always in our timing. When we're desperate, we search. We seek out understanding, reasons, answers, wisdom, all kinds of noble things. But then, somewhere along the way, we realize it was the very absence of the thing we were seeking that gave birth to the desperation in the first place. The thing that holds the answer is the same thing that causes the question."

"Grandma, what's the point of all this?"

"Nathan, if everything I ever told you was simple and clear, then you wouldn't have to work for any insight. You can only take credit for insight into something you yourself labored to discover. What I'm trying to say is this, son — steward the mystery of life with fervor. And don't let the lack of answers steal your hope for the things you dream of."

Nathan was quiet for a moment, there was silence between the two of them for a while until Alex opened his mouth. He was still sitting off the edge of the tailgate manning the rear gun. "Hey! Check out that McDonald's!" he exclaimed, pointing to the rubble of a building with its trademark yellow *M* blown to pieces, hanging upside down. "Bet you anything," he said with conviction, "if there's any french fries in there, they'll still taste the same. That's the one thing in this world I don't think will ever decompose — Micky D's fries."

Nathan was caught off guard. There he was,

passively struggling with the anxiety and fear of the Sarx, the future, the unknowns, and Alex has some off-handed comment about fries. "Haven't had those since I was five," said Nathan. "Forgot what they taste like." He knew in a world of starvation it was easy to get caught up daydreaming about food.

Iris piped up again, as if she had been brooding in her thoughts the past few minutes. "Listen to me, Nathan. You need to know something. I was not a smart girl," she said in a stern voice. "*Dumb* would actually be a better word to describe my youth."

Nathan wasn't sure why she was venting or what she was getting at, but he listened.

"I always felt behind other people, like I needed to catch up, everyone else was a hundred miles ahead of me. I struggled to read, I stuttered; it was almost impossible for me to memorize anything. Always thought everybody else's minds were made of moldable clay and mine was hard as stone. I had a very difficult time, and halfway into the second year of high school I decided that school wasn't for me. We were nothing more than an uneducated farm family — all grit and no brain. Dad dropped out, mom dropped out, so I did too. I was *convinced,* no one could tell me otherwise, that I was born with a two-cylinder mind and everyone else had six horsepower. Just couldn't seem to find my place amidst anything intellectual. So when I gave up on school, with pride, I hid myself in the soil of our family farm and declared my destiny there as a common working girl who'd spend the rest of her days with dirt on her face."

Iris continued, "*But,*" she said with emphasis, "all that time there was a cry that never left my soul. There were so many things I couldn't comprehend with my mind, but in my heart — oh, in the deepest places of my heart — there was a cry for wisdom that I couldn't ignore. Every night

I went to bed, looked out my window into the sky and longed for something. I wanted understanding, to know the meaning of life. No matter how hard I tried, I couldn't deny the feeling that there was someone out there listening, tending to my groaning, and leaning in with a desire to know me. Many times I stuck my head through that window and called out all sorts of absurd things. Mom and dad thought I was just talking to myself, yelling into the air. For years, I never heard a thing — no response, nothing. And you know what? It didn't matter. The silence on the other side? The lack of answers? It didn't end my hunger; it fed it. I called out. Complained. Questioned. *Why'd you make me like this?* I asked. *DUMB! Why can't I be smart? What use am I other than to be a dirt-girl?"* And then, one night, I heard something. Not sure if I was asleep or awake, can't recall, but what I heard was something that's become the rudder for my life, my anchor of direction and purpose."

Iris got quiet as she recalled what she was about to say. In a way she was hesitant about sharing some of the most vivid words she had ever received. The *words* she was about to share were engraved on her heart. Yet trusting that it might help her grandson, she opened herself up.

"A voice spoke," continued Iris, "but I heard it not just with my ears but with my soul. With my soul, Nathan. It said: *I made you different from the others. I withheld from you, only that which would fuel the fire of your search for me. What you lack will be nothing less than the soil from which I cultivate your true identity. What I have reserved for you is more precious than knowledge, more valuable than intellect,"* Iris paused briefly. "And then the voice said this: *I fashioned you to be a mistress of wisdom. To you belongs the discernment of the ages."*

Like Annak sharing his story, Nathan was intrigued. "How old were you when that happened?" he asked.

"Seventeen," she answered. "I never finished high school, never stepped foot into the halls of college, never found success in the intellectual world. I just ran the farm. And you know what? I was ok with that. That farm became the school ground where the Navigator began to impart wisdom into my spirit. In the furrows he taught me about the process of life — the sowing of seeds, the reaping of harvest, the death of a thing, the life of a thing. Nathan, there's a lot I still don't know and haven't figured out. I would have never made a good banker or a business woman or anything like that. But I'll tell you this — when a storm is on the horizon, I'll be the first to guide helpless victims through the darkness. I'm not a knowledgable woman, but I have wisdom. I know life. I know heart, I know blood, tears. I know evil, I know virtue. I can discern the spirits of the age and recognize the facades of our world. And I can take the pulse of the seasons and hear the voice of the One who means more to me than anything else. The success of my life, if it can be measured at all, can only be measured by one thing: was I able to hear His voice and did I obey Him? I may have lacked many of the gifts that others were given, but I was never without His presence. *Presence* is life, Nathan. Life!"

Iris was fired up as she kept talking, "Think about it. What gives life greater meaning — facts about someone you love or the presence of someone you love? Aren't you glad you and I get to be together rather than just hearing rumors of who I was as your distant, never-knew-you, grandmother? Life's about presence, Nathan. But most of all, it's about *His* presence. That's why I'm ok with not having all the answers, cause His presence makes all the difference. Whether I'm stewarding the *question* or the *answer*, the *mystery* or the *revelation*, it doesn't matter; because He's with me in both. And the best part about all this is that His same presence is available to you as soon as you are ready to open up and acknowledge him. He watches over you from a distance until He's welcome. But as soon as He's welcome, He will be nearer to you than your very own breath. One day you'll see what I mean."

Nathan was still quiet. Iris was a mouthful, but she was honest. Feeling the urge to get some other things off her chest, Iris persisted in turning the focus from her own heart to his. "You're empty, son."

Nathan glanced over quickly and gave her a defensive look, yet part of him knew she was right.

"It's true, Nathan, and you know it," said Iris. "We can only give out what we've got. What's inside us always comes out. When all you have inside you is *you*, then all you have is *you*. There's a limit. But when you open the door of your desperation to Him, the One who's limitless comes inside, and then there's no end to what you can do. I live out of His abundance, not my lack — out of His river, not my pond. Life's exhausting only because so many have to sustain what they produce in their own strength. Whatever you plant, you'll have to harvest. Whatever He plants, He'll have to harvest. The glory of life is not in being the source, but being the vessel...the channel."

Iris leaned over toward Nathan and rested her hand on his shoulder, "It's a lot of work being a *dam,* isn't it?" Simultaneously, as Iris asked the question, she was seeing a vision of Nathan's chest in the form of a thick concrete blockade, holding back a massive amount of water. In the concrete wall was a doorway marked by a single keyhole at the center, one to which only Nathan held the key.

Nathan shrugged, not knowing how to respond.

They were crossing Ross Island Bridge as it overlooked a section of the Willamette River. "You see that water?" Iris asked. The mass of the river bed was dried up except for one area. Nathan looked down and saw what she was referring to — a sick collection of stagnant water that probably came from a small amount of melting snow; it was mirky, infected, and undoubtedly reeked of rot and death. There was an infested mass of alkali flies swarming over it. "That's what our souls look like when we harbor disappointments against the Navigator that He didn't cause."

The words stung Nathan like a needle injecting a painful elixir. In an instant, Nathan was reminded of his parents' disappearance. He could hear their screams echoing through his skull. He saw their faces, but they were blurred and unrecognizable. Then suddenly, another memory broke in, Nathan felt his father's stout arms wrap around him as he helped him cast a line into the lake. He heard his voice, a whisper, *I love you, Nathan.* Nathan could feel the whiskers of his beard tickle the back of his neck.

"If I could just see them again!" complained Nathan. "It's not fair. They were taken from me and I never had a chance to do anything about it!"

"You were never meant to hold back all that water, Nathan. One day it will drown you if you don't let go. Rivers were never meant to be stopped. Use the current of that pain! Let the waters create a new channel."

"But...Mom? Dad? It doesn't make sense!"

"Nathan, there's still hope. There's always hope." Iris took a deep breath and let the cold oxygen course through her lungs. She sighed, "There's something," she hesitated for a moment, "something I never told you —"

Iris was brutally cut off by a massive explosion that rocked the bridge, *BOOM!* A surveillance drone breached through the floating clouds and whipped by. The second Crawler behind Annak was hit. Nathan gasped as he saw Silas and five others violently blown to pieces and sent hurling off the edge of the bridge.

Annak whistled and called out, "GNAT!"

"Alex!" yelled Nathan. "Get your eyes on that thing!"

Alex was startled as he flung the artillery gun around as fast as possible, sighted the drone and opened rapid fire. *Tat! Tat! Tat! Tat! Tat! Tat!* Tons of shells went flying, yet every single bullet missed the drone. The drone maneuvered and shifted like a mechanical humming bird, from a distance firing multiple shots that spread out across the asphalt of the bridge and ricocheted off the Crawlers before circling back around and swooping low.

Max was with Annak, manning the front gun. He did not hesitate to open fire in the opposite direction, aiming right at the oncoming drone. Max's 4-foot barrel gun cried out, *chink, chink, chink!* Then *BOOM!* The drone was finally struck by the inferno of Max's artillery. It burst apart, sending shrapnel and shards of metal all across the bridge. Bits and pieces came down on the heads of the onlookers and smashed into the cabs of the Crawlers.

Nathen sped up toward Annak's vehicle. Easton, Max and the others were there. Nathan cussed with vivid despair. "They're dead! They're all dead! No! No!" He got out of the vehicle, ran to the edge of the massive steel-concrete bridge and peered down over the wreckage, where he pulled out his machine gun and fired purposeless rounds into the air, nothing short of a purposeful exhale of his anger and rage as he yelled at the top of his lungs.

"Nathan!" said Annak, coming up behind and grabbing him. "Get a hold of yourself, there's nothing we can do — they're gone!"

"NO!" Nathan screamed again as he fired one more shot and kicked his foot against the edge of the railing.

Max grasped Nathan's arm, "They know we're here! We gotta go! GOTTA...GO...NOW!" he yelled, pulling Nathan and forcefully throwing him back into the Crawler.

Annak yelled at everyone else, still in shock, "Pick

up the pace! Keep up!"

With no time to mourn, Annak rushed the group off the bridge and exited the cityscape where they recklessly made their way into the off-road that paralleled I-84. Most in the group were, by now, bitterly awakened to a new level of panic. Nathan's hands gripped the suicide knob so hard it could have broken had it not been made from solid metal. He clenched his jaw, ground his teeth and forcefully locked his eyes on Annak and the others tearing down the road, kicking up billows of dirt and rock. Alex was still on the back, barely holding on with all his strength, aiming the gun back and forth.

Barely outside the city, two more drones appeared out of nowhere. Sustaining minimal casualties from their assault, Alex was so on edge he was able to shoot them down before they raised serious havoc.

It seemed like they screamed through those backroads forever before Annak finally slowed down. At a certain point he veered into an old mechanic's bay that was built into an old Texaco. Annak broke the chains off the doors and opened them up. The place still had the car lifts inside, and used oil barrels knocked over on the ground — empty and corroded. It was in disarray, but likely the only place around they could find shelter from overhead visibility. When everyone was hidden inside, it appeared that despair was pacifying any sort camaraderie. The smell of defeat was more staunch then the fumes of putrified animal feces and rusted car parts. No one moved. They simply lingered with their heads down.

Annak, Iris, and Easton were a bit different. Not that they callously dismissed what just happened back at the bridge, but they were somehow more resolved, more capable of moving forward through tragedy than most of the others.

Annak was not ignorant of the dismay in the atmosphere but knew they could not afford to lose time mourning anyone's death, not even Silas's even though he was one of their best and closest. He walked over to a window ledge and looked outside. "There's nothing I can say about what just happened. I hate losing people. I know what it feels like to lose fellow soldiers more than anyone in this room. But I refuse to believe that casualties are just a normal part of the game. The truth is, we should've seen that thing coming...and we didn't. The Gnats must be getting quieter; that one didn't even show up on our scanner. There's no doubt they've been alerted to our presence now." Annak tightened his fists, "We're just outside Horsetail Falls. We can't drive any further. There's still seven miles between us and the Bonneville. We cover the rest on foot. When we get there we'll do our best to assess how the place is laid out."

Easton interjected somewhat timidly, but loud enough to be heard, "I can get us to the powerhouse, just depends on which one." Annak was silent, and skeptical for a second, then took into account the sincerity in Easton's voice.

"How?" asked Annak, watching what Easton did next.

Easton quickly started pacing around the garage in search of something to write with. Oddly enough it did not take him long to find a cheap pen lying on the floor. Unable to find anything to write on, he swept his arm across the wooden mechanics bench and cleared the junk off of it. "Look" he said, waving his arm at Annak and Iris. They, and everyone else but Nathan, circled around. "My parents used to take me here as a kid," said Easton.

"What, you grew up around here?" Annak asked, a little surprised. "You just happen to know the layout of the Bonneville dam?"

"Well, yeah," answered Easton. "Hood River, actually."

"You were a kid," stated Annak. "How well could

you have known?"

"You wouldn't believe me if I told you," answered Easton. "I have a good memory."

"Try me," said Annak.

"My dad was one of the civil engineers who maintained the dams along the Columbia. He used to take me with him sometimes for work."

Nathan's ears perked up a bit.

"You're right," said Annak, "I don't believe you. Show me."

Easton did not hesitate to share, acting almost as if he was giving a lecture. "This place is complex," he said, as he started sketching a humble map on the wood bench. But the pen wouldn't work. Iris looked around, bent over and pulled a half-sharpened carpenter's pencil from a shattered coffee cup and handed it to Easton. "This place is kinda laid out like a prison, hard to get into. But I know...I know how we can get into the powerhouse where the turbine canal is."

Easton stopped talking, finding it difficult to draw while speaking. He took the next few minutes to lay out an elaborate blueprint of the entire Bonneville. "See those?" he asked, pressing his finger onto the table. "Those are the three islands that span this section of the Columbia: Cascades Island, Bradford Island, and Robins Island." Annak was listening, but slipped away for a moment to look out the window again, then came back. "Right there's the southern fish hatchery. In between the hatchery and Robins Island is the navigation lock. I guarantee this area will be heavily active if the Screeners have any cargo vessels moving in and out of the dam." Easton pointed to one of the rectangular objects he had drawn, "That's the first powerhouse. Right there between the first and second islands, next to the fish ladder. The second powerhouse is clear across the river on the other side of Cascades Island; right there, across the spillway bridge."

Alex scratched his head and piped up, "Where did this guy come from?"

Easton, seemingly not one to understand sarcasm, answered, "I told you, Hood River."

"Go on," said Annak. He was standing next to Iris, who was quietly intrigued, listening. Inwardly she was pondering the peculiar timing of Easton's arrival at Adullum, just days ago.

"Here's what I'm trying to tell you. There's hardly anywhere around the dam that we can go unseen. That right there is the single bridge that spans the length of the whole dam. No other way to get access to the powerhouses other than going on that bridge, and it's right out in the open. If we go out on that narrow bridge, we'll be trapped. You see that? That's the first powerhouse and the spillway wall." He looked at Annak.

"What are you suggesting?" asked Annak.

"We use the layout of the dam to our advantage. We take the high ground just outside Tanner Creek." He pointed again to the sketch right next to the southern fish hatchery, "The Screeners' only open point of visibility should be from that bridge. Instead of us getting caught on it, we draw the Screeners out, and take as many down as we can from a distance."

"You mean shoot them?" asked Annak.

"Yeah," Easton answered, "from the high point of Tanner Creek. Hopefully we can draw them out...they will bottle-neck on the spillway wall."

Annak pressed his thumb and index finger down on the point between Tanner Creek and the spillway, "How far is that distance?"

"Probably 900 meters."

"And the North side?" asked Annak, as he pointed to

the opposite end of the dam.

"I'd say 1500 meters."

"You crazy?" asked Nathan, joining the conversation. "You know how far that is? That's almost a mile!"

Max joined in, "Come on, you guys can do that!" he exclaimed, looking at Nathan and Annak. He knew what they were capable of.

"Longest confirmed kill in military history was 1.5 miles," said Annak. "Anything is possible."

"Mexican guy, right?" asked Alex, proudly referring to his own ethnicity.

"British, struck down two Taliban machine gunners in Afghanistan. But even the best marksman still have a hard time hitting targets at 1500 meters."

Easton spoke up again, "Hey, I don't know what you guys are capable of, but all the other options here are not good. We use the narrow channel of the powerhouse walls, and the spillway, to funnel them into a line. It can work. That's all I can suggest at this point."

Annak stepped back and thought about the plan, he liked the idea. He was not only surprised by Easton, he was impressed. Annak had never been to this dam before, and had only seen it through digital imagery. Easton appeared to know more about the layout than anyone else, which meant he was either a spy working for Geospark, or he was genuinely trying to help. Had Annak not been aware of the blue flicker inside his eyes, and there being no chip inside his right wrist, he would have suspected the former to be true.

"Iris?" asked Annak.

Iris looked at Easton briefly, "I think he knows what he's talking about," she answered.

"And what about the distance of the shots?" asked Nathan. "1500 meters?"

"I've never seen either of you shoot that far,"

answered Iris, referring to Nathan and Annak, "but I have confidence it's possible."

Annak thought about the plan, then gave a warning, "There's no negotiation with these sickos, absolutely none. When you see these guys face to face, there's no time to think about anything other than a kill. They've made this place a wasteland. If you show them mercy, you'll never get it back. They live for one thing and one thing only — to control these waterways. They laugh while the rest of us dry up to death. If any of you...any of you hesitate, even for a split second, just remember all the children who died of thirst, all the family members who've been killed or used in slavery; all the slaughter! For the sake of our six friends now dead back there in the Willamette, we take the dam at any cost! Don't hold back! If you hold back you're going to get more than a slap in the face, you'll get a bullet through your head."

Annak paused, then lowered his tone, "And listen to me very carefully, very...very...carefully. Unless you have the Blue Flame, do not go up against a Nephilim with anything less than a cartridge of ammunition. You cannot fight one of them in your own strength. Though they're part human, they're uncommonly strong and will tear you apart."

It was interesting Annak wasn't more encouraging at this point. Nathan swallowed nervously; he could feel his Adam's apple sliding up and down in his throat. He had only heard about the Nephilim by rumor yet had never seen them in the flesh. There were uncomfortable stories about them actually eating some of their victims alive. Not sure what to expect, the thought of taking as many of them out from a distance certainly sounded like the best plan.

SIXTEEN
Sight of the Gun

"Time to go," commanded Annak.

Max had just finished getting his shoes back on, his socks were scrunched and damp with cold sweat.

"Grandma, tell me you're packing something," said Nathan.

Iris looked at him confidently, "I'm always packing something."

Nathan looked back at her in a demeaning way, "You know what I'm talking about — a gun."

"Nathan, you don't need to worry about me," said Iris.

Nathan became frustrated, remembering what had happened just days ago with the bear incident, knowing that Iris could have helped if she would have been carrying a weapon. "We can't mess around anymore! We're in uncharted territory here! Who knows what we're about to encounter over there." He glared at her, "If you'd had your gun back there at Badger, you could've shot that bear."

With calm, Iris replied, "Nathan, I know you don't get me, and that's ok. We're different, son — you're a shooter, I'm an overseer, an intercessor; you're the arrow, I'm the covering. My job's to keep watch over you, His job's to keep watch over me."

Nathan shirked and said nothing more.

"My refuge isn't behind a trigger, it's behind His presence, just my personal preference."

"Takes a whole lot more faith to live that way than just picking up a gun doesn't it?"

"Not for me, son," answered Iris.

The next seven miles were heavily wooded.

The terrain was littered with fallen timber, the tree line separated by sporadic patches of open visibility. There was a nervousness that silenced everyone as they could hear Screener activity all along the roadside off in the distance. Nathan was not sure what to expect, his proximity with the Screeners had been far and few up to this point. *Are we talking ten, thirty, a hundred? How many?* There was an intensity Nathan could feel the closer they got to the water. By now, most of the country was abandoned, desolate and unpopulated, the real estate surrounding the waterways was by far the most dangerous territory in the land.

After running out of the Texaco and down into a ravine where they disappeared into the forest, they stayed close to the inside cliff of the Columbia River Gorge and lingered as far away from the water's edge as possible. Within a couple hours they reached a rock mesa that over looked the dam; it was just outside Tanner Creek, adjacent to the southern fish ladder. "That's the spot," whispered Easton, as he led them into a cleft in the rock in between two large boulders.

Max stayed low and looked around, seeing the dam off in the distance. "Not gonna get any better than this," he said.

Annak signaled to Max and Alex, both panting because they had been carrying heavy artillery on their shoulders the whole way. "Before we fire the first shot, you guys need to get set up behind us." In the back of his mind, Annak was concerned about drones being released once their shooting position inevitably gets compromised.

Very methodically and mechanically, Max and Alex set up their tripods and prepared their guns. "Ready," they said, in unison.

Annak and Nathan both laid down, rested their bellies on the cold rock, and situated their rifles. Iris crouched behind them and folded her arms. She was quiet, but very aware of everything that was going on. Annak's gun was an old German HK416; it was heavily used, but would have looked like an antique had he not taken such good care of it. Nathan's similar — a gift from his mentor, Annak; a 7.62 millimeter distance rifle with a scope mount and a large silencing barrel fastened to the tip. They both tweaked their sights and set their calibers.

"Conditions seem too perfect," whispered Nathan.

"You sure about that?" Annak asked.

"Yeah. I mean, could be worse."

"Let me know when you feel it."

Nathan held still for a moment, long enough to sense an almost unrecognizable breeze brush across his face.

"Surprising for this canyon," said Annak, "that little wind is coming and going every few seconds, more than a couple miles an hour. But at this distance, everything matters — your heartbeat, the weight of your bullets, the light, the wind. Everything." Other than the sound of the rushing river echoing off the canyon walls, there was not much noise from where they were positioned. "Hardly anything, but take note of it. You feel the direction it's coming from?"

Nathan waited, "Yes."

"For every shot you take, barely aim to the right, into the wind," instructed Annak. "Let me see your rounds."

Nathan unlocked his magazine and showed one to him. "Empty that thing out," said Annak, as he handed him a different cartridge, "too lite." Nathan took the 16.2 gauge LockBase bullets from Annak and put them into his rifle. "You ready?"

"I'm here, aren't I," answered Nathan.

"I mean, ready to kill?" Annak asked again with more clarity. "Once you look through that barrel you have to be ready to pull the trigger."

"I know," said Nathan, "I'm ready."

Annak knew that his protégé had only been trained hunting game, they killed wild beasts because they had to so they would not starve to death. But, today was different. This was the first time there was something on the other side of Nathan's telescope that had a human heart. Down the nose of his ignited barrel would be the lifeless remains of a man, not an animal.

Suddenly, Nathan felt the urge to urinate. He hustled back behind the boulder and relieved himself, then came back. "I'm ready."

Annak could tell Nathan was nervous, and recognized a sliver of doubt in his countenance. "Remember, these aren't victims," he said to Nathan. "They're our adversaries."

"Annak...I know. Just leave me alone, ok!"

"Everything to the *right* of that bridge belongs to you. I got the left," said Annak.

At once, Annak and Nathan both pressed their eyebrows up against the cold metal sights of their guns and aimed down onto the dam. Annak was so quiet, Nathan questioned whether or not he was even breathing. Nathan sensed a heavy focus begin to settle. As he tuned everything out, he could feel the heaviness of his heart beating, sending blood and pulse through his limbs.

Without looking over at Nathan, Annak spoke softly, "Clear the navigation lock first... powerhouse ledge, second."

Nathan lifted his sights across the I-84, then scanned the sage brush prairie that lined the river banks until finally he had a visual of the lock. Right away he saw movement. A slew of men stood watch on top of the concrete balcony, all of them clothed in black parkas, and darkly advanced military gear bearing Geospark insignias on the shoulder — the image of a mammoth's head with a crown on it. Nathan shifted his aim to the farthest right corner of the lock and embraced his first target. The Screener's facial details were hard to make out as were many other characteristics. The tall frame was walking along the wall, bearing a shaved head with an elongated gun slung over his shoulder.

Annak looked through his own sight, still and motionless as he lay on the rock with his rifle pitched across his left forearm, "You first, Nathan," he challenged.

CRACK! Without hesitating, a shot rang out from Nathan's rifle, his shoulders jolted back from the force. He watched as no one went down, his first bullet missing everything but air. He fired again, the second shot passing through the Screener's chest, dropping him to the ground. Nathan could not help but feel a punch of euphoria overtake him. At first the feeling scared him, knowing he had just killed someone, but then all of the sudden it was as if he had been shaken; something inside of him was opened up. He took a deep breath and at the same time had a flashback of Silas's body being thrown off the bridge. His anger intensified as he fired a third shot. *CRACK!* The body of another Screener shuddered and fell dead.

Annak's rifle resounded, and in a split second a third Screener at the opposite end was brought down. Quickly alerted to the attack, other Screeners started scurrying back and forth along the wall. They struggled to assess where the shots were coming from as they braced themselves behind the steel railing and took cover. Amidst the shuffle, Annak sunk another bullet into one of them before they could duck.

Nathan's heart was beating faster and faster as he searched for a target, all of them seemingly tucked behind the wall, occasionally lifting their guns over the railing and firing in various directions. It did not take long for them to realize that the shots were coming from the southern ridge rock wall, though none of the Screeners appeared to have long range rifles. Yet one by one, sporadically, they aimed their guns and fired shots back in Annak and Nathan's direction — all of their bullets missing; ricocheting off the rocks and disappearing.

Annak set his eyes on one of the Screeners through a break in the wall. He was holding a voice box up to his mouth, undoubtedly calling for backup and sounding the verbal alarm that intruders were present. As soon as he could, Annak pulled his trigger twice, one bullet blowing apart the Screener's hand, the other piercing his head. Nathan's gun sounded at the same time, a failed shot that hit the railing. He fired again. Missed. Then fired again, this time hitting a Screener dead on.

Between both of their shots, more bodies dropped. As far as Nathan and Annak knew, there could not be more than a couple of them left. They waited and watched for a while without seeing any movement. Then suddenly, one of the Screeners came out from behind the wall and ran toward the back edge of the lock, attempting to escape into the trees of Robins Island. Annak's rifle fired. *CRACK!* The bullet pierced the Screeners back right between the shoulder blades, forcing his body over the edge into the river below.

It appeared the navigation lock was almost clear by now. "Last one's yours," said Annak, as he quickly reloaded his rifle.

Nathan waited and waited. "You sure there's another one down there?"

"He's there," answered Annak. "Don't take your eyes off that wall."

Nathan got the feeling the Screener was crawling along the backside of the wall in an attempt to escape down the ladder on the left side of the lock. Submitting to his inclination he shifted his aim toward the top of the ladder and held it there. Minutes went by before abruptly, the Screener leapt for the ladder. Nathan sent a bullet whistling through the air, piercing the soldier's leg, and then another through his chest. The Screener was left bloody and lifeless with his hand clutched to the edge of the ladder.

"There's more, get loaded," warned Annak.

Without delay, Nathan stuffed another magazine into his rifle and aimed, this time beyond the navigation lock toward the powerhouse. Knowing the distance was further and the shots would be more difficult, he closed one eye and squinted the other up against the sight just as a blaring siren shrieked through the canyon.

Max was sitting on his butt just behind Nathan, peering through a pair of binoculars, "Up top!" he yelled. "Up top!"

Annak aimed onto the roof of the powerhouse, where he barely made out a rotating bulk of heavy artillery. The massive gun boasted at least four cannons, all locking and swiveling in their direction. A Screener was wired into a seat situated behind a bulletproof metal shield. Within seconds the gun was fully rotated, sending a mass of heavy fire in their vicinity. *BOOM! BOOM! BOOM!* All over the place, bits and pieces of the canyon wall were busted apart and thrown everywhere. Easton was hit, a gash opened up across the side of his head. Everybody ducked, except for Nathan and Annak, who were still firing shots at the gunner, his body pulsating violently as the artillery cannon shook his chair. Yet one after another, their bullets were amiss.

Round after round, the gunner pummeled the side of the rock canyon. Then, running out of bullets, there was nothing but smoke and silence surrounding Nathan and the others — all of them briefly looking at one another to see who had been hit. Annak lifted his head and kept his eye on the target, glimpsing another Screener trying load more cartridges into the gunner's chamber. Annak fired, immediately killing the one Screener, and then with another successful shot sent a single bullet through the square sight hole of the gunner's shield. Instantly the trigger-man was struck dead.

There was no time to celebrate, Annak aimed back down onto the powerhouse wall where Nathan had not stopped firing shots. More Screeners were flooding through a doorway and spreading out across the spillway wall. Unceasing gunfire was rudely exchanged back and forth. Annak and Nathan tried their best to engage the timing so that one of them was always covering the other while each reloaded.

Together, both of them fell into a beautiful rhythm, immersed in a deep place of focus. With mechanical regularity it was as if a switch flipped on inside them. After running out of ammunition, they would methodically reload and then keep pumping bullets through the air, then with uncanny precision they hit their marks, one after another, left to right, right to left. Enemy bodies dropped everywhere. Easton, Alex and the others looked on in bewilderment, astonished by the accuracy of their shots. Max observed them and thought their seemingly supernatural achievement might have something to do with Iris, who was behind them, mumbling with her eyes closed. She appeared to be interacting with the One no one else could see.

Losing count of how many kills they had, Nathan and Annak watched as more and more Screeners continued to appear. They were showing up everywhere — in small window openings, pivoting themselves along the corridor wall and down below. Annak wondered how long it would be before the — still sounding sirens — would cause drones to start flying in their direction.

Ready behind their artillery guns, Max and Alex were on high alert. On top of the massive structure was a network of over twenty-six towers, all supplying electricity to power lines running down river. Enemy targets dispersed and hid behind them, scattered across the entire roof. One after another, Annak and Nathan did their best to spot them and shoot. Everything seemed surprisingly triumphant until the Screeners stopped pulling their triggers. The activity atop the powerhouse subsided.

There was a long pause before Alex yelled out, "Hey! Looks like those fools couldn't take anymore, huh?"

Annak knew better, and responded, "Just stay quiet, and get ready."

Nathan kept looking through his telescope and carefully scanned the entire dam. There was hardly any activity.

"We move, or what?" asked Max.

"I don't think I like this," stated Nathan, sensing something was off.

Iris was still quiet and beseeching.

Then, without a command from Annak to do anything else, they watched as out from Bradford Island three drones started soaring in their direction. Annak, more than anyone, knew that sniper rifles would not do much against drones, they were machined and fashioned with super metals — lightweight carbon, graphene, and near impenetrable. More so, even with heavy artillery they were hard to destroy given their maneuverability. Geospark drones were mechanical and operated by an autonomous software; they flew through the air like hummingbirds, many carrying revolving machine guns and nukes that dropped with more accuracy than manned jets.

Nathan's heart sank, "Here they come!" he cried.

Max was next to Alex, his knees shaking the gun between his legs. Both of them nervously clutched onto their simultaneously firing triggers and tried to wait for the drones' to come within range. In no time, the drone's stuttering machine guns unleashed their misery. Wrath was poured out in tremendous power. The amount of ammunition coming toward them in the cleft of the rock was overwhelming. It appeared no one had a chance.

Nathan did not have to think hard about how to respond. Taking his rifle, he grabbed Iris, slid down the jagged boulder and collapsed onto a pile of dead wood. Annak followed, as did the rest, leaving only Max and Alex behind. Max unleashed like a mad man, grinning his dirty teeth from ear to ear as empty shells went flying in all directions. Alex did the same. *TAT! TAT! TAT!* Huge shots rang out as equal gunfire exchanged across the grey-gunmetal skyline. Bark, rock and dirt exploded everywhere. And then, *BOOM!* A massive explosion ignited in the air as one of the drones blew up. Amidst the gunfire, Alex took credit and erupted with a howl.

Max, on the other hand, was not ignorant enough to claim victory, even though his shots had just sent one of the drones into a tail spin. He watched as it smoked and spiraled into the valley below.

"I got the right side! I got the right side!" yelled Max, ducking his head to evade gliding bullets.

All of the sudden, Max and Alex's collective gunfire blew the third drone into pieces, but not before it approached the cliff and released a whirling missile that plummeted at their feet. Helpless, the force of the explosion sent Max and Alex flying off the plateau, a couple others still near them on the cliff suffered the same.

Down below, Nathan was trying to recover, his ears ringing from the explosions. He rushed over to Max and Alex as soon as he saw them hit the ground. Alex lie there — stunned. Max was in shock and bloodied more than ten feet away. Both of them were blanketed with silica dust and bits of metal.

"Don't touch me," Alex moaned, barely breathing.

Nathan quickly scanned over and saw the two other Reapers, their bodies were badly mangled and lifeless, then focused on Alex again. All he could see was a solitary piece of metal protruding from his shoulder. It appeared to be a piece from one of the drones, a shiny antenna-looking stick no more than eleven inches long. Nathan could hardly believe it was Alex's only injury.

"Don't move!" Nathan commanded, as he pressed down on Alex's chest and yanked the metal from his shoulder. Alex gritted his teeth and screamed. "Now get up," Nathan said with little apathy. The painful moaning issuing from Max's quivering lips was more disconcerting than Alex's. Nathan immediately crawled over to Max.

In excruciating pain, Max could hardly get the words out. "It's not good. I'm afraid to move."

Nathan studied Max's body, already unkempt and dirty. A cold feeling came over him when his eyes settled on both Max's legs. The sight was horrible, as Nathan could barely look at the compound fracture from the knee below. The other leg was no less unsettling — bent backwards, broken. Nathan felt helpless and knew something like this could slow them down or force them to turn back, let alone the fact that he grieved for Max.

Max tried to lift his head to look down, he could see the ghastly expression of hopelessness on Nathan's face. Catching him just in time, Nathan covered Max's eyes, "You don't want to see this," he said.

Alex came over and saw the same thing, merely letting out a sigh, "No…"

Out of nowhere Annak appeared in their midst. Without saying a word he pushed Nathan and Alex out of the way and knelt down next to Max. Nathan stumbled backwards, unable to understand what would happen next. Annak, with an unflinching posture toward the grotesque wounds, removed his gloves and confidently placed one hand on each of Max's legs. Then — his eyes illuminating with embers of a spectral world — started whispering commands in an un-coded tongue.

Not quite instantly, but soon enough, Max looked as if a hot numbing liquid was being poured over his legs, both of them starting to shake. Like an anesthesia being administered, he could feel the nerves in his body being persuaded from chaos to peace, coming under the command of something much stronger than leaking blood, broken bones, and torn ligaments.

Nathan and Alex witnessed what was happening with both their jaws dropped to the ground. Nathan could not decide which was more frightening, the explosion causing the fractures, or the sight of seeing the bones move back into place on their own. His disillusion only intensified when the blood went away and the skin closed back up. For some odd reason all Nathan could think about were some of the few cartoons he watched as a kid, particularly Tom and Jerry, and all the times that persistent cat kept getting destroyed, then healed again. Yet Nathan knew that what he had just glimpsed was no cartoon, there was nothing comic or jocular about it. The exchange that took place between Annak's hands and those two snapped legs was abnormally beautiful and alluring, and something that Nathan could not write off as a fantastical scene. It was supernatural.

Max finally braced himself up and looked down at his legs, "What happened?" he asked. Neither Nathan nor Alex had any response, only astonishment. All Nathan could do was keep looking at Max's healed legs and then at Annak like he was a phantom of some sort. At that moment, the rumors Nathan had heard about Annak's ability to heal had just been realized. Iris and Easton, no less disheartened by the other two deaths and Max's injury, were somehow able to comprehend the miracle more easily than the others.

Annak got up, looked at Alex and Easton, "You guys alright?" He could see the blood still issuing from Easton's head as well as the dark crimson stain on Alex's shoulder.

"Whatever you got, I'll take it," said Alex.

Annak pressed his palms against both of their wounds and at the same time closed them up. Nathan was no less beside himself. With a couple circles, Alex waved his arm around and rubbed his shoulder with his other hand, much perplexed.

"That explosion destroyed our guns," said Alex.

"Nothing we can do about it now," said Annak.

"What about them?" Max asked, nodding at the two other dead Reapers.

"It's too late," said Iris.

"We gotta go," commanded Annak.

Pieces of doubt were still inside Nathan, but for some reason, after witnessing the healings, the apparent inability to raise those two bodies from the dead did not sit right with him. A tug inside him wanted to be the missing link to console that disconnect. There was no time to think about it any further. Running by the head of one of the drones, Nathan was bewitched by what he saw — it was steaming on the ground, the mechanical connections inside its shell still jerking and sparking like a pin was pricking its electrical circuit. Inside was what looked like a single surveillance eyeball, made of solid black glass...a small, perfect globe. Intrigued, Nathan knocked it loose from the rest of the parts and stuffed the ball into his pack.

SEVENTEEN
Nephies

Before long, Annak, Iris and the others slowly crept out of the tree line and into the open where they reached the road that ran alongside the dam's fish hatchery. The road eventually turned into a bridge that crossed over to the navigation lock. When they were back at Tanner Creek the dam looked somewhat small, but up close, the massive bulk of concrete and steel was now enormous. The Bonneville Dam was no less reminiscent of an old military prison outpost. The walls, easily more than sixty feet high above the water, were covered with an array of green and black moss. As they made their way up the rebar ladder that led to the top of the lock, Nathan noticed how uncomfortably calm things were. Breeching enemy lines was feeling a little too easy at this point, and he wondered why there were not more Screeners.

They kept advancing quickly, but with caution, clearing the place. Max, Alex and the others did not hesitate to collect some of the abandoned weapons. Iris stayed close behind Annak, Nathan was not too far behind them, as were the rest. Occasionally, Nathan kept glancing over his shoulder to see how Max was doing, still in awe of his legs, amazed that he could even run. All across the dam were the dead Screeners that Nathan and Annak had shot out just moments earlier. There was an odd uniformity that characterized them. Their wicked, sleek black garb was unsettling. The dominant feature about them was their apparent good health, unlike the Reapers, who were mostly frail and malnourished. Nathan felt even more dirty just looking at them. Yet every time he stepped over one of their bodies he felt gratified. The memory of his lost parents and the stolen lake only solidified that.

Now across the concrete bridge, the river below their feet was already loud, but when they reached the central doorway to the powerhouse, the sound of rushing water escalated and became deafening. The rapids running through the Kaplan turbines created so much resonance it made it hard to hear one another. As he knelt down outside the doorway, Annak started throwing hand signals, motioning for everyone to stay low. Then forcefully, Annak kicked open the door and rushed in with his gun held tightly to his cheek. One by one, the rest followed suit. Surprisingly, the building appeared to be empty.

Once inside, it was easy to become awestruck by the immensity of the place — a long factory like corridor more than a thousand feet in length and over seventy feet high. Concrete walls towered above, fragmented by a profusion of small glass windows with iron grids lining the top of both sides. The place was dreary and uninviting.

"So much different than I remember it," said Easton as he ran his fingers across some of the crumbling white plaster. "Used to be…touristy, I guess. Scary in here now."

"You feel that?" yelled Alex, looking at Nathan.

Nathan knew he was referring to the Columbia River surging underneath their feet. The ground was solid, but shaking. Twenty-one generators were vibrating, powered by the turbines.

Nathan raised his voice, "Any of you think it's strange no one's in here?

"Not sure what's going on," answered Annak, "but we need to be ready at any moment. The panel for Adullum's either up here on the first floor or down in the basement. We need to find it as soon as possible."

Nathan threw another question at Annak, "Even if we do find the power, how are we going to keep them from just shutting it back off again?"

"Be quiet," said Annak, perking up his ears. He commanded everyone to stay low and spread out. He crouched down, leaned up against a wall and aimed his gun toward the building's northern entrance, opposite the one they had come in through.

Nathan ducked down beside Annak and held still, trying to listen for any sound beyond that of the growling generators. Despite how cold it was, nervous drops of sweat were trickling over his brow. Soon enough he heard what sounded like troops marching outside the doorway. He had the feeling chaos was about to ensue again.

"NEPHIES!" Annak shouted.

Nathan's eyes went bloodshot when he saw what came ripping through the doorway. There were three of them, hardly small enough to squeeze through the large opening in the corridor. The first one he could see in the distance — a beast of a man, easily nine feet tall, carrying heavy assault guns in each hand, and a massive body arrayed in stout technical armor. The other two were no less fearsome.

The Nephilim let loose the full adrenaline of their gun-power, bullets spreading out across the place. Nathan watched as a few of the Reapers were instantly assaulted to death. The Reapers did their best to reciprocate fire, unloading as much ammunition as possible. The grotesque giants rushed forward, continuing to unleash. They charged like rhinos, destroying anything in their way. Bullets whizzed everywhere, ricocheting off the side of generator cylinders. With every step, the Nephilim lurched forward, shaking the ground.

Nathan flung his body behind a pillar, perched up on his elbows and kept shooting. Three of his shots sunk into the flesh of one of the giants. He watched in defiant shock as the giant's arms drooped and its body continued to surge forward for a while. Nathan unloaded more ammunition on it until finally its massive body caved onto the ground. *Thump!*

The other two Nephilim kept rushing forward, one catching a Reaper in its grip, and then smashing him to death. Nathan caught a glimpse of the other giant going down, most likely from Annak's shots, and then realized he was cornered. The Nephilim dropped the mangled body over the railing and set its beaming eyes on Nathan. Without hesitation Nathan lifted his gun, aimed at the giant's head and pulled the trigger. *Click!* No bullets, his cartridge was empty. Nathan searched the pocket of his pants for more ammo, the giant running right toward him, no more than twenty yards away by now.

No one else was shooting at it. "Someone help!" Nathan screamed. "Someone take that thing down!" His cry was hopeless. It appeared he was not the only one reloading or scrapping for a gun.

Nathan got the ammo in his hands, but was shaking so badly he fumbled the cartridge to the floor. And then, a writhing foe more frightening than his darkest nightmares — took hold of him by the neck. Nathan dropped his rifle and immediately reached for his knife. He tried to slash it across the giant's flesh, but was unable to compete with the reach of its outstretched arm as it dangled his puny body in the air. Compared to the giant, Nathan was just a small piece of trash.

The giant tightened its grip around Nathan's neck. Nathan felt the blood vessels in his forehead about to pop as he helplessly stared into the face of the Nephilim. The thing was distorted and beyond grotesque. Its features — eyebrows, jaw-line, bone structure — were all exaggerated by a plethora of injections and chemical enhancements. It was near impossible to see a human being in its eyes.

The Nephilim looked at Nathan momentarily, admiring him like a bear would its kill just before sinking its claws into the victim's belly, and then with its other arm, pulled out a protracted machete. The blade glistened in the colorless light that was pouring through the windows of the powerhouse, one side of it perfectly sharpened, the other notched with terribly deep teeth. Unable to yell, unable to cry out, suffocating, Nathan stared in slow motion as the giant reared back and then brought the blade around in full swing. Abruptly — what was left of Nathan's splintered, short life — flashed before him. Nathan closed his eyes and braced for pain.

And then, just before the blade was about to cleave his body, two bullets from an unknown gun went right through the giant's neck. The Nephilim's body jolted. Nathan stayed fast in its grip and swayed back and forth while the giant stumbled all over the place. Then another bullet cut through its body. Nathan felt the tension in his neck leave as the giant's hand let go. Barely able to land on his feet, Nathan slid across the floor and watched the giant hit its knees and topple over.

Lying on the ground in shock, but feeling as though he had been resurrected to an extent, Nathan could hardly believe what he saw — standing directly behind the dead Nephilim was Iris, holding a rifle up under her chin. Nathan was lost for words.

Iris did not say anything. She reached out, helped Nathan to his feet and embraced him for a short moment. For now, no more Screeners were penetrating the building. Nathan looked around and realized not many Reapers were left — Iris, Annak, Easton, Max, Alex and only a few others. The team had greatly diminished.

"Please tell me there's no more of these out there," said Alex, looking down at the Nephilim.

For a moment there was no response. No one was in the mood to talk. By now their losses were too great, and their calls were too close for comfort. Reaper bodies, many of those who had been at Adullum for years, were now lifeless at the edge of their boots.

Breaking the silence, Easton knelt down and ran his hand along the chest of the dead Nephilim, "They used to be normal human beings," he said, "Now...just some of Geospark's normal experiments. They mess em' up from birth. Brainwashed to kill, bred to be monsters."

"From birth?" added Max, wondering how a sick corporation like Geospark could get their hands on babies and grow them into killing machines.

No one seemed to know the answer until Iris responded, "Their *mothers* are the ones who chose to give them up in the first place."

"What do you mean?" asked Alex.

"They abandoned them," said Iris. "Geospark took the babies as a means to save them, but instead used them for science and war."

"That's disgusting!" exclaimed Alex. "How can they do that?"

"Because..." complained Easton, "there's no one to stop them, no one to tell them what's wrong and what's right anymore."

"When I was part of the military, we used to fight alongside them," said Annak. "They would send them into battle like sacrifices. The government could only keep them a secret for so long, hiding it from the public. But once Geospark took over, things changed."

Nathan looked down in pity at the dead giant. He did not have anything to say. He was sick to his stomach at the thought of what had been done to them.

"There's hardly anything left of us," said Alex, looking throughout the powerhouse corridor. "What now?" The dam's emergency sirens were still sounding in the background. "I don't like this place at all."

"It's time to find the control room," said Annak with a tone of urgency. "We didn't come this far just to bail out now. If we give up, everyone who's died will've died for nothing. You three stay up here to guard the doors, the rest of us will search the basement." The three designated by Annak picked up what weapons and guns they could find and split up at the doorways. "Alex and Nathan, you two stay together. Easton, you're coming with me and Iris."

Nathan took one more sobering look at Iris, pointing a stare at her that was filled with gratitude, yet lacked words. Then walked away.

EIGHTEEN
Counting Fish

I con — Geospark's nerve center at Redfish Lake — was alerted to the commotion down river. Gabriel had not returned for more than a couple of days before Onyx was summoning him back up to his glass balcony.

Gabriel walked slowly through the large mechanical doors and into the foyer of a great room that overlooked the lake. Onyx was standing there, his back facing Gabriel, staring into an immense, complex master screen. The screen was a huge rectangular terminal, lit up with a vast array of buttons, probes, blinking lights, and an elaborate geographical map. On the display was a complete layout of the northwestern watershed — from the southern tip of Canada to the base of Idaho, spreading through seven states to the western shores of the Pacific ocean. Every lake, every river, every creek, every stream was marked out, with more than sixty dams being showcased throughout. Some of the jagged lines on the map were lit up like fissures with the colors blue and purple, some red, others various colors by degree of importance and visibility.

Onyx pressed his finger against one of the blinking squares, a digitized live image of the Bonneville dam expanded on the screen. He nodded at Gabriel, not saying a word. Gabriel moved closer and looked at the panoramic view of the dam — the place was smoldering, remnants from explosive activity and dead bodies were strewn all across the navigation lock and powerhouse bridge. Gabriel cringed and clenched his fists with rage, thinking back for a second of the insignia he had just discovered all over the petrified fish at the Dalles.

"Visitors," said Onyx, in a cold voice. "The

Bonneville's energy supply is too valuable."

"I'll take care of it," said Gabriel.

"They've taken the first powerhouse."

"I'll put an end to it."

Onyx peered into Gabriel's eyes, "Find out who's in charge of this and keep them alive. Don't spare anyone else." Onyx tweaked his neck as he spoke, flinching his eyes in an odd way as he always did; a reminder to Gabriel that he was under the reign of a half-human, half-software commander.

Gabriel nodded his head cordially in response, sending a signal of compliance as Onyx turned back toward the screen in silence, clearly commanding the phrase, *now get out of here.*

Gabriel made a quick exit outside onto the floating dock, "Rook!" he voiced into a microphone situated on the edge of his forearm.

A couple of seconds, then a response, "Yes Gabriel."

"The Bonneville."

"All of us are ready," Rook answered.

Gabriel lowered his arm and stared across the Sawtooth Mountain range. He was angry, but paused long enough to notice what looked like the contours of a man's face carved into a section of the mountain. Standing there silently, he was triggered by something, a flashing memory, but gone too fast to catch. There was a density to his heart, a heavy emptiness strong enough to box every other feeling out, except for those of vengeance and biting criminality. Gabriel was aware of one thing only, his identity defined as the enforcing arm of Onyx's power — nothing more, nothing less. He was blind to anything beyond that purpose. Yet as he looked at the mountain, he could not shake the feeling of there being loose ends to his life. At this point, if there were any, they were forgotten and almost nonexistent. His safety rested in his detachment from others and in his loyalty to Onyx. Gabriel was untouchable, lifeless, vicious and unwavering in his determination to kill at any cost. Whatever was taking place at the Bonneville, he was determined to snuff it out.

◻

The basement room was dark and empty inside. "Alex, get the light!" yelled Nathan.

Alex flipped a switch, the room was illuminated by a fixture hanging from the ceiling that resembled an old barn lamp with a single Edison bulb. Both of them sniffed around, poking at things. The front wall was encased by a huge glass window that looked out into the river water, letting Nathan and Alex both know they were well below the surface. Nathan hit another switch that seemed to turn on an exterior light that lit up the water, they could see the bottom of the river bed.

Alex pressed his face against the glass and looked around for a moment, "What kind of place is this?" he asked.

"I think it's where they count the fish," Nathan answered. "Check these out," he said, sifting through some papers scattered across the desk next to the window.

Alex looked down at what appeared to be a bunch of numbers and migration graphs.

"Counting fish? Seems like a boring job to me," Alex snickered, as he kept rummaging through all sorts of junk. There were various maps of what appeared to be the northwestern river system, most dominantly Oregon's.

"WHOA!" cried Alex.

"What?" asked Nathan.

"Did you see that thing?"

Nathan looked at him in a funny way.

Alex stuttered, "Th...th...that...thing!" he

exclaimed, pointing through the glass into the dark river water.

Nathan leaned closer and stared out the window. Instantly, a river-monster flashed before his eyes and then disappeared. Nathan jumped back.

"You see it?" exclaimed Alex. "Looked like a prehistoric shark to me!"

"That's a Sturgeon! Must be your first time seeing one?"

"Thing's gotta be eight feet long!" said Alex

"Amazing," sighed Nathan. "I've never seen one up close before." He and Alex both watched in awe as the fish lingered, swimming back and forth right in front of them.

"Didn't think there were still that many fish alive out there," said Alex.

"Hard to tell what's alive and what's dead anymore." Nathan said, entranced as he peered through the window. He was grieved by the rare fish just as much as he was intrigued by it. "I remember some of the Salmon that would swim into the lake every year — they were huge!"

"By the way, how'd that place get its name in the first place?" Alex was well aware that Redfish Lake had been Nathan's home before the war broke out.

"Forgot, you were a city boy, weren't you?" responded Nathan.

"L.A. baby! Best city in the world!"

Nathan laughed, "You have to be kidding me."

"You've never been so you wouldn't know," argued Alex.

"Doesn't matter...I know."

"Let me ask you something, you ever had a taco from El Pollo Loco?"

Nathan looked at him like he was crazy, "You see the world we live in? Do I look like I've had a taco from *whatever-loco?*" he responded as he pulled up his shirt and smacked his skinny belly a couple of times.

"I am older than you, aren't I? What about In-N-Out...*animal style?*"

"Animal what?"

"It's just a burger, man. Grilled onions and stuff." Alex laughed, but was soon disheartened at the thought that Nathan really had no life outside of the cave, or the lake

"Alex, you're making me hungry. Why do you always have to be talking about food?"

"Alright, alright. Aside from the best food, let me just say this, if you've never seen a sunset in Los Angeles, then you haven't seen one at all."

"Disagree," argued Nathan. "I prefer the wilderness... city boys are just weak."

"Tell me you didn't just say that." Alex crinkled a piece of paper and threw it at Nathan, "The wilderness is nothing compared to the streets I grew up on — concrete jungle, man!"

Nathan laughed, "A jungle where you can survive on tacos and burgers I guess, huh?"

"Well, yeah...man."

Nathan pulled back his collar and revealed a scar on his neck.

"Looks like a good one," Alex admired it.

"It's from a mountain badger," Nathan boasted proudly. "Got attacked by one when I was ten."

"You win?"

"You stupid? Course I did, I'm standing here, aren't I?"

"Check this out," Alex pointed to something below his right eye.

Nathan moved closer and saw the mark of a teardrop, "What, did you cry a lot *surviving* on all those tacos?"

Nathan was still being sarcastic, but Alex settled into a serious tone. "You get one of these with your first kill," said Alex.

"First kill?" asked Nathan.

"A person...murder."

"You serious?"

"Yes. But that was a long time ago."

"Well, now killing's just normal these days," replied Nathan. "Come on, let's finish up down here." Alex followed him as they left the fish counting room and made their way down a long corridor lined with massive generators.

"Hey, you never answered my question," said Alex.

"What question?" asked Nathan.

"The name of the lake?"

Nathan was quiet for a moment, then responded, "Because of all the sockeye salmon that would migrate there to spawn. The scales on their backs were red. So many of them would come that it made the appearance of the lake from clear blue to red."

"Hmm," said Alex.

"One of the most beautiful places on earth."

"Maybe we'll get to see it one day," said Alex.

"Yeah, if we can ever get through the walls they've built. It's a different place there now. Geospark took paradise and turned it into a black market. They built mass structures all over the place."

"Hey!" a voice came from behind Nathan and Alex.

Nathan was startled, quickly turned around, and aimed his gun at the person's head. "Easton? Crap, man. You can't be sneaking up on us like that."

"Sorry, you guy's find anything?" Easton asked.

"Just fish," answered Alex.

"Place seems empty," said Nathan.

"I heard you guys talking about *the lake*...Icon,"

inquired Easton.

"I prefer not to call it that," answered Nathan. "It's Redfish Lake."

"What do you guys know about it?" asked Easton.

"It's where I lived when I was a boy," Nathan answered.

"You're joking, right?" Easton was surprised. "The earth's entire fresh water system collapses except for one lake. The last clean lake on earth? And you grew up there?"

Nathan was quiet, not really wanting to talk about it.

Easton continued, "So...you were there when they took it then, right?"

"Don't remember much of what happened," answered Nathan, "kind of a blur. My Grandma won't tell me the whole story."

"Wow! That lake's the greatest miracle phenomenon known to man! All over the world, people struggled with their lives to get to that lake, and you were there!" said Easton.

"A lot of crap happened to me cause of that lake, not something I like to talk about," warned Nathan.

"A lot's happened to all of us because of that lake," added Alex.

"It's not the lake, it's the Screeners," Easton reminded. "It's a different world over there."

Nathan perked up, "You've seen it?"

"Recently," answered Easton.

"Wait a second," barked Alex, "how does someone like you get that close to Icon?"

"It's a long story," said Easton, "there's a whole city there now, creepy though; factory like, weird skyscrapers and such. There's even this crazy looking structure coming out of the Sawtooths that overlooks the lake, it's all glass and steel." Nathan and Alex were listening intently. "Supposedly the leader of the Screeners lives there, hardly anyone's seen him, though."

"The leader of Geospark?" asked Nathan.

"It's the same guy," answered Easton, "said to be half-human, half computer or something — name's Onyx."

"How the hell did they do something like that?" asked Nathan.

"He was one of Geospark's only successful experimentations in the area of infusing embryos with software," said Easton.

Nathan shook his head, "That stuff's hard to believe."

Easton continued, "Onyx is the one behind all this, he was Geospark's prized creation — programmed, devoid of morality. But it wasn't until he got older that they realized they messed up, they lost control of him. Not even the scientists who formed him were able to stop his programmed madness. All they wanted was to create a perfect, limitless human being. They certainly got that, but didn't realize he was a machine without a heart."

Nathan was perplexed, somewhat disgusted, and curious to know more.

"Through Onyx, they always wanted to create a new society," said Easton, "one where there's no toleration for spirituality. Technology is the only deity, programming is the only supreme; science rules. The collapse of the water supply is what they always needed. Some bait, some way in which they could corral society into a one-world system — *join the Screeners, renounce all association with the Navigator, or die of thirst.* The Redfish Lake watershed is bloody real estate, the currency of the new world; more important than gold, silver, coal…fuel. They've wanted one thing all along…"

Nathan's gut was uneasy as he listened, not sure what to make of Easton's breadth of information. His eyebrows curled with suspicion as he pointed his rifle at Easton's head. "You're a spy!" Nathan insinuated.

"Whoa, Nathan!" yelled Alex. "Calm down!" Easton just stood confidently, holding still, giving off the impression that he was not about to retaliate.

"Tell me!" commanded Nathan. "How do you know all this? You just show up to Adullum all of the sudden out of nowhere?"

"Nathan, put...the...gun...down," said Alex, slowly.

"Tell me!" yelled Nathan again, ignoring Alex completely.

"Nathan," Easton answered calmly, "listen to me. I promise, you need me. I'm part of your generation. I want nothing to do with them, I'm on your side. TRUST ME!"

Nathan stood firm, glaring at him, not sure what to believe.

"Look at his wrist, Nathan!" blurted Alex. "He doesn't have an implant! Come on!"

Nathan glanced over at Easton's wrist, he knew there was nothing there. All Screeners were forced to get the implant. "Doesn't matter," said Nathan. "What if they allowed him not to have the chip so he could easily spy on us?"

"Nathan, Iris would have discerned that and you know it!" said Alex.

After a few minutes, Nathan slowly lowered his gun, raised his chin as he looked at Easton and took a deep breath.

"I'm on your side," Easton reassured him again. "I was captured and escaped from there a year ago. Listen, the one we need to watch out for is Onyx's commander."

"Who is he?" asked Nathan.

"I don't know his name, but he's like the Screener's general. He's insane and twisted — like Onyx, he's supposed to know this area better than anyone else."

Nathan thought to himself, *I'd love the chance to take a shot at that guy!* "I'm not sure about you yet, Easton. But you're different, you're definitely different."

The intensity between the three of them settled down as they kept traipsing carefully through the generator aisles.

Alex was still curious, "So…Easton, since you seem to know so much, I got a question for you. How does the earth's entire water supply get poisoned, yet only Redfish Lake, and all the rivers connected to it, stay clean?"

"Huh," Easton laughed, "not sure about that one. I have yet to meet anyone who has the answer to that question. Either the Navigator preserved the lake miraculously or it has something to do with those vibrations in the ground — just a guess."

"Whatever those vibrations are," said Nathan, "I think that's where all the poison is coming from. Tell me I'm not the only one who's bothered by all the alkali flies everywhere."

"I definitely don't think the water contamination was an accident," added Alex. "Hey, check it out!" Alex was in front of Nathan and Easton, pointing to the door in their way. There was a white square sign on it with red letters that read: *CONTROL ROOM.* And then in small print, *Breaker Panels.*

Nathan placed his hand on the doorknob and opened it up as Alex and Easton spotted him. They were greeted by Annak and Iris standing inside, both of them admiring a huge wall of switches, knobs, tubes, wires, and an elaborate spiderweb of electrical conduits.

"You two alright?" asked Nathan, as he walked up behind them, admiring the wall.

Iris turned around and nodded with a grin on her face, "We're standing in the room we came eight hundred miles to see."

"So is it here?" Nathan asked.

"Look," said Iris, pointing to the wall.

Nathan lifted his eyes in the direction of the upper right corner. There it was — a massive panel labeled: *ADULLUM*. There was duct tape strapped across it with sharpie writing that read: *No use*. "You've got to be kidding me," he said. "You weren't joking!" Nathan grabbed Annak by the shoulder, "It can't be this easy?"

"Maybe it can," responded Annak.

"If you don't know what or where Adullum is, then there's no reason to pay attention to this breaker box," added Iris.

"But how could they not know after all this time? It's labeled right in front of their faces," said Nathan.

"Because," explained Iris, "Adullum is underground. They probably flipped this on and didn't know where the power was going. No way to trace it, no way to find it. So they left it off."

"Blows my mind, that after all these years, Geospark still doesn't know about Adullum," Nathan shook his head. "What are we waiting for? Turn it on."

"Just wait a minute," said Iris.

Nathan wondered what the holdup was.

"Everything's going to be different once we flip those switches," voiced Annak. "Once we get that power on, there's no going back."

"That's the point, isn't it?" Nathan asked. "Things need to be different."

"If this works, and the cave's power comes on, then the Screeners will know our location. They'll find Adullum," responded Annak.

"Thought you just said they couldn't because it was underground and undetected underneath the granite?" asked Nathan. "They never found it before, right?"

"Their technology's different now," said Annak.

"It's true," declared Alex, "one of the last Gnats we captured at the tower had some weird stuff going on with it."

"Well, it's only a matter of time before they find out either way," replied Nathan.

"Yeah, but now, we're broadcasting our location on purpose," said Annak.

"Gotta do what we gotta do," expressed Nathan, "so be it."

"Nathan," said Iris, in a maternal tone, "we know. We're just taking a moment. Adullum's been my shelter for years now; many of us have taken refuge there for so long. I've practically raised you there since you were a boy, Nathan. The place has become like a home for me. All these years the Navigator has provided for us within those walls… taken care of us, kept us alive, fed us."

Nathan listened. As much as he was ready for things to be different, he knew that Adullum was special to Iris. "I'm just ready to get our real home back…the lake," he said.

"I know," she replied. "But for some of us, Adullum's been a lot more than just a reminder of the drudgery and depression of the last days."

The room was quiet.

"When you're ready," said Annak, looking at Iris.

"I am," she replied.

Annak walked closer to the breaker box, easily the size of a barn door, flipped open a few latches and opened it up. Inside were seven large levers, lined out vertically in the *off* position. Iris reached up to the top lever, and with both hands, pushed it into the *on* position. She worked her way down and did the same to the next one, and the next, and the next, until all seven were in the *on* position. When she was done, Annak closed the door, repositioned the latches, and touched up the duct tape as if it had never been opened.

In the moment, nothing changed; no one heard anything, nor could they verify that anything had been altered back at Adullum. There was no option, other than by faith, to believe that things would be different when they got back. An image ran through Nathan's mind of what could be taking place at the cave if the power did come on; the bewilderment on the people's faces, as all throughout the tunnels and caverns, lights flickered on, maybe even the heat from the HVAC system.

Yet the moment was soon cut short when Maxed rushed into the room, his eyes were wide and bone-white, "We got a problem!" he exclaimed.

NINETEEN
Open Your Mouth

Max turned and bolted down the hallway, hustling his large body back up the stairs. Everyone ran behind him. Annak cocked his rifle and was the last to leave the mechanical room, while in front of him Nathan did the same — checking to make sure his cartridge was full.

When they reached the top of the stairway, Max handed Annak a pair of binoculars. Annak held them up to his face and peered through one of the broken windows. From up the river valley, a distant aircraft was moving toward the dam. Thoughts of whether or not the power came on to the cave quickly vanished as everyone started preparing themselves for the unexpected.

"Let me see," said Easton. Annak handed him the binoculars. Easton looked and immediately his countenance turned cold as he slowly lowered the binoculars. "That's him..."

Nathan grabbed the binoculars and looked out. "The general you were talking about? Under Onyx?"

Easton nodded to affirm. "These guys aren't like the others."

Iris got a mischievous look on her face when Easton mentioned their leader, though nobody noticed.

"Listen up!" said Annak. "We came here for a reason and we've accomplished what we set out to do. We're too low on men and ammunition to worry about the navigation lock at this point. Nathan, get on the roof and find a shoot point," ordered Annak. "Alex, take the last heavy gun and go with him. If that other gun is still up there...use it. Easton, go with them. Iris and I will stay down here and post up through the windows. Max, you and the others watch the doorways and windows facing the North. Now go!"

Iris grabbed Nathan by his arm, "Be careful, son!"

No one hesitated. Nathan, Alex and Easton ran up the stairway and broke out upon the roof of the powerhouse. The place was embellished with an array of power poles and utility towers. Nathan set up underneath one of them and rested his rifle on the wall ledge. Alex distanced himself about twenty feet adjacent from him and braced up with his own gun right next to the other dead gunner they had shot down from Tanner Creek. Easton stayed close to Nathan with a readied weapon.

All three of them kept still and watched. The humming sound of the Adler became stronger as it moved down the neck of the river. Nathan watched as it dropped onto Bradford Island and disappeared behind a thick cluster of trees.

"Nathan," said Easton, "Pay attention. These guys aren't gonna be easy targets."

"We'll see about that," he answered, "to me they're all the same." Nathan puckered his lips with intensity as he watched back over the ledge through his telescope. "Any of you guys find it odd they didn't just fly over and shoot us out? Why'd they land so far away?"

"Maybe they don't know we're at the powerhouse!" yelled Alex.

◻

From fifteen hundred yards up river from the powerhouse, Gabriel and the other fifteen filed out of the aircraft. They were trimmed in exceptional war gear, covered in black from head to toe. Gabriel was different, however, maybe because for this excursion he did not waste any time changing out of his musky cabin getup prior to leaving Icon.

He stood out awkwardly from the rest, archaic, seemingly not concerned with blending in — standing tall on the raw Oregon soil, wearing a pair of stout cowboy boots made from buffalo hide, and draped with a long raggedy leather rancher's trench coat that was colored with stains. In his right hand was a single Colt, top-break automatic revolver, pulled from his hip, and the same seventeen inch blade undoubtedly tucked away behind his back.

"You seem to know exactly where they're at don't you?" asked Rook, the foreman of the other fourteen Screeners. He was clean cut, shaved, dirty blonde hair, tall and sleek — yet prepped with a hidden, cold-killer face.

Gabriel answered, "You see that navigation lock and powerhouse wall when we came in?"

Rook nodded.

Gabriel continued, "The engineer who signaled the alert retreated from the first powerhouse. Says they haven't moved past that point, seventy-five men and three Nephilim dead already."

"Not your typical ragpickers, huh?" said Rook.

"Doesn't matter," said Gabriel, "they're all dead in the next hour."

The two pilots stayed in the cockpit while Gabriel and the other Screeners started making their way through the heavy woods of Bradford Island.

☐

"You see anything yet, Cowboy?" yelled Alex.

"No," Nathan yelled back.

"Why didn't they just drop a bomb on this place and take us out?" asked Alex.

"The powerhouse is too valuable," answered Easton. "The Bonneville's one of their top four power producers."

blue flame

"What are the others?" asked Alex.

"The Mcnary, John Day, and The Dalles," responded Easton.

"You know what," said Nathan, "I got a new name for you, Easton — *Professor*. How do you know all this stuff?"

"Doesn't matter," he answered.

Alex laughed to himself.

"Tell me this," said Nathan, "how do those alkali flies live off of the same poison that's supposedly killed all the clean water?"

"It's simple," answered Easton, "the acidity. The greater the uranium, the chlorine, the sulfur — the more they thrive. Just how they were made, I guess."

"See, Nathan," piped Alex, "some people just function better on McDonald's french fries!"

"Enough with those ridiculous fries!" yelled Nathan. "I don't want to hear about burgers, fries, tacos, or anything that has to do with food. No more! I'm starving! As a matter of fact, maybe I should've eaten one of you two already. Especially you, Easton, you look tasty." Nathan pulled off the telescope and grinned.

"What? Because I'm black?" said Easton.

"That doesn't matter to me," answered Nathan, "you just smell better than Alex."

"Oh yeah whatever," Alex argued, "not like any of us are clean around here."

Nathan refocused, looked back through his lens and began to notice sparse shadows moving throughout the trees. "They're close," he said, waiting, aiming. Before long the shadows turned into a figure that dashed from one tree to the next. Nathan fired a shot. Nothing. He waited again until suddenly one of their shots returned and broke against the concrete wall right next to his head. Nathan tucked himself away behind the ledge as fast as he could. "Whoa! How'd they find my position so fast?"

Easton periodically started firing random shots down into the enemy's vicinity just as a few more bullets ricocheted off the power poles atop the roof.

"Guess they got some shooters too, huh?" shouted Alex.

"Blow something up down there, would ya!" yelled Nathan.

Alex tweaked the dial on his gun, cocked a lever back with his right hand and opened up machine gun fire. *Chink! Chink! Chink!* Repeated blasts sent tree limbs, pieces of dirt, and shards of bark all over the place — everything except for Screeners. Alex let the smoke from his gun clear and held his finger motionless on the trigger. No sooner did Nathan poke his head over the edge that another myriad of bullets flew by, barely missing him. He ducked and hid again.

Anxious, Nathan slid his body across the back part of the wall and poked his rifle out again. Creeping his head just above the ledge he looked, caught a target in his sight and fired two shots. He watched as both rounds passed right through the chest of one of the Screeners. Nathan aimed again and before the Screener could crawl behind a tree for refuge, ended him with a third shot.

Instantly, a vast amount of gunfire opened up from below. Nathan, Easton and Alex stayed low and held their positions until it subsided. Nathan could hear intermittent shots coming from inside the powerhouse windows.

Rook grinned at Gabriel from behind an opposing tree, "Ducky's dead."

Gabriel looked, but did not respond; he simply kept moving forward.

Shifting across the forest floor, Gabriel continued leading the others as they zig-zagged through the maze of trees and gained footage on the powerhouse. Though one of them had already been brought down, they were stealthy, and took turns moving, then firing shots, moving, then firing shots. The canyon walls reverberated with the sound of rushing water and gunfire.

"They don't look normal!" said Nathan, catching fleeting glimpses of the approaching Screeners. "The one's we took out on the dam looked like grunts compared to these guys!"

After a generous amount of exchanged shots took place, Nathan was more than discouraged by the fact that he had only brought down one Screener. For too long, he, Alex and Easton all watched helplessly as their collected efforts did nothing. It was not long until all Screener gunfire ceased and went dormant.

What the hell are they doing? Nathan asked himself, unable to trace where any of them had gone.

Then, like an unwelcome firework display, an erratic assault was loosed on the powerhouse. The walls shook, glass windows shattered. Up top, Nathan was caught off guard by an almost unnoticeable, *tink.* He felt something small hit his thigh and bounce off. Immediately, from out of the grenade-like flask, came a harsh fumigation of gas.

"Move! Move!" Nathan cried, already sensing the fumes stifling his lungs. Easton and Alex got up like anxious deer as another flask landed on the roof, then another. Lingering like a dust cloud, the substance was unbearable. Visibility was brought to nothing.

"Where you guys at?" Nathan yelled. Easton and Alex tried their best to grope their way to something familiar as they listened to Nathan's voice. Alex yelled back, as did Easton, their three-way communication beginning to break down for lack of breath and having to shut their burning eyes. Unconsciously, they were forced to split up. Clarity disappeared from Nathan's mind while mayhem ensued

— shots and screams, noises and explosions spinning and twirling all around him. He could feel chaos shaking beneath his feet as distinct voices were blurred into one. The event was nothing short of a tumultuous war circus. Amidst it all, as if by some sort of directionless chance, Nathan was able to make his way off the roof and down the stairway, assuming somehow Alex and Easton would be following.

"Annak!" Nathan yelled. "Iris!"

Everything progressed naturally the way it ought to given the shape of the powerhouse. The building was a large rectangle. The ten massive generators lined the middle, each of them easily the size of a small city water tower. Ladders went up to the top of each generator, and elevated hallways protruded from the walls on each side, guarded by nothing more than a see-through metal railing. The Screeners entered through the north side of the building as the Reapers backed themselves against the south side where they had originally entered. Since the generators were shelled with heavy steel and reinforced concrete, they stood as shields for both sides. Rounds of vengeance blazed everywhere simultaneously as both sides bottlenecked.

Nathan did his best to catch the sound of Annak's voice, recognizing the noise of his rifle's gunshots, and eventually discovered him at the southern entrance lying down behind one of the railings. Iris was right next to him.

"Get down, Nathan!" yelled Iris.

Nathan backed up bchind the same railing off the opposite wall paralleling Annak and started pulling his trigger. Some shots were worthless, others were not. Here and there, Nathan watched as one of his or Annak's rounds dropped one Screener, then another. For a moment, it actually appeared like things were turning in their favor. That was until Nathan noticed how many Reapers were getting stung and shot to death. The few survivors they did have, Nathan witnessed them drop, one by one. His attention soon drifted, when out of the corner of his eye he kept getting entranced by the man in the rancher's coat. In and out of every shadow, the man would appear then disappear, somehow evading every bullet. With only a pistol, almost aiming carelessly, he was hitting Reapers like they were standing still.

Nathan became engrossed, and with rage made it a point to stop him. He let loose all the bullets he possibly could from his rifle, but no matter how hard he tried, was hindered from a successful kill.

And then, everything slowed down. Nathan felt his shoulder kick back and a compacted *whoof,* pulse in his ears. It was like the sound of a fist smacking into a dense pillowcase. Not sure what had just happened, but feeling a strike of shock take hold of his body, Nathan lowered his chin and saw blood pouring from a hole between his chest and shoulder.

The room was deafening. Nathan's ears were ringing with white noise. With diminished concentration he unknowingly kept firing his weapon and tried to ignore the pain. Nathan got the feeling that he was not the only Reaper with a crumbling resistance. "I'M HIT!" he yelled, looking for some sort of sympathy or aid.

"Nathan!" Iris yelled back, not discounting his hit. "Where's Easton?"

"What?" Nathan hardly heard her voice. Not only that, but he could barely comprehend the fact that he had just alerted them to the fact that he had been shot, and all Iris cared about was finding Easton.

"Where's Easton?" she yelled again, "Where…is… he?"

Easton yelled over at Iris from Nathan's left side, "Here!" He was crouched down, firing shots toward the North side of the building.

Iris looked beyond Nathan and yelled at Easton, "Open your mouth!"

Verbal exchange was not easy amidst all the noise. "What?" Easton yelled back.

"Open your mouth!" she shrieked from the top of her lungs.

"No," Easton answered, "too many bullets!" He was scared now, not only of the Screener bullets, but of Iris's demand.

Nathan was curling up in pain and perplexed. *Open your mouth? What the hell is she talking about?*

Iris shouted again, commanding Easton with even more vehemence, "OPEN...YOUR...MOUTH!!!"

Finally, without any further argument, something happened; something that was beyond mystifying — way, way, way beyond. What Nathan witnessed was so insanely opposite of what one should even consider doing in a time of war. Within such close proximity with the Screeners, in the middle of all the assault, Easton stopped shooting, stood straight up and did exactly what Iris commanded him to do — *opened his mouth.*

And then, of all the things he should have done with that mouth — he did not yell, he did not scream, nor did he shout or taunt, or warn, or do anything that would have been considered normal nature — no.

Easton liberated a melody, with a power and pitch that was terrifying. It was as if a bird had just been let out of its cage.

From the depths of his gut, with his mouth flung wide open, he sang louder and more pronounced than anything Nathan ever thought imaginable. The resonating tone that swept through the place was beyond human. If the all the bullets and explosives had not broken the windows, Easton's voice would have. The sound was just simply and absolutely beyond description.

Instantly it was as if the gravity of a heavenly realm had been kicked open and was breaking forth with waves of mystery.

Nathan would have continued to take in the unnatural wonder of what he was witnessing, but as Easton's singing grew louder, Nathan felt his ears start to crack and go numb, followed by an excruciating pain that surged through his body, much different than that of the bullet wound. The insides of his intestines buckled and cramped.

Just before losing complete visibility Nathan looked around and noticed that all Screener gunfire closed out. One by one, he watched the Screeners panic, madly trying to scrape away at their ears and scurrying about like lost rats. Easton's voice was booming, paralyzing almost everybody, Nathan included.

Suddenly, Nathan remembered Iris's words back at Adullum: *Only those with the Blue Flame are braced enough to receive the freedom of his gift. If you don't have the Spirit, you'll be torn up from the inside out.* Mysteriously, all but one Screener was affected, the man wearing the rancher's coat was still possessed with a darkened countenance, unmoved by Easton's voice as he continued reloading his pistol and taking shots toward the southern doorway.

Losing control of his eyeballs, Nathan felt them roll back in their sockets. "STOP SINGING!" he screeched, "GET ME OUTA HERE! STOP IT! STOP!"

But Easton, unaware of Nathan's cry, kept pouring out unearthly melodies into the atmosphere. His voice thundered over the racket of the generators and the turbines.

Nathan yelled again, "HELP!" The pain was so unbearable now, he knew he could not be far from death. Almost completely unaware, but cognizant enough to detect two strong hands reaching around him, Nathan felt his body being dragged across the floor and then taken outside the powerhouse. He could still hear Easton's voice rumbling in the distance, though quieter now. Nathan looked up and saw Annak, frantically trying to get him as far away from the powerhouse as possible. With a *thud*, Annak dropped Nathan to the ground and then ran back into the building.

Nathan laid there, still rolling around in pain, trying to cover his ears, and watched as Annak came flooding out of the powerhouse doorway, this time dragging Max. He dropped him next to Nathan, then ran back again. The next person to be carried out was Alex, looking half-dead.

Iris and Easton were not in the building much longer before they both came running out. Annak tried to help Nathan, Max and Alex recover; shaking them, looking into their eyes, bringing them *to*. Nathan's hand was braced across his chest, trying to keep the blood from pouring out. He was growing weaker. Annak took hold of the wound by pressing the palm of his hand over Nathan's. Instantly, Nathan jolted as energy resurged back into his body, forcing his wound to fade. It was nothing short of another moment that reminded Nathan he was part of a world he had yet to understand. Within less than twenty-four hours he had experienced his life being miraculously preserved twice, and the weightiness of the reason why was no less stirring.

TWENTY
An Uncomfortable Conversation

"We're all that's left?" asked Nathan, as he and the other five made their way to the edge of the powerhouse wall with the intent to cross back over to Robins Island.

"Everybody else is dead," said Iris.

"Annak, why can't you go back in there and heal them?" asked Nathan.

"Because, I can only heal," answered Annak.

"Exactly, so what are you waiting for?"

"Nathan, once they're gone, they're gone. I can't raise people from the dead. I can only heal wounds."

"So, just like that, we lost everyone?"

"Nothing we can do," said Iris.

"Stay focused and keep moving," urged Annak.

It was deep into the afternoon by now. The sky was darkened and overcast. Nathan was not the only one discouraged because of all those they had lost. Yet his body and mind felt vitalized by Annak's healing release.

Pacing himself behind the rest, Annak had the strange feeling someone was quietly lurking behind him. A few times he dismissed his hunch, but continued to periodically look back, each time not seeing anyone. Then, just before reaching the edge of the navigation lock, Annak looked back once more and without warning was violently tackled to the ground.

The others came to a halt, hearing the commotion. One look told Nathan who Annak was wrestling with along the edge of the lock, the man wearing the rancher's coat. Annak and the other man — both victims of one another — were grunting, trying to take the edge on the other's strangulation.

The combat was intense, punches being thrown equally and mercilessly. Only one thing clicked for Nathan — run right into the fight.

Annak 's cold knuckles landed across the man's stone chin, sending a spit of saliva from his mouth as he toppled over. Without flinching, Annak straddled him and clenched his throat. Unable to escape, the man pulled out his blade and swiped it across Annak's rib-cage. Annak was forced to let go and stumbled backwards. Both out of ammunition and within close range of one another, Annak pulled out his knife, and like cats, they raged and thrashed at one another, expressing a tumult of furry that was hard to watch.

Soon enough Nathan's momentum carried him close and with full force, he hurled himself onto the Screener's back and broke the blade free from his grip. Both of them rolled across the bridge to the edge of the navigation wall, yet somehow kept themselves from falling into the river. Nathan was belligerent and filled with rage. He had been trying to shoot this Screener with too many failed attempts, and now he was threatening Annak's very life. But Nathan was younger and quicker. Nathan pegged the Screener, now with no weapon, and thrust his knee into his chest. He punched him, kicked him and did absolutely everything that was necessary to bring him down. No prowess or technique about it, just pure grappling.

Taking some hits, but eager to kill, Nathan pulled out his own knife, reared it up over his shoulder and then looked right into the Screener's eyes. For a split second, he felt something inside his heart. Staring into the man's face gave him an uncomfortable familiarity; something so recognizable, yet so eerie. In the moment the two of them could not have been farther apart, yet triggered by an odd intimacy. Nathan sensed his executioner countenance slip away and hesitated to plunge his knife into the man's chest. Still, as if preserved by bitterness, Nathan's coincidental mercy was short lived. He snapped out of it, and with intensity started to thrust his knife down upon the man.

Simultaneously, Iris's screamed, "NO!" Followed by her arm that held back Nathan's knife. She held Nathan down as best she could, allowing the Screener to jump to his feet. Quickly, the Screener loaded one last bullet into his pistol and aimed the gun at Nathan's head.

"GABRIEL!" Iris stepped out in front of Nathan, her eyes were burning with ardor. The Screener was about to pull the trigger, his pupils dilated like he had just been confronted by a ghost from hell, yet he did not say anything.

Iris put her hand out and yelled again, "Gabriel!"

Gabriel stood there motionless, his face dirty. To Nathan he appeared to be the most intimidating man he had ever seen. There was so much emptiness, yet he seemed possessed by rare vexation and depravity. Nathan's heart was beating fast, not sure who was going to get shot, confused no less by the fact that Iris called out the man's name with such conviction and amity.

"Gabriel," Iris said a third time, her voice stern.

"You," said Gabriel, quivering with a slight stutter. "Hard to believe it's you," he said in a calm voice. He was still poised to shoot, with a scrutinizing look of disgust and revenge smeared across his face. Then in a burst of anger, yelled, "You tore us apart!"

"You left me no other choice," Iris responded.

"You ruined everything!"

"Gabriel —" Iris started to speak, but he interrupted her. All eyes were on both of them.

"EVERYTHING!"

Everyone was quiet. Nathan, Annak and the others crowded around, not sure what to make of the exchange that was taking place.

"Put the gun down," commanded Iris, this time taking a step towards him.

"How could you?" he answered.

"Put...it...down," she said again.

"I won't put down...what I am."

"Gabriel, listen to me!"

"Your words mean nothing to me anymore!"

Iris took another step towards him, "Just put the gun down. I had to...you know that."

"You disgust me, old woman. What you did...was poison to my soul!" he cried. "I've had nothing to live for because of you! Because of you! Your insanity! I searched for years! For years, Iris! YOU'RE A THIEF!"

Iris continued to plead, not so much as a victim, but more for Gabriel's sake. "I used to know you, Gabriel. This isn't who you are. I didn't take anything from you that you didn't lose. I couldn't allow us to live that way. To be taught their ways? To become part of their dark world? To become like you?" Iris paused, "Look at you! Look at whose side you're on!"

"You're wrong! This is the chance I've been waiting for all these years — to finally redeem what's mine! This is your last chance to give an answer for what you did. And then you're going to pay for it."

"I won't," answered Iris, "Not like this. It's not too late to change, to take it all back. Things can be different. You have to let go!" Iris paused, everything was quiet except for the sound of rushing water coming from below. "Gabriel! It was never the Navigator's fault!"

"I'd thought you would have seen things clearer by now. You're still blind, Iris! Of course it was His fault! All of this is! He was supposed to be watching over us — protecting us! And He didn't. He's the reason she's gone. All those years I spent honoring Him! Serving him!

Worshipping him! Devoting my life…TO HIM! And then… when I needed Him, where was He? Where the hell was the King who's supposed to be ruling over everything?" Gabriel came closer, pointing his gun now at Iris, "NOWHERE!!!"

"Gabriel…you're wrong!" she yelled.

"This is your last chance or I'm pulling the trigger," warned Gabriel.

Iris stood firm, sharpening her stare at Gabriel. Suddenly, Gabriel's gun went *click* as he pulled the trigger, yet no bullet came out.

"Annak!" Iris yelled.

No sooner did Iris give the signal, Annak, who had already picked up a gun from one of the dead Screeners, fired and sent a bullet soaring through Gabriel's arm. At no more than a few yards away, it was obvious the shot was not intended to be fatal. The reason, however, was known only to Annak and Iris, no one else. Immediately, Gabriel's pistol fell from his hand. He roared in pain.

Annak kicked Gabriel's pistol over the edge and then gave him a vivid warning, "Come after us and I'll make sure the next shot doesn't miss." Gabriel was without words. "Let's go!" charged Annak.

Nathan could not seem to move, standing there, puzzled by what he had just seen. He felt slight pity, his judgment weakened by the choice to stay with Gabriel or take off running with those he had been close to for years. Too much happened too fast. Too much was spoken and unspoken. The words exchanged in those fleeting seconds only brought more questions, more confusion.

"Nathan! Now!" demanded Iris. Max came up alongside Nathan and began dragging him to a steadying run. Nathan took one last look at Gabriel and then jetted.

"Don't let them get away!" commanded Gabriel, seeing Rook and the other Screeners coming out of the powerhouse. It was clear by their shifting and yawning jaws they were still trying to get the ring of Easton's voice out of their ears.

Rook started shooting at the Reapers scattering across the way. Annak stopped, turned around and fired off what little ammunition he had left, then kept moving. In no time, Annak and the rest crossed the entire length of the navigation lock, sprinted through Tanner Creek and dispersed back into the woods they originally came through. Momentarily, Rook turned down the pursuit.

Gabriel roused to his feet, wrapped his arm, and led the rest back to the Adler. By now he was at a level of indescribable paranoia. "That woman!" he cried. "We have to capture her alive!"

"Who?" asked Rook.

"Iris," he answered.

"She's behind all this?" asked Rook.

"She's behind a lot more than that," answered Gabriel.

"How did that guy do that to us?" Rook asked, still caught off guard.

Gabriel did not have to guess that Rook was referring to the one who opened his mouth. "He's a singer," Gabriel answered, with great displeasure. In the back of his mind he thought to himself, *Must be the last of his kind.*

"A what?" Rook asked again.

Gabriel stopped and turned his sobering attention to Rook, "No one at Icon hears about what happened back there. Do you hear me?" he warned. Rook nodded. "Now signal for reinforcements. I want eyes on everything from here to Portland!"

The gorge would soon be engulfed in darkness as the sun tucked itself away behind the hills. Seeing Iris, seemingly thinking she was dead after all these years, had caused Gabriel to snap. Rook noticed him, his demeanor was slightly different, Gabriel was passively mad as usual, but there was something else, a vulnerability was there that was not before. Gabriel may have seen glitches here and there, some occasional assaults. But they were rare, they were weak, they were nothing, and he always refused to tolerate them.

Over the years, more and more people died off, and there was less that stood in the way of the Screeners' initiatives. Yet for the first time in twenty years, Gabriel was confronted by the reality of the greatest assault he had ever felt upon his life. Feelings that were somewhat dormant for decades were all of the sudden pouring through the caverns of his heart at the sight of Iris. The rules of the game seemed so much more costly. Gabriel was not just feeling the responsibility of being the Chief Steward over Geospark's resources; now, he was on the hunt to regain a piece of his own personal property and to try and recover that which was lost in his life.

TWENTY ONE
To the Mountain

At the same time, as Nathan and the other Reapers ran for their lives, little did he know that miles and miles away, a woman was hoisting her little boy up onto the back of a beast and setting him on a makeshift saddle made from scraps of metal and strands of leather.

"This is it, mom. I know it," said the boy.

The woman simply looked back at him, trying to hide the doubt that was in her heart.

"To the mountain is where everything changes. I know it," the boy said again, making himself comfortable in the saddle, and somehow reminding his mother that the trip would be worth the risk.

Yet inwardly, she knew the excursion would expose her and her son beyond any sense of safety, and she was fully aware that there was a grave chance they would not return alive. She found it hard to cling to anything of substance, save for the foolish faith that was in the childish eyes looking back at her. But perhaps those innocent little eyes would be enough. Regardless, she had nothing left to look to for hope anymore. With one leap, she pulled herself up behind the boy, grabbed the reigns, kicked her heels into the beast and left behind all that she was familiar with.

TWENTY TWO
Trap Door

"**H**ey!" yelled Alex, "I need to stop for a second!" He braced himself up against a tree, exhausted and panting. Nathan came up behind him, dipped his flask into the river, handed it to Alex, and then took a drink for himself. Alex wiped the excess water off his face. "Seem weird to you what all that was back there?"

Nathan was not sure what to say.

Annak drew back, "Hurry up and keep moving!" he urged.

"Just getting some water while we're close to the river," said Nathan. "We're drained."

"They're gonna be on our trail any second, Nathan. We need to get to the gas station and back to the Crawlers soon as possible," said Annak.

Iris was at the front with Easton and Max, the three of them had yet to stop and rest. It was odd, but true, that she was somehow in better shape than anyone else — somehow constant in her ability to keep moving. It was no secret that everybody was getting by on fumes, yet they all knew the opportunity to rest was gone the moment they decided to leave Adullum a few days earlier. Their journey was only just beginning. The task of getting home alive was filled with much uncertainty. Food and ammunition were scarce.

"Now! It's time to go!" Annak commanded, pulling the flask of water down from Nathan's thirsty mouth.

Nathan let the water's moisture grace his chapped lips and dry throat, took some deep breaths, then continued pacing himself alongside Alex. Little by little they moved through what seemed like a labyrinth — the scattered forest trees being permeated by fragmented rays of twilight.

Within less than two hours they were back at the gas station. Nathan did not hesitate to go in and kick on the Crawlers so they could make a quick exit and maintain momentum.

Alex stopped him. "Wait," he said, listening intently to the soft hum of Gabriel's aircraft gliding over-head, followed by the blinding search lights that started piercing through the clouds. The lights flashed and strobed constantly, moving back and forth in all directions. Annak looked out the window and saw what appeared to be six other Gnats spread out as part of the flock. They were organized and seemed to move by invisible square and triangular patterns. Immediately, Annak cleared back and pushed everyone to far corner of the garage, trying to get clear of the slightest visibility.

"They've got the whole ground lit up!" exclaimed Max. "How we supposed to get out of here?"

Annak did not pretend to have the answer. Neither did Iris, she had not said the slightest word of anything to anyone since commanding Annak to shoot Gabriel.

"This is it," Nathan grumbled. "We're trapped."

Annak looked at Nathan, wanting to say something, but held back.

"Why didn't you kill him?" asked Nathan. "You never miss." He posed the question not so much as a prosecutor, but as a child groping for understanding of something he had no sense of.

Annak was quiet, trying to evade the question.

"Tell me," said Nathan. "It didn't look like he would have hesitated to kill you. And you shoot him in the arm?"

Annak still chose not to respond, his attention being drawn to the flickering lights outside.

"I know you know something I don't," Nathan stated clearly.

Iris interrupted the moment and was quick to break up the looming conversation between the two of them. "We need to get to the corner of Sixth and Davis," she said.

"Sixth and Davis?" asked Annak.

"What happened to the retreat point?" added Max.

"Retreat point's not going to work anymore," answered Iris. "We never got separated. Sixth and Davis is where we need to get to." She said it in such a way that she was not inviting any objections, nor was she willing to entertain other options.

"That's Chinatown," said Annak.

"It's in the heart of *old town* Portland," responded Iris. "If they release heavy airstrikes, they'll blow up the entire city looking for us."

"Doesn't make any sense to me," said Nathan. "If they shoot the city to death, why are we going back into it?"

"Guess you're just gonna have to trust me," Iris answered.

Even Annak was in the dark on this one, convinced only by his track record with Iris and an awareness of her keen edge on certain matters.

"We go, but no lights," Annak warned. "Everything has to stay off."

"Doesn't matter," said Alex, "Gnats can still track our every move."

Annak did not answer back. He knew what the drones were capable of.

"Just get us to that street corner," urged Iris.

Annak looked around the garage, "What's left for ammo?"

"I barely have anything," said Alex.

"Nothing for me," followed Easton.

"I'm out," Max declared.

Nathan looked at his rifle, it was empty. Then his

side-arm, "I've got three bullets left in my pistol. And my knife."

Annak's supply was equally despaired.

"I have enough," said Iris. Nathan glanced at her, wondering if she was referring to bullets or faith.

"Why can't we wait it out here for the night?" asked Max.

"It won't be long before they send foot soldiers from the other half of the Bonneville. They'll rake this whole area by morning," answered Annak.

"The fact is, we're outnumbered," complained Alex. "Like mice running through a maze. The chances of us making it all the way back into downtown is crazy!"

"Maybe you should be focusing more on the *will* and less on the *odds*," whispered Iris.

A fleeting thought ran through Nathan's mind, *you can only keep secrets for so long, Grandma.*

With one motion, sensing what was inside him, Iris put her mouth up to Nathan's ear, "If you only knew, son," just loud enough so that he was the only when who could hear.

In silent consensus they started up the Crawlers, made a clean exit from the garage and veered into the backroads. No more than half way through the forest, just outside of Troutdale, Nathan got sick to his stomach. He knew the feeling by now and was beginning to grow uncomfortably familiar with it. Even though Annak was in the cab right beside him, he was no less struck by a heavy onset of loneliness and insanity. His ability to think clearly dripped away like melting wax. He did not have to guess where the feelings were coming from. Even with his eyes closed, he could see with his mind that same death-pale shadow running through the trees alongside the road. The Sarx was again accompanying him as if he had never left. Nathan buried his cold face inside the frozen stiff collar of his jacket and slouched in his seat. Yet the physical cloistering did nothing to help him ignore the demon's presence. The dark beast felt closer to him than anything else, somehow touching a part of him that no one else could seem to reach. The gnashing of teeth, the jeering, the taunts, the demoralizing whispers of a thousand depressed and roaring voices — "You're mine. You belong to me, Nathan. Wherever you go, I'll find you." — it was all there.

"Annak." Somehow Nathan summoned enough courage to speak up.

Annak pointed his chin in Nathan's direction, "What is it?"

"That thing's out there, following us."

"The Sarx?"

"Yeah."

Annak stretched his arm across the cab and grabbed Nathan by his shoulder. Nathan looked out again into the passing forest and realized no sooner did he give voice to the reality of the demon, it disappeared.

"You're gonna have to make a decision at some point Nathan," said Annak. "Who you gonna give your life to?"

Nathan could still feel the slight residue of the demon's presence. He shook it off as best he could and remained somewhat alone in his thoughts, uncertain how to respond to Annak's question. Part of him could not help harboring ill feelings toward Iris. Inwardly, he questioned the extent to which he was being deceived by all the secrets she was keeping, real or imaginary. He found it impossible to get the pressure of her and Gabriel's exchange out of his mind, and was feeling eaten away by it.

Scattered thoughts raced through Nathan's head as the shattered urban landscape started to thicken. He watched as the timber and dirt of the wilderness gave way to crumbled buildings, abandoned subdivisions, and torn up city streets. Annak continued leading the humble caravan, maneuvering in and out of overturned vehicles and bits of rubble. By now they could not have been more than five miles from Iris's designated street corner, and for some reason it appeared they were still unnoticed. Annak wondered if Gabriel's entourage was too occupied scanning the forests instead of the city. But there was no way things could stay quiet for long.

Alex was on high alert in his normal tailgate position, chewing on a piece of dried meat from wild game weeks earlier. He refused to take his eyes off the dark sky while he kept his machine gun pointed out into the air. For some reason no one else could hear it, but his ears started to pick up the subtle cackle of static electricity coming from Nathan's seat. Ignoring it at first, Alex kept his focus on the rear. Seconds later the sound grew louder. *What is that?* he asked himself. His mind did not stay blank for long. Just then he made the connection and deciphered the sound as the exact same resonance he had heard dismantling other drones back at the tower.

"Nathan!" said Alex. "You got something going on in your seat." Nathan could not seem to hear anything, his ears less tuned than Alex's. "You got something in your pack?"

Soon enough Nathan was able to hear it. He reached down into the pack next his feet. Opening it up, his face was immediately aglow. Inside was the mechanized eyeball from the drone they shot down in the gorge — illuminated and sparking wildly. Nathan pulled it out so Annak and Alex could take a look. Annak kept driving with one hand and with the other grabbed the orb from Nathan. Bringing the Crawler to a complete stop, Annak held still and listened, feeling only a slight breeze blowing through the streets.

"This ain't good," said Alex. "I'm telling you, it's not."

Annak stepped out of the cab and held his head in the air. "Alex," he whispered, "how many shells did you say you had?"

"A strip," he answered, "maybe fifty bullets."

"There's two Gnats coming in behind us!" said Annak. "One from the West and one from the East. Don't miss!"

The small orb was even more provoked by now. Alex shook his head nervously to acknowledge Annak's charge. He turned around and braced himself for what was about to breach the clouds.

Annak leapt back into the drivers seat, clenched the suicide knob and called back to Max driving the other Crawler, "KEEP UP!"

"Cake! Man!" Alex's nerves were stressed to the point where he unconsciously started blurting out senseless fantasies of food. "Just gimme some cake!"

The Crawler's sped off as Annak searched for some sort of cover. It seemed impossible to get out of the open. *WHISP!* Suddenly, a small object hissed right past them and exploded inside an abandoned RV just to their left.

"They're here!" yelled Alex.

Annak swerved and raced down a side street. Two drones came into the rearview, gliding airborne side by side and unleashing a blanket of bullets. Holes were blown open all over the place, penetrating the bodies of both Crawlers. Annak and Max forced the gas pedals so hard that the others could barely hold on.

Soon enough, Alex reciprocated fire, his body being flung from side to side in his seat. Nathan looked back and caught a glimpse of the drones. One was small and spider-like, probably no more than six feet in diameter, and rapidly loosing rounds of bullets. The other was larger and looked similar to a floating human hand that carried heavy artillery.

Nathan saw enough but could not hold his focus for long, Annak's driving was making him nauseous.

"Alex!" Nathan yelled. "Hit one already!"

Alex was too scared to answer back, his nerves wrecked by the rapid assault. He was trying his best to calculate and time his shots so as not to waste any, but the drones shifted and maneuvered with unusual agility. They were not easy to tag.

Another explosion shattered the street just in front of them. *BOOM!* Everyone in the Crawlers felt the force as the vehicles shook, the tires feeling as though they had been blown off. Without slowing down, Annak quickly passed right through the middle of the flames, Max followed blindly. They shredded their way through the city streets until finally breaking through a gateway that lead them into a park. With limited options, they crashed through what was left of a metal swing set, in and out of some fallen trees, until finally spilling back out onto the city streets. The drones moved without glitches, coming too close for comfort. They separated, then came close to one another, moved up, moved down, shifted laterally. The smaller one took a nose dive, spiraled and spilled out more bullets at a magnitude that was hard to evade, while the larger one shot out what seemed to be another rocket. The explosion broke right behind Max, his Crawler barely escaping. A huge crater opened up in the earth where they had just passed. Nathan was having his doubts about being able to escape their mechanical dragnet.

At the same time, while the rat-chase chaos ensued on the ground, Gabriel was in the sky, gritting his teeth, hanging one-armed halfway out the Adler as it flew low. The aircraft was soaring just east of downtown Portland before being alerted by the drones. Gabriel's eyes were intent, glaring, focused and unshaken by the cold air that roared against his face and through his dirty grey hair. Rook and the others were prepared to deploy at any moment.

"Turn there!" yelled Iris, pointing down the street, still clenching the roll bar with her other hand. This was the first time she had spoken up during the chase. Annak did not bother to question. He surged and cut the corner hard and then instantly, by the light of the moon could see the massive Hawthorne bridge right front of them. Confidence was fleeting as sections of the bridge were blown apart, the entire structure looking as if it were barely holding on. The complete stretch of suspended, broken road was less than promising — an old school bus was overturned on one side of it, almost eliminating all through access. The large steel arches and support beams looked like oversized frayed violin strings, ready to collapse any second. Yet with nowhere else to go, Annak sped forward and took his chances.

As they raced across it, Nathan swallowed with a stiff neck and tried to ignore the feeling of the entire structure shuddering and swaying in the wind. The bridge groaned. The bullets and explosive artillery, fired from the drones behind them, hit parts of the bridge and only made it worse. Sections of the street caved in around them, large pieces of asphalt fractured and flew through the air. The situation worsened as they reached the middle arch of the bridge. Nathan looked over the edge for one second and imagined a dead fall to the barren Willamette river bed below. His anxiety was well beyond manageable as he began whispering to himself, *Come on Alex, hit one of those things.* Nathan closed his eyes, then opened them and looked over at Annak. He closed his eyes again and then opened them. *I cannot believe we're not dead by now.*

Finally, Nathan sighed when they reached the end of the bridge. The skyline disappeared as they accelerated into the blocks of Old Town. The buildings left standing were reminiscent of China. Oriental signage and rusted out metal advertisements dangled outside the storefronts. High above, Iris caught a glimpse of the corroded historic Portland water tower, holes blown into the sides of it, and the once-lit neon, 'State of Oregon' sign, with the token frame of the leaping dear, somehow still standing.

"Go there!" Iris commanded again. She pointed forward into the distance toward a cluster of crumbling edifices.

Just then, Nathan heard Alex scream from the back of the vehicle. Nathan turned around and in shock, watched as the hand-like drone plummeted to the street and blew apart.

"About time!" Yelled Nathan. Alex continued struggling to hit the other one. Max was behind still trying to keep up.

Annak swerved and cut into a narrow alley. "Here's your chance, Alex!" exclaimed Annak.

The drone ripped around the corner in pursuit and was soon corralled between the brick walls of two opposing buildings. Alex aimed, pulled the trigger and fired his last two bullets. *Tink! Tink!* He watched with dumbfounded celebration as the drone was punctured and sent curling into the side of the building.

"GNAT'S DOWN!" cried Alex. "GNAT'S DOWN! Just gimme some cake!"

Annak did not have to ask, he knew Alex was out of ammo.

"Get me into the subway station!" Iris commanded Annak, as the Crawlers left the alley and came out into an open street.

In the distance Annak could barely see anything, yet pulling closer, there was a stairwell that disappeared underneath what was left of the sidewalk. Annak stopped, stuck his head out of the Crawler just in time to see the Adler come into view behind them. The aircraft was more intimidating than anything else like it. They were all close enough to see Gabriel hanging out the side as the black mass hovered a few stories up.

Rook looked into Gabriel's eyes with a temper that communicated it was time. Gabriel did not have to guess that the pilots had already locked the self-guided rockets on both Crawlers. Gabriel just shook his head in response, making it clear to Rook he wanted them alive. Down below, Annak and the rest looked on in silence, while Gabriel's eyes honed in on no one else but Iris.

"GO!" charged Iris.

Soon enough Annak and Max hit the gas pedals and tumbled down the concrete stairwell, somehow staying upright. *Thud! Thud! Thud!* The tires smacked against each step, causing everyone's head to bobble. The only thing in front of them was a dark tunnel.

"They can't go anywhere down there," said Gabriel, watching as they vanished beneath the city streets.

Annak fishtailed at the bottom and screeched to a halt. Max pulled up alongside him. They switched on the headlights and looked around.

"This is a dead end," said Max. The entire subway tunnel was crammed with too much to mention. The place was murky and reminiscent of a thrift-store gone terribly wrong. The smell was near unbearable, a residue lingering with the reek of people having taken refuge there before they died. The place was an underground morgue of death, starvation and thirst. Not even the unsettling hiss of rats and their dragging tails echoed off the walls. The place was deader than dead, with no outlets of escape in sight.

"Grandma, did you lead us into a trap?" asked Nathan. "Where the hell are we supposed to go?"

The stench of wild animal feces was strong. Bones, broken grocery carts, oil barrels, car doors, rusted bicycles, and empty gasoline canisters, littered the place. Nathan frantically looked around, finding it odd that there was an old 1970's metal military desk pushed up against a particular wall — with one lonely cheap lamp standing on it.

"I'm not liking this one bit," repeated Nathan.

Iris, less observant of the surroundings than the others, did not seem to care about responding to any of the doubtful remarks. If anybody looked like they had a plan, it was her. "You guys can either follow me or go right back up those stairs," she said. "Your choice. There's no time for answers right now." Everybody but Annak took one more look at the stairway that led back up to the streets and did not say anything.

In silent agreement, taking what they could carry out of the Crawlers they followed Iris as she led them down the tunnel. Nathan was confused, did not have a better plan, and was no less perplexed when she showed them the way through the door of what appeared to be the remains of a hoary-old sushi restaurant. Nothing was left of the glass windows and the place smelled of rot. Nathan braced his nose with his forearm and crept over an array of scattered dishes and broken bar stools.

No one had to guess that Gabriel and the others had already flooded out of the Adler. Easton was the last to go through the restaurant and was already hearing their marching footsteps coming down the stairway. From a distance he could barely see the telescope lights of their guns spreading out across the walls. "They're not far behind us. Move! Move!" he whispered to the rest.

Nathan wanted to ask Iris, *where are you taking us?* But she looked beside herself and delirious. He knew she was not in the spirit to talk. For the moment, all he could see was no way out of the corner she was leading them into. Soon enough, all six of them were huddled inside the restaurant's cramped kitchen.

"Hurry! Get this stuff out of the way!" commanded Iris.

Max and Easton quickly started moving a stack of boxes and clutter that blocked a walk-in freezer door. No sooner did they finish, Iris undid the latch and thrust it open. Acting as though she had been in this room before, she walked in, did not look up, did not look side to side, but bent down, placed her hands on a large metal clip, and tried to pull up a small rectangular piece of the floor. Nothing budged, everything apparently frozen solid. Easton stepped in and cranked it open. The hinges creaked. Nathan shined his flashlight through the trap door opening, then rested his eyes on a rickety wooden ladder that lead down a shaft.

"What the —" Max said hesitantly, but failed to finish his sentence.

Nathan just shook his head back and forth.

"You first," Iris told Nathan, stretching out her arm to push him down the ladder.

Nathan disappeared through the floor, followed by the rest. Annak was the last to go, shutting the door overhead behind him. As twelve feet settled on the cold dirt ground there was a synchronized cough, brought on by a cloud of floating dust. If *old* had a smell, this was it, and its ability to gag a throat was no less pungent. Encased by cold earthen walls, the place was stale and felt like a dungeon.

"I don't know where we are, but it's strange down here," said Alex.

"Ghostlike!" echoed Max.

Easton's breathing was heavy, no less than anyone else's, all of their hearts still pounding from the chase that emerged from clear back at the dam. Nathan's light shone back and forth, exposing multiple tunnels that headed off in different directions.

Annak simply shook his head at Iris, "Is this what I think it is isn't it?"

Iris nodded.

"What?" asked Nathan.

"The Portland tunnels," said Iris.

"I like to call them the Shanghai Tunnels," added Annak. "A lot of people thought they were a myth, hidden from the public."

"Well, here they are," answered Iris.

"What kind of tunnels are these?" questioned Max.

Annak continued with a history lesson, somewhat entranced by where he was standing. "Not a lot of people knew about these. Their existence was always questionable. The city of Portland…they always tried to cover up what took place down here and blew it off as though it never was — just a fairytale. Believe it or not, this town was once called the Forbidden City because of its underground vices."

"Vices?" asked Nathan. "Like what?"

"No time to talk about that right now," said Iris. "Annak, we have to head South — at all times. South! Do you hear me?"

"No problem," he answered.

"Nobody has a compass here right?" asked Easton.

"Annak's never needed a compass," said Nathan, "it's inside of him."

Annak quickly picked a tunnel and started down it. Nathan followed, but was still unsettled. It was difficult to shake off the uncertainty of what lie ahead of them. Even after everything he had seen — the miracles, the fact that they were not dead yet — all he had to go on was the peculiar chance that Iris was being led by the Navigator's voice. Nothing more, nothing less. Yet even then, the spiritual inclination of Iris was troubling at times. They were low on water, low on food, and now they were on foot. Iris led them to a point where they were forced to abandon the Crawlers, and now the question lingered in Nathan's mind: *How are we supposed to make it back to Adullum eight hundred miles on foot?* Nathan groped for an answer. Running through the tunnels, thoughts raced. *Trust? How can I continue trusting you? All these years. All this time. All I've done is trust you, Grandma. And what have I gotten? Unanswered questions.* Nathan was beginning to sense that Iris knew more — way, way more about the world than he was aware of. This was obvious given her age, but what she knew was not necessarily what bothered him, it had to do with what she was withholding — the secrets she was keeping. Her reserved quietness was troubling him. Even though Iris had saved his life back at the dam, Nathan could not ignore the fact that he felt like their relationship was diminishing.

□

Rook circled around the two Crawler's abandoned in the subway station. "Where did they get these?" he asked

Gabriel did not care to respond. He and the others were spreading out, carefully sweeping the place. Gabriel knew they were close, oddly feeling as though they were right under his feet.

"They're here," said Gabriel. "There's no way they could've gotten out of here."

The rest of the Screeners scoured and searched the station from corner to corner, ceiling to floor; overturning everything in sight, and found no one. Hours passed. Gabriel's rage deepened. His leather cowboy boots were dirty and bloodied. In his left arm he carried a freshly loaded pistol, while he held his wounded arm close to his belly. The adrenaline of the hunt was still serving as an anesthetic.

"Gabriel," said Rook, "we've searched the entire tunnel. The street's caved in at the other end. The only way out of here is the way they came in."

Gabriel was puzzled. He looked over at the damaged subway train derailed from the tracks with all its windows broken out. "You look there?"

"Searched it already," answered Rook.

Gabriel was quiet for a moment. "You checked behind every door?"

"Every door," answered Rook.

"Every door?" Gabriel asked again.

Rook paused for a second, "Well yes, but…"

"But?"

"Except for one." Rook pointed across the way, "The refrigerator door in that restaurant." Rook got a resilient look on his face as if to imply the obvious, *there's no way all of them could fit inside that refrigerator.*

Without concession, Gabriel immediately made his way toward the small restaurant until he was face to face with the refrigerator door. Holding his pistol straight out in front of him, he kicked open the latch. The walk-in fridge was empty. In spite of that, Gabriel stepped in and examined every square inch. Then, standing still in the middle of the small seven-by-seven square room, he noticed his boots made a hollowing sound over part of the floor. Slowly pressing his chin to his chest, he looked down and saw the trap door. He moved aside and looked at Rook. "Open it," he said.

Rook had a sinister smirk on his face like he was drooling to kill someone. Right away he crouched down and pulled open the door. The other Screeners pressed in to see what was going on. Admiring the underground passage, Rook was baffled.

Gabriel, on the other hand, was already pushing Rook out of the way and climbing down the wooden ladder with one hand, his boots hitting the cold dirt at the bottom. Unwilling to stop until they were found, he picked a direction and started moving down one of the tunnels. The rest of the Screeners followed suit.

TWENTY THREE
Snake Oil

The tempo of panting was like music within the walls. The darkened tunnels twisted throughout the underground of Old Town like a maze. Their lights intermittently lit up areas lined with thick dark clay, occasional rotted wood posts and various masonry retaining walls — all made from English bond-brick and mortar, pieced in with a collage of cobble stones and morsels of rock. At every turn, the place was strange and unwelcoming.

Annak and Iris seemed to have the most vitality, both of them racing at the front while the others made every effort to keep up. There was no time to talk. Not enough energy. They had been running though the tunnels for hours. Nathan could only hope Annak knew where he was going.

Apparently and intuitively moving southward, Annak was constantly making decisions on whether to go left or right. His focus was determined until he heard a loud clap just behind him. *Thud!* It was Nathan. His body hit the ground, sending his warm face smacking into the dirt. His dry tongue draped slightly from his mouth as he closed his eyes.

"Hold up!" Max called to the front, stopping and kneeling down next to Nathan's limp body. Max slapped his face a couple of times, "Come on man!" Nathan looked as if he had been knocked out, his eyelids twitching and his eyes rolling back into his head. "Nathan!" Max called again, "get up!" Nathan's clothes were damp with sweat and dirt. "Nathan!" Slowly, he came to and tried to open his eyes, but his vision was blurred.

Iris drew near, knelt down, and with her thumb and index finger she squeezed Nathan's cracked lips and forced them to pucker. Then, lifting his head, from one of her small containers she poured a few drops of water into his mouth. The water was quickly absorbed by his lips, then trickled down his throat like it was pure gold.

Nathan almost forgot how to drink, he choked. "I got nothing left," he mumbled.

"You can't quit," said Iris. "Not now."

Nathan did not have the strength to say anything more. He slumped his head to the side and laid there quietly looking off into dark space. Barely able to see, his attention was tempted by something. Trying to lift his head, he looked more intently down one of the tunnels. Without saying anything he pointed at what appeared to be a room. Iris looked in the same direction and aimed her light. Through an opening in the brick, headed off by a steel ledger, there were crates lined up inside along the wall. Annak did not miss a beat. He walked right into the room and broke open one of the crates.

"You need to see this," Annak called back to Iris, before breaking open another crate, and then another.

Iris got up and walked toward Annak. She entered the room and looked around. There was stuff stacked up to the ceilings all along the walls. There was an aged cast iron cauldron situated at an angle within a makeshift blacked out brick fireplace. A huge tarnished wood burning furnace was in one corner, surrounded by an array of nostalgic artifacts, all cluttered and in disunity. There was a baby carriage situated on top of four handmade wooden wagon wheels, an old rocking horse with faded turquoise lead paint, dirty mason jars, a wood carving of a Native American Indian hunting atop a horse, and tarnished garden tools. Decrepit copper plumbing pipes lined the walls, intermixed with shelves that held various crates and scraps of metal. Large distillery cylinders were tipped over on the ground. Chairs, easily more than a couple hundred years old, and mattresses were piled up throughout the room.

Annak nudged her on the shoulder and directed her attention to one of the open crates. "Look," he said.

Iris reached inside an pulled out a glass bottle, dusted it off and read the aged label, *Genuine Snake Oil - 1945.*

"Alcohol," said Annak, looking surprised.

On the antiqued label stuck to the glass was the small depiction of a medieval door knocker — a troll's face holding a ring in its mouth with a snake swirled around it. Iris put the bottle down then rummaged through the rest of the crate only to find more and more of the same. The crates were full of it.

"If only it was water," noted Iris.

Annak lifted another crate off the ground and set it on top of the pile. He and Iris looked inside, this time not seeing bottles but bags of unopened white rice. A few more crates were full of the same.

Easton walked in, "Unbelievable!" he exclaimed.

Alex followed right behind, "No way!" He picked up a bottle of the old clear liquid and kissed it, the bottle leaving a residue of dust across his lips.

Max pushed them all out of the way and beheld the crates. He was speechless for a moment and then yelled back at Nathan, "You gotta get in here!" Yet Nathan was still too weak to move.

There was a new excitement that rushed upon everyone. Annak rummaged through more crates and boxes. More alcohol, more rice. Alex and Max did the same. It was not until Annak reached the bottom of one of the piles that he discovered stacks and stacks of tightly packed sardine cans inside one of the crates. There was not time to wait; he pulled out his knife, cut open the can and scarfed down a mouthful of slimy, salty fish.

"Here!" said Annak, as he sorted through the cans and started tossing them throughout the room. He opened another can and handed it to Iris. She closed her eyes in a moment of silence, poured the tiny fish down her throat and then consumed the residual oil from the can.

No matter how much delight was breaking out inside the room, Nathan's body was frozen stuck to the cold dirt of the tunnel floor. All the racket, the slurping, the moaning and grunting, tickled his ears but was not enough to move him. Motionless, he lay there with his eyes closed, starting to shiver, his sweat turning cool until finally he was startled by Alex's voice.

"Open your mouth, man!" said Alex. Nathan did not respond. Alex was too thrilled to be patient. Without permission he cracked open Nathan's mouth and slapped a slimy sardine onto his tongue, then finished it off with a handful of uncooked rice. Nathan felt like someone had spit a massive loogie into his chops and then threw sand in it. With hardly any strength, he chewed the best he could with a stiff, rigid jaw. But soon he started to choke. Alex immediately pulled him into the upright position and swatted him on the back a few times. Nathan threw up. Alex just took it as a sign to feed him more food, "Eat, man! Eat!" he cheered.

Slowly, swallow after swallow, Nathan started to look less like a torture victim of Alex's childishness. His strength began to return. "Gimme some more of that!" Nathan begged, asking not so much for more rice, but for fish. He snatched the can out of Alex's hand. Alex gave it up with delight, as well as the bottle of glistening cold liquid. Nathan gulped and chugged the stuff like it was water.

Soon, Annak could not help but notice what was happing outside the room, and rushed into the tunnel. "Whoa! Easy!" he interrupted, ripping the bottle out of Nathan's hand. Annak looked at both of them like they were two kids greedily devouring a chocolate cake. "You guys want to be sicker than sick? You have any idea how much alcohol is in this stuff?"

"It's drinkable, right?" Alex stuttered.

"It's not for the faint of heart is what it is," answered Annak. "Just take it easy."

"Well, I'm thirsty!" cried Nathan. "Give it back!"

"No!" declared Annak. "You'll be sick to death!"

"Guys!" Easton yelled from inside the room. "Hurry!"

Alex and Annak pulled Nathan up off the ground and helped carry him into the room, Nathan's legs were still numb. When they got in, Iris's light shone on Easton. He was in the back corner by the furnace holding up two large glass jars sealed with a tin lid, each two gallons worth. They both appeared to be filled with water.

"Just found these! Can you believe it?" said Easton.

Right away Max, Easton, and Nathan started grappling with one another to get a drink.

"HEY! HEY!" shouted Iris. "Everybody stop it!" She forced her way into the middle of them and grabbed the jars.

They all calmed down and then in a quiet, awkward moment could not help noticing Alex — he was in his own world, head cocked back, swigging a bottle of alcohol, trying to quench a thirst that was seemingly unquenchable. With the tip of the bottle still pressed against his lips, he sensed everyone staring at him, and then with a funny look on his face, lowered the bottle and asked, "What?" He saw Annak shaking his head, "You guys act like we haven't been living on crap for the last...how many years? This place is a goldmine!"

Iris kept staring at him, "You're no good to us if you get sick."

"Alright, alright," Alex responded, he kept the bottle

in his hand, but did not bring it back up to his mouth.

There was a plethora of Mason jars in the room. Iris randomly picked six of them and set them on top of the furnace. One at a time, she filled each one a quarter full of water. "Let's make this last," she said. "No telling what's ahead of us." She passed out the water.

Everyone was quiet, no one wanted to speak. They all held the water in their hands and embraced the sacred moment. It was shocking to have stumbled upon such ample supplies in the underground slums of Portland.

"We should toast or something," said Alex.

"I think so," said Max.

One by one they raised their jars in the air, tapped, and then drank away. The water was sharp and old, but it was good. It was water.

Trying to enjoy his water, between sips, Annak looked over at Alex and laughed. Alex was trying not to break his teeth while chewing the hard rice. "You're going to be constipated," said Annak. Alex's hunger was too possessive, he did not care. He kept chewing. A short lived humor made itself present in their midst. A strike of joy pierced everyone's hearts while just for a moment they all became ignorant of the world they lived in.

Annak finished half of his water, walked over to the cauldron, took a piece of torn cloth from the ground, and wiped it out. "Get me some wood," he said as he hung the pot back on the hook protruding from the brick wall. Alex and Max grabbed a couple wooden chairs and broke them down, making a pile underneath the pot. Annak ripped open a bag of rice, poured it into the pot and then flooded it with bottles of alcohol.

Looking for some kindling, it did not take Alex long to find a stack of vintage newspapers inside the baby carriage. He picked one off the top. *October 9th, 1925.* The title to the

article read: *Portland's Shanghai Tunnels! Myth or Reality!*
"Crazy," said Alex, "looks like the very same room we're standing in." He held up the clipping and showed the picture; it was a blurry, black and white photograph of what appeared to be the same room they had just discovered. "Well, I couldn't care less about history right now, I'm hungry," he said, handing the newspaper to Annak. Annak crinkled it up and stuffed it into the small pile of wood and then lit it.

There was a mattress leaning against one of the walls, Nathan knocked it over and then flopped his exhausted body onto it.

"So what is this place anyway?" asked Max.

"My grandma will tell you, she knows everything," Nathan barked, with a hint of sarcasm.

Annak crouched down beside the boiling cauldron, the fire underneath it making the room glow. Alex handed him a bottle of alcohol, motioning for him to take sip as some sort of celebration drink offering.

"Not for me," said Annak.

"You serious?" said Alex. "This stuff's amazing!"

"Don't care," answered Annak. "Don't drink."

"You telling me if this was your last day on earth, you wouldn't drink this?"

"Nope," said Annak.

Alex grumbled, not understanding Annak's position, and somewhat offended by Annak's refusal to join in his sprightly binge.

"You gonna tell us or not?" asked Nathan, nodding at Iris. "How'd you know all this was down here?"

Iris was sitting in one of the old oak chairs, leaning her head back, still sipping her glass of water, and eating sardines. "I don't know," she answered.

Nathan was quiet for a minute then piped up again, "How do you explain the odds? You take us to a dead end corner in an abandoned subway station and then…you just happen to find a doorway in the floor? And now here we are in a room filled with supplies?"

"It happened back at the gas station by the dam," she answered.

"What did?" asked Nathan.

"When we were back there…while you guys were worrying about the Gnats flying overhead, I was invoking the Navigator — asking Him where to go, calling out the One who I know always knows the way."

Nathan did not have to question Iris's sincerity, he knew she was not kidding. For her, faith in the unseen had seven times the substance of what was seen, probably more. Still, he found himself shaking his head.

Iris looked at him. "I hope you're seeing things by now, Nathan. You wouldn't be eating fish and drinking that water if it weren't for Him."

"We would've gone right past this room if I hadn't fainted out there."

"Two ways to see a circumstance, Nathan," said Iris. "He uses our weakness at the right time to lead us to a banquet. Our frailty slows us down so that we don't miss His provision." Iris moved away from her theological stance and shifted back to the story, "Before we left the gas station I saw a series of visions, each one lasting no more than five seconds. That metal trap door in the floor? That was the first vision. Then I saw the refrigerator opening, then an image of the sushi bar." Everyone listened intently to Iris's explanation. Max and Alex were slightly more shocked than the rest.

Iris continued, "I saw that subway station sign that was out there near the stairwell. After that I saw the street corner, and lastly, the Oregon sign with the deer on it. That was it."

"You saw everything in reverse?" asked Easton.

"What do you mean?" questioned Max.

"She saw every marker, backwards in the order we discovered it," answered Easton.

"That's how He speaks to me," said Iris, "doesn't show me everything...just enough."

"Iris, you didn't know these tunnels were here?" asked Annak.

"No, I just saw the visions, same way I discovered Adullum," she answered.

"You mean to tell me, you know nothing, absolutely nothing about the history of these tunnels?" Annak questioned again, with more curiosity.

"Nothing," she said, rather composed.

Annak shook his head in amazement. "You certainly are a *seer*," he said, "always have been."

Nathan's arms were folded behind his head as he relaxed on the grubby mattress, "Annak? So you know what this place is?"

"Didn't know they existed until now, but yes," he answered. "The Shanghai Tunnels — I'd only heard myths about this underground world. When I was stationed here off the Pacific, guys would joke around about Portland's dark culture underneath the streets. I never believed them."

"What about it?" asked Nathan.

"It's not pretty," answered Annak. He poked his head into the pot to see how the rice was coming along and poured more alcohol into it. "These tunnels were dug for the purposes of kidnapping and running a black market. It was called *shanghaiing*. They would capture people and sell them illegally to the captain of a ship when they needed crewmen."

"Slavery," mumbled Easton.

"Yeah," added Annak, "but supposedly they weren't

just black slaves, they took anybody. The ships would then head off toward the Orient and the slaves would work for free without pay. There's supposed to be basements all over this city under hotels and bars that link all these tunnels together. Illegal goods, like that Snake Oil, were moved all over the place. Underground. Out of sight. If the myths are true, then all these tunnels eventually lead to the Willamette River Basin, where the old shipyards used to be."

"These tunnels were for kidnapping?" Alex looked disgusted. "That's messed up!"

"Men and woman both," answered Annak, "most of them sold for no more than fifty bucks a head."

"I knew there was a reason I never liked big cities," said Nathan.

"Either way, the tunnels once meant for evil, have become our refuge," added Iris.

"So what about this room?" questioned Nathan.

"Gang bosses," answered Annak, "those in charge of drugging and kidnapping slaves and moving product, would use these rooms to keep prisoners until they sold them. That's why all this is down here. I just always thought this place was imaginary. It's hard to believe these provisions have gone undiscovered until now."

As Alex continued to drink from one of the bottles, an unease came over him. All of the sudden the alcohol did not taste so good. He did not like the thought of sharing the same bottles as those cold-hearted thugs. "I don't feel well," he moaned, knowing that most of what he was feeling had nothing to do with remorse, but the onset of alcohol poisoning.

"I told you," said Annak.

Suddenly Alex hurled chunks of fish and rice all over the floor. After a period of wailing he collapsed on the ground and moaned in pain the rest of the night.

"I think I'm all done with that too," echoed Max, as he put his bottle down.

"There's no way they can find us down here, right?" asked Nathan.

"There's no way!" said Easton. "How can the Screeners know about this place?

"I don't think anyone does," added Max.

"Probably not," said Annak.

Iris had a fleeting memory about Gabriel and was reminded how clever he was — persistent as a ravenous fox. "Hope not," she said.

"Don't think we should stay here too long though," said Annak.

"I just need one night of sleep," cried Nathan. "I can't go on any further. I can't even think straight."

"Did you ever think straight?" joked Alex as he continued rolling around on the floor, moaning and clutching his arms around his belly.

"I don't think you're in much of a position to say anything," answered Nathan.

"I need to sleep, too," said Max.

Annak did not like the idea of staying overnight; he wanted to rest briefly and then keep moving. He was conflicted. "What do you think, Iris?" he asked.

"Maybe not the whole night, but for a little while," she said.

"Alright," said Annak. "Just for a little bit. The rice is done. Throw me some of those empty cans." Without delay a pile of empty cans were at Annak's feet, everyone seemingly still starving. One by one he scooped out the steaming rice and passed it out.

Immediately, Max stuck his fingers into the rice and stuffed his mouth, "Definitely much better cooked," he mumbled.

"I think Alex will be able to keep his teeth now," joked Nathan.

"Eating that hard rice reminds me of the first time I had sunflower seeds," said Max. "I was just a little kid, no one told me you had to break the shell first and only eat the seed. Well, I ate the whole bag — shell and all! I couldn't go to the bathroom for two days!"

"That's torture!" laughed Easton.

After a while, everybody was able to settle down a bit, joking casually as they immersed themselves in the provisions.

"So Easton?" asked Nathan, "How did you do that?"

Easton was busily eating his rice, using one of his sardines as a utensil, "Do what?" he replied.

"Your voice," said Nathan.

Easton tried his best to respond with a mouth full of food, small grains of rice falling down his chest, "Not sure I have an answer for you," he said honestly.

Iris did not look surprised at Easton's response.

"What do you mean?" asked Nathan.

"Whatever it is that happens when I open my mouth, I still don't understand it. Never did. All I know is what I feel — like there's a lion that grabs me by the throat and then starts to roar."

"Has to be one of the craziest things I've seen," said Alex, "and felt," he added regretfully.

"Could you always sing?" Nathan asked.

"Actually, no. I had a stuttering problem, got made fun of a lot when I was a kid. My throat was always raspy and embarrassing so I stayed quiet most of the time to hide from people's remarks. Besides, we never played music in my house — too much fighting and yelling going on for that." Easton took a few more handfuls of food into his mouth. "Then one day, after I received the Blue Flame, I went to talk and the only thing I could get out was a song — no stuttering, no nothing, just a melody. It scared me to death though, like I was possessed by something I couldn't control. Took a long time, but now I can handle it to an extent. It's not something I like to tell everyone, so I keep it to myself."

Iris spoke up, "You're the only one of your kind I've ever seen with my own eyes. When you first came up to me at Adullum, just by standing next to you, I could hear the melodies inside you. Melodies...melodies unlike anything I've ever heard before. You know, a long, long time ago, people endowed with your gift used to be the *elite*. When going into battle, the people on the front lines weren't the archers or the ones carrying the swords or the foot soldiers. No, the *singers* were the ones who led the army into battle! And as they marched forward with their mouths open, a great trembling would move through the ground: walls would crumble, the enemy would panic, unseen angelic atmospheres would be unleashed, thick places in the unseen realm would suddenly be made thin. As the *singers* marched, no one could stand in their way. Without shooting a single arrow into the sky, whole armies would be laid low by the voices of the Navigator's anointed. Just like you Easton, there used to be thousands just like you — all carrying the same gift, the same roar."

By now Easton had stopped eating and was listening to Iris's encouraging words; they meant a lot to him. Easton had seen his gift ruin people and did not always feel proud of what he carried.

"What do you mean *thick* places becoming *thin*?" asked Nathan.

Iris answered, "*Thick* places are where mankind has set up stout walls between itself and the spiritual world. *Thick* places are where victims are entrenched in vice and immorality, where men trust in their own naive intellect, where they refuse to abandon themselves to anything greater than themselves. *Thin* places are where the boundaries between our world and the spiritual world of the Navigator have been loosened, broken open. When a singer opens their mouth, in that very location something's cut loose, like the rope anchoring a ship to its dock. Easton's voice alone has the power to command pneumatic activity and to release the supernatural power of the Blue Flame.

"Wait a second," said Max, "pneumatic?"

"*Pneuma*," declared Iris, "they're the Navigator's angelic army."

"I don't believe that," said Nathan. "I've never seen one of those my entire life!"

"You're still young," answered Iris. "They're all over the place, hundreds of thousands of them, all commissioned and functioning within twelve different tribes, coming and going between earth and heaven."

"What do you mean *tribes*? Twelve?" asked Max.

"Tribes represented by twelve precious stones of the earth, all of them functioning with a different purpose, yet in complete unity," answered Iris. "Jasper, sapphire, agate, emerald, onyx, carnelian, chrysolite, beryl, topaz, chrysoprase, jacinth, and amethyst."

"*Ame-what*?" retorted Alex. "Never knew half those existed! What's the point?"

"Too much to explain in one night," said Iris, "but the strongest of the twelve is the *Onyx* tribe, it represents purity. The Onyx-Pneuma were created with such fine appearance that they eventually fell in love with themselves. Pride crept into their hearts and stole their allegiance to the Navigator — they became plagued by narcissism. Because they refused His authority, they were sent to earth and permitted never again to enter the courts of the Navigator's presence. All those belonging to the Onyx tribe have since been denounced and renamed Sarx."

When she said that, Nathan had flashbacks of the familiar demon running alongside them in the trees. For a moment, he could even smell the stench of the thing's breath. "Stuff just gets more and more complex with you, Grandma."

"Sorry, Nathan. I didn't make these rules and I didn't write the story. Theres a whole unseen world out there, and I can't pretend like it doesn't exist. Those couple days I was out there in the mountains fighting for your soul, you know who tended to me?" Nathan looked at her with peaked interest. "Pneuma," she said. "As soon as you're ready to open your eyes, son, as soon as you're ready, there's a whole other playground waiting for you. There's entire hosts of Pneuma waiting to come to the aid of those who are ready to fulfill their calling. Annak has the gift of healing! Easton has the gift of singing! And you? Who knows what gift is waiting for you once you surrender your life to the One who made you. His hands are open to you, Nathan. A whole treasure chest of doves is waiting to escape, when you're ready. Only when you're ready. Same for you, Max…Alex."

Nathan was unresponsive. As he lay there he looked up at the clay ceiling and pondered her words. *Maybe,* he thought to himself, *maybe.*

"Onyx?" asked Easton. "That's the name of the one who leads the Screeners."

"Yes," said Iris.

"Is that just coincidence?" asked Easton.

Iris continued, "For every human agenda on the earth, theres a spiritual one behind it. The Sarx of the Onyx tribe have been crawling the land for years and years, whispering their purposes into the ears of anyone willing to listen. Geospark is perhaps their crowning achievement — a company of demonic puppets."

"Why'd one of them come after me?" asked Nathan.

"Wait, you've seen one of these things?" asked Alex, excitedly. Nathan looked back at him, reluctant, and not proud of the fact.

"Unfortunately," he grumbled, his face half hidden behind the dirty color of his jacket.

"Why haven't you said anything?" Alex asked again.

"Trust me, it's not something to brag about. Wish I never would have encountered that *thing*," answered Nathan.

"Why haven't I seen one?" complained Alex.

Iris interjected, responding to Nathan's earlier question, "They lean in on the plans of the Navigator and try to destroy those with a destiny."

"Oh, nice," joked Alex, "I feel very important now. Only important people get pinned, huh?"

"But if you can influence an entire corporation like Geospark why waste the time going after one man?" asked Nathan.

"Because one person entirely filled with the Blue Flame, can do more in a day than a spiritually empty corporation can in years," she answered.

"No one could have ever imagined what Geospark would do to this land, no one!" exclaimed Nathan. "It's gonna take a lot more than one person to undo the greedy mess they've made…if it can undone at all."

"It can," answered Iris, "but not if people don't realize who they are…and who they're called to be."

Nathan rolled his eyes back into his head, just the conversation about the Sarx was making him squirm. There was not much that intimidated him, but that *thing* did. "I'm just sick and tired of this so called *spiritual world* trying to mess me up," he complained. "I mean, aren't there boundaries between us and them? Why can't I just figure things out on my own?"

"There are, son. And you can," responded Iris, "but sometimes, the boundary lines get blurred. If someone is turned in on themselves enough, in their own pride, they place themselves outside the Navigator's protection."

"Protection?" Nathan barked. "How exactly do you define *protection*? Losing the lake? Losing the land? Millions of people starving to death? Thirsting to death? Having no access to clean water? You call my mom and dad being murdered *protection*? Looks to me like I was always outside His protection — if it exists at all."

Annak sipped on his water and kept quiet by the fire. The others did the same, resting, listening in. Iris sighed, then spoke up again. "Nathan," she said calmly, "you can ask all the questions you want, tens of thousands of questions. You can yell 'em, kick 'em, scream 'em and spew 'em from your mouth. But until the light's turned on, you won't get any answers." Iris paused for a moment before continuing, "All the answers you want, reside in His will. And you can't get His will until He gets yours first. The best thing you can do in the dark is hold still and ask for help."

"So what about *that* Screener, what did you say his name was?" Nathan asked as he looked over at Easton.

"Gabriel," replied Easton.

"When Easton sang," added Nathan, "why wasn't that man affected by his voice? Grandma, thought you said everyone without the Blue Flame was crippled by Easton's gift." Iris closed her eyes and put her head down, as if to communicate the fact that Gabriel was someone she really did not want in the room at the moment, not even by means of conversation. "So?"

Reluctantly, she felt compelled to respond, "Once you receive the Spirit, you never lose it."

"You're telling me — that scum, that piece of crap, who kills helpless, innocent people, who works for Onyx, selfishly guarding the waterways — has the Blue Flame?" argued Nathan.

Iris refused to say anything.

"I just don't believe that," added Nathan. "That sicko deserves to rot and be eaten by worms! Once you're a Screener you can never go back." Nathan leaned forward and sat upright on the mattress, "And how'd you even know who that was?"

"I really don't know how to tell you," she answered. "It's just not the right time."

"Well, when is *the right time*?" asked Nathan. "Annak, I know you shot him in the arm on purpose. Almost like you and Iris communicated beforehand and she told you not to kill him." Annak just stared back at him silently. "You guys and your secrets, you're just as bad as they are!" Nathan's face was well ignited with intensity by now. He sat upright. For a split second he imagined himself throwing his glass jar clear across the room and watching it shatter against the brick. Answers that evaded him still triggered rage. "You going to tell me or not?"

Iris listened to his plea; she thought about it. A surplus of reactions, consequences, memories, doubts, fears rushed through her head like cold water. She knew things could not go on like this forever. Nathan had a right; he had claim to the answer. He had every reason to feel what he felt. Nonetheless, one small sliver of unease settled in Iris's gut and she found it hard to answer. "I don't know, Nathan. Not here. Not now."

Nathan took a few deep breaths and leaned back. He looked around, seeing Easton, Max, Alex, and Annak all staring at him before refocusing again on Iris. "I've always loved you, Grandma. I've always trusted you. I've always followed you." Nathan thought about what to say next, a whirlwind of gritty emotions turning inside him. "As long as you're holding your secrets back, there will always be a part of me I'll hold back from the Navigator."

In the moment, Iris did not want to say anything. She did not feel like pursuing Nathan in any way. Instead she considered the blame that was upon her shoulders for how she had tried to raise him. And for a second she became aware of the fact that maybe she was responsible for so much of Nathan's struggle for truth. She and she alone knew the reason why she withheld so much from him, even at the cost of vexing his inner confusion. The day caught up to her and she became tired. Nathan knew by the look on her face that he would not hear another word from her the rest of the night.

The others continued to enjoy the provisions until their bellies were beyond satisfied. A hush fell throughout the room. The mood settled down on its own, except for the occasional slip of a sardine down a throat and the pressing of teeth on rice. Alex knocked out, sleeping sideways as his head rested on his inner bicep with his arm stretched out and the other flung the opposite way. Easton laid on his back, the stack of old newspapers underneath his neck, his hand folded perfectly across his chest, sleeping so quietly it appeared he was dead. Max, with his stout body, fell asleep sitting down, both forearms leaning on each knee and his head slouched low, causing his blonde hair to drape across his face. Nathan sat there watching one by one as each person drifted off to wherever they go at night — dreams, nightmares, black. Yet Annak just sat still next to the fire, his eyes intent on the flames, his body motionless as stone, seemingly far from falling asleep. Eventually Nathan fatigued from watching him and closed his eyes.

TWENTY FOUR
The Scroll

Nathan's eyes were closed. There was no telling what time it was or how long he had been asleep. His mind was somewhere distant, somewhere uncomfortable. All he could see was the helpless face of Silas — his cheek bones and eyebrows cringed as the explosion flung his exposed body over the side of the bridge, and in slow motion thrashed him against the river rocks. His back was broken, his arms went limp. Nathan pressed up against the railing and looked down below, searching for a way to help him, wishing the event could have been reversed. Yet all he could see standing there beside Silas's mangled body, was the Sarx happily watching over the tragedy in pure approval of the gruesome death. The Sarx snarled and grinned in celebration.

Nathan could not believe the same dark principality he had encountered at Adullum — the *levitator,* the *breath taker* — was now staring up at him as he watched his friend's decimation by a Screener Gnat. Like a professional undertaker, the Sarx was smiling, laughing with a sinister scold, pointing his finger at Nathan, twitching madly, as if to say, *You're next!* Its eyes cut through every sense of security and peace that Nathan desperately tried to cling to. In fear and disgust Nathan tried to look away, but could not seem to peel his eyes from the scene. It was as if something was holding him there, preventing him from running.

Then, without warning the Sarx yawned, not as though *it* were tired, but as though it were unleashing something from inside itself, and exhaled a modest draft of black smoke. No larger than the size of a man's fist, the smoke moved upwards toward Nathan and then turned into a mass of flying locusts. Just before being engulfed by them, Nathan covered his face and everything went black.

Soon, in a moment of timelessness, like a flare had been lit in a dark room, the scene changed. A scroll opened up within a whirlwind of particles, seemingly unseen static, electrical currents, and airwaves of a metaphysical atmosphere yet to be comprehended by human eyes. Shafts of light, large and small, were all over the place. Light spread out like countless veins from a pounding heart. Whatever the place was. A realm? A sphere? Nathan was inside of it, not so much forced, but brought. The unfolding scroll was alluring, more than anything else, and was arrayed with a litany of blurred words exuding with red ink. Nathan moved closer to it, somehow knowing that it had not been written by human hands, and finding himself so attracted to the scroll that it was as though it was nothing less than one of his own missing bodily organs. As he approached the scroll some of the words came into focus, none of them on a single line, but scattered, crisscrossed, encircling one another. He did his best to read:

Marked at birth
Destined to reign
Formed for Glory
Fashioned for Fury
Dead Raiser

And then, more words flooded the scroll; sentences, declarations, phrases all intertwined with one another and spinning like a myriad of intersecting wheels, yet none of them crashing into one another. In an instant, Nathan perceived the words were not just *words* — the words were WORLDS. Worlds that were seemingly in womb form, alive, living organisms, potential realities yet to be discovered. As he read he could feel the pulse of each one, bursting with life, each word holding a universe like an atom holds energy.

Instantaneously, more words and phrases appeared and disappeared, without permission, sporadically. Without communication, without a personal commentator, Nathan knew he was in the presence of something, and in his soul could sense that the scroll was the totality of all his moments — past, present, and future. Yet no sooner did he receive the revelation of what he was looking at, the words disappeared. And after a moment of blackness, on the scroll, appeared three rivers; separated by columns, containing three sets of new words. The words were on the waters and underneath the surface, flowing, drifting like foam. Nathan was caught off guard and could not seem to understand what was going on, but found himself watching the unfolding scene, speechless and spellbound.

The first river was murky — its waters dark, and its current strong. Yet Nathan could read the flowing words and sentences in it clearly. There was a rainbow-like banner over it, yet colorless, that bore the name, *BITTER*. Underneath it the words streamed and formed a lamentation, laying out a series of events in Nathan's life that tore up his heart, that disappointed him — his worst memories, his most wretched hours. They spoke of the time he almost drowned in the lake, sinking like an anchor down to the bottom with all the rest of the decomposing salmon graves. The day his parents disappeared from his life. The time he broke his leg falling from a cliff in Northern Stanley. The first time he ever saw Reapers die, shot to death by Screeners. There was more, much more; the list went on as the river kept flowing, seemingly boundless and unrestrained.

The second river was less murky than the first but still dirty. The banner over it was named, *SWEET*. In its current flowed phrases and sentences that recounted Nathan's most treasured moments, the ones he thought held the most significance and value. His childish attempts to climb Rock Man. Running through the forest with the family hounds — Chub and Nino, wrestling with them in the newly fallen pine needles as they slobbered all over his face. There were the moments when his mother held him and read him books, sang to him. Nathan watched as other memories drifted by. Yet as he tried to read the words in the second river, they were less clear than the words in the first, even though the water in the first river was darker.

Then as if he knew to move on, his eyes set on the last river — it was like champagne, as lucid as a glacial river, clearer than glass. It flowed wonderfully and swiftly, yet without rapids or eddies. There was a blue tint to the water, and as the sun reflected off its surface it looked as if there were threads of flaming azure and sapphire weaving in and out of it. The river was stunning, unearthly. Yet unlike the first two rivers, it was nameless. And rather than flowing side by side with the first two rivers, the third river formed where the first two forked and was composed of both their waters, flowing as one divine river. Captivated, Nathan slowly started to see the words spilling down from the horizon. Soon there were sentences and phrases all over the place, but no matter how hard he tried he could not read them — they were too blurry and convoluted, even though the water was the clearest of all three rivers. He rubbed his eyes, squinted and looked again, but to no avail. Unlike the first two rivers, every word in the water of the third river was uninterpretable and sadly, beyond Nathan's comprehension.

After repeated attempts, unable to read the words, Nathan became anxious and found himself crying out for justice, calling out for someone to claim responsibility, someone to hand him the keys of interpretation so he could read the words. Complaining to the point of exhaustion, now well beyond a frustrating panic, Nathan heard a thundering voice speak over the waters concerning the third river, *Outcome of first two rivers, as seen through hope, or despair.* No sooner did he hear the voice that he saw a banner shoot out across the river, bearing the name, *MY REDEMPTION,* followed by the sudden appearance of two shadowy figures standing on the shore, their outline alluding to the presence of a woman and a small child, though he could not make out their expressions or details. For some reason Nathan did not pay much attention to them, his eyes simply diverting back to the water.

Nathan was stunned. By now the river had run beyond the edge of the scroll and was flooding the space where Nathan stood. He was barefoot and could feel the water quickly trickling in between his toes and running up his heels. All at once he was in turmoil over the third river, yet at the same time desirous of it at a level that was deeper than words. There was something divinely terrifying — yet wonderfully attractive — about the third river. Nathan stood there looking into its waters and felt something hard bump into his shins. Surprised, he peered down and saw an antiquated canoe with no oars. There was no question as to whether or not he should get in, the choice was his. Yet just as his foot stepped over the bow, without warning, the waters receded and shriveled up.

All of the sudden, the rivers and the words were gone and all Nathan could see was an unwelcoming sight — two crippled, rotting hands that ruthlessly rolled up the scroll. Catching only a glimpse of the sickly fingers, boney knuckles and pale skin; Nathan knew whoever it was, lacked reverence for his life and viewed the scroll like it was nothing more than a newspaper about to be used for fly-killing and then tossed into the trash. Nathan's eyes followed the arms connected to the hands, upwards to the shoulders, then the neck, then ultimately to the nightmarish face of the Sarx.

Then all at once, no sooner did he see its face that Nathan had the feeling his feet were set in a block of concrete. He tried to move but was unable to. With nowhere to go, he watched, victimized by the Sarx stuffing the scroll into *its* mouth and eating it. Then, chewing but not swallowing, the demon pulled from its lips the regurgitated scroll in the form of one word, *MISERY*.

Nathan held still as the Sarx held MISERY in its hands and then hurled it at him as if it were a spear. The word flew through the air. Immediately, just as Nathan felt the tip of it hit his chest, he woke up only to realize a blitz of sickness rushing through his body. His limbs were shaking uncontrollably, cold sweat pouring from his brow, his breathing staggered and intermittent. Delirious and not knowing where he was, with barely enough strength to lift his head, Nathan looked around and slowly realized he was still in the thug chamber of the Portland tunnels. As soon as he was reminded of the reality of his location, the back of his head hit the cold dirt again. Feeling as though there was a five hundred pound weight on his chest, he knew his temperature was well over 107 degrees. He mindlessly passed in and out of consciousness, fading back and forth between reality and darkness. He groped for a cornerstone, some reference point from which he could *come to,* something familiar. Yet, rapidly opening and closing his eyes, the only thing he could make out was the silhouette of Iris's face. Her long silvery grey hair draped low as it covered her eyes and rubbed across his forehead. She was bowed over him, chanting, saying things in an uncommon language and prophesying. Nathan was too unaware and out of reach to understand much of it, but occasionally, her determined, poetic, broken language would fall back into English where Nathan could decipher just a few of her vocal convictions.

"You will live and not die...you will live and not

die…you will live and not die!" she declared over and over again.

Nathan — black out. Nothing.

"I break the stronghold of all curses against you…I break! I break all curses!"

Black out. Nothing.

"Where You go, he will go! What You say, he will say!"

Black out. Nothing.

"Revive!"

Black out.

"Revive!"

Nothing.

It was evident Iris knew what was going on. The Sarx's curse was still waging war against Nathan's soul, yet she was unreserved and bold in her pronouncements against it, "Revive him according to Your purposes! Take his heart of stone and make it flesh! Make it flesh! Flesh! Flesh! All of You, none of Him! All of You, none of him!" Iris repeated.

Black out for the rest of the night.

TWENTY FIVE
Hopeless Containers

Hours later came a voice, "Wake up."
Nathan slowly opened his eyes; his fever was gone. He felt a warm, strong hand on his chest.
"Wake up buddy."
Nathan looked up, it was Annak. "You had a rough night."
"Where's my Grandma?" Nathan felt a longing to be close to her.

Annak pointed out into the hallway where she was pacing back and forth, watching the tunnels. Nathan looked around the room — the fire was glowing, the rest of the guys were still knocked out, seemingly getting much better sleep than he did. He had a few sips of water and took his time waking up.

"I didn't drink any alcohol last night," said Nathan.
"I know," replied Annak.
"Why did I get so sick then?"
Annak looked at him firmly, "You're being tormented by something way more potent than alcohol."
"The Sarx was in my dreams, he was standing next to Silas's dead body, he was…" Nathan was not quite sure how to put into words what he saw.
"I know, Nathan. One way to see it is that the Sarx is tormenting you, but that's not what I think."
"Then what is it?" asked Nathan.
"You're being tormented by destiny."
Nathan was puzzled, "That's what *destiny* feels like? Sure doesn't feel too good. If that's the case I want nothing to do with it."
"You don't have a choice about your destiny, Nathan.

You either embrace it or run from it. The only reason you'd choose to run from yours is because you're scared of your identity. If someone's created with purpose, and one purpose only, than a refusal to live out that purpose will only result in destruction. As long as your neck is stiff toward your calling, you will always be left wide open to the gates of darkness. And those devils aren't shy about coming in to feast on a rebel heart."

"I'm not a rebel," said Nathan.

"No?" asked Annak. "You want justice so bad, you grope for meaning so frantically, that you become like a kicking and screaming child. There's *you're* way, then there's *His*. You only need one little ingredient to be a rebel — *pride*."

"Yeah, but can't *pride* be a good thing?" asked Nathan."

"Only when it's governed by *humility*. Other than that it's reckless. *Pride* apart from *humility* is like *knowledge* apart from *wisdom*. You can have all the knowledge you want, but without wisdom — you're a mistress with no husband."

"What do you mean?"

"In order to get knowledge, all you have to do is study the natural world. But wisdom is only attained by seeing what isn't seen. You can catch fish with knowledge, but knowing when to eat and when to release? That's a matter of wisdom. Knowledge gets you to the door, but wisdom gets you through, over the threshold, and helps you interpret what's on the other side. Knowledge can define power, but wisdom knows how to use it."

Annak continued, "On the other hand, *meekness* is a gift to those who've been broken of themselves. And only through brokenness can one steward *pride* in a way that's redemptive and not destructive. *Knowledge* is *you* governing your *own* will. *Wisdom* is giving your will over to the One who made you. You *cannot* reign the pride in your heart apart from the meekness of your Maker."

Nathan was somewhat overwhelmed by Annak's words. He and Iris had that effect on him. Often times they were philosophers more than they were comforters, but somehow he knew their intentions were good.

"Let me just say this, Nathan. The thicker the veil, the greater the revelation when the veil is lifted. Nothing's hidden that won't be revealed, and nothing's hidden that's also not valuable. When the answers to all your riddles unfold, it will all be worth it, you'll see."

Even though Nathan was unsure why, he was feeling better. "The problem is that most of my riddles come from you and my grandma. Any chance you could put that in sailor terms?" Nathan asked.

"You really can't appreciate the solid ground until you've experienced months out in the open sea," answered Annak.

Nathan looked at Annak in an unsurprised manner, "See what I mean? You're still confusing. You guys are always speaking at a higher level than me."

"It's not that, Nathan. When you have no one in your life speaking riddles, then you have no one in your life worth listening to. If everything's under your feet, then you have no reason to look up. Your grandma and I know about the hereafter because, and only because we've tasted the dust of the earth and had the courage to look up and ask for help."

Their conversation was quiet, parsed between an occasional gaze into the fire. Annak prodded, "So, what happens when you get the lake back, Nathan?"

"Huh?" Nathan was somewhat caught off guard by the question, but then answered confidently, "Everything! We find out the secret of the clean water, we find a cure!

Everything goes back to normal again."

Annak listened, "Normal? Then what?"

"We rebuild. We go out there and find others who are alive and we bring them to the water!"

"Let's say all that happens," Annak hypothesized, "then you die. Your body departs from the earth and you're forced to leave all your dreams, your fears, your ideas. Then what?"

"Then...nothing, I guess."

"Nothing? Nathan, life's more than the *lake*. Getting Redfish Lake back is just the beginning. If all your hope is set on the *lake,* once you find the *lake* you'll be lost. But if you set your desire on the city beyond the lake — you'll get the lake, and much more."

"That's just not gonna happen. I can't see anything beyond the lake, Annak"

"There's more than just the lake, Nathan. The lake's a shadow, it's just a representation of the substance that exists behind our world. Beyond the lake there's a city — Zion." Nathan listened quietly. "It's where everything is reconciled, where everything makes sense, where everything begins. It's where there's a banquet table prepared for those who are starving. It's where the crippled run. Where the mute shout, the deaf hear, the dumb rule, the blind see. It's the city that belongs to the seekers, the warriors of virtue who don't compromise, the restless, the broken. The city where children reign, violence ends, where the weary ride on the wings of the wind."

Nathan's ears perked up, "I could believe in a city like that." He did not doubt the validity of Annak's words. Nathan had seen the miracles, he had seen glimpses and wonders that reflected that celestial place. But still, the place felt far away and out of reach. "Hope you're right."

"Remember this, it's not about being right, it's about

being alive," said Annak. "It's about someone digging six feet down and breaking you out of your coffin. You ever been to New Zealand?" asked Annak.

"Of course I haven't. I've been raised in a cave in northern California all my life."

Annak really was not trying to be sarcastic, he was focused on making a point. "I thought I knew what *color* was until I set foot on those islands. I've seen some beautiful places here in the States, but I swear, when I saw the colors of Milford Sound, the moss growing over the old graves of Christchurch, the blue, the pink, the red — its as if all my memories of home turned to black and white. There's no *green* like New Zealand *green.* There's a city built with such glorious density that it makes our world look like a paper house, if that." Annak paused, and then looked at Nathan with a thrill of excitement, his face lit up not so much by the tangible fire, but by unique solace, "The journey's only significant because of where you haven't been. Momentum's defined by your destination. Don't just go after the lake, Nathan. Go after the city beyond the lake."

Nathan was about to ponder Annak's point, but his attention was stolen when Iris rushed into the room, "They're here!" she exclaimed with a cold look on her face. Annak jolted to his feet and rushed out the door where he quickly realized in the muffled distance that footsteps were too close for comfort.

Annak yelled back at Nathan, the only one awake in the room, "Get these guys up!"

Nathan roused himself and began shaking each body from its sleep, "Easton, get up! Get up now! Max, Alex, get up — now!"

Annak took as many boxes of alcohol as he could and smashed them throughout the tunnel.

Max, Easton, and Alex were startled not so much by

Nathan's plea as much as they were by the sound of glass breaking.

"What? What's going on?" asked Max.

"We gotta go!" urged Nathan, as he grabbed him by the shoulders.

Alex got up; he did not need to guess why they were in such a hurry. The look on Nathan's face communicated one thing clearly — Screeners. Nonetheless, he took some time to stuff his jacket full of sardine cans before making haste amidst the commotion. Easton did the same, until everyone was ready at the doorway.

"We have to keep heading south down this tunnel," said Iris, as the sound of oncoming footsteps grew louder.

"Nathan, give me your flint knife!" blurted Annak. Without thinking, Nathan tossed it into his hands. It was dull. The bottles were smashed and spilled across the tunnel floor. Annak started shucking the knife against the side of the brick wall, as fast as he could, again and again.

Then, abruptly, amidst the monotony of Annak's flinting for sparks, Gabriel appeared from around the corner, though still somewhat off in the distance. His gun was in hand and the outline of his dark body was highlighted by those following behind him with sawed-off shotguns, shining their rifle-mounted lights in Annak's direction. Annak's eyes lit up like a raccoon. Within seconds bullets started screaming and whizzing by Annak's head.

Annak ducked and yelled, "GO! GO! GO!" urging Nathan and the others to take off.

Easton could tell Nathan was not about to move, he did not want to leave Annak. So with his stout arms, Easton wrapped himself around Nathan and started dragging him.

Iris, on the other hand, had full confidence in leaving Annak. She was already running southward yelling at those behind her, "Run!"

Alex and Max shared the same opinion, neither of them were in the mood to get struck with a bullet. They caught up to Iris. Annak stayed behind, vigorously trying to produce sparks. Over and over he swiped the knife against the brick until suddenly, *Flink!* A small spark drifted onto the puddle of alcohol. The combustion of a blazing inferno lit up the tunnel. The flames became a firewall, raging and stout, that separated Annak from the charging Screeners so that they were unable to pass. Even so, bullets continued to soar through the flames, the Screeners on the other end anticipating a kill. Annak proudly stood back and admired the blaze for a moment before turning to run in the opposite direction. He could see the back of Alex's heels just ahead.

Gabriel halted, coming up against the flaming wall like a bull. He grinned, his eyes riddled with hate, dilated from having not slept. They had scoured the tunnels all night, all directions, back and forth with pure vengeance.

Rook stood next to Gabriel, not saying a word. The flames were roaring and obstructing a long section of the tunnel, making it impossible to pass without sustaining severe burns or perhaps being burned to death. Still, exclusive in his options, without the courtesy of a response, Gabriel slowly backed away from the heat until he was a substantial distance away from the flames. With his shoulders squared, moving up and down as he breathed, he stood there for a short moment like a psychotic patriot, letting the orange-umber and deep red of the flames dance in the reflection of his pupils, and then in an expression of mindlessness, stormed headlong into the inferno. Rook and the others pushed their backs up against the wall as they watched their leader run right into the fire tunnel; the tail of his rancher's coat swooshed as it trailed behind his fanatical body and disappeared into the thriving underground oven.

Unconscious and unaware if he had been burned or

not, Gabriel broke through to the other side and kept running, numb, and hardly showed any concern for whether or not the rest of his men were following behind. Like a cinema screen hung across the inside of his temporal lobe, all he could see was Iris's wrinkled face of betrayal — he loathed it. Whatever or whoever was behind him did not matter so long as he was on her trail. Whatever needed to be done, he was willing to do it himself. He was willing to get the blood of victims on his own skin. For Gabriel, there was no conception of status, or glory, or fame — just life, just death; that was all.

Meanwhile, after a few paces, Annak heard something behind him. In spite of the fire he had set, he knew they were still being followed. For a moment, he was shocked at how fast someone could have passed through that blazing wall. Gabriel's heavy feet were trampling the dirt on Annak's darkened trail. Annak, knowing that he, Nathan and the others were out of ammunition, was not sure what to do in the event of them catching up. Annak knew that without bullets, guns are not guns — just metal. At this point, Annak and the others were strapped with nothing more than knives and the gritty calluses of their own bare hands.

Unlike Gabriel, Rook and the others waited for the remaining fumes of alcohol to be consumed before scurrying across the hot earth — small flames here and there still burning and smoking. They ran, unknowingly passing the infamous thug room, and tried their best to catch up to Gabriel. For the rest of the early morning it was nothing short of an all out foot race through the web of tunnels. Collectively, everyone underground could easily feel the Worm shifting, alerting them to what time of day it was. The Worm was more intense than normal and shuddered heavily, making Nathan and some of the others nauseous.

After a frantic and strenuous move southward,

Nathan could hear Iris's voice in front of him. "Come on!"
she yelled. She could see minimal shafts of light penetrating
through what appeared to be a sealed wooden doorway.

Soon, everyone caught up to her. Nathan started
swinging the butt end of his rifle into the wooden door. Max
joined in and did the same. But for all their force they were
met with rigidity. Unlike a normal door, this one was thickset,
made from true wood 4x8 planks, fastened together with
robust six-inch nails; most of them already melded together
by rust and corrosion. Easton joined in. One after another,
the blunt force of their blows started to splinter the wood and
loosen the boards. Then, *CRACK!* One of the boards went
flying. More light broke through and a cold wind brushed
against their bodies. Immediately they were coddled by
the fangs of nature's biting winter. *CRACK!* Another board
broke loose. *CRACK!* Then another. Finally, there was a
fragmented opening. Annak pushed everyone through, then
exited last. No sooner had he came out the other side of the
door, bullets started breaking through the wood.

Immediately, Nathan looked out upon a wide open
space. The pungent smell of rot and sewage took hold of his
nostrils as it crept up through the sickly river basin. They had
rushed out of the tunnels only to find themselves underneath
a tattered, leaning dock, its decomposing beams and support
posts looking as though they could collapse at any moment.
In front of them was the dead bay of the Willamette River
Basin; the inlet of Portland's abandoned shipping yard.
Struck not only by the horrid smell but by the indecision
of where to go next, they looked out across the morbid
landscape, knowing that no matter what direction they ran
they would undoubtedly be left out in the open. Uncertain
where to run, they ducked and dodged as more gunshots
blew through the wood panels.

"There!" yelled Easton. He pointed to a capsized

cargo ship that lay dead in a field of scattered shipping containers. In the distance they could barely make out some of the blurred logos, *Maersk, Evergreen, K-Line, Hanjin, Tex.*

Annak was not too concerned where to go as much as he was concerned about continuing to move. "GO!" he yelled. "I'll catch up!"

"Are you crazy?" Nathan questioned. "You can't fight these guys alone!" He was the only one who protested.

Annak grabbed Nathan by the collar and gave him a reassuring warning, "I know what I'm doing, now go!"

Reluctantly, Nathan slowly took off, following Iris, Easton and the others. Their arms flailed and they kept their knees high as they ran viciously across the earth's cracked surface. Directly in front of him Nathan could not help noticing a bottle of alcohol hanging halfway outside Alex's pack. Half of it was slapping against his butt as he ran. He would have had time to laugh had the circumstances not been so intense. But all he could think about was the unease of leaving Annak behind. All he had to go on when push came to shove was the fact that Annak was not good at making bad decisions. Once Annak's mind was made up, there was no way to change it.

Trying to keep moving forward, Nathan intermittently looked over his shoulder, occasionally watching Annak swing a huge beam as he repeatedly struck one of the dock's rotting support pillars. With every hit, the whole structure lurched and shifted. Again and again, Annak swung, splintering the wood from the pillar. The vibrating of the massive dock intensified. Then at last, with one final swing, the wood beam collided with the pillar and all at once — wood by wood, piece by piece, corroded bolt by corroded bolt — like a massive tree being axed by a sweating sawyer, the dock swayed and crashed to the ground.

Nathan took another look back and watched the scene unfold, it was beautiful. Annak was now en route. Nathan was certain the crumbling dock was enough to trap the Screeners behind the door, leaving them with no choice but to stay inside the tunnels.

Halfway across the bay, they entered the maze of massive metal shipping containers — they were scattered all over the place, countless numbers of them. Most were overturned, some broken into, some still locked up because the large bifold doors were bent or smashed up against one another.

Nathan had one thing on his mind, finding whatever he could for a weapon. The thought of having a bullet-less rifle and a single hunting knife did not console him even though he was prepared to grapple if necessary. He and the others collectively searched one container at a time, yet found nothing. Most of the materials that would make a good defense had already been scoured long before they arrived.

One after another, Nathan swung open the huge metal doors to multiple containers. He pried open boxes, but to his dismay kept discovering only computer hard drives and an array of software chips. An occasional container had cheap clothing and what seemed to be miscellaneous industrial building materials. There was nothing of value, not in the moment. Alex, on the other hand, was able to lay his fingers on a bottle of cologne and the proceeded to take the time to spray it on.

"Are you serious?" yelled Nathan.

Alex did not answer back. All he had was a childish swag look on his face.

"There's nothing but useless crap in all of these!" shouted Max. By now Annak had caught up to them.

"We can't run any further," said Iris. "We need to hide out in one of these."

"No way, we have to keep going," Nathan argued. "Who knows how many of them are back there."

"We wait it out," said Iris. "Chances are they will think we kept moving and will search beyond the basin. Then we can make our way back to the Crawlers."

"I'm not liking that," Nathan shot back. "We outrun them and find a better place to hide. There's no way they're getting out from underneath that dock anytime soon."

Just then, to everyone's dismay, a bullet ricocheted off the side of one of the containers. Nathan could hardly believe the Screeners had tracked them so quickly. How they were able to break through and get out from behind that doorway was beyond him. Now there was certainly nowhere to go.

TWENTY SIX
Run

For a second, Nathan wondered why Easton could not just simply open his mouth again. He thought about circling back around and taking Gabriel from behind and slitting his throat. He considered making a stand and swinging the butt end of his rifle at the heads of as many Screeners as he could. A flash of thoughts undoubtedly rushed not only through Nathan's mind but everyone else's too. Yet, in a fraction of a moment, in the end the unspoken consensus was to hide. Nathan, as well as the others, silently slipped into one of the containers and hid against the back of the cold metal wall where he crouched down behind a teetering stack of boxes. There was a good chance if he was found he could take on at least one of them at a time. Whether or not Nathan was alone in the container was not certain, though it sounded like everyone had split up in different directions. He could not sense anyone next to him. It was dark.

Nathan was anxious and struggled to lighten his breath as he heard intimidating machine guns carelessly being fired, not at any of the containers, but into the air. Nothing else made a sound. There was no Reaper retaliation, no fighting back, no signs of Annak, Iris or any others. Then abruptly, like a circuit had been cut, after a few rounds everything went quiet. Nathan's heart was pounding.

What seemed like a world went by and then, a savage yell broke the silence, "GET THE HELL OUT HERE!"

Nathan knew, even from inside the muffled metal box, that it was Gabriel's voice. Almost equal to that of the Sarx, the man's presence made Nathan's skin crawl. With one hand, Nathan wiped the fretful sweat from his forehead;

and with his other, he quietly pulled his knife out and held it tight to his chest.

Another voice rang out, this one different from Gabriel's. It was Rook, "You're done!" He continued taunting, "We know you've got no ammo left!"

Gabriel stayed silent, scraping the end of his new pistol across the outside of one of the containers — its paint chipped and fading. The sound of metal on metal was a horrifying groan. Gabriel stopped, swung out the revolver of his pistol and capped it off with six more bullets.

"You're all dead, you know that?" Rook continued. "How about we make it easy on you. Surrender, and perhaps we'll give you one last chance to join us." Rook followed behind Gabriel, lingering in his shadow like a hellish secretary, outlandishly verbalizing the thoughts of the Screener's world.

In his trepidation, Nathan's mind was a circus of thoughts, reminding him of how Geospark and the Screeners had been selfishly raping the earth for years. Now more than ever, within the hearing of their voices, their darkness was more real than ever.

"I find it odd that none of you want the chip!" teased Rook, in a serious tone. "How could you resist it? You're never the same after getting the chip. You'll have a nature like ours, an all-access pass to life, to the water!" Rook snorted and licked the upper left side of his lip, running the point of his tongue across some of his short scruffy facial hair.

Nathan was growing more uneasy, not so much by Rook's chattering mouth, but more so by Gabriel's silence.

Rook kept talking, "One of you is going to pay for shooting my commander's arm. There's — "

Gabriel interrupted, "IRIS!" His tone was intense, and colder than the desolate weather. "You can't hide from

what you've done anymore. THIEF! How could you live
with yourself this long?"

Not knowing where Nathan was in all of this, Iris
listened from inside one of the containers adjacent to his.
She was grieved at the sound of Gabriel's voice and chanted
to herself, invoking the Navigator in matters only He and
she were aware of. Regardless of how much hate there was
for her inside Gabriel's heart, she harbored not one sliver of
bitterness towards him — only hope, only mercy.

Simultaneously, Nathan had never been more
perplexed. He could not ignore the gross intimacy Gabriel
seemed to share with Iris. From a young age he always knew
Iris was unique because of the inside information she kept.
But the tension of the moment was growing more awkward.
Nathan knew something was about to break from exposure.
The line between Screeners and Reapers had invariably
been drawn. Yet Gabriel had a strange way of blurring black
and white into gray. There was something wonderfully
uncomfortable about him, a shameful familiarity in his voice
— the way he was calling out to Iris, his questioning of
her virtue — that reminded Nathan of his own inquisitions
regarding Iris's secret world, one he had yet to completely
grasp. So many times throughout his life as a boy as well as
a young man, Nathan questioned Iris. He doubted her from
a cramped place of insecurity. There was so much about her
that seemed dark, threatening and bizarre. Nathan trusted Iris
— at least he thought he did. He wanted to, yet some small,
isolated, ignorant part of him still doubted who she was. She
guarded her privacies well behind a shroud of spiritualized
fabric, a seemingly *holy* veil of wisdom and honor.

But now, not that Nathan was forcing it, he could
feel the changing of a tide like the New England shoal.
Gabriel did not have to say much for Nathan to feel his
heart resonating with something. In an odd way it was as

if there was a clarity to Gabriel's voice, like he knew more about what was going on in the world than anyone else. Yet perhaps most alluring was the way he appeared to be crying out for justice. Despite the outrage that poured from his lips in just a handful of syllables, Gabriel's voice was laced with a tone of conviction that was nothing short of a plea for fair-play. Whatever it was, if indeed it really was there, was not far from the same oil that ran through the gears of Nathan's own heart — his cry for the lake, his cry to find out what happened to his parents, his own cry for justice. Whether good or bad, right or wrong, Gabriel, like Nathan, was crying out for an answer, for vindication, for the return of that which was lost, for the broken to be made whole, for the fractured to be made right. And in a moment, in the fleeting blink of an eye, Nathan felt something strange happen. Whereas before he felt like he was in the presence of an enemy, all at once he was caught off guard by the feeling of being accompanied by a fellow ragamuffin — another man struggling to eat of the scraps falling from the table, trying to make sense of things. It was the dark chorus of a cry he could easily join himself to. And now, rather than being repelled by Gabriel, Nathan was being drawn into whatever it was he was carrying. So much so that he could not tell who was his enemy and who was not. The certainty of he and Iris's uncertain relationship was brought to the edge.

Though Gabriel remained mostly quiet as he searched the containers, Nathan could almost hear the unspoken thoughts running through Gabriel's head. A sort of telepathy maybe, he was not sure. He did not have time to think about it. Gabriel's thoughts passed through Nathan's head like they were being broadcasted through a bullhorn. *You're here...I know you are! Where are you, Iris? I can't believe it's you leading these attacks. I should've known it was you all along. You're a dead woman. You betrayed me! You dishonored me!*

And you know it, you must know it! Nathan did not know it, but outside Gabriel gnashed his teeth and looked as if he were about to tear his clothes in anger. The excursion from the headwaters of Icon had become way more personal than anticipated. *By now, if you're not tormented by what you've done, it only means one thing — your heart's just colder than mine. You claimed to be such a woman of light, a woman of the way! If indeed there is a way at all. You claimed to represent the One who supposedly made all of this, the One who fashioned us, who joined us bone to bone, flesh to flesh, life to life! The One who hovered over the face of the earth's waters and spoke life into existence!*

Nathan tried to get the sound of Gabriel's voice out of his head, but he could not. He had no choice but to lean in on his thoughts, alluring as they were. He felt pulled. He had no awareness that he and he alone, unlike the others within earshot, was the only one hearing the unspoken. And then, not in reality, but in silence, he heard Gabriel cry out from his bowels, *I...TRUSTED...YOU! The very person I would have never imagined, of all people, it was you — who betrayed me. You disappeared! I spent months, year after year, going out into the wilderness, overturning every rock, searched every building — looking for you! Looking for him!* Nathan knew Gabriel was referring to Iris.

Gabriel suddenly kicked open one of the container doors, braced himself and fired a couple shots into the dark. It was empty. Nathan continued listening, *He belongs to me...and you know it. He was always meant to be a part of who I am, what I stand for. All that mythical crap! That Navigator crap! That Blue Flame crap! All that metaphysical crap you've sold your life to! It's not for him! It's not! You can waste your life on that stupidity, but not him! If he's still alive, I'll make sure he sees the truth.*

Nathan was way beyond uncomfortable by now. Too

many tumultuous emotions were blitzing his psyche — anger, confusion, sadness, excitement, fear. And over it all was the heavy question, *Who is this Gabriel?* Gabriel flinched as a shooting pain from his wounded arm ran through his body.

More of Gabriel's thoughts came into Nathan's head, wave after wave of them. *Time's up Iris. You know, I held off from releasing an airstrike. I called off drones that could have leveled this valley by now. I could have released a hundred more troops to come and slaughter you. But... because I know it's you, I'm relenting. With all that wisdom you have, why can't you realize I'm trying to give you one more chance to do what's right? Don't you understand? Not just you, Iris, but all of you — there's no future for you! You can't survive any longer apart from us. You have no choice. The world is governed by our system and our system only. Anyone trying to scrape by outside of that system will eventually be brought to an end. Everything's under our control. Your days are numbered. The Navigator never was, never is, and never will be. The Blue Flame never was. You think our world could have come to this if there really was a supreme being? And even if there was, what kind of monster would He be, having allowed all this?*

Nathan could imagine Gabriel shaking his head in bewilderment, *you attach your silly little lives to something that doesn't even exist. The only thing remotely triumphant about you people is your ability to stay blind to the reality of what's really going on. You're persistently stupid! Trusting in One who's only allowed sickness, death, disease, and war! If He exists at all, he's sitting on a sofa in another world, watching our starvation, our greed, our chaos through his television, drinking a beer! He's nothing but a coward! Unable and unwilling to come to the aid of those who needed Him. Your faith is dead, Iris.*

Nathan proceeded to hear Gabriel's arguments, *We,*

on the other hand, have the technology, the science, the power, the last resources of fuel, oil, gas. The advancements of mankind belong to us. We hold the reigns on the direction of life. And may I remind you, most of all, we have the W.A.T.E.R. Gabriel slowed his voice and whispered the word *water* in a sinister slither. *Without water you have nothing. The ones who control the water control life! Looks to me like the Navigator's not the one with the authority!*

Nathan was not sure why, but he felt his grip naturally begin to loosen around the handle of his knife. He could not tell if he was harnessing a power to hear Gabriel's thoughts or if Gabriel's thoughts were controlling him, but he felt as if his will was bound to something he could not turn away from. Nathan perceived a strong urge to leap out of that Maersk container and surrender himself. He so badly wanted to come out of the darkness and into the light, if indeed the light is what Gabriel was offering.

Yet concurrently, Nathan caught the edge of a small whisper that barely made itself known above Gabriel's slew of thoughts. It was hardly anything, but just enough, delicate as the soft evening wind — *Don't do it.* Whatever it was that kept him from surrendering he did not know, but it also did not tell him to hold still. Being paralyzed by schizophrenia, would not have been out of the question, Nathan's mind, more than anything, was at war. As enchanting as Gabriel's telepathic emanation was, Nathan found himself slowly starting to recount the things he had witnessed — Annak rebuking the Sarx as it was suspending his helpless body off the ground, the blue fire in Iris's eyes, that invisible power that pierced the mother back at Adullum, the miraculous healings, Nathan's own gunshot wound being closed up, the roar of Easton's voice, the dreams, the sobering conversations with both Annak and Iris.

By now, Nathan was well beyond the point of

disbelief in the spiritual realm Iris spoke of and lived by. No longer could he ignore what he had seen — the signs, the wonders. The memories might have been enough to guard Nathan against completely being swayed by Gabriel, but in a sense they fell short. Rather than being hot or cold, Nathan found himself succumbing to a lukewarm torment, a place where he could not fully trust either side. Whether or not the spiritual was real was not the question anymore. He needed to come to realizations on his own. He did not discount what he had experienced in Iris's world, but poised in the middle of conflict, he also was not willing to deny the validity of Gabriel's chants.

In a way, two fishhooks had been dropped into the water, and both had a deep hold on Nathan's lip. Inside Nathan's chest an inner compass was broken and had lost control. Numbness set in. So, in an attempt to get away from all the confusion, the madness — to somehow flee from all those who reminded him of the myriad of unanswered questions plaguing his life, to somehow go somewhere he had never gone before — he broke out of the container and ran. Whether or not bullets whizzed by his ears, he could not tell. Whether or not anyone saw him take off, he did not know. He ran and ran, and after a while assumed he must have outrun any Screener resistance, merely surviving by chance.

Even if Nathan was not fully aware of the reason he took off running, nonetheless, it was the only thing that made sense to him in the moment. He wanted to be alone, completely alone. He needed to find out what was at the core of who he was, and in an instance of intense insecurity, yet brutal certainty, amidst the clash of two opposing worlds, he ran with every fiber of his being. He ran with all his heart. He ran and ran, as fast and as far as he could, without the slightest desire to look back, raptured by a climactic typhoon of soul-searching.

Like a scared little boy? Perhaps. Like a worm trying to escape the sunlight? Maybe. Yet maybe he ran like a lightning bolt simply trying to strike something solid so it could release its charge. Maybe he ran like a man in search of a test that would finally unearth the material he was made of. Maybe he ran because some small part of him knew that every salmon has to make it upstream on its own eventually. Maybe he ran because he needed to feel the grit of the journey apart from the crowd — by himself. Like he needed a blank page, one that had not yet been cluttered and lined with the spills, the blots and the ink of other's experiences — their testimonies, their opinions. Maybe he ran like a mustang dying to get free of the bridle, ruthlessly flinging its neck in opposite directions and using its mighty hind legs to kick up dust in the air. Maybe he ran in an attempt to escape the *hot*, the *cold,* and to see what *lukewarm* felt like. Maybe there was more than just the option of *left* or *right*? Maybe chasing after nothingness was the real way to move forward.

Maybe.

Perhaps Nathan himself did not even know why or what for. The fact is, the moment came in his life when the only truth he could conceive of was running, regardless of what he thought or felt. He stepped into a new reality, one where there was no beginning and no end and no ultimate destination — just running. Just the simple movement of one foot in front of the other in a direction that did not promise any finish line — running for the sake of engaging in the warfare of losing himself in the process. Maybe that was all.

TWENTY SEVEN
Frozen Coffin

umb, but alive. Caught up in the euphoria of escape, Nathan lost track of how far he had run, or for how long. He was unaware what time of day it was or even why he had taken off running in the first place. He knew not how many days he had been running, or even how he was being sustained for so long. The intoxication of his own adrenaline had disintegrated all sense of bearing. His heart beat for a direction that was undefined by north, east, south, or west. He was hit by the enticement of isolation and driven by one thing only — getting as far away as possible from everyone and everything he was familiar with.

Though he was not cognizant of it, he had run across the Willamette Bay, through the eastern streets of Portland, through the surrounding rural neighborhoods, far past the outskirts of town, and miles into the deep wilderness. Yet even then he did not stop. He kept going for what seemed like a timeless period, being carried along by sheer will or perhaps something else until he finally collapsed.

As he lay there, drenched in a cold sweat, panting, his chest moving up and down, he looked up and beheld towering trees all around him. Most of them, even though standing, were dead and barren, and all leaned to one side from being windswept for so long. Wherever he was, he noticed the glow of dusk settling throughout the forest. Nathan was more than in a daze, he was near unconscious, dwindling off his last nominal ounces of energy. In the moment he tried to recall what had happened from the time he had bolted from the bay, but there was no memory of seeing Annak, Iris or any of the others. For a second he felt ashamed for having left everyone behind, but then he was not even sure he valued his own life enough to care about anyone else. The only thing to do now was lay on the forest floor. Nathan was unable to feel his legs or anything else, except for the hunger pains growling in his gut. He was too tired to move anymore.

Then, hours later maybe, he heard an unexpected sound. The sound was soft but familiar. Leaning his head to the side and rolling his cheek into the dirt he saw where the noise was coming from — the trickle of a stream caused by a small amount of melting snow. The water was running down a staggered path between the trees.

Wheezing, Nathan rolled over and squirmed on his elbows toward the water, dragging his lethargic legs behind him. When he reached the trickle, without thinking he plunged his lips into the flowing water and slurped like a dog. He sucked up water and particles of dirt and filth. He drank, and drank, and drank, until his stomach hurt. Then he stopped. To an extent he was satisfied and thankful, until, with blurred vision, he looked up and down the small creek and was reminded of how sick the earth's water system was. He had been too thirsty and failed to notice sections of the creek releasing small pockets of bubbles that popped with gas, revealing a fuming vapor that contrasted against the cold winter air. Unlike times in the past, the sight did not make him nervous. He crawled over and stuck his nose to one of the emissions and was overcome by its smell. It reeked of sulfur, acid, pneumonia and unpleasant gases. He knew it was emitting enough toxins that if he had a match he could have lit the water on fire. Nonetheless, he was much too thirsty to care about poisoning. At this point, if sickness infected his body it would not matter. Again he stuck his face into the stream of water and slurped mindlessly until his body could not hold any more, then backed away and rolled over.

It was dark now. Nathan had no food, no supplies, not even a gun, just his hunting knife. Not much was clear other than the fact that he knew he was not far from a mountain peak just a few hundred yards away. He could see the peak through the trees and had the slight notion he might be on Mt. Hood, though he had no realistic explanation for how he could have ran that far from the bay. Not that it mattered, knowing his coordinates would not make a difference. His body was too weak to try and find food, and his adrenaline was gone. By now it was nothing shy of a miracle that he had even survived for so long. So depleted of calories, exhausted, he could feel his stomach trying to eat itself, the water only filling him up temporarily. Nathan knew it would not be long before he had absolutely nothing left. The thought of giving himself over to death seemed appropriate.

Nathan lay there, slowly scanning his mind for reasons, strategies, and ways to stay alive. *But what for? I'm done. I've lived long enough — I'm ok. I can't go on any more...no reason to. I can go now...no more struggle, no more pain.* He wanted to quit. His mind grew tired of trying to come up with reasons to live. With the back of his head resting on the cold earth, his arms sprawled out and eyes open, he uttered one last phrase with as much sincerity as he could levy, "Navigator, help me." He waited, but there was no tangible response. Unable to stay awake, he closed his eyes and drifted off.

Two more days passed by. Nathan was comatose but somehow not frozen to death. Gradually, his blacked-out vision became blurred with fragmented shimmers of light, specs and flashes trickling through the dark. *I must be dead*, he thought. His rigid body was frozen like a piece of steel. He could hardly shake his head free and open his eyes. It was dark but slowly, he could see a splintered flare of light burning in the distance. He opened his eyes wider, then looked again, this time realizing it was a fire coming off the nearest peak. Seeing it, but lacking strength to get there, thinking it was perhaps just a hallucination, he let his head slump back down.

Moments passed by. Nathan was unable to get the glow of the fire out of his mind. How easy it would have been to just lie there in his icy coffin, helpless. Nothing in life was being demanded of him any longer. The effort involved, had he allowed his body to simply break down and pass away, would have been next to nothing. Had it not been for that tiny flicker of light, he would not have been stunned by the lure of intrigue, and the possibility of life going on. Closing his eyes then opening them again, that tiny light began to draw him. There was no voice, no waving of an arm, and no invitation other than that of warmth. If there was a fire, there was a chance someone was over there. Whether they were good or bad did not matter, only the prospect of warmth meant anything at this point.

So, in one last attempt to go on, summoning just enough strength from a place that was beyond words, Nathan slowly got up. His ligaments and bones cracked. His muscles were tight and strained. He felt as though he had forgotten how to use his legs, if indeed they were still there. Crawling inch by inch through the darkness, up the hill toward the fire, he felt like a block of ice thawing. He would move forward a little, then collapse onto his chest and bury his face on the ground. He would get up and move some more, and then brace himself against a tree. A little more, then collapse again, barely able to lift his neck enough to see the fire still burning ahead of him. The situation was terrible, the fire seemed lifetimes away, but options were limited. Where he got the energy to even move in the first place was a mystery, but it was there, and it was just enough.

Nathan was breathing heavy. A substantial amount of

time passed before he finally came close enough to the fire. He tried to quiet his huffing so as not to be noticed. Like a stalker, he braced himself behind a tree. His throat was numb and stiff, his lips parched and withered, his hunger pains ⁄almost unbearable. His mouth was so dry that the inside of his cheeks kept sticking to his grimy teeth. In desperation he took few deep breaths, pondering what to do next. With the tips of his fingers he could feel the soot and dirt layered on his face, touching himself for no other reason than to check if he was still alive or not. His features bore the makeup of homelessness, the wilderness having done its job to baptize him in nature's grit.

Without looking, rolling his eyes back in his head, he could hear the crackling of the fire behind him. He was close enough to smell the smoke rising from burning timber; it smelled good. Other than gasoline, the scent of smoldering wood was one of Nathan's favorite things on earth. For him, smoke had become the cologne of life, a sign that someone was either getting warm or cooking — a reminder of the simplicity of the times.

Breathing in the smoke through his nostrils, he could not shake the thought of how ridiculous it was to light a fire at night, no one who wanted to stay alive did that. More so, the fact that whoever it was had lit the fire not only at night, but on the summit of a mountain top — out in naked visibility. With Screeners raking across the land and the sporadic drone flight flooding the skies, no one in their right mind, at least no one who's been alive for the last twenty years, would dare light a fire at night — it was a death trap, a sure broadcast to say, *Here I am! Here's my white flag!* Nonetheless, in this instance, if someone else's foolishness meant warmth, and perhaps food, then so be it.

Soon enough, however, it was no longer just the fire that intrigued him, Nathan was caught off guard by a voice singing. The voice was melodious and reciting lyrics in an unfamiliar tongue. The language reminded him of Iris's own private recitals from time to time. Nathan thought his ears were playing tricks on him. There was just no way out here in the middle of the wilderness he was hearing what he heard. But he was. Not turning to look, but listening more intently, Nathan could make out the tone of someone who had certainly not hit puberty. It was nothing less than the pitch of a little boy or girl. Nathan did not know what to do; the singing actually made him nervous. Yet, the intensity of his own starvation was too overwhelming. He had to find out if there was food, regardless of who it was. He poked his head around the tree and saw what now was a raging bonfire. The small child was singing and dancing around its flames. Nathan quickly scanned the area to see if there was anyone else around. He waited. He waited some more, but there was no one else, just the child. *There's no way*, he thought. *A child out here in the dark?* It was odd. Nathan started to reason with himself, *Just a kid. I can't take his food.* Nathan sensed something was strange about the situation, yet his ability to think clearly had been drained like a bathtub being emptied of its water. He was too hungry to surmise moral decisions. If a little child stood in his way of getting warm, of getting food, then he was not about to hold back.

Not thinking about it any further, with bully-like tenacity, Nathan pushed himself off the tree and started to creep toward the fire; pursuing, not so much with evil intent, as much as with the intent to simply stay alive and fend for his life. The child was still joyously dancing and singing, but in a rather eccentric way. It was not the sort of dancing and singing one would expect from a young one — foolish, immature, un-calculated — it was quite the opposite. The child moved with rhythmic passion and sang with conviction and awe. The child was immersed in something, barely even aware of the fact that Nathan was approaching behind him. Yet, rather than feeling remorse for what he was about to do, Nathan accepted the child's mindless abandonment as a means to take him by surprise. Nathan simply moved closer. He could tell now that the child was a young boy, no more than six years old.

Without hesitation, Nathan sprung forcefully out into the open light and snatched the little boy in his arms. At first the boy panicked and tried to scream, but was unable to. Nathan had him bound tightly to his chest and the dirty palm of his large hand pressed against his tiny mouth. The boy struggled and squirmed like a lamb caught in a lion's mouth, but even though Nathan was still weak, the boy's little body had no chance of getting free.

Holding the boy tightly, Nathan interrogated him, "FOOD!" then looked around frantically again to see if anyone else was around, considering momentarily that he might have walked into a trap. "Where's your food? TELL ME!"

Mumbling and groaning, the boy was unable to speak. He tried, but could not open his mouth big enough to bite Nathan's hand. Nathan was asking questions, but all the while unaware that by covering his mouth he was preventing the boy from answering.

Dragging the little thirty-five pound body with him, Nathan circled around the fire, forcefully searching for supplies until finally laying his eyes on a dark leather satchel. "I know you can't be out here alone," declared Nathan, foaming and salivating at the mouth. Nathan was as forceful with the boy as he would have been with a Nephilim or a full grown man. Not letting him go, he knelt down, picked up the satchel and emptied its contents all over the ground. A modest amount of dried meat fell out. With the swoop of his hand, Nathan stuffed all of it into his mouth, scarfing it down so intensely that he had to keep himself from choking to death. The boy continued to swing his arms in a panic, groaning with all the force he could muster. Nathan continued clutching onto him with one hand and eating with his other, even picking up lost pieces on the ground that had crumbled down his chest.

"Who are you, kid? Who do you belong to? Do you know how stupid it is to be dancing out here by the fire?" *Stupid! Absolutely stupid,* Nathan thought. Intermittently, Nathan tried to size him up, looking at his wrist for signs of a chip, but did not see one. The little boy, still being held by the mouth, was clothed in scraps of animal skins like a rag picker; he was dirty and unkempt.

Then, discovering a jug with a small amount of water in it, Nathan wrapped his fingers around the handle and chugged it so carelessly that the excess water ran off his chin and down his neck. He tossed the jug into the fire. As soon as the plastic started to melt, from behind, Nathan felt a brute body collide with his. The boy was quickly flung loose from his arms and sent tumbling across the ground. Nathan toppled over from the force and hit a pile of rocks. The oncoming body did not hesitate to tackle him, giving him no chance to recover. Nathan felt the brawn of this person that had jumped on top of him. Now the wrestling match was fair, Nathan was no longer fighting a boy.

The person wrapped their hands around Nathan's neck and began to ruthlessly strangle him to death. Nathan tried to pry the grip, repeatedly punching the attacker in the side. Still weak, he was somehow able to break free, back away, stand to his feet and create some distance between him and the person.

Swaying back and forth in an attack stance across from the other adult-size body, Nathan struggled to get a clear look at who the person was. Just like the boy, the person was covered in animal skins and raggedy clothing, wearing some sort of camouflage wig made from rope and straw. Aside from that, Nathan could not make out the face that was hidden by a shroud made from what appeared to be fish netting. Amidst the fight, Nathan was surprised by how tactical the person's garb was.

Yet the momentary observation was short lived. Not able to react quickly enough, Nathan felt the wind get knocked out of him as a knee sank into his groin. He hunched forward and felt his body stumble backwards at the same time, almost falling into the blazing fire but catching himself just in time. In excruciating jolts of pain and struggling to breathe, Nathan took his knife from the sheath and prepared to stab the adversary. But, no sooner did he lift his arm in an attempt to plunge the blade into flesh, he was kicked, the laces of the other person's boot colliding with his wrist, sending the knife flying through the air. Nathan watched in slow motion as the blade disappeared into the night and was then tackled to the ground again. Both bodies rolled violently over the fire and scattered hot coals across the ground. Nathan ended up the on bottom and felt the punch of a cold fist sink into his jaw, *SMACK!* And then another, *SMACK!* In seconds, his lip began to swell and oozing blood filled his mouth.

In a fit of rage, Nathan was able to throw the attacker off. He backed away, readied himself and tried to think about what to do next. Yet, as he charged forward, his feet were abruptly kicked out from underneath him. His body hit the ground, and this time he was pinned down again with more force. In an instant he felt the other person's knee press hard into his Adam's apple. He watched in fear as the oppressor pulled out what looked like the jaw-bone of a horse.

Suddenly, the little boy came back into the scuffle, "MOM!" he cried. "LET HIM LIVE!"

Hearing the boy's voice, Nathan's attention was drawn to the fishnet shroud as he considered who might be behind it. *A woman?* he thought. Nathan was certain he was about to be slain by a female. It sort of made sense in the moment — raised by a woman, killed by a woman. Yet even if he wanted to live, he was too weak now to fight any longer.

Unwilling to entertain the boy's plea for mercy, the woman behind the shroud proceeded with her attempt to brutally end Nathan's life. As she lifted her arm in the air, the sleeve of her jacket receded. In the glow of the fire, Nathan's eyes were quickly drawn to what was revealed on the tanned skin of her wrist and the markings running up her forearm. He could scarcely believe what he saw. It looked like a tattoo — markings depicting a train of flying doves, similar to that of Annak's divinely inflicted scars. In that moment, Nathan's thoughts became clear again. Immediately, he thought of the piece of paper he had found in the theatre and quickly tried to speak out the words, "No! Wait!" But he could not. The pressure from the knee on his throat hindered him.

The boy screamed again, "MOM! DON'T DO IT!"

Nevertheless, the woman paid no attention to the request and wrote it off as nothing more than a silent commentary of youthfulness that was unaware of the heaviness of an adult situation.

In a last ditch effort of panic, Nathan attempted to reach into his pocket and pull out the piece of paper, desperately trying to ease the tension and create some commonality amidst the death match. But he was not fast enough. Whoever it was on top of him had made up her mind and was not about to change it. Nathan cringed as the jaw-bone swooped down with great force. Sharp and strong, the weapon struck his head and sliced it open. The last thing he heard was the crack of bone on bone. For Nathan, everything went black. That was his end, as far as he knew.

TWENTY EIGHT
Drawings in The Wind

Nathan's mind was bleak, but still he could hear sporadic whispering. He sensed traces of a gentle wind blowing that carried the shimmering hues of a sunrise. The chuckling of a boy's voice faded in and out; it was scratchy and carefree. *Am I alive?* He wondered. Sporadically he could feel his body moving up and down, jerking abruptly like he was being hauled on top some kind of beast. He knew there was no way it could be a horse — they were all extinct. But then again, if he was dead, maybe there were horses in the afterlife. Whatever it was, as he lay on top of it, he could feel the beast's throbbing muscles underneath his belly. Unable to think about it any further, he slipped back into nothingness, overtaken by the intense throbbing of his forehead.

Moments passed in and out of each other before a stinging itch on his nose brought him back to reality again. He tried to lift his finger to scratch it, but could not make his arm move. Smearing his snout across the animal's coarse hair, he began to get the sense that his hands were bound with ropes and tied down. Whatever was underneath him smelled terrible, yet it was not an odor he was unfamiliar with. In some strange comforting way, he let the stench of the sweating beast sink into his nostrils and was immediately taken back to a time he was just a child. An old memory flashed through his mental hard drive without an invitation. His arms were clutched around the waist of his father as they rode their black mustang around the lake. It was a small part of his childhood he had forgotten all about until now.

There's absolutely no way I'm on a horse, he thought. *They don't exist anymore.* But to his disbelief, he was. As his eyes gradually pried open, stuck together by some kind of watery pus, he caught a glimpse of the beast's flowing mane — it was burnished blonde with hints of yellowish brown and white. In some weird flurry of peace, Nathan rested his cheek firmly against its hair and then faded back to sleep.

It was not certain how much time had passed before Nathan woke up again, but it could have easily been measured in days. How he wished he would have been dead after having come alert to the discomfort and pain that was coursing through his body. His pants were damp, cold and wet from what he assumed to be his own urine. His feet were cold and felt as though his toes had fallen off. His head was thumping. All he could do was clench his teeth and stiffen his cheeks as a means to cope. The pain was enough to keep him from opening his eyes. Yet after a while he tried to open them, first the right one, then the left.

It did not take him long to realize he must have been brought to some kind of huge abandoned warehouse. He looked up and saw sections of the ceiling caved in and gaping holes blown through the steel rafters. The place was lit up just enough for sufficient visibility from the sunlight streaming in. It felt like the first time he had seen the sun in weeks. He shifted his focus downward, leaned forward and realized he had been lying on a soft row of chairs, five or six of them, all lined up.

Sitting up and trying to put his feet on the ground, he reached his hand up to hold the side of his head and felt something thick encased around it — a wrapping of some sort, or gauze. He ran his fingers across the stiff fabric and scratched away at the scab of dried blood encrusted along the outside. A flashback of the horse's jaw bone slashing across his head came to mind,. How far or near he was from Mt. Hood was uncertain. He tried to figure out where he could possibly be, finding it odd that in front of him was some sort of stage, littered with broken guitars, pieces of an old drum set and smashed instruments.

"He has a plan for you," a little voice said.

Nathan was startled as he looked around, but did not see anyone.

"He does," the small voice said again.

"Who is that?" questioned Nathan, in the kind of voice one would expect from someone waking up with a hangover and a killer headache. "Who's there?"

Pillars of light were breaking through the upper rafters, separated by the inner dimness of the building. From a dark corner the little boy came out into view. He was tossing a dirty baseball up and down, the threads on it frayed and the leather almost completely worn off to the point where its inner twine was showing. Nathan recognized him — it was the same boy who was dancing and singing by the fire.

"My mom tried to kill you, you know," the boy said. "She broke your head open. You should have died. But you didn't."

Nathan was not so sure what to say. The boy's words were comforting to an extent but made his head hurt even more at the thought of what had just happened to him.

"Thought you were dead...laid there all night... bleeding...you didn't move," the boy said. "But when we got up the next morning you were still there. I told mom you were still alive. Mom told me you were dead. I told her, *no*. Mom wanted to leave you, but I told her...told her you were breathing. Mom didn't want to listen to me, but I told her there was a reason."

Nathan engaged in the conversation, as if he had a choice in the matter given the terse persistence of the boy. "*Reason...*" Nathan said softly, "for what?"

"A reason you were still breathing," the boy answered.

"A reason, huh? I could've killed you, kid. And you

think there's a reason I'm not dead?"

The boy answered confidently, "I know...but you didn't. And I knew you wouldn't. If it was meant to be, it would've happened." The boy paused. "You were just hungry...and scared. Mom didn't believe me, but I told her you were different. You're different, I know it! I told her we couldn't let you die."

"Who are you, kid?" asked Nathan, still delicately rubbing the side of his head and squirming in his wet pants.

"My name's JUDAH," he said proudly, widening his eyes as he emphasized the '*ah*' sound on the end. "Know what that means?" The boy asked, and then refused to wait for Nathan to respond. "Means *worshipper!*" he exclaimed with a unique smile, as if he had a secret pocketful of rare marbles or something.

The excitable tenacity of the boy was a little much for Nathan at the moment. His body was sluggish, to say the least, and felt like he was coming out of a coma. Perhaps because of his pain, Nathan probably came across somewhat rude, responding to the boy more like a critic than a companion. "That's it?" replied Nathan, "Seems pretty week to me. Why not *warrior*? Or *fighter*? Sounds to me like you drew the short straw with that name."

"Short straw?" the boy asked, confused.

"Nevermind," said Nathan, shrugging him off, knowing the boy had no sense of sarcasm. "Good for you, *good name*."

The boy glared at Nathan, not in a mean way, but in an edgy, sympathetic way. "Yeah...well at least I know who I am. What's your name?"

"Nathan," he answered in a weak voice.

"*Nathan*? What's it mean?"

"I actually don't know."

"YOU...DON'T...KNOW?" the boy exclaimed

slowly. "How could you not know?"

"Because it doesn't matter…it's just a name. A name. That's all."

The boy shook his head for a moment as if time stopped and then took a break from throwing the rugged baseball up and down. "Yeah! But what would you be without a name?"

"I'd be the same thing I am now, without a name. Names don't matter in this world, kid."

The boy was puzzled. "But…but…you can't just go around not knowing what your *name* means! Have you ever asked Him?"

"*Asked Him?* Asked *who?*"

"What do you mean *who?* You don't know?"

"Know *what?*"

"Know Him?"

"Who's *Him?*"

"The One who knows your name!" the boy said, almost shouting. "The NAVIGATOR! Everybody knows who He is."

Nathan was in disbelief, his heart just about exploded. He could not comprehend the fact that by fleeing those who loved him most, and by trying to steal some innocent child's food on top of Mount Hood, that he had inevitably found himself in another conversation about the Navigator. He immediately recalled the moment lying helpless on his back, *Navigator, help me.* "You're following me, aren't You?" Nathan whispered under his breath, addressing the Navigator, barely loud enough for the boy to hear.

"What?" asked the boy, coming closer.

"Oh, nothing," said Nathan, "and no…I haven't asked Him."

"So you know the Navigator?"

"Wouldn't say that," answered Nathan. "I know

about Him. Didn't believe in him for a long time, but I think..." Nathan paused momentarily, "I think now I've seen enough."

"Well, you must know Him," said the boy without the slightest flinch of doubt. "And you need to ask Him what your name means. You can't know your destiny until you know your name. And you can't know your name until you know Him."

"Who told you that?" asked Nathan.

"Uh, my mom of course," the boy said, communicating very clearly with his chin raised in the air so that Nathan would not argue the issue.

"Are you a prophet or something, kid?"

"The Navigator told me we couldn't leave you. Not a prophet...just a listener, that's all."

"Listener, huh?"

"Yep," the boy paused, "He's always speaking."

Nathan sighed, "Hmm," keeping the rest of his comments to himself for the moment while he watched the boy start throwing the baseball up in the air again. When the leather ball came back down it hit the skin of the boy's hand with a sublet slap — it was the loudest sound in the place aside from the flicker of dust particles floating around in the scattered rays of sunlight. Nathan's eyes followed the ball up and down for a few moments and then let his gaze wander throughout the room.

"What is this place?" Nathan asked.

"Bethel," Judah answered casually, not taking his eyes off the ball. "You're in Redding."

"Redding?" Nathan paused. "Redding, California?"

"Yeah. You know what *Bethel* means?" Nathan was thinking to himself, *No more name stuff, don't care, in too much pain for that right now.* Yet, same as before, unwilling to give Nathan a chance to respond, the boy answered his own question. "It means *where the Navigator dwells*."

"He dwells here, huh?" Nathan asked, thinking about how the place looked nothing like a divine house at all; it was dumpy and thrashed just like the rest of the world.

"Well, yeah. But *Bethel's* wherever *He* is. It's not a building."

"You know...you're pretty brave, Judah," said Nathan. "Coming over here, talking to me by yourself. How do know I'm not dangerous? How do you know I'm not one of them — a Screener?

"Because..." Judah shook his head quickly and puckered his lips as if Nathan had just asked an ignorant question, "I just know."

Nathan did not have a response, he changed the subject. "So...where's that horse at?"

"Oh, Stardust?" answered Judah.

Nathan got curious look on his face, "That's his name?"

"*Her* name," Judah said, correcting him. "Stardust is a girl."

"Corny name for a horse don't you think?"

"Nope," Judah answered quickly.

"*Stardust?*" said Nathan, as he raised one eyebrow, and subconsciously shifted his legs. By now the wetness of his pants was making him extremely uncomfortable; he could feel rashes on both sides of his inner thighs.

"Yeah, 'cause she's the fastest horse ever, faster than a shooting star," Judah said confidently. "We keep her out there," Judah pointed toward some sort of lobby just outside the main room they were talking.

Nathan looked over his shoulder, but the distance was too far to make anything out. "How the hell do you have a horse? Those things don't exist anymore."

"Hey, don't say that word," warned Judah.

Nathan felt terrible that he had offended the boy, "Sorry. It's not a swear word, you know."

"To me it is," said Judah. "We found her, well... mom did. Out in the wilderness...long time ago. She told me Stardust is a Pneuma. Did you know Stardust is a Pneuma?"

"And why would she think that? Aren't those supposed to be some kind of *divine messengers* or something? Angels? Not horses?"

"Because she's not a normal horse. Mom says *Stardust* is different. I can't explain it. You'll have to see for yourself. She doesn't run like a normal horse."

Nathan was not quite sure whether or not he should believe there was anything angelic about the horse, to him it was just a horse. Regardless, he was still beside himself that they even had one. "Well, *Pneuma* or not, the fact is you're the first people I've met with a horse...haven't seen one since I was your age, actually."

Suddenly, a stern voice came from out of the shadows, "JUDAH! Get away from him!" Giving substance to the voice was a woman. She came up behind Judah and pulled him back, stepping in between him and Nathan. She stared at Nathan with disgust while she braced her arm against Judah's chest.

Nathan was anything but offended. He knew what he had previously tried to do to her and the boy. She had every reason to loathe him and to not want Judah anywhere near him. Still, Nathan found himself looking back at her, unresponsive, admiring her as if she was the best thing he had ever seen. At this point there was no fishnet veil covering her face. Whoever she was, aside from the soiled commando clothes and the grubby long black hair, she was absolutely beautiful and alluring. Nathan could not help feeling possessed by her to an extent, stunned by her enchanting face. In one sense it was sharp and carved by the tenacity an endurance of survival, yet in another it was gentle and serene. Somehow he could see right past her repulsion of him. He guessed, by the tone of her skin, her slightly raised cheek bones, and the dark brownish-green purity in her eyes, that she must have been Native American. Never in his life had he seen anyone quite like her. And somewhere deep in the midst of it all, buried behind the woman's eyes, there was a force that reminded Nathan of Iris. Just by looking at her, Nathan was temporarily relieved of the pain in his head, or at least unaware of it.

"If you ever!" she hissed strongly. "If you ever try to touch my little boy again...I won't hesitate to kill you!" Nathan knew she was not bluffing, her face was stoic and uncompromising.

Judah was standing behind her, trying to break loose from her motherly grip, the top of his little head barely at the small of her back. "Mom, it's ok!" he tried to assure her.

"Be quiet, Judah!" She silenced him with a fearsome stare and then looked back at Nathan. "You should be dead right now!" she declared. "If it weren't for my son, I'd have never carried you back here. Never!"

"He's different, mom...he's different!" Judah spoke excitedly but cautiously, hiding his face again behind her back after pouring out his words.

"You better have some answers if you wanna live!" she demanded. "You took our food! Our Water!"

Nathan was still at a loss for words, finding it difficult to speak. He was no less struck by her presence regardless of how threatening she was being. Nonetheless, he tried, "Well...between the both of us I don't know who's got more questions." He was quiet for a moment, then reminded of his discomfort, "You don't happen to have any pants do you?"

At first she thought he was joking and trying to be rude by making light of the situation. But then she noticed how cold and wet Nathan was. He was shivering, yet it was not enough to get her to offer any help.

Judah piped up, excited to be of service to someone other than himself and his mom. "Got all kinds of stuff around here! I'll find you some!"

A new rush of head-pounding pain forced Nathan to close his eyes. He leaned his head back against the top of the chair and stayed quiet until Judah came running back into the room and threw something onto his lap. Nathan looked down, and of all things, it was actually a pair of half decent Levi's — clean, aside from a spatter of red paint on the butt pocket and a few tears down both legs. Soar and achy, Nathan could not act fast enough to get them on.

"How 'bout thanks?" said the mother.

"Sorry," Nathan answered as he looked back at her and then at Judah, "thank you."

"Yeah…yeah, anything you need I can get it for you," assured Judah.

"Judah," said the mother, "you won't do anything for this man without asking me first."

"Mommy, his name's Nathan."

"Come on." She grabbed Judah's hand and pulled him out of the room, leaving Nathan by himself.

As best he could, he untied his boots, inched his pants off and slowly slipped on the jeans. Neglecting to put his boots back on because it felt so good to be barefoot, Nathan steadily tried to stand up for the first time in days. Leaning himself on the back of the chair, shaky and unbalanced, he struggled to stand up straight and put one foot in front of the other. Little by little, not allowing himself to drift too far away from something he could hold on to, Nathan gradually made his way through what seemed like a large church sanctuary. The immense auditorium-like room had almost completely been blown to pieces by the war but still provided decent protection from the outside. Nathan stumbled a little, noticing a large Chevy pickup truck crashed through one of the walls to his left. He grabbed onto the truck's bumper and tried to balance himself.

"HEY!" he called out, after a while, not seeing the boy or his mother. "Where are you guys?" He held still, waiting for a response — a sound — but there was nothing more than the racket of his own wheezing. "HEY!" he yelled again, still trying to move one foot in front of the other.

Then, a whisper, "Pssssssst! Over here!"

Nathan heard Judah's voice and looked in the direction of the noise but saw only the little boy's head poking through a doorway just ahead of him.

"Can't get me!" Judah taunted, just before disappearing.

Nathan tried to pick up the pace as he carved his way around rows of empty chairs and attempted to follow Judah, not really knowing where to. Leaving the large room, he entered a hallway just in time to catch a glimpse of the Judah's foot as he bolted up a stairway and vanished around the corner.

"Crazy kid. Not really in the mood to play tag." Nathan said to himself, hobbling up the stairs with one hand inching along what was left of a drooping metal rail.

Slowly reaching the top, Nathan looked down another long hallway where Judah again vanished from sight. *You have got to be kidding me!* Thought Nathan, as he desperately tried to catch his breath, never mind the thought of why he was even chasing the boy in the first place. *How did the kid get the authority to set the pace, after all?* It did not really matter, after not using his legs for so long, the challenge felt quite good.

Nathan moved his body down the hallway, periodically inhaling the stench of the place through his sinuses; it smelled like homeless people had been living there for a while. Nathan was not surprised. The majority of urban America was all the same — beaten up and run down. People tried to survive where they could. Safe havens did not exist anymore outside of Adullum, at least not to anyone's knowledge. For Nathan, it was hard to fathom how this one mother and her boy could seemingly survive in such a place for so long, apparently without the help of anyone else. *There have to be more people here,* he thought. *Something doesn't make sense here.* He kept searching for the boy.

"See me?" yelled Judah from a room to Nathan's left.

The boy was having too much fun, yet by now Nathan was agitated because of how painful it was to move. His legs were stiff, and his head hurt with every step. *How much farther do I have to go to catch up with this kid? The world is falling apart, I have almost died more than once, and this little boy wants to play hide and seek? Ridiculous!* All around, the reality of life was morbid and depressing, yet Judah's playfulness alerted Nathan to the fact that the boy was somehow unaware of that reality, or was just simply not encumbered by it. *What's a child supposed to do when the world's crumbled around him? Play amidst the rubble, I guess.*

Finally, Judah decided to stop at some point, and Nathan was able to catch up to him in an upper room that looked like their main living quarters. For a second, Nathan could see Judah's shadow jolt from one wall to the other. Then, as he walked into the room, Judah suddenly ran up from behind and tackled his leg.

"Gotcha!" yelled Judah. Nathan just about fell over, his hand catching the door jamb just in time to stay standing.

"Judah, calm down!" said the mother poised next to a large shot out window that overlooked the building's parking lot. Judah was excited. He let go and went to fidget with a junk collection he had in a box.

Not sure what to do because of the awkward tension between himself and the boy's mother, Nathan slowly made his way over to the window and stood next to her, sure to leave at least a few feet of distance from where she was. Looking out across the view it was apparent that winter was on the heels of Spring. Below was the ruined city of Redding — demolished, unattractive, barren, trees burned to the ground.

Nathan was not sure what to say.

"It's still our home," the woman said in a firm, but somber voice.

There were gaps of silence in their conversation, intermingled by the sound of Judah tinkering with things just a few feet away.

"At least you can still look at yours…haven't seen my home in twenty years," said Nathan.

The woman glanced at him quickly with a slight pity, but not much, then redirected her gaze back out the window, "Where's home?"

"You wouldn't believe me if I told you," answered Nathan.

She waited and did not say anything.

"Redfish Lake," Nathan finally answered.

She squinted, "You're right, I don't believe you." She waited for Nathan to say something back or argue the fact, but he did not. His silence made her question whether or not he was telling the truth. He was not quick to defend or explain.

"Are you serious?" she asked. "Stanley, Idaho?"

"Yep."

Suddenly, she could tell by the sincerity in his eyes that he was being honest. "That's Icon!" she exclaimed, "That's their headquarters! The center of this whole world war! The headwaters!"

Nathan did not respond immediately, he just looked at her with his eyes clearly open in such a way so as to communicate the simple fact, *I'm aware.* And then once again got caught off guard by her beauty.

"So...you were there?" she asked.

"Yeah, but I was just a boy," answered Nathan. "Judah's age probably. Don't remember much of what happened though."

"Where have you been all this time? How have you stayed alive?" she asked.

"I'm not quite sure, exactly, been living in a cave mostly.

"Cave?" she asked, glaring at him with curiosity.

"Yeah, El Capitan, in Yosem - "

She cut him off, "I know...*Yosemite!* There's only one El Capitan, but a cave? There's no cave there."

"Adullum," answered Nathan. "It's been kept a secret. Not a lot of people know about it. *They* still don't."

"So how do you know about it?"

"My Grandma."

"I don't get it," she said, confused.

"It's a long story. I need to get back there as soon as possible."

"Your grandmother? Are there others?" she asked in shock.

"Yeah, about three hundred people are hiding there."

"I don't believe it! Didn't think there were that many left out there who weren't Screeners. That's a big cave!"

"It's massive. And weird...a lot we still don't know about it."

She was amazed and was not quite sure what to think, "So...you're a Reaper then, right?"

"Guess that's what we've been called," answered

Nathan. "What about you? How'd you get those marks on your arm?"

"What do you know about those?"

"I saw them right before you hit me." Nathan reached into his pocket, but it was empty. "It's in my other pants," he said to himself.

"What is?"

"A picture," answered Nathan. "Well, it's a drawing actually."

"A drawing? Of what?" she asked, rather intrigued.

"Kind of what's on your arm," answered Nathan. "Some doves flying out of a treasure chest." Those were the last words Nathan got out of his mouth for a while as he watched the woman's jaw just about hit the floor, looking like she had just seen a ghost. All of the sudden she was speechless and nervously tried to gather her words, waving her arm frantically over at Judah. Immediately something clicked in the atmosphere. Nathan simply stood by and watched the magnificence unfold.

"JUDAH!" she yelled. "Go down there and get me those pants!"

Judah did not react quickly. He just looked at her and continued to play with his stuff, not really sure why his mom wanted them.

"RIGHT NOW!" she yelled. "Hurry!"

This time Judah took her seriously and did not hesitate to obey. He threw a dirty stuffed animal to the ground that had an orange beak and a black and white body resembling an Alaskan Puffin, then dashed out the door. While she waited for Judah to get back upstairs, the woman paced back and forth, not saying a word, not talking. Nathan was silent.

A few minutes later, Judah rushed back into the room, holding the pants out in front of him. Nathan took the pants and pulled the piece of paper from the pocket, unfolded it and then handed it the woman. Timidly, like she was afraid, almost not wanting to open it, she held the drawing and looked at it, opening her mouth and then putting her hand across her lips as if to let a slur of unspoken words escape into the air. She continued to look at it, not taking her eyes off the paper and then started to cry, trembling with tears in her eyes.

"Mom," said Judah, "what's wrong?"

With her lips quivering, shaking her head back and forth, she quietly handed the piece of paper to Judah.

Judah's eyes shot open like an owl as he shouted, "HEY! THIS IS MINE! I DREW THIS! I DREW THIS!"

"What?" said Nathan, captivated by the fruition of a circumstance he was still trying to figure out.

"I DID! I DID! THIS IS MY PICTURE!" Judah kept shouting. He was excited while his mother kept crying, now with her eyes closed and both hands to her mouth. "MOMMY, I TOLD YOU! I TOLD YOU! I TOLD YOU!" Judah repeated.

Looking at her then at Judah, Nathan asked, "Will one of you tell me what's going on here?"

Ignoring Nathan for the moment, the woman knelt down and took Judah into her arms and held him tightly. He kept declaring as his face was pressed against her neck, "I KNEW IT MOM! I KNEW IT! I KNEW IT!"

"I have the feeling there's a lot more to this picture than I'm aware of," said Nathan.

"We have to show him, mom! We have to!"

Judah took his mother's hand and started pulling her out of the room. "Come on!" he shouted at Nathan.

Trying to keep up, Nathan followed them to an attic ladder that led them out onto the rooftop of the building. When they broke through the doorway, Judah took them to the northern corner of the roof.

"Tell him, mom! Tell him!"

She did her best to speak, "This is the spot."

Nathan listened.

The woman gathered herself and tried to get a hold of her emotions. "We've lost all our family," she said. "Everyone...they've all died. I thought we were the only ones left who hadn't joined the Screeners." And then, almost as if she had forgotten Nathan was there, the woman started talking to herself, "I can't believe it, I just can't."

"Come on mom! Tell him!" cried Judah, wagging his mother's hand.

She continued, "Judah likes to draw...always did. He's always drawing. One day he saw this picture in his mind — that...that on the paper," she pointed to the drawing, "the doves leaving the treasure chest. The first time he drew the picture he did something I hadn't seen him do with any of his other drawings. Out of the blue one day, he just decided to come up here to this spot. He stood on the edge, right here and then...let go of it. The wind just took it away."

She paused for a moment, "Then...the next day he drew it again, the same thing! When he finished he came up here again to the same spot and let go of it, again giving it away to the wind."

Judah was smiling, nervously shaking his body like it was Christmas morning or something, looking up at his mom as she recounted the events. "Then he did it again... and again...and again," she said. "Again and again and again — day after day! He didn't miss a day! I didn't understand it at first, I just watched. Then one day, I asked him, '*Judah, what are you doing?*'" The woman started talking to herself again, "I just can't believe it. I can't believe it."

"He told me he was drawing the pictures," she continued, "and then sending them out, hoping that others like us would find them." Hoping the pictures would lead them to us, that the Navigator would somehow anoint the pictures and help us find anyone else out there — anyone alive, standing their ground, doing the same we've been doing. At first I knew he was just being a kid, just foolish and wishful. He needed something, some kind of ritual to give him hope around here. And so...I went along with it. Every single day, coming up to this roof and letting go of another picture, over and over again for the last year. But nothing happened. Nothing ever happened. And then, some time ago, I had enough. I told Judah he couldn't send out any more pictures, that I would only let him draw one more, just one more and let it go, but that was it. After this last one, no more. No more!"

Nathan was listening so intently that he almost forgot to breathe. The woman kept telling the story, "This last winter was scary," she said. "The snow's been less and less each year. Finding clean water's been getting more difficult. I was constantly plagued by the thought that Judah and I weren't going to live much longer. We weren't going to make it. Something needed to happen. After Judah let go of the last picture, that one you're holding in your hands..."

"What do you mean?" asked Nathan. "How do you know this is the last picture he drew?"

"Because," she answered, "he never marked any of them, not one. But the last one he signed with a *J* — the same *J* right there on that piece of paper! After that last picture I wouldn't let him send anymore out. Judah and I packed up Stardust and rode to Mount Hood in one last ditch effort to find some sort of breakthrough, one last chance at staying alive."

Nathan was fascinated by all of this, "Why Hood?" he asked.

"Mount Hood," she answered, "was the place my parents used to take me to worship. We'd go there once a year and stay three days just to seek the Navigator. I'd given up though, since they died. I refused to go back to that mountain for years; it was getting too dangerous. And with just Judah and I, didn't want to take many more risks than I had to," she paused. "But something inside me said to go one more time. Just one more time to worship and seek the face of the Navigator. And then while we were there on our third night, what happened? You came and tried to kill my son and took our food! I Thought, *there's no way this could be His will, no way!* I was sure you were dead. But something was different about Judah, I could see it in his eyes. He was crying, not because he was scared, but because he was drawn to you. He told me not to leave you there. And for some reason, I blindly trusted him. And now? Here you are with his little picture in your pocket — the last one he drew. The last one, by faith, he set free in anticipation that it would somehow lead us to something, someone who could somehow help us to not give up, to keep going."

Nathan was awestruck as he recounted the woman's story. "My head's spinning," he said. "I don't know what to say." Nathan looked at Judah - he was still grinning, his eyes glowing.

"I just can't believe it," she kept whispering to herself, looking off into the distance, then turning her gaze toward Nathan. "What were you doing out there? How did you find us on the mountain?" she asked.

Nathan was stunned by all of this. He grunted, "Huh...I don't know," he said. "I was running, running from something, for something...I guess, still not sure."

"But you must have known we were there!" she exclaimed, "He must have told you!"

"Actually, no," said Nathan. "I wanted nothing to do with the Navigator, and I wasn't *hearing* anything. As a matter of fact, I've never felt more lost."

"Makes sense," she muttered, "it all makes sense."

"What does?" asked Nathan.

"Sometimes those who are the most confused are the ones He's leading the most," she answered.

"Uh, I don't think so," said Nathan. "My Grandma always told me He leads those who seek Him. And I haven't been seeking him."

"Sometimes, but His ways are higher than ours. He can use the path of someone's rebellion to run right into His will. I don't know how to explain it, but there's a reason you were brought here!"

Gradually, the woman's guard against Nathan slowly began to break down. Judah clutched onto Nathan. Nathan was comforted by the boy's touch.

"You're the first person he's trusted besides me, his entire life," she said.

Nathan was quiet, not sure how to react. He thought back to how he had asked the Navigator for help, and then realized He had rested the salvation of Nathan's life upon the hope and discernment of a young boy. He wrapped his arms around Judah and let him cling as long as he wanted to. The touch of the little boy was the closest Nathan had ever felt to the Navigator. The moment was sober and holy. It was evident that Nathan's path had crossed with this mother and her little boy for a reason, even though they may not have been aware of the full magnitude of everything at the time. There was certainly much ahead of them they had yet to realize.

"This city has nothing left," she said, "I've searched almost everything down there for food and water. We don't know where to go from here."

"Well, I have to get home," answered Nathan, "and you and Judah are coming with me." Nathan looked into her eyes, still glazed over, "What's your name by the way?

She hesitated, not sure whether or not she wanted to trust Nathan at this point, but at the same time knowing that the incident with her son's drawing was no coincidence. She looked down at Judah one more time, deep into his eyes, and then back at Nathan. "Meridian," she answered. "My name's Meridian."

Nathan could have never predicted the turn of events that would occur the moment he decided to run out of that Maersk container — it was an entrance, not an exit. No matter how hard he tried, there was simply no way he could have imagined meeting Meridian and Judah. There was something powerful and resilient about them. Whether or not he was able to convey what he was feeling through words, he could sense that by meeting them a shift was taking place. He felt more hope than before. For the first time, he looked forward to something other than just getting the *lake* back. Meridian, whoever she was, fascinated him. Being in her presence felt like the result of an invisible force bringing them together for something magnificent — a joint calling, a remarkable union that was somehow essential to the next phase of their journey. There was definitely more going on in the spiritual realm than he was able to comprehend in the moment.

Amidst the whirlwind of revelation that was unfolding on the rooftop of Bethel, Nathan still had no idea what had happened to Iris, and Annak, or any of the others. He had no idea if their dead bodies were strewn across the bottom of the Willamette Bay or if they had been taken captive by Gabriel. In the back of his mind, just the thought of them made him uncomfortable. He regretted having left them behind, but at the same time he could not deny the divine encounter that he had now been ushered into. He had yet to taste the true fullness of the Blue Flame and still had yet to discover his own supernatural gifting. He tried his best to get the clutter of racing thoughts out of his mind and for the moment, simply refused to let go of Judah. The power that was present was too much to ignore.

TWENTY NINE
Only the Beginning

abriel's hand was cold and bloody as he dragged the pale deceased body behind him. Why he cared enough to not simply leave it rotting there was a riddle to those watching. Despite all that had happened, he knew this was only the beginning and refused to return to Icon empty-handed.

Simultaneously, Nathan had no clue that Meridian had picked his pack up off the ground and brought it back to Bethel. Still on the rooftop embracing Judah, he knew not that down in the sanctuary the same glass orb was inside of it, acting up, flickering wildly with static electricity.

WWW.ZNARNSTAM.COM

Stay on the lookout for book two, *Cold Fire*, as well as for other stories from Z.N. Arnstam. To get connected, visit the website above and engage in the ongoing blog, or conversations via Twitter. An up and coming YouTube channel will provide videos, readings, and discussions. To contact the author, write to znarnstam@gmail.com. Thanks for reading *Blue Flame*!

'lA information can be obtained
w.ICGtesting.com
'n the USA
0036120817
BV00005B/181/P